THIS IS
MY
BRAIN
IN
LOVE

THIS IS MY BRAIN IN LOVE

I. W. GREGORIO

LITTLE, BROWN AND COMPANY

New York Boston

Cover and interior illustration of brain copyright © Nick Kinney/Shutterstock.com. Cover design by Karina Granda. Cover copyright © 2020 by Hachette Book Group, Inc.

Little, Brown and Company
Hachette Book Group
1290 Avenue of the Americas, New York, NY 10104
Visit us at LBYR.com

First Edition: April 2020

Little, Brown and Company is a division of Hachette Book Group, Inc. The Little, Brown name and logo are trademarks of Hachette Book Group, Inc.

The publisher is not responsible for websites (or their content) that are not owned by the publisher.

Library of Congress Cataloging-in-Publication Data
Names: Gregorio, I. W., 1976– author.
Title: This is my brain in love / by I. W. Gregorio.
Description: First edition. | New York: Little, Brown and Company, 2020. | Audience: Ages 12+. | Summary: Rising high school juniors Jocelyn Wu and Will Domenici fall in love while trying to save the Wu family restaurant, A-Plus Chinese Garden.
Identifiers: LCCN 2019033954 | ISBN 9780316423823 (hardcover) | ISBN 9780316423847 (ebook) | ISBN 9780316423854 (library edition ebook)
Subjects: CYAC: Restaurants—Fiction. | Cooking, Chinese—Fiction. | Anxiety disorders—Fiction. | Chinese Americans—Fiction. | African Americans—Fiction. | Love—Fiction.
Classification: LCC PZ7.1.G7415 Thi 2020 | DDC [Fic]—dc23
LC record available at https://lccn.loc.gov/2019033954

ISBNs: 978-0-316-42382-3 (hardcover), 978-0-316-42384-7 (ebook)

Printed in the United States of America

LSC-C

10 9 8 7 6 5 4 3 2 1

*For O and G, as a promise to walk with you through
doubt, fear, anger, and sadness*

Prologue

This is a mostly happy story. It's important for you to know this because if there's anything I hate the most, it's a book that makes your emotions feel like a child's overloved comfort toy being flung around a washing machine. The ones where it seems like the story's all beautiful and nothing hurts, until someone kicks the bucket at the end, tearing a hole in your belly and removing organs that you didn't know existed. I'd rather know ahead of time whether to bring tissues. It's just better for your heart, you know?

I say this to you because I want you to be reassured. I want you to know so when the story ends with me staring at a pill bottle, wrestling with what to do with it, you're prepared.

It'll all be okay.

I promise.

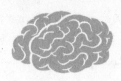

This Is My Brain
on Bankruptcy

JOCELYN

Irony: The year I decide that central New York isn't a total dump after all, my dad finally admits that it was a mistake to move here.

It's one of the rare days that my whole family gets to spend together. Usually my parents trade off running the register downstairs in the restaurant, because they're incapable of trusting anyone else to do it, but when our water main breaks in the middle of the lunch rush, we can't get a plumber to come in until dinnertime.

My brother and I greet the news like it's a snow day. Family meal! Amah, our grandma, won't be doing prep work, so she can help Alan with his algebra! We won't need to help with cleanup after we've finished our homework, so maybe I'll finally have time to work on the screenplay I'm writing with Priya!

The excitement dims pretty quickly, though, when I see that my mom's almost at the point of tears when she writes the CLOSE FOR REPAIR sign that I edit to read CLOSED FOR REPAIRS.

I start to get really worried when I watch my dad pour Pepto-Bismol for his dinner instead of his usual chrysanthemum tea, so I pay more attention than usual to the heated conversation my parents have in their bedroom. I basically speak Mandarin at the third-grade level, never really having applied myself at the Mohawk Valley Chinese Association's weekly language school, but even I can pick out the words "expensive" and "no money" and "back to New York City."

After a long phone call, my dad finally sits down at the dinner table. It's littered with the usual hodgepodge of microwaved kitchen leftovers. The moo shu pork looks particularly deflated.

My mom looks at him expectantly, almost hopefully. He nods and looks at the rest of us. Amah and I look at him, but my brother is too busy stuffing his face with a day-old egg roll to actually notice that my dad's joined us.

"Alan," my dad says sharply. He waits for Alan's five-second attention span to focus before he says, "Second Uncle says manager at Queens branch of his restaurant go back to China. May be time to go back to the city."

The silence after his announcement is suffocating, like someone's hoovered away all the life in the room. Living over a restaurant, you get used to a constant soundtrack of activity underlying your life. There's always the sound of chopping, or the clank of a wok banging against a stove, or someone shouting or cursing in Chinese.

My amah is the first one to make a sound. It's a soft,

noncommittal hum. Two notes, questioning, neither approving nor disapproving.

Alan, still chewing, manages only a shrug and a "Huh," which makes no sense because he's the one who's spent the majority of his life here.

So it's up to me to say loudly, "No." Because we can't move. Not now, after I've found an actual bubble tea place in this god-forsaken backwater. Not now, when I've finally got a chance to take a film class at the local college. Not now, when I've pains-takingly identified a group of people I can tolerate as friends, and even found a best friend.

My mom's looking down at her hands, and my dad's glaring at me, so I elaborate. "Dad, please say you're kidding. I've literally spent the last six years of my life complaining about moving to central New York, and you want to give up the restaurant now?"

My dad bristles at my tone (I swear, there are actual hairs at the crown of his head that stick up when he's agitated). Alan's eyes dart back and forth between my dad and me. With his cheeks still full of food, he looks like a squirrel watching a tennis match.

"Xiao Jia" is all he says, his voice low and warning.

I back down and try a different tack. "But...what about the schools? They're amazing. You know I'm already set up to take a college class in the fall. And the restaurant has a following now." Not a big one, but there are definitely regulars. "What if Alan takes over my deliveries so I can work the counter more and we, like, start a Facebook account or something. For free advertising. Check-ins, you know. It's a thing."

"Why are you only thinking of this now?" Dad asks. "You

have been working at restaurant for forever, and never do no thing." The worry lines on his forehead have morphed from frustration into suspicion. It's a subtle shift, but a familiar one.

I don't say: "Because the place sucks the soul out of the living."

Instead I say: "I didn't realize how desperate things were. I thought we were doing okay." Looking back, I can see the signs. When Mr. Chen went back to Kaohsiung to be with his family, we never replaced him. My mom worked double shifts instead, and my dad started to do his accounting and ordering at the restaurant so he could lend a hand when things got busy. Suddenly a lot of little things make sense: why my mom would scold me when I'd leave the light on after leaving a room, why Alan couldn't go on his sixth-grade field trip to Great Adventure, why they canceled our Netflix subscription so I had to "borrow" Priya's log-in information to feed my prestige TV and film addiction.

"Has this been going on for years?" I ask my dad, horrified.

His bowed head, and his silence, are my answer.

A few years ago, there was a 5.0 earthquake on the East Coast, with its epicenter in northeastern Pennsylvania. It was a pretty big deal and caused some minor property damage (coming from the West Coast, of course, Priya rolled her eyes and sent out a meme about lawn chairs being knocked over). I'll never forget how my body felt in that brief moment of shift: paralyzed yet at the same time pushed by an outside force terrifyingly beyond my control.

I feel the same sensation right now. And I think: This is it. This is the "Nothing Is the Same Anymore" trope.

When I started hanging out with Priya and really started

getting into film—not just watching movies, but analyzing them—it was kind of a buzzkill to realize that so many of the movies that gave me joy as a kid were actually pretty formulaic. Priya and I would have "Name That Trope" movie nights during freshman year (I usually won, because her parents majorly limited her screen time, whereas mine were so busy with the restaurant I could usually sneak in some TV with my amah). But as our game evolved from a joke into a way of seeing life, I realized that tropes are more than just clichés. They're neither good nor bad. They simply are, like earlobes and Winnie-the-Pooh. They're a reminder that all stories are cut from the same cloth, with patterns that are recognizable, even when they're unique and surprising. Seeing these patterns helps us make sense of the world, helps give us a framework for navigating what might come next.

What comes next for me is the "Big First Choice" trope. Am I going to go gentle into that good night, or am I going to be dragged kicking and screaming from the life I've finally built for myself?

Come on, like you really had to ask.

I start off with appealing to my dad's natural tightwad tendencies. "You can't really want to move back to New York. Didn't you mention last week that Second Uncle's parking space costs more than our rent?" We left the city when I was pretty young, but I remember him constantly complaining about the traffic, the rude customers, and how Second Uncle lorded over him. "Where would we live? Alan and I are too old to sleep in the same bedroom anymore."

"You think I haven't think of this?" my dad grits out. "You think you so smart?"

"Aiya, Baba," my mom murmurs, putting a hand on my dad's arm before things escalate. "Ta xiang bangzhu ni."

Dad's nostrils flare as he takes a deep breath, and he rubs his hand over his eyes.

I regroup and try a different approach. "Baba. Mom's right. I'm sorry I haven't been more involved in the restaurant. I just want to help. Let me look at the numbers, brainstorm some strategy—that commerce elective you made me take has got to be worth something, right?"

Even as I say it, I get the sinking feeling that my dad's right. It's arrogant for me to imagine that I can swoop in with ideas from a high school Intro to Business class and turn around a restaurant that's been floundering for years. It's a measure of how desperate the situation is that my dad just throws up his hands and mutters, "Haoba, suibian ni," which is the equivalent of "Fine, try it your way."

I take it as a win. For now.

This Is My Brain
on Summer Vacation

WILL

It's the last day before summer vacation, and I may be the only one at St. Agnes High School who's apprehensive about it. The twenty-four-hour news cycle of my mind is on overload. Manny is practically bouncing off the walls, high-fiving all his buddies from the soccer team and yelling "T minus one, baby!" He's got a sweet gig at Amazing Stories, the local comic book store, so he's essentially going to get paid for sitting around reading manga all day. Javier's floating through the hallway wearing his shades and noise-canceling headphones, with a particular spring to his lanky step, telling everyone who will listen about the internship our computer science teacher helped him get at ConMed. If our local Students Against Destructive Decisions chapter were to see them, they'd put Javier and Manny into an ad depicting people who are "high on life," right next to their retro THIS IS YOUR

BRAIN ON DRUGS posters where the subject's neurons are eggs cooking in a pan—meant to represent the perils of substance abuse.

I'm the only one of my friends who doesn't have a headline, and the worst thing about it is that I have only myself to blame.

My anxiety only ratchets up when Javier and I walk into the media studies studio, which feels strange because for the past ten months it's been my favorite place at St. Agnes. When I enter the classroom, Mr. Evans grins up at us like we're prodigal sons returning.

"Will! Javi! Grab your chairs. I'm getting ready to give out my superlatives." About a decade ago, St. Agnes's staff got rid of yearbook polls after a voting scandal led the administration to proclaim that "all our students are likely to succeed, so there is no value in suggesting that popularity can predict future achievement." That didn't stop Mr. Evans from making his own superlatives list as a way to announce next year's editorial staff for the *Spartan*.

When I go to collect a chair from the bank of computers lining the room, it slips from my sweaty fingers, making an ungodly clatter. In my mind, I'm already making up my own superlative: William Obinna Domenici, Most Likely to Have Clammy Hands. No one seems to notice the racket, but my face still burns as I take my seat.

Mr. Evans perches himself on the edge of his desk, pushes up his horn-rimmed glasses, and thanks us all for a fantastic year. "You all should pat yourselves on the back. Online clicks were up ten percent, and we had an increase in ad revenue as well. Kudos to our business team." He nods in my direction, and next to me, Sanjit Mehta (senior, business manager) puts out his hand to high-five me (sophomore, reporter) and Javier, (sophomore, photographer). The knot in my chest loosens up a fraction.

All day, I've been trying not to hope too much. A fair and impartial review of my prospects concludes that I'm too young to be one of the executive-level editors. When Mr. Evans sent around his end-of-the-year survey of staff, though, I figured it would be reasonable to throw my hat in the ring to be business manager since Sanjit is graduating. Barring that, I'm hoping to be a section editor at least. Opinion is my first choice—even though I hate arguing in person, I love being able to construct an argument on paper—then Features or News. Those are the high-profile sections that would get the attention of a school with a prestigious journalism program.

Mr. Evans starts off by acknowledging the graduating staff. Our editor in chief, Julia Brown (Most Likely to Be Incarcerated to Protect Her Sources), is going to Northwestern to study journalism; Sanjit (Most Likely to Retire at Forty) to Penn for business. Next, he announces the new editor in chief, executive editor, and managing editor, all juniors. I try to be a team player and look happy when three upperclasswomen snag the sections I wanted.

When Javier (Most Likely to Insta His Own Kompromat) is announced as business manager, though, I can't completely hide my disappointment. Everyone else is laughing, because it's true: Javier's Instagram is filled with compromising pictures that would probably torpedo any future attempts to run for public office, but the best I can manage is a barely convincing smile.

"Congrats, Javi," I say, slapping him on the back. "You're going to be awesome."

As I wait for my own assignment, I focus on slowing down my breathing and on stopping my knee from jiggling so much it causes another furniture malfunction. Finally, after it seems like Mr. Evans has acknowledged every other sophomore on staff, his gaze turns to me.

"To Will Domenici, I'm delighted to bestow the title of Most Likely to Respond to a Tech SOS Within Thirty Seconds." A ripple of laughter goes through the classroom, and my face feels like it's going to spontaneously combust. Does Mr. Evans realize that he's implying that I have no life? Apparently not: "With his history of reliability, tech savvy, and eye for design, I think you guys will agree that the *Spartan* couldn't have a better assistant online manager."

My classmates burst into applause, but for the second time in less than an hour, I have to force a grimace into a smile, and when I say "force" I'm describing a Herculean effort of acting and facial control that is probably Oscar-worthy, or at least deserving of a Daytime Emmy.

Of all the positions at the *Spartan*, assistant online manager is the booby prize. You're not a reporter. You're not an editor. From what I've seen, you're nothing more than a coding minion and social media gopher. It's not that I don't appreciate the fact that the web team is an integral part of the success of any paper, it's just that I feel like I have more to contribute.

I try to explain as much to Mr. Evans after class.

"Just because you're assistant online manager doesn't mean that you won't also be able to write," he reassures me.

"I know, but…" My voice cracks, and I study the worn linoleum floor by Mr. Evans's desk. I take a deep breath and try not to sound pathetic. "Is my writing not good enough? Do you not trust my editorial judgment?"

"Oh, Will." Mr. Evans leans in toward me and looks straight into my eyes, like he knows I'm the type to be skeptical of any praise. "You're an excellent writer. Your attention to word choice is phenomenal, and you are always clear and precise in your reasoning. Your fact-checking is top-notch."

I wait for the caveat for five excruciating seconds.

Mr. Evans's eyes flick away for a second, and when he speaks again his voice is gentler. "I've noticed, though, that you rely a lot on secondary sources and e-mail correspondence for your stories. Next year, I want you to focus on going behind the scenes to really dig deep. Make that extra call. Drill down and ask the hard questions that make sources squirm."

He makes it sound so easy. How can I tell him that he might as well be asking me to fly to the moon?

As if to illustrate my failure, my smart watch buzzes. My parents got it for me a few years ago after my last panic attack, and it's set to go off when my heart rate goes above one hundred beats per minute. It's supposed to be a cue to do my mindful breathing and centering exercises.

I open my mouth, but it feels like I'm drawing in air from one of those tiny plastic-straw stirrers you get at coffee shops.

Five seconds in, five seconds out.

The slow breaths do nothing to quiet the heckling questions that fill my head like an out-of-control press conference: *Mr. Domenici, why are you so afraid of making cold calls? Don't you think that you're constitutionally incapable of asking the tough questions? Do you really think that someone who can't even order* pizza over the phone without breaking out into a sweat is going to be the next Bob Woodward?

"Will, are you okay?" Mr. Evans's round face is creased with concern. "I don't want you to be discouraged. You're only a sophomore, and you've already got the most important attributes of a good journalist. Integrity. Attention to detail. Work ethic. It'll come."

"Sure," I manage to get out. "Thanks, Mr. Evans."

"Did you end up applying to any of the summer programs on the list I sent out? That's one way to start honing those investigative skills."

It's a struggle to keep the self-loathing out of my voice when I answer. "No, it didn't work out. I couldn't find the right writing sample." The truth is, I'd started the applications to three programs but chickened out when it came time to ask for letters of recommendation.

Mr. Evans brightens. "Well, that's something you can work on over the summer—some kind of long-form piece that'll show them both your investigative skills and your analytic ability. Remember, there are lots of ways to learn leadership skills. I'd like to see you take on a bigger role on the staff next year, so look for a summer job where you can learn how to manage a team and start thinking of the newspaper as a business whose readership you can grow."

Furiously, I scribble down my assignment: Write a long-form piece. Make the calls and ask the hard questions. Learn how to manage a team. Grow a business. They're only sound bites for now, and developing the story is going to be my big summer challenge, but all I can do is try.

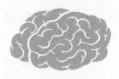

This Is My Brain
on the Impossible

JOCELYN

Within the first day, I'm panicking.

"He set me up, Priya. It's basically the 'Impossible Task' trope." It doesn't take a Nobel Prize in economics to realize after looking at my dad's books that A-Plus has been operating on razor-thin margins for months. "The worst thing is, there isn't enough data to figure out how to do better. I have no idea what dishes really sell the best or what our foot traffic is."

It's truly depressing. When it gets too exhausting to think about it, I do what I always do when I can't deal with my life: I binge-watch a TV series.

When we first moved to Utica six years ago, Netflix saved my life. I'm not exaggerating.

I was ten years old when we moved, and to say that my family experienced culture shock moving from the "greatest city in the world" to a place where Red Lobster is high-class dining, well, that's an understatement. Honestly, most of my classmates probably thought I was kind of a snob. There are only so many times you can start a sentence with "In the city, we used to..." before people stop talking to you. Which is why I spent most of middle school glued to a screen so I wouldn't have to think about the fact that I had no real friends.

When Priya Venkatram moved here from San Francisco in seventh grade, she latched on to me right away when she heard I had lived in NYC. After we bonded over our mutual love of *Orange Is the New Black* and *Better Call Saul*, we became BFFs. She'd come over to the restaurant, and we'd put on a show with descriptive audio so I could listen as I did cleanup. I trust her judgment on TV shows 100 percent, so when she tells me that I might want to check out *Restaurant: Impossible* and *Kitchen Nightmares* for ideas, I do.

It only makes me feel more hopeless. "All the places on that show are sit-down," I say. "Ninety percent of our business is take-out. Also, I can't get a professional chef to come in with a full design team and do ten thousand dollars' worth of renovations. You know this place is like a hamster wheel. There are only so many hours in a day, and we have to answer phones, make take-out bags, fold menus, prep food, do deliveries and inventory and purchasing....How could I possibly have time to do community outreach on top of that?" I'm starting to hyperventilate just thinking about it.

"Can you guys hire someone part-time?"

I've thought about that, too. "My dad's just going to yell that we can't afford it," I say.

Sure enough, the next day, that's exactly what my dad says.

"Aren't you always saying that our Yelp reviews complain about wait times?" I argue. "If we get more help our revenue goes up and they pay for themselves. Like with the sushi bar. If we get that cranking and sell four or five rolls a night, it'll be worth it." I still feel stupid calling a twelve-inch glass case that holds stuff to make California rolls a sushi bar, but whatever.

"We can't even afford to bring someone from China," my dad says. By that he means an under-documented "business associate." "No one want to come to Utica."

"We could hire a local student or something with the money in my savings account," I suggest. I've squirreled away more than a thousand bucks from delivery tips. Because it isn't like my dad actually pays me, of course.

My dad turns a dark orange. "If you have extra money, should go to your college fund!"

"If I have more time to study I'll get into a better college," I counter.

As I watch my father wrestle with an Asian parent's version of a no-win situation, I haul out my laptop. Within minutes I've got an ad up on Craigslist.

Then I print up a HELP WANTED sign with little tabs you can tear off, and I hope to all the gods that it will be enough.

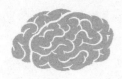

This Is My Brain
on Unemployment

WILL

When my eleventh-hour effort to see if the *Observer-Dispatch* has any job openings fails, my mother wangles me an interview for a data mining internship at the hospital. It's the first summer where I've really felt pressure to get a summer job. My family is well-off enough that I've always gotten an allowance just for doing chores and homework. My sister and I have never wanted for anything, a fact that started making me feel vaguely guilty around freshman year, when Manny got a job to save up for a used car.

This year, my mother is strongly encouraging me to "seek gainful employment." I think she's desperately afraid that I'm going to end up like my cousin Nick, who lazed around in the summers and is now going to what my mother deems a second-tier college, with my uncle Chris paying out his nose for him, too.

"It will be good for college applications, William," my mother tells me as she pecks me on the forehead before rushing out the door to perform a C-section. "Everyone judges a man by the work of his hands."

When my father drops me off for my interview, he hands me the container of hibiscus tea with honey that my mother made for me and reminds me to do some of Dr. Rifkin's centering exercises if I get nervous before the interview.

I started going to Dr. Rifkin in third grade. I had begun complaining of stomachaches; the pain happened at random, and my mother went wild trying to figure out if I was hungry, or lactose intolerant, or allergic to gluten. I was paraded in front of pediatric specialists and went for ultrasounds where they kneaded my belly like it was pizza dough.

My father was the first one to notice that the stomachaches often coincided with exams at school, or with times I'd gotten into fights with my friends or my sister. He had seen my aunt Louisa struggle with anxiety when she was a teenager and suspected that was what I had. It took him a while to convince my mother that I should see someone.

"Will has always been a nervous child. Let us start by giving him some guidance rather than pathologizing his issues," she told my dad. She filed away the list of child psychologists he'd given her and arranged for me to have a sit-down with my youth group coordinator instead.

Five months later and I had had guidance from pretty much everyone at the St. Agnes Lower School, up to and including Father Healdon (twice), and my stomachaches had progressed to bouts of nausea with the occasional vomiting episode thrown in for fun. When my nne nne visited from Chicago, she took one look at me and exclaimed, "Oga, na devil work," before whisking me away to pray.

Finally, my father had had enough and set me up for a Skype session with Dr. Rifkin. My mother conceded that it was the right thing to do when my really bad symptoms stopped after the first month of cognitive behavioral therapy. The anxiety has mostly been manageable since, except for a couple of panic attacks that I had at the beginning of middle school.

After I check in at the front desk of the hospital for my interview, I'm directed to a waiting room. In a couple of minutes, the door to the administrative office opens, and a middle-aged guy with brown hair steps out. I kid you not, he's wearing a cardigan in June.

"Mr. Domenici?" he calls out, staring around the room until his eyes land on a rumpled-looking white man sitting two chairs down from me. I wonder how he can seriously think that man is an intern applicant. The guy looks like he was born in the first Bush administration.

"Yes, hello. Mr. Johnson?" I stand up.

Mr. Johnson's welcoming smile freezes infinitesimally as he gives me a once-over. I rub my wrist and can feel the fluttering of my pulse beat faster. I've seen The Look—that little panicked surprise when people realize that William Domenici isn't a white male like they've assumed—so many times in my life you would think that my body would have gotten used to it by now, but nope.

My sister, golden child that she is, relishes getting The Look. It's like her own little sociology experiment—her opportunity to catch people off-balance when they realize her skin tone is more Halle Berry than Drew Barrymore. "How people recover from that initial surprise says a lot about who they are and what kind of assumptions they hold," she told me once.

I still prefer not to get The Look at all, because invariably it leads to The Question, which can range from cloyingly polite (So, tell me about your parents, Will?) to offensively blunt (What are you?). Waiting for The Question always makes my anxiety level go up.

Mr. Johnson leads me into a corner office overflowing with files and scraps of paper. I sit on a worn leather chair and clasp my hands on my lap to weigh down my jiggling legs.

Five seconds in, five seconds out.

Mr. Johnson leans back with a sigh into his mesh office chair and clicks on his computer screen. "So, William—do you go by that or by Will?" He plows on before I can even answer. "What makes you want to be an intern here at St. Luke's?" He says it the way a checkout clerk asks you if you would like a receipt with your purchase: with minimal inflection—practically a negative inflection—giving you the impression that they have an equally negligible interest in your answer.

I'm embarrassed to realize that I don't have an answer. Of course I don't *really* want to be a scanning drone in the basement of a hospital. I like the idea of having my own money, and I want my mother to think that I'm not a freeloader.

When I hesitate, Mr. Johnson prompts, "Are you premed?"

"I'm not sure yet," I say. "My mother works here, so she told me there were some opportunities."

"Oh." Mr. Johnson's face breaks toward actual interest. "Is she a nurse?"

It's one of my mother's biggest pet peeves to walk into a patient's room, only to have someone assume that she's a nurse or an orderly. Suffice to say, I learned the term "microaggression" before I went to kindergarten. "No, she's a doctor. Dr. Ogonna. Ob-gyn."

He nods knowingly, as if to suggest that it finally makes sense why I'm applying. "Did you have questions about the job?"

I bring out the folio my dad gave to me and run through the questions we prepared last night. I barely register Mr. Johnson's answers, transcribing them to my reporter's notebook like they're algebra homework to be solved later. He asks me a few questions about what electives I'm taking, and we talk about my extracurriculars, but really it seems like the point of the interview is to make sure that I have a pulse.

Before I leave, I think of one more question. "What is the stipend for the internship?"

When Mr. Johnson laughs, he laughs with his whole body. "Oh boy. I'm sorry if your mother didn't know, William, but St. Luke's has a policy that teens aren't eligible for our paid internships unless they have a high school diploma. If you want big bucks, you'll have better luck with construction. I have a buddy who might be looking for an apprentice."

When my dad asks me how the interview went, I don't know what to say.

"It was okay," I manage. I stare at the reporter's notebook I wrote my interview notes on and grimace at the "responsibilities" of my job at St. Luke's: Scanning medical records. Data entry. Running utilization reports. Then I flip back to Mr. Evans's sound bites from the day before.

"You know what, Dad? I think I'm going to look around some more."

♡

After my interview, I go to drown my sorrows at Amazing Stories, where Manny (aka Mansur Fathi: Most Likely to Succeed at Breaking Will Domenici Out of a Thought Spiral) is newly employed. The space used to be a nail salon, and sometimes if you breathe in really deeply you can still smell the carcinogens.

Manny, Javier, and I have a standing gig taking a first look at that week's trade-ins, including some pieces that the owner, Jordan, gets off eBay. It's not a particularly good haul this week, mostly 1990s X-Men that's already been digitized on Marvel Unlimited, so it doesn't take too long. Still, my stomach is rumbling by the end. Or maybe it's just leftover nerves. "Guys, can we go over to the deli? I need a BLT or something."

"Bring me something back," Manny says, adding an unnecessary, "no piggie." Manny isn't a particularly observant Muslim, but he's pretty firm about the no-pork thing. "I just don't understand why you'd want to eat an animal that literally eats garbage," he says whenever I have a ham sandwich.

"We didn't ask you how your interview at the hospital went," Javier says as we walk to the deli down the street. He does that a lot—replays conversations in his head so he can follow threads and tease out social cues that he can act on later.

"The interview went okay, but they can't pay me, so it's probably not worth it. I'm just afraid my mom's going to make me do it 'for the experience.'" I make air quotes.

"You can always look for another job that pays," Javier says.

"Yeah, because jobs for high school sophomores grow on trees around here."

"There's a job right there." Javier points to a sign literally in front of our faces, on the window of A-Plus Chinese Garden:

HELP WANTED:
SEEKING SUMMER MANAGEMENT INTERN
TO HELP GROW OUR BUSINESS.
WEB PAGE DEVELOPMENT EXPERIENCE PREFERRED.
COME BE PART OF AN
A-PLUS TEAM!

I look at the sign and I can't help it. I bark out a laugh. "Um, no," I say, shaking my head.

"Why not?" asks Javier curiously.

I blink, and think. I do that a lot when I'm around Javier. Not only because he's brilliant, but because he has this utterly objective view of the world that occasionally forces me to rethink my own biases.

When I contemplate it, I laughed because of the visual image of me passing out fortune cookies and rolling sushi. It could easily be a *Saturday Night Live* skit, with the lyrics "One of these things is not like the others" playing in the background.

My hunger pangs twist into shame. I think about my sister, and how she says that your reaction to cognitive dissonance says volumes about who you are.

Five seconds in, five seconds out.

I close my eyes and breathe in the warm June air. The scent

of fried rice mingles with the smell of yeast from the bakery down the street.

The unsettled feeling in my stomach calms. I look back again at the HELP WANTED sign. It's a good poster. The job's an opportunity to manage a team and grow a small business. I have at least one of the skills they're looking for. Whoever made the poster has hand-illustrated it with little anthropomorphized sushi rolls and dumplings with thought bubbles saying things like "A-Plus needs YOU!" In addition to a call-back number and an e-mail address, each of the little tear-offs at the bottom has a different emoji.

As gently as I can, I tear off the tab with the shrug emoji.

This Is My Brain
on Twitter

JOCELYN

I would love to describe my family's restaurant as a dive, but honestly it's not cool enough to be considered one.

To be clear, the restaurant isn't dirty—it's just old. When my dad first visited A-Plus Chinese Garden, he was pleasantly surprised. There were no rat problems or fire hazards, and the building breezed through inspection. The decor wasn't awful for a place that wasn't really a sit-down spot—there were four booths with mostly intact red vinyl coverings, and room for a few tables. The walls were plain but didn't need repainting. I hated the name, though.

"Isn't that the name of a convenience store? Can we change it to 'China Garden' or something?" I knew there was no way he'd take the "Garden" out of the name. The word for garden in Mandarin is "yuan," which is a homonym for money. You don't mess with those things.

"No, no, no," my dad insisted. "Keep A-Plus and we always be at top of search engine list." I think he just didn't want to spring for new signage. Six years later, same name, same '80s decor. One winter I tried to dress the place up for the holidays, but my dad wouldn't okay the purchase of Christmas lights. "You can't turn a sow's ear into a silk purse."

Basically, when I look around the restaurant for a background image for our new Facebook, Instagram, and Twitter accounts, I have no idea where to begin. It's like how you can enter a room where someone's thrown a banana into the trash, and at first you're like, "Oh, shit, someone ate a banana?" Then you wait a few minutes, and you don't even notice it—you've been desensitized to the smell.

I'm a little desensitized to design when it comes to our restaurant. I know it doesn't look quite right, but it isn't jarring to me anymore. More importantly, I have no idea how to fix it. I can't even imagine it looking good, to be honest. Maybe if we made it completely dark and put in strobe lights. At least the floor doesn't have any obvious stains—it's a drab brown low-pile carpet that could probably hide a mass murder.

"Do you think we should take pictures in the bathroom?" I ask Priya when she lugs her camera and lighting gear in. "That's the nicest part of the restaurant since Dad wallpapered it."

"Don't worry, I brought some tablecloths and scarves we can use as background, and we can put some food on some special serving plates," says my genius friend.

Priya's dad is an applied science professor at the college and her mom is a nurse, which means that she and her brother knew from an early age that they had to go into either engineering or medicine (personally, I also had business and law as options, which made my parents seem really open-minded). We had been friends for about two days when she told me her plan to sabotage her grades so that her parents would let her go to film school to study cinematography.

"Doesn't it bug you, to have your parents think that you've failed?" I asked when she told me how she intentionally put down a few wrong answers for a math test.

"Getting a B isn't failure," she said, even though she knew that it kind of was, in our parents' eyes.

"But don't you ever think, 'God, if I'm not any good at this crappy school in the middle of nowhere, how am I ever going to succeed in life?'"

"Einstein failed high school."

"No he didn't. That's a myth." My dad looked it up once when I used it as an excuse for getting a B plus.

"Fine, then. There are plenty of other people who didn't get straight As who did great in life. You know how all those college counselors say that you don't need to be well-rounded, if you're well-flat?"

"Is that some sort of comment about my bra size?"

The point is, Priya's determined to go to film school, and I'm 110 percent certain that she's going to make it. She's aces with a lens, whether it's an iPhone or a video camera. She has an eagle eye for the essence of things and always knows how best to frame objects to make a picture more than a bunch of pixels. To make it into art.

I run upstairs to grab our nicest serving plates—the ones that stay in our curio cabinet all year—and a pair of lacquered wooden chopsticks. I bring my amah, too, because she's the most photogenic member of our family.

When we get downstairs Priya has set up lights and draped cloths to create a shockingly gorgeous background, accented with some jade jewelry.

"Oooh, that's pretty. Where'd you get that necklace?" I ask.

"It's your mom's."

I look over to where my mom is readying the register. "I've never seen those!" I say.

My mom gives a small smile. "Priya need something pretty. I never get chance to wear my nice things." It's true. My mom does so much prep work at the restaurant that she never even wears her wedding rings. Her hands are perpetually chapped and Band-Aided to cover her bleeding cuticles.

I swallow hard. "Thanks, Mom." Then I ask Priya, "What other dishes do you think will look good?"

"How about some kind of sushi and sweet-and-sour chicken?"

"Okay, one Cali roll and one ABC chicken coming up...."

"I thought chicken and broccoli was ABC chicken?" says Priya.

"No, that's ABC broccoli."

It's no secret that what's served in American Chinese restaurants isn't close to what most people in China actually eat. The sad thing is I'm such an ABC (short for "American-born Chinese") that I'm used to "fake" Chinese food and find most of the dishes my amah cooks to be kind of bland. Except her dumplings, which are perfection.

When we're done, Priya loads up her images and I show them to my grandmother.

"Amah, this one with you is the best one. It's so terrific. I'm going to put it on the web."

"Ai-yo, why didn't you tell me I gain so much weight?" she laments. "You should tell me early. I put makeup on."

"Don't worry, Mrs. Wu. We can use a filter." Priya taps some buttons, and voilà. Covergirl Grandma.

Amah clicks her tongue and gives a nodding frown, her way of saying "not bad." She watches with interest as I load the image to Instagram and Twitter.

"What is that?" she asks. "Some kind of…what you call it? Message board?"

"It's called Twitter," I explain. "It's like…it's a way to send texts out to the whole world. We're trying to get the word out about the restaurant."

"So…whole world can see this?"

"If they follow us, yes."

"What you mean 'follow'?"

And we go down a twenty-minute rabbit hole. By the end of it, Priya has gathered up all her stuff and sent out five tweets about me trying to explain social media to my grandmother. #DontLetGrandmaTweet. Her hashtag doesn't trend, but we do get twenty new followers.

Even better? That night I get a résumé for my job posting.

This Is My Brain on the Unexpected

JOCELYN

Because pretty much all my clothes are hand-me-downs, or from Goodwill or Target, I call an emergency fashion consult with Priya on the day of my very first employee interview.

Ultimately, we throw together the black slacks that I wore once for a middle school chorus concert with a blouse that my auntie Lei got from Taiwan. I even sneak into my parents' bathroom, steal some lipstick, and comb my hair. Checking myself in the warped bathroom cabinet mirror, I have to give myself props. Pretty good "She Cleans Up Nicely" trope.

At 1:50 I head down to the restaurant. The place is pretty much dead except for the sounds of Jin-Jin cleaning up the kitchen in the background, so I bring out my laptop and transfer the questions from Monster.com onto a legal pad, as if that were somehow more official.

At 1:53 I grab two glasses of water, feeling only a little silly when I set them on cocktail napkins, because it's not like Formica forms water stains.

At 1:58 the bell jangles as someone comes in. It's a tall black guy in a navy-blue suit that doesn't quite fit him. He looks almost lost, and there's a furrow between his brows as he scans the restaurant before settling on me.

"Can I help you?" I ask. "We're still serving lunch if you need anything."

"I'm, um, William Domenici."

I puff a laugh. "Oh, of course. Sorry," I stammer, and give my head a shake, only barely resisting an actual facepalm. Way to get off on the right foot. "Sorry. Please come in."

Oh, God, I'm such a screwup.

WILL

The girl at A-Plus is quite pretty, or would be if her mouth wasn't twisting in dismay. She has shoulder-length hair that frames round, full cheeks and brown eyes with thick, quirky eyebrows.

"Sorry. Please come in," she says.

"I wasn't who you expected," I say grimly, a familiar tightness growing in my chest.

"No, not really." She smiles crookedly. "You just look so professional I didn't take you for a high school student." At that her smile breaks open, and the pressure under my breastbone recedes. She stands up and beckons me in to sit at her table.

"Hi, William. I'm Jocelyn Wu," she says as she extends her hand. I try to subtly wipe mine against my pants before holding out my own. Her hands are soft and dry. They feel like my mother's favorite blue silk scarf.

"It's Will. Call me Will."

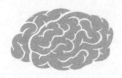

This Is My Brain
on Chemistry

JOCELYN

Will sits across from me and I slide the glass of water over to him. He nods in thanks and fiddles a little bit with the corner of the napkin. It's the smallest sign of nerves and reminds me that I'm supposed to be running the show.

It's hard to feel in charge when he's wearing a suit and I'm in an outfit Frankensteined from my thrift-store chic wardrobe. I feel…short sitting across from him and straighten up a little bit. But it's weird. He doesn't act tall, and his shoulders slope a little bit, almost apologetically. It's cute. Or it would be if I weren't concentrating on interviewing him. Which I totally am.

I clear my throat and peek down at my notes.

"So, Will. What makes you interested in working here at A-Plus?"

WILL

I swallow, and suddenly I can feel my heart throbbing in my ears. This is the question that I've dreaded the most, that I pondered all last night as I second-guessed my decision to accept the interview. I'm still not sure if I'll get it right.

"I've eaten your food before and think that it's great. I like that you can use my web skills, and it'll be cool to get behind-the-scenes in the restaurant game. Plus, I work for the St. Agnes school paper and my adviser wanted me to learn how to manage a team and grow a business."

She nods, expression neutral. I want to see that little sliver of a smile again, so I add, my voice shaking only a little, "Also I thought your sign was cute."

If you were to measure it, her lips probably tick up only a millimeter. But it brings me miles closer to calm.

JOCELYN

I knew the emojis would be a hit. I knew it! My dad frowned and said it looked "not professional," but I was right. I let myself preen for just a second and then settle down to business. Who is this guy and do I want to pay him with the money I shredded my soul to earn?

"You said you work for the school newspaper at St. Agnes?" That's the local Catholic school. No wonder I didn't recognize him.

"I just finished my sophomore year."

"Me too. I'm at Perry High." Weird, to be interviewing

someone who is the same age as me. My eyes flick toward the legal pad with questions from Monster.com.

"Tell me about your greatest strength? And your biggest weakness?"

Will nods and looks straight at me, and wow, effective use of eye contact. While his skin is a smooth medium brown, his eyes are dark, almost black, kind of like mine. "My greatest strength is probably that I am very detail oriented and careful. I think before I act and try to consider all the consequences of my actions before I do anything. That's how my parents raised me."

He says the last part almost as an afterthought and breaks our gaze to take a sip of water.

WILL

My parents raised me to be thoughtful, of course, because when you're black in America you need to consider the consequences of your actions in a way that other people don't.

Sometimes, though, thinking too much can paralyze you. So when Jocelyn asks me what my biggest weakness is, I tell the truth. "I guess the flip side of thoughtfulness is that I can think too much. Once in a while, it takes me too long to get things done. My sister, Grace, calls me a camel." I grin, thinking of last Christmas when she gleefully packed my stocking with dromedary-themed stuff. "I can agonize for hours over things that seem trivial to others. But the thing is, I feel like when I make decisions, I can stand by them."

JOCELYN

Will's honesty catches me off guard. "Good answer," I blurt out a millisecond before the silence gets uncomfortable. I blush. God, how condescending.

He takes it in stride, and I wonder if it's because he's been told too many times how "articulate" he is. "Thank you."

I look at question number three. "So, what do you want to know about us?"

"What are the general duties you mentioned in your e-mail?" Will asks.

I shrug. "Whatever needs to be done. The main thing I need help with is social media and outreach. We need to get more customers. But the more customers we have, the more we might need someone to help with processing credit cards and delivering. Do you have a car?"

Will nods.

Thank God. If Will can drive, we can expand our delivery radius—right now we only deliver to where my brother and I can bike. We really aren't going to find a more perfect candidate. The restaurant might actually have a fighting chance.

"Anyway, that's the deal. I think you'd be great for the job. We can't really pay you more than minimum wage plus gas mileage, but you'll also get some money from tips. You could probably get thirty to forty dollars if it's a good night. And of course, we'll provide a meal each shift."

This is the part that I dread: I watch him do the mental math, and I step back for a second and consider this from his point of view. He has a good résumé, excellent references. What the heck do I think A-Plus Chinese Garden can offer him?

Nothing.

I close my laptop and finish off my water in one gulp. "I can give you a few days to make your decision. I know you've probably got a lot of options. But if it sweetens the pot any, I can also add the Netflix password that I stole from my BFF into your compensation package."

He grins at that, the corner of his eyes crinkling, and I feel a pang that it might be both the first and the last time I ever see his smile.

WILL

When Jocelyn offers me a job on the spot, our role reversal is so absolute it's dizzying. All of a sudden, I'm no longer the supplicant. I've been chosen, and I don't know what to do with my newfound power to reject.

I don't respond immediately, and Jocelyn's face falls, and I'm surprised by how keenly I feel her disappointment in my own chest. It seems out of proportion to what I could offer as an employee.

If I'm being honest, I applied to the job to prove to myself and to Javier that I'm an equal-opportunity job seeker, and I agreed to the interview mostly because it seemed like a low-stakes way to get another interview under my belt. But then today when I told Manny where I was going, he got really excited. "Did you know A-Plus is the only restaurant in that strip mall that hasn't closed in my lifetime?"

It made me wonder if there is a story there. In the *Spartan*, we're always writing about stores that are opening. We've never really done a piece on the restaurants—the Utica institutions, really—that *stay* open. Just last fall, Javier went for a photo shoot for an article about a new gastropub; I remember laying out his photos and being surprised by how trendy it looked, and thinking that the owners must have spent a fortune on interior design.

That gastropub closed within eight months. And yet A-Plus, with its battered Formica tabletops and minimalist decor, has been around for as long as I can remember.

There *has* to be a story there.

Jocelyn stands up and bites her lip. "Well, thank you for your time."

I blurt out a response without thinking about it.

"I'll take it."

Jocelyn's eyes bug out comically. "You...Seriously?"

Watching her light up ignites a warmth in my belly that cements my decision, my use of power. "Yeah," I say, taking in the bare-bones restaurant. It's clean. Rough around the edges, for sure, but it's not trying to be anything that it isn't. "This place has a lot of potential."

JOCELYN

Maybe I'm not the only one who's desensitized to design.

I reach out my hand, happiness and hope bubbling up inside me.

"Welcome to the A-Plus team, Will. You can call me Jos."

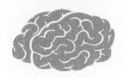

This Is My Brain on Hope

JOCELYN

That afternoon, I'm so stoked to tell my dad I hired someone that I actually hang out in our living room, something I haven't done since middle school.

Amah pulls me in to de-string some snap peas, taking advantage of my public appearance. I look over at my brother fiddling around with his Nerf basketball hoop in the front hallway. "Hey, why isn't Alan helping?" I complain.

"He no good at doing this. Take ten times as long and pea look like been chewed on by dog," she says.

"Can't he at least fold some napkins or something?"

"I did them already," Alan says, bouncing off a rim shot. "Amah promised I could play for a while when I was done."

"Five more minute, then homework," Amah reminds him.

My poor bro almost flunked math last year so Mom and Dad put him in summer school. That's one of the reasons we're so shorthanded—it's not like Alan can do much (he only just turned twelve), but even having someone to do busywork like folding napkins and filling up the little take-out containers of soy sauce keeps us afloat.

The three of us in the room is as close to a family gathering as we can get when we're not in the restaurant; my mom is already downstairs, cutting and marinating meat. When I was younger I used to wonder if this was the life she thought she'd have when she first came to America as a teenager. Did she imagine that she'd come home from a twelve-hour shift every night with her hair reeking of sesame oil and cornstarch trapped under her fingernails? She knew when she married my father that he was in the restaurant business, of course, but maybe she thought she'd be a cheongsam-wearing hostess at a fancy sit-down dim sum restaurant in the city, the kind of place that uses nondisposable chopsticks and charges five bucks for a pot of chrysanthemum tea.

In sixth grade we had one of those personal history assignments for school—the kind where you make a family tree and interview your parents. I actually asked my mom what she had wanted to be when she grew up, if she wished she'd done something different with her life.

She surprised me: She didn't regret anything. She didn't seem to resent the hard work, the dreariness and exhaustion, or the fact that we hadn't had a family vacation in twelve years.

"You were my dream, you and Alan," she said. "This is my dream, that you grow up and have good life, be happy."

The question that kept nagging me afterward, though, was this: If I'm not happy, does that mean I'm killing my mother's dream? Because I can honestly count on my hands the number of times in my life when I've felt unadulterated happiness. I've never been a bouncy Tigger, or a kind and steadfast Piglet. I'm an Eeyore, plain and simple.

I can tell when my father gets back from his supply run because the muffler on his ten-year-old Honda Accord broke three months ago and he hasn't bothered to fix it yet. I wait for the sound of the trunk slamming shut and run down.

"Baba!" He's unloading drinks into the display case. My hand moves toward a pink lemonade Snapple, but at his sharp gaze I grab a Nestea iced tea (twenty-five cents cheaper) instead. "I hired someone for the internship today."

He grunts. "You think he reliable?"

"Yeah, I do," I say. "He's a high school student, but he's in the honor society, so he's got to be pretty responsible."

"It's good he a student. Minimum wage only—don't have to listen to him begging for more money for his children." Frowning, he lifts a carton of produce over the counter. "Still don't know if we can afford. He work for one month, we see if we can keep him on."

"I probably have enough money to cover him for two months," I say.

My dad grimaces like someone who's just bitten into a sour orange. "Do not be silly. The restaurant pay him."

"Are you sure?" It's a legitimate question—he actually looks physically pained.

"One month. At end of month, if he not pay for himself…" My dad makes a throat-cutting gesture, and I know it's not just Will who'll get the ax.

It'll be my life as I know it.

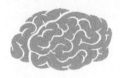

This Is My Brain on Action

JOCELYN

By Tuesday, I feel like someone should be playing "Eye of the Tiger": It's time for the "Training Montage" trope.

For Will's first day, I've printed out the Yelp pages, websites, and social media stats of our major competitors, including the No. 1 China Restaurant two towns over, whose Stone Age marketing plan makes me feel much better about myself.

I also may have taken a peek at the copy of *Running a Restaurant for Dummies* at our library, but you'll never be able to prove it. Ten minutes of browsing through that book made it clear how little my parents know about running a business. When I started looking at my dad's files—they are still mostly on paper and written in that crisply uniform handwriting that is so typical of people who grew up writing Chinese characters—I remembered that he never finished high school in Taiwan. He was pretty much my age when he came over to help my uncle with his business.

Basically, everything he knows about restauranting, he learned on the job. He definitely didn't have any pro forma sheets or business plans in any of his files. If you were to summarize my parents' advice on how to run a restaurant, it would boil down to two things: hard work and sacrifice. Everything else is just noise.

When I come down the back stairs to the restaurant dining room, Will is already there and I'm struck by a sudden panic. He's not wearing his suit, obviously, but with his slacks and navy button-down, he still looks like he should be the head waiter at one of the bistros downtown with outdoor seating. He's carrying a leather folio and a cardboard cup holder with two hot drinks from the overpriced café that just opened up by the college.

In other words, he couldn't look more out of our league if he'd tried.

WILL

Jos is wearing flip-flops, a Hufflepuff shirt, and cutoff jean shorts that are so revealing that in my attempt not to ogle my new boss, I'm rendered completely unable to remember the greeting I rehearsed.

Instead I blurt out, "I got coffee," and shove the cup holder into her hands. Except she's holding a legal pad and a water bottle and I manage to crowd her just enough that she can't easily put the things down, leading to some excruciating seconds of awkward juggling that I eventually resolve by admitting defeat and setting the drinks back down on the booth where I was sitting when she came in.

"Thanks," says Jocelyn when the cups are back on stable ground again. "You didn't have to do that. Aren't I supposed to be the one providing fringe benefits?"

I feel myself blushing. It's early enough in the day that it's still relatively cool, so I don't feel any actual beads of sweat on my temple, but I can feel the heat building at my hairline. Right on cue, I hear my mother's voice reminding me to *just breathe, William, and say something.*

I don't give myself a whole five seconds to inhale, but I get to a count of three before I give a shaky smile. "I didn't have time to make coffee at home and the place was on my way in. You really don't want to see me trying to solve problems when I'm under-caffeinated. My sister tells me it's like watching a slow-motion replay of someone missing a dunk."

Jos grins, and I get down to business so I don't have to come up with more small talk. "So how do you guys do things around here? Do you have an electronic ordering system?"

Jos rolls her eyes. "I wish." She waves a paper order pad. "We have two cases of these in our basement, and I'll bet you real money that my dad would say we can't waste the rest, and we shouldn't transition to digital until we use them all up."

A warm slice of recognition melts away the last of my residual anxiety. "My grandmother hoards stuff like that. She still drives a 1997 Peugeot that she shipped over from Nigeria. 'It is still working; why would I replace it?'" I mimic the standard retort she uses every time my mother offers to buy her a new car.

"As you can see, we're a bit of a fixer-upper," Jos says. "I have a plan, though."

JOCELYN

After a while I realize that Will's preppy getup and the overpriced drinks make him more adorable than intimidating. It's more of a "tries too hard" than "thinks he's better than anyone else" vibe.

Also, he seems to get the restaurant and isn't afraid to tell me what it needs.

"There's a lot to work with here," Will declares. "I mean, the potential of the online stuff is unlimited, and free. There are also easy changes we can make here in the storefront."

"Our website really needs help, though." Right now ours is only a landing site with our phone number and a photo of our menu that's at least two years out of date.

"I can upgrade it. Do you want me to make you an online shopping portal?"

I gape at him. "You know how to do that?"

"Uh, yeah." He looks sheepish, so I assume I'm looking at him like he's just barfed up a pile of gold, which he kind of did, when you think about how much money he could potentially be saving us. "It's not like I'm a computer genius or anything like that. But my mother made me go to programming camp a couple of years ago, and that was one of the things they taught us."

I shake my head, unable to believe my luck. One improvement down, approximately 574 to go. "Now, what do you think we should do about Yelp?"

WILL

At around ten o'clock, we get our first preorder for lunch pickup at noon, and Jocelyn brings me back to do a tour of the kitchen when she relays the order.

When I walk through the kitchen door, I understand for the first time why Mr. Evans was pushing me to go behind the scenes for my stories. Five seconds of standing there taking in the sights, sounds, and smells of the kitchen gives me more fodder than a dozen e-mails, more detail than I'd be able to pick up with hours of online research. I'm struck first by the wall of sound. There's the baseline hum of the refrigerator units, the on-and-off susurration of the dishwasher, the woodpecker sound of chopping. One of the cooks, a burly, pug-nosed Asian man who Jocelyn introduces as Jin-Jin, is cracking eggs into a giant vat of soup. A younger woman named Miss Zhou is cutting carrots with a daunting efficiency. An older woman, reed thin with heavy-lidded eyes, sits at a corner table making dumplings.

Jocelyn brightens. "Come meet my grandma." She jogs over to the back and introduces me to the older woman. "Amah, this is Will. He'll be working with me on all the online stuff that Priya and I were talking about."

"But I'm happy to help out around the kitchen and up front as well," I insert. I don't want it to sound like I'm afraid to get my hands dirty.

Jocelyn's grandma puts down the wooden dowel she's using to roll the dough and wipes off her flour-covered hands briskly with a wet rag. "Very nice meeting you," she says in gently accented English. "You work in restaurant before?"

"No," I admit.

Her face breaks into a wide, eye-crinkling grin. "That what I think. You too skinny. Do not worry." She pats me on the arm consolingly. "We fatten you up. You like pot sticker?"

"Sure, they're great," I say.

"Be careful," Jocelyn warns. "You'll want to marry those dumplings when you're done."

When I bite into the finished pot sticker, which is still piping hot, sublimely crispy on the outside and juicy and bursting with flavor on the inside, I can't say that she's wrong.

"Holy cow," I say, so overcome that I talk with my mouth still full. If my mother were here she'd be scandalized by my manners. "Why are people not lining up outside your door to buy these things?"

Jocelyn thinks about it. "I dunno. Most of our orders are take-out, so maybe they're just not as good when they've been sitting in a box for twenty minutes? Or..." Her eyes open in horror. "I know why. Because we don't actually have pot stickers on the menu. Only boiled dumplings, because that's faster and easier."

Then she grins like a maniac. "Good thing there's an easy fix for that."

JOCELYN

The back entrance to the A-Plus parking lot is open except for the screen door, so I can tell my dad is in a foul mood before I even see him. "Zenmegaode, ludo dou mai?" he mutters as he unloads the boxes of produce from our van. When I look over at Will he's got a little crease between his eyes. There's no way he can know that my dad is complaining about our supplier's lack of green beans, but I'm pretty sure it took him about a millisecond to peg my dad for a grouch.

The screen door screams as my dad pushes it open using his elbow, and he unloads two boxes with a groan and a "zhong si." He's panting with his hands on his hips, his back turned to us, when I decide to rip the Band-Aid off.

I give Will a smile that is probably more than a little apologetic. He's going to have to meet my father eventually; might as well know what he's getting into from the start.

"Hey, Dad. This is Will. Our new employee."

WILL

When Jocelyn introduces me to her father, I freeze immediately, because that's what I do when I'm introduced to new people out of the blue. Dr. Rifkin says it's a survival tactic that allows me to observe the stranger, put on a neutral expression, and let the other person speak to me first, so as to set the ground rules of our interaction.

Mr. Wu eyes me up and down. He's wearing jeans and a Hawaiian shirt that's now patchy with sweat, and I feel like a tool in my button-down.

After what seems like an eternity, he asks, without any preamble, "What your GPA?"

I blink and answer automatically, because that's what I do with adults. "4.35."

Mr. Wu squints at me. "How you get GPA more than 4.0?" he asks suspiciously. "What kind of school you go to?"

"I go to St. Agnes, sir. You can get above a 4.0 if you're taking AP classes."

Jocelyn's dad sniffs and nods as begrudging a nod as I've ever seen. His eyes are a dark brown, kind of like his daughter's, but they lack the openness that hers have. "You ever be arrested?" Mr. Wu continues in his interrogation. "Do drugs? I have friend at police station, I can check."

The outright aggression of his question (nothing micro about that one) leaves me speechless. Thankfully, Jocelyn has my back. "Dad!" she hisses. "Of course not. I asked about that stuff on the application. He got the Citizenship Award last year for crying out loud."

Her indignation goes a long way toward giving me the words to answer her father's question. When the sting of his accusation dissipates, I hear my mother's voice in my head, reminding me to turn the other cheek, to kill with kindness. It's not as if these aren't questions that any employer would want to know, even if they don't have the nerve to ask them to my face.

"Sir, my record is perfectly clean," I say, in as steady a voice as I can muster. "I can have one of my references, Father Healdon, call you if you have any questions." I figure it'd be laying it on too thick to add that I was an altar boy and still sing in the church choir.

Mr. Wu frowns and squints at me again, and my brain starts generating rogue press conference questions like a mofo. What if Mr. Wu thinks that I'm too arrogant? What if he decides to call up Father Healdon, who tells him about the time I left my cell phone on and Led Zeppelin's "Immigrant Song" from *Thor: Ragnarok* (Manny's distinctive ringtone) went off in the middle of Communion? What if Mr. Wu looks through my résumé and thinks I'm exaggerating my business experience with my "selling ads for the school newspaper" line item?

Finally, after what feels like decades of scrutiny, Mr. Wu lets out a breath through pursed lips and waves at me dismissively. "No, no need to make call, too much trouble. You work hard, there be no problem. But Jocelyn will keep close eye. No hanky-panky! I want to see results! Now come help me carry in grocery."

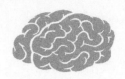

This Is My Brain on Smiles

JOCELYN

I almost pass out from relief when Will doesn't quit on the spot after my dad's questions about drugs and arrests.

Seriously? Like my dad doesn't know what it's like to be racially stereotyped?

There is one moment where the shock on Will's face almost tilts into anger, but then he closes his eyes, and when he opens them he's composed again. Even respectful, though my dad barely deserves it.

Over the years, I've gotten good at keeping any exposure my dad has with my friends—and potential friends—to a minimum. He's just too embarrassing, on so many levels. But Will's an employee now. It's not like I could shield him from my father forever.

I wonder if it's weird that I've already started to view Will as a potential friend, as a person I want to hang out with. A person I want to not just respect me, but like me.

Because I like him. Not, like, *like* like him. Though the guy does look good in a suit.

Basically, Will is a pretty darn likable dude. I'm most impressed by how calm he is when my dad gives him the third degree. Actually, "calm" is the wrong word—the way he holds himself almost soldier straight suggests there's some sort of tension buzzing under the surface. He's…deliberate. But it isn't a calculating, manipulative kind of deliberation that a pro would throw at you during a job interview. He's thoughtful. Wanting to give an honest answer.

Which is good, because the Wu family bullshit radar is military grade.

Given how much of my time the restaurant eats up, I don't have that many close friends. Priya has a ton of them and I kind of hate her for it.

Another thing that doesn't help is my resting bitch face, which my mom has been trying to train me out of since middle school: "Why you frown all time, Xiao Jia? You so pretty when you smile! How you find husband if you always look so moody?"

I always thought it was ironic that she'd bring up my future mate (assumed to be male, of course), when it's always been a given that she and my dad won't let me date until college. I guess the point my mom was trying to make was that people don't consider me welcoming, because I only smile when given a reason to. And what's the matter with that? It takes a lot of effort and a significant amount of muscle control to be a walking smile emoji all the time.

Bottom line: I don't meet potential friends often, so I'm glad my dad didn't scare Will away.

I make sure to plaster a big smile on my face when Will comes in with the last of the broccoli. He's panting a little and has rolled up the sleeves of his button-down, revealing well-toned arms that my gaze does not linger on at all, I don't know what you're talking about.

When I manage to tear my eyes away from the glorious lines of his forearms and shift to his face, he's grinning at me, too, and I feel my forced smile relax into something more natural, more true.

I'm really looking forward to those muscles getting more use.

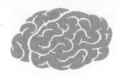

This Is My Brain on Work

WILL

No amount of research, no phone interview, could ever prepare me for how hard it is to run a restaurant. Behind the curtain, the action never ends. If you're not prepping for a meal, you're cooking it, or serving it, or packaging it up. Then you're cleaning and closing out the register, and then it's time for another service. Rinse and repeat. It's never-ending and exhausting and humbling.

I tell Jocelyn as much after the lunch rush is over and ask her how her parents have kept up the pace all these years. She shrugs. "It's what they do to survive. They don't know anything different."

The words she uses so casually to describe her parents' motivations cut deep. They do it *to survive*. I've always known that I live an economically privileged life, but it's possible that today is the first day I've ever understood what it is like to be a little bit desperate that you won't be able to make ends meet. In just a few hours I can see the toll it takes on Mr. Wu, with his constant scowl and complaints about the cost of produce. It makes me sad, and determined at the same time. I took the job practically on a whim, but after just a day I want to stay because of how I might be able to help out.

"I just wish I could have done more," I say. "Thanks for a good first day."

Jocelyn shakes her head. "No. Thank you," she says with a force that surprises me. "Half the time we're at DEFCON 1. Having even one set of extra hands makes it basically a party."

And that's why I leave A-Plus shaking my head—that anyone in their right mind would ever imply that I bring the party with me.

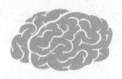

This Is My Brain on Hormones

JOCELYN

"Pri," I moan over the phone as soon as I get into my room after we've closed the restaurant. "You have to help me. I think I'm falling for the 'Nerds Are Sexy' trope."

"NO WAY."

"Yes way, and it's terrible."

"Who is it? Is he googleable? I need pics ASAP."

"You know that ad I put out? I hired this guy Will. He's gonna be a junior at St. Agnes in the fall. I can see if he's on Insta or anything."

"He goes to Catholic school? Is he totally straightedge?"

"Kinda? But in a totally sweet, adorable way, not in an annoying judgy way. He's black, or maybe mixed race, I think. He works for his school newspaper and is just really a solid guy, super thoughtful. My dad met him today, and he only asked one racist question that made me want to die." I tell her about how he's going to redo our website basically for free, and how he both passed my dad's GPA test *and* aced Amah's pot sticker challenge.

"Did your mom meet him?"

"No, it was already too lunch-busy when she came back from her errands. I think it'll be weird to do a formal introduction. Better to just let him grow on her."

The truth is, Will isn't the first person that my family has been biased against, and he won't be the last. Case in point: The day after I got my period, my mother sat me down to do her version of the birds and the bees talk, which included a rundown of who it was acceptable to marry in my hypothetical future.

"American boys only want one thing. You should marry an Asian guy." Except she then proceeded to contradict herself by eliminating every other Asian subgroup based on their worst ethnic stereotype, concluding, "As long as you find someone who is Taiwanese, that okay."

Priya got her own special brand of South Asian mom xenophobia, so she gets that white people haven't cornered the market on bias. In fact, she was the one who explained to me, after her family trip to India, how colonial powers encouraged intraracial prejudice—the better to keep everyone down.

"Sliding the guy in under the radar is a good strategy. It'll give you time to get some mom-bait details, play the long game. Maybe you can pretend he wants to be premed and make him come up with nutritional information for your menu. Oh! Or have Amah fake a heart attack and have him do CPR on her."

I roll my eyes. "You've been watching too many telenovelas. Will's got plenty of mom bait up his sleeve; we don't have to make anything up." I realize what I've just said and make a face. "OMG, why are we talking about whether my mom will approve of my marrying Will? It's not like he's going to want to date me or anything."

"Can't hurt to try. This guy sounds incredible! You sound like you're glowing."

"Give me a break, you can't hear light." I sigh, still smiling.

"You know what I mean. You haven't sounded this excited about a guy since…your birthday." She catches herself, but I can hear the name that she didn't want to say out loud anyway. And it's this bruise of a memory that dampens the expanse of my feelings and makes me remember where I am. Who I am. What I need to do, without distractions.

I can feel the smile melt off my face. "Who am I kidding," I mutter. "I'm sure I'm not his type."

"Jos, don't do this."

"Do what?" I ask, daring her to say it.

I hear Priya's deep intake of breath and brace myself. "You know, the thing you sometimes do where you admit defeat before you even start the game."

"It's not like that," I insist. "No games, Pri. I promise. I just got excited. It's only a crush that will run its course. I'm psyched that I found someone who can help the business, that's all."

"Jos."

"Gotta go, it's bedtime. See you tomorrow night to do some storyboarding?" We're working on a short film to submit to the All American High School Film Festival. I'm writing the screenplay and Priya is going to direct.

After we hang up I stare at my ceiling, and despite myself, I can't stop thinking about my last big crush. Rob Bradley comes into A-Plus at least twice a month to pick up takeout for his family, and sometime after Christmas he started making small talk about little things, like our English homework and who we thought was writing our school's anonymous advice column. When Priya told me she'd convinced him to come to my birthday dinner at Carmella's, I wanted to hug her and puke at the same time.

Turns out, Rob only came to my party because he wanted to mack on Peggy Cheng, the other Chinese girl in our grade, aka the one I always get mistaken for.

Months after my party, I still feel like a deflated balloon thinking about it. Rob only gave me a cursory "Hey, happy birthday" before beelining to grab a seat next to Peggy. When I remember how he leaned his head down to laugh with her, there's an echo of pain in my chest.

The most embarrassing thing, though, what I'm maddest at myself for, is that I had thoroughly convinced myself that Rob was interested in me. I still don't know how I was so delusional. What, did I think that my attraction to him would magically make him attracted to me? Animal magnetism doesn't quite work that way.

I'm not going to make the same mistake twice.

Sluggishly, I plug my phone in, but my arms give up on anything more complicated than that. I'm so bone tired that I can't even get the energy to slide off my bed and get ready for sleep.

I figure, why bother brushing your teeth, if you just have to brush them in the morning?

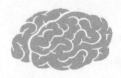

This Is My Brain
on Confusion

WILL

When I get dressed for my second day of work, I make a point to wear jeans and a dark polo shirt and remember to put on sneakers so my feet won't be killing me again by the end of the day. My mother frowns at me as she gets ready to leave. "Looking rather casual, aren't you, Will? I thought you were a management intern." Today's an operating room day for her, so she'll change into scrubs when she gets to the hospital, but she's still wearing a dress and pearls.

"My boss told me to wear clothes that I didn't mind getting dirty," I say, trying not to sound defensive.

"Well, as long as you remember you mustn't look like a hooligan if you expect to get any respect from your coworkers." She punctuates her comment with a kiss on my cheek, and I have to remind myself that her crisp British English makes everything sound harsher than it should.

"So how'd the first day go?" Grace asks after my mom leaves. Her voice is sympathetic. I can't help feeling sad when I think about her going to Yale in the fall.

"It went okay," I say. "The people are nice, and it's cool seeing how a restaurant works. I'm thinking about maybe writing a piece on restaurant turnover and how it can affect the micro-economy of strip malls. Kind of like that feature Julia Brown wrote on the new construction downtown? The one that got published in the *O-D*?"

"Really?" Grace asks. "Are you going to write a Chinese food version of *Kitchen Confidential*? Adventures in the lo mein underbelly?" She fakes a movie trailer voice-over: "What's really in that pork fried rice, and what day of the week should you avoid the moo shu?"

"Ha ha," I say, not impressed. "Hey, have you ever had real pot stickers here in Utica before? You know, the kind of dumplings that are crispy on the bottom but steamed on top?"

"I don't think so. Mom and I had some that time we went to New York Chinatown. On my college trip. Why, do they make them at A-Plus?"

"Not yet," I say. "Quick question: Last year when you ran in the Boilermaker, there was a food court, right? I'm wondering if maybe A-Plus could be a vendor. There's a ton of foot traffic."

"It's kind of late to be planning this. The race is in, like, two weeks."

"Isn't Maria Bertozzi's dad one of the big organizers behind it all, though?" I ask.

"Sure, I guess I can try to get his number for you."

There's a meaningful pause during which my sister looks

right at me, her eyebrows raised as if daring me to say something else.

I know what Grace expects to hear. She's waiting for me to ask if she can call for me. She probably even knows all the arguments I'd make: The Bertozzis know her well, so won't it mean more coming from her? She is the one who ran the race, wouldn't she know more about what kind of opportunities there might be?

She knows that I know she would never make the call.

You would think I would prefer talking on the phone to conversations in real life. It's safer, right? The person on the other end doesn't see you and can't make a snarky judgment of you based on your appearance. You never have to make an effort to look the person in the eye or stress out about their microexpressions and what they mean.

With my anxiety, I should be the type of person who would thrive as a telemarketer, but no. Phone calls are my Achilles' heel. I particularly hate the silent moments, when there's no body language or facial expression to tell me whether someone's bored to death or just thinking about their response. On phone calls, I can second-guess myself to the point of hysteria. This is not an ideal match for journalism, I admit. But luckily, these days most sources are more readily available by e-mail or a text. I've also been known to bike two miles across town to speak with someone in person and have cultivated a lot of friends who are willing to be middlemen and middlewomen when I need to make requests of others.

Grace is not one of those middlewomen. In fact, she is the anti-middlewoman. She is an endwoman. She's my mother's daughter, too, so she's done her homework and decided that the way to fix me is exposure therapy—forcing me to do the things that make me the most anxious to help make them less anxiety-inducing. In the hierarchy of fears that Dr. Rifkin made me chart out, phone calls ranked even higher than public speaking and my anxiety about the mobile roller coasters at the Booneville-Oneida County Fair.

As I dish out some Greek yogurt, blueberries, and granola, Grace sends a series of texts. She's rewarded with a response within a minute, because of course she is.

"I'm forwarding you Mr. Bertozzi's number. Maria says he should be in his office."

"Grace, at least let me finish breakfast first."

I eat my breakfast super slowly just to mess with my sister, but the joke's on me. As I get up to wash my dishes by hand, instead of putting them into the dishwasher like I usually do, she finally loses patience. "Okay, Captain Avoidance, time's up. I've gotta get to work." She grabs my phone, dials a number, and puts it on speakerphone.

I swear and frantically de-suds my hands while the phone rings once, twice. And of course I don't catch a break as Mr. Bertozzi's secretary picks up on the third ring.

"Lisowski and Bertozzi, how may I help you?"

These words should not strike fear in my soul, I know they shouldn't. But I don't need to look at my smart watch app to know that my heart rate has probably doubled. I grab the phone and turn off the speaker. My voice only shakes a little as I answer.

"Um, hello. My name is William Domenici. I was hoping to speak with Mr. Bertozzi?"

The minute I'm put on hold, I hiss at my sister, "I'm going to tell Mom and Dad. You know Dr. Rifkin said exposures are supposed to happen in a safe environment, right?"

Grace rolls her eyes. "Please. You're in our kitchen. Doesn't get much safer than that. Good luck, bro." She grabs her blazer and is out the door before Mr. Bertozzi picks up the phone.

"Will! How can I help you? My daughter just texted something about the Boilermaker?"

"Yes, sir." At least I'm so pissed off at my sister that I can't concentrate enough to be too anxious. "I know the deadline has passed for vendor applications, but I wanted to know if it's possible to make an exception for a small food cart?"

When it turns out that there are a few more openings left, it's maybe a little bit irritating to have to admit that Grace's strong-arm tactics worked. It's worth it, though, to be able to show up at A-Plus with the opportunity in hand. Jocelyn is already staging the bags for that afternoon's lunch orders when I get to the restaurant. She looks up from her work using a box cutter to make rectangles of cardboard and nods at me.

There's something off about her. It's not just that she's frowning with concentration (she is)—it's that her movements are slower than usual. When she showed me the setup routine yesterday, her movements were impressively quick and efficient: open the paper bag with a flick of the wrist, slide it instantly into a plastic bag, line it with cardboard with one hand while grabbing two fortune cookies to throw in with another.

"I should've brought coffee again, huh?" I ask, joking, but when she doesn't smile, I hover awkwardly for a minute.

How could everything that felt so natural yesterday feel so wrong today?

This Is My Brain on Frugality

JOCELYN

My brain feels like a giant ball of lint.

Will, in contrast, comes into work all eager, like a Saint Bernard with a tennis ball in his mouth. I nod at him in greeting, because words seem too hard at the moment.

"I should've brought coffee again, huh?" he jokes, and for a moment it irritates me. Is he basically saying that I look tired? Or worse, cranky? I swallow a snarky response and wave to the kitchen.

"Amah has some green tea already steeped if you need some caffeine."

"No, that's okay. I'm good," he says a little too quickly, like he's trying to manage my mood, for God's sake. I shake my head to clear out the cloud of negativity in my head.

Snap out of it, Wu.

"So," I say. "What's in the folder?"

"Oh!" Will lays down his folio and starts pulling out computer printouts. "I couldn't sleep last night, so I made some mock-ups of a new website."

"Wow," I say after some stunned blinking. "These look awesome!" I mean, anything that uses a font more sophisticated than Arial Black would win an A-Plus design competition, but what Will has come up with is both functional and super slick.

He flips through some different views of the drop-down menus and spouts some technobabble that I mostly ignore, before he asks anxiously, "You like it?"

"Are you kidding? It's ridiculous. You did this in one night? My dad will freak out." At least he'll be happy when he finds out it was free. He's always ignored our website except for the annual grumbling when he has to renew our hosting service.

Will gives a bashful smile. "And, oh, I've got another advertising opportunity. You know the Boilermaker?"

I laugh. "Do I know the Boilermaker?" It is the biggest event of the year in Utica, with literally thousands of runners flooding the city, seeking carbs and electrolytes. "It's a freaking zoo every year. Dad tripled our order of water and Gatorade last year and we still ran out. Why? Are you thinking of running in it?"

"No, it's just…have you ever thought about doing a food stand in the Expo?"

"I don't know," I say dubiously. "Like I said, it's our busiest day of the year."

"Sure, I get it, but we would only have to do the Friday before, not race day. It could expose tens of thousands of people to the restaurant. You and I could run the booth. I think the focus should be your grandma's pot stickers. The smell alone will have hundreds of people following their noses, and when they come by we can hand out samples. I'm sure we'll sell at least a thousand dumplings—and people are going to be ready to pay concessions prices."

"Let's do five for five dollars," I suggest, warming up to the idea. Then I look at the vendor application that Will has already partially filled out, and my eyes goggle.

"It costs FOUR HUNDRED dollars just to have a freaking food stand?" That is more than what we net some nights.

"Look, I know it's a lot, but I swear, it'll be worth it. Even if we don't make up the vendor fee through direct sales, the exposure is priceless—you'll be listed in the program, we can have huge signage. We can hand out menus, too."

I shake my head. "There is no way in hell that my dad is going to shell out four hundred bucks for the 'privilege' of having a booth. He'd sooner take his money and try to deep-fry it."

Will bites his lip. "What if he didn't have to?"

"What, you can get them to waive the fee?"

"Not exactly." Will cricks his neck like he's gearing up to throw a pitch, and he takes a deep breath in and out. "You don't have to give the whole amount up front. There's a fifty-dollar deposit, and then you can put the rest on a credit card the day of the event. If we don't make up the booth cost, I'll pay you back from my tips, or volunteer extra overtime hours without pay."

"You'd take that risk?" I ask.

Will looks down at his feet. He's ditched the wing tips he wore his first day, thank God, and is wearing black-and-white Adidas tennis shoes that look pristine except for one foot's front edge, which he is currently dragging back and forth across our already threadbare carpet.

"I mean, it's my job to help this restaurant succeed, right? And I really think doing the Boilermaker will help. Think of this as a money-back guarantee."

"At one dollar a pop, we'd probably have to sell about one hundred and twenty orders of five to break even, assuming we spend about two hundred dollars in ingredients and supplies," I muse. "You're absolutely sure this is doable?"

"Absolutely."

For the first time since I met Will, I allow myself to stare at him. He meets my eyes without flinching, like he's used to the scrutiny, and when I think about it, I guess that's probably pretty accurate given the town we live in. I'm used to it, too—the gazes that linger just a second longer than they would if I were white, the frank assessment that people make when they add up the sum of your parts and think, *Other*.

"Okay," I say grudgingly. "I'm on to you, you know. You're the fairy godmother of this story."

"The what?"

"The fairy godmother. You know, the deus ex machina that allows the plot to progress?"

"Um, okay."

"Someone needs to start reading more TVtropes.org. Pro tip: Use tabbed browsing. And also, I'm going to draft up a formal agreement where if we don't make up the four hundred dollars with sales from the day of, we'll pay you in pot stickers instead."

Will's eyes dance. "You know that was my master plan all along, right?"

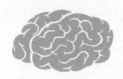

This Is My Brain on Pot Stickers

WILL

The next day is food prep boot camp. Jocelyn is honest in laying out her expectations.

"Your first few jiaozi are going to look like lumpy little bags of crap," she says bluntly.

"Wow, tell me what you really think about my fine motor skills," I joke. It's okay that she's candid. More than okay, if I'm completely truthful. When my father asked me yesterday what I thought of my new job, I said that the work was interesting and that my boss was smart, fair, kind, and completely 100 percent free of bullshit.

Sometimes you don't realize how people layer their lives with a bubble wrap of concern for other people's feelings, until you meet someone who's unvarnished—what some people would call rough around the edges—and realize how refreshing it is not to have to sort through their protective wrapping and suss out who they really are. It just makes you that much more likely to peel off your own buffers against the world, to let yourself breathe.

As Jocelyn explains to me the steps of dumpling making, I can't help but notice that one side of her bottom lip is just a little plumper than the other, and that she has a tiny mole on her left cheek, near her ear.

"Earth to Will, want a pop quiz?" Jocelyn snaps me back from my distraction.

"No need. I got it. Cut off about an inch of dough. Roll it into a ball, flatten it, and use the dowel to thin out the edges while moving it around to make it symmetrical. Put in about a tablespoon of filling. Then you do the twisty thing."

"Not twist!" Grandma Wu scolds. "Pinch." She demonstrates the way to crimp the edges of the dumpling wrapper together. Her moves are as perfectly fluid and graceful as a concert pianist's. I kind of wish we had ESPN here to offer a super-slo-mo replay.

"Do you think you could do that again, maybe not as fast? It looked a lot easier in that *Crazy Rich Asians* scene," I say.

"Best way to learn is to do, no to watch," she insists, waving her dowel. And I prove Jocelyn wrong. My dumplings aren't lumpy little bags of crap.

They're lumpy little bundles of crap that pop open and spooge raw pork onto my T-shirt.

After I manage to make four passable jiaozi in the time it takes Jocelyn and her grandmother to make two hundred, we take a break to transfer the dumplings to the walk-in freezer so we can store them for the race. Then we regroup with Grandma Wu and work in assembly-line fashion. We fall into a synchronized swim of movement, my initially awkward motions smoothing out into a clockwork of activity that hums along with the Wus'.

Our rhythm only breaks once, when Mr. Wu comes in after a supply run. He's glued to his phone and his forehead is furrowed and pinched like one of our jiaozi seams. "...cannot raise rent by ten percent. It unreasonable," he shouts. "I give you five percent. We have been good tenant for many years."

He listens for a few minutes, his breath audible in the suddenly quiet room. Beside me, Jocelyn is frozen mid-wrap, straining so hard to hear the conversation that she's vibrating.

Still listening, Mr. Wu starts shaking his head. "You want to do that? You try. We talk again in July and see what happen." He jabs his thumb to end the call, his mouth twisted in a rictus of frustration. My reporter's curiosity is killing me. What's up with their landlord? Are they really in danger of being kicked out of their space? Mr. Wu puts his left hand over his face and stands there for a second, then storms out of the kitchen to the dining room.

As the swinging door flaps shut, Jocelyn's shoulders stiffen. Her mouth tightens. And grimly, with increasing speed, she keeps on folding.

♡

Before I know it, we have another five hundred jiaozi cooling in the freezer unit, and we call it a day. My T-shirt is gray with flour and there are spots of grease on my jeans that will take a mighty pretreat to remove. When I get up to wash my hands, my stomach rumbles.

Grandma Wu gets a glint in her eye and barks out some commands in Mandarin. Within minutes she's shepherded Jocelyn and me to the front and laid out plates like the staff do for their end-of-the-day meal, with side dishes that don't show up on the menu: smashed cucumber salad, sautéed bok choy, and stir-fried "glass" noodles that Jos says are made from mung beans.

"Why aren't these noodles on the menu?" I ask as I stuff my mouth. "And these cucumbers? They're ridiculously good." They're obscenely flavorful—salty and sweet, tangy and nutty all at the same time.

"I dunno," Jos says. She's barely eaten anything on her plate, using her chopsticks to make a series of mounds with her noodles instead. "My dad just copied the menu my uncle used. Also, mung beans aren't exactly a big draw here in central New York."

I nod, but think to myself that the noodles seem like a no-brainer addition—extremely tasty and made from generally low-cost ingredients. On the other hand, I'm beginning to understand that cucumbers are relatively expensive as fresh veggies go. But it could be an in-season special for August and September, when local farmers are drowning in cukes. I could even ask Mrs. Peabody next door for some the next time she comes around trying to offload her extras. If the restaurant's rent is going to increase, a new popular item could help. I'm dying to ask Jocelyn for their landlord's contact information, but it's pretty obvious that now is not the right time.

Jocelyn's noticeably down for the rest of the afternoon, even though we get a few more followers on Instagram and Facebook. I try to cheer her up by showing her my mock-up e-commerce interface.

As Jocelyn clicks through the steps customers would use to order, I see the clouds begin to lift. Pretty soon she's blazing with excitement. "Will, this could be a game changer," she says, bug-eyed with wonder. "Even two or three orders a night will make a huge difference."

Ten percent, I think. That's how much their rent might go up by. Surreptitiously, while Jocelyn's taking a phone order, I google "average restaurant margins" and find that they average from 3–6 percent.

No wonder Jocelyn's stressed; just looking at the stats makes me queasy. Suddenly, the offhand comments she makes to Alan, along the lines of "You better pull your weight, or we'll have to move again," make sense.

"I'll get the online ordering up and running tonight," I promise Jos.

Before I leave, I remember to tell her that I'm going to be a little late tomorrow because I have a doctor's appointment. I tell her I'll stay an hour after closing to make up for the time.

"Oh, is everything okay?" she asks.

"Yeah, it's just a skin condition." It's a fib I've been telling for years whenever I've had to explain why I have to skip out on something for a therapy session. Dermatology is one of those things that's almost always an instant conversation stopper, and Jocelyn's no exception.

I can't help hoping, though, that someday I won't have to lie about where I'm going.

♡

I don't get to go home and change before heading over to hang out with the guys. I collapse onto Javier Diaz's basement couch, more tired than I realized. Tim Rosenthal is our fourth player today. He's wearing his "Tolkien White Male" T-shirt.

"Javi and I call France," Manny says, loading up a game of *FIFA*.

The background roar of computer-generated stadium noise washes over us as we settle into our normal trash talk. I'm a little slow to start, my muscles aching from the repetitive motions earlier in the day. Manny scores first off a header and tears his shirt off, running around the basement as the in-game commentators go wild. Of the four of us, he's the only one who plays soccer for St. Agnes. Tim's not the biggest fan of anything that requires him to break a sweat, and team sports aren't really Javier's thing. I played youth soccer for a few years—my uncle Akunna was my coach for the first year—but only lasted a couple of months of travel league. I begged my mom to let me quit after the time I almost hyperventilated going back onto the field after missing a penalty kick.

The next year, my mom signed my sister and me up for tennis lessons. We started playing mixed doubles as a family, and that satisfied my mother's desire to keep us active. By that time I was seeing Dr. Rifkin, and he taught me all the little ways to trick my mind into calming down during a match, like focusing on the feel of my right toe in my sneakers, counting the ridges on my racket, and recalling how a perfectly hit volley reverberates in my shoulder.

"Missed you yesterday, Will," Manny says. Yesterday—Wednesday—was, of course, new comic book day. "Marvel's gearing up for their next crossover."

"Pfft," says Tim. "Getting ready for the next crappy money grab, more like it."

"Someone's bitter," Manny sings. "Did you rewatch *Justice League* last night or something?"

If we're honest, the four of us all read across distributor lines, but Manny and I have always been more Marvel than DC fans, mostly because of Black Panther and Kamala Khan. Tim, on the other hand, was raised in a die-hard DC family. There are literally pictures of him being toted around in a baby carrier dressed as the Robin to his parents' Batman and Catwoman.

After *FIFA* we play *Mario Kart*, because at the end of the day there isn't a multiplayer that's a more straightforward adrenaline rush. Plus there are enough random power-ups, shortcuts, and pitfalls to equalize the competitive advantage that Tim has as a hard-core gamer (and who doesn't like a game where you can throw banana peels at your friends?).

By the second run, my bone-weary fatigue is gone, and my shoulders have finally relaxed. Javier waves his hands excitedly as he throws a blue shell and rubber-bands into the lead with an outraged shout from Manny. I laugh out loud as Tim hoots at Manny's comeuppance and gets so distracted by his gloating that I use a Mushroom and race into first myself.

For the first time all day I'm completely loose, my brainpan unoccupied by business strategy, family pressures, or uncertainty about my future, gleefully mindless as I race around a physics-defying fantasy world with my buddies. For these few precious moments, life is easy.

On the way home from the Diazes', I pass A-Plus. The open sign is no longer lit and the curtains are drawn, but the lights are still on. I imagine one of the Wus sitting at a booth tallying up a spreadsheet on their crusty Dell laptop that needs to be plugged in at all times because its battery won't hold a charge anymore, and I feel a pang of guilt. I'm pretty sure Jocelyn didn't spend her evening playing video games. She was probably stressing over that day's take and what that spreadsheet would look like after a rent increase.

For the first time, I wonder what she does outside of the restaurant and school. What makes her happy? Does she plan on taking over A-Plus, or does she have other dreams? And does she find having fun as difficult as I do?

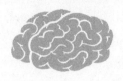

This Is My Brain
on Drama

JOCELYN

A couple of nights before the Boilermaker, Priya and I Skype to work on the short film we want to submit to the All American High School Film Festival. Before we start brainstorming, though, Priya announces, "I think our film should be set in a restaurant. Specifically, this one."

"You want to make a film about A-Plus?" Why would anyone with two minutes to spare want to waste it watching a movie about our eyesore of a restaurant? No offense to eyesores.

"Well, it wouldn't be, like, a documentary. The story would still be original. It'd make it so much easier for you to be involved— you wouldn't have to take time away from the stuff you're already doing, and we could set shots up when things are slow. This is what I'm thinking." Priya puts on what I call her "auteur look." "The heart of the movie should be about how food can be a vehicle to show love. It's a cliché because it's true, right? The way to a person's heart is through their stomach."

I nod slowly, the pieces of the story falling into place in my head. "So one character is the 'Eating Lunch Alone' dude who comes into the restaurant at the end of a long, hard workday. Is that too tropey, though?"

"Maybe we can invert the trope?" Priya says, scrunching up the side of her mouth in concentration. "It's not the customer who's tired, it's the waitress."

"Maybe she just started working there, and she's totally not into the job. And he's a regular customer, so he orders all these things not on the menu and she's, like, totally confused."

"Yeah, so the *guy* is the one to take the *waitress* back to the kitchen and feed her the real stuff." Priya goes distant the way she does when she's framing shots in her head. Suddenly, her eyes widen. "What if the first part is in black and white and when she heads back into the kitchen it goes full color? Deliberate monochrome, like in *The Wizard of Oz* or *Pleasantville*?"

"Yes! We can have a lot of color: red peppers, carrots, green beans, bright shrimp."

After a bit more brainstorming, Priya has to sign off (her parents are actually around to enforce an electronic curfew). Not for the first time, I wonder what my life would be like without Priya Venkatram. It's one of the reasons I'm so desperate to stay in Utica—I'm pretty sure I'd be a miserable witch without her. Right now I'm only a melancholy one, which she's apparently okay with, but sometimes my fear that she'll realize that I'm the butt end of a cool-kid-and-loser friendship makes me so desperate that I want to chain myself to her person. Other times, for the same basic reason, I pull away from her, try to play it chill so that she'll be less likely to see my weirdness.

Growing up, Alan and I didn't really have the best role models for friendship cultivation. My parents' lives consisted of work, nagging my brother and me about our homework, and sleeping. Our family's social calendar was perpetually blank, except for the occasional Mohawk Valley Chinese Association meeting that Amah dragged us to.

That's where Peggy Cheng and I began our long frenemy-ship. Alan and I were the new kids on the block, used to living in a city where you could walk down the street and hear half a dozen different languages. It was honestly kind of disconcerting to realize that all of a sudden diversity wasn't the default—it was an oddity, something to be pinned like a butterfly and examined with a magnifying lens. Maybe it's because of this that the Asian kids in Utica seem to have this constant desire to blend in. It's funny to me because a lot of my friends in NYC were the exact opposite. Some were a little too militant about their Asian pride and used to dis people for being "bananas" (yellow on the outside and white on the inside) for the silliest reasons: wearing the wrong kind of graphic T-shirt, being too devoted to Taylor Swift, or preferring Oreos to mochi.

They had no idea how white a Chinese person could be. Utica is home to some next-level Twinkiehood.

The thing is, I don't blame the kids here at all. Pretty much everyone just wants to fit in at some point or another; Taylor Swift really is a great songwriter, and Oreos must have some sort of drug in them, they're so addictive. Plus, it's not the fault of the kids in the Mohawk Valley Chinese Association that their families wanted to assimilate. Peggy, for instance, barely knew any Mandarin at all, because her parents were both second-generation. That's how we first met: Alan was six at the time, and he literally could not keep his eyes off Peggy's shiny new iPad. She was doing some sort of Mandarin language program with flashcards of apples and trains, the sort of graphic catnip that Alan could never resist. After a while he started blurting out the answers to each question, and that was history.

"You're the new family from New York!" she exclaimed. "Your Mandarin is so good," she told Alan. "Are you fluent?"

"Meh, kind of?" I said, because compared to her, I was.

"That is awesome. My mom has been all over me about learning it. She says it's super useful for business these days."

I was new, so I shrugged and figured it'd be as good a way as any to make a friend. When the school year came around, Peggy made an honest attempt to introduce me to her social circle, but it soon became clear that aside from both being Chinese, Peggy and I had nothing in common.

She was relentlessly cheerful to the point where I started to seriously wonder whether there were substances involved. (There couldn't be, of course. She was way too Goody Two-shoes.) And why shouldn't she be happy? Peggy's family is rich, so she wore all the right clothes (first Justice, then Abercrombie and Banana Republic) and got to go to fancy summer camps that had the words "Cove" or "Retreat" in their names. She had long, shiny, aggressively treated hair that didn't have an endless halo of fly-aways and split ends like mine did. She did all the right activities: student council, volleyball, marching band. Nowadays, I would recognize her instantly as the "Girl Who Has It All."

For a couple of months, I hovered on the fringes of Peggy's social scene like a shriveled, misshapen pea in a pod, until the day when I overheard Sarah Martin say, "I don't know why Peggy is friends with that Wu girl. She's so negative. Does she ever smile?" Sarah said the word "negative" in the way that other people might say "herpes" or "alcoholic."

It stung because I knew Sarah was right. I drifted away from their group. They didn't try especially hard to keep me in the fold. Then Priya came along. Our puzzle pieces slotted together perfectly, and I tried my damnedest not to sabotage it, the way I do everything else in my life.

Here's the thing: If we move back to NYC, my family might have more money, more help, and more free time. To me, none of that is worth having less Priya Venkatram.

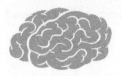

This Is My Brain
on Sales

WILL

At six AM on the Friday before the Boilermaker, we load up the Wus' van with the big stuff—the stove on wheels that can be hooked up to a portable tank (a remnant, Jocelyn says, from its former life as a component in a Mexican food truck), the food warmer, and boxes upon boxes of serving supplies, soy sauce packets, and water bottles. That leaves my car as the dumpling-mobile, with over a thousand dumplings crammed into my trunk and back seat.

When we get to the Expo area and start putting up our A-Plus Chinese Garden banner, Jocelyn steps back to make sure it's level. "Are people really going to come?" she asks when she returns to help me zip-tie it to the booth's awning.

"There are more than twenty thousand people registered. The foot traffic is going to be beyond anything we've ever seen."

There's no way to predict how much we'll sell, but Jocelyn's hoping for a profit of $400 that we can use toward a booth next year. Privately, I think that our goal should just be to break even. Even if we lose a little money, it'll still be worth it for the publicity and exposure.

"What if people don't stop to eat? What if they just pop in to get their bibs and leave?" Jocelyn waves over at the other food trucks setting up. "There's so much competition already."

"Wait until we start giving out samples," I reassure her.

We make short work out of setting up the cooking area. As I'm emptying ice into a cooler for the water bottles, a plump, shortish South Asian girl walks up.

"Good-looking booth," she says, eyeing our banner.

"Priya!" Jocelyn's entire demeanor changes when she sees her. She practically tackles her in a hug. "Will! This is my friend Priya. She's our social media consultant. Her Instagrams are the ones you put on the new website mock-up—that is literally her picture up there," she says, pointing to the dumpling banner.

"Nice to meet you," I say. "You're a great photographer." She is. I've scrolled through enough student galleries—including Javier's—to appreciate what she does with lighting and composition.

Priya shoots a few candids of us setting up and then pitches in herself. With another pair of hands, we're ready to go in no time. Because of the volume we have to cook, Grandma Wu came up with a shortcut that only marginally affects the flavor—we preboiled the dumplings and will panfry them to get the all-important crisp.

Jocelyn takes over video duties and livestreams Priya biting into her first dumpling.

"Mmmmghhhh," Priya moans. It doesn't even seem exaggerated. "Oh my God." She barely pauses to wipe some juice dribbling down her chin before inhaling her whole serving.

"Hashtag Boilermaker. Hashtag Expo Eats," Jocelyn declares. "This is awesome! Okay, Will, you're next. This can be our thing. Dumplings on the street."

Priya gets out her phone. "I'll live-tweet it, too." She types furiously on the phone.

> If you're gearing up for @boilermaker #ExpoEats, make sure to get some killer pot stickers from the @apluschinese booth. It's a religious experience.

She attaches a picture of herself gazing rapturously at a dumpling. Then she turns to me and cocks her head to the side like she's looking right through me. "Okay. Stand with your back to the booth so I can get the signs in the shot."

I do what I'm told and try not to feel too self-conscious as I stage my own first bite.

"Don't look at me," Priya barks. "Pretend I'm not here."

Easier said than done. The sun's coming up higher, and we're exposed and out in the open at the edge of a large field. With the kitchen area already generating heat, I'm beginning to feel dampness in my pits. Thank God I wore a dark shirt.

Priya misreads my hesitation. "Do you want to use a fork?"

"No, that's okay." To prove that my family ordered Chinese takeout as often as any other working American household, I grab a pot sticker with my chopsticks and dunk it into some soy sauce mixed with vinegar and ginger. Because I'm not allowed to look at Priya while I eat, I look at Jocelyn instead. She's looking at me, too, with an intensity that kicks my heart rate up a notch.

There's a moment before the food hits my mouth when I'm suddenly afraid that we have screwed it up. That the two-stage cooking method isn't going to hold up to the traditional way of panfrying them all at once. What if my memory of the flavor of that first dumpling that Grandma Wu made me has become legendary in my mind, something that can never be replicated, like when I was five and waited all year to go back to the Jersey Shore to have boardwalk pizza, only to be disappointed when it wasn't actually that special after all?

Then the first taste of warm, velvety jiaozi hits my tongue, salty slick, and I bite into the wrapper that gives away effortlessly, releasing that incredible synergy of pork and cabbage and green onion that does not disappoint. The pot sticker is the gift that keeps on giving—continually surprising, as the crispiness of the bottom contrasts with the soft boiled part that wasn't panfried, as it gives way to the complex overtone of ginger and a bite of garlic. It isn't until I've swallowed my last bite that I realize that I've closed my eyes to savor the experience.

When I open my eyes Priya is grinning.

"What?"

"Cut!" she says. "Hashtag Food Orgasm."

Jocelyn turns pink. "Priya!" she stage-whispers with her eyes wide open in horror.

My face is a little hot, too, but I have to laugh. "You're not wrong. Those things are as amazing as anything I've ever eaten."

"I'm going to quote you on that," Priya says, composing another tweet.

By eleven, people are trickling by to get registered, and Jocelyn cuts some jiaozi in half (she just couldn't accept the idea of giving away a whole dumpling for free), and skewers them with toothpicks. She and I each take a plate and fan out around the booth while Priya sits at the booth and pretends to be checking her phone while secretly lining up shots.

"Excuse me, would you like to try some handmade dumplings? It's my grandmother's secret recipe," Jocelyn tries.

The first few people have kids in tow. They don't even stop for a sample.

Then, "Ma'am—care for a free sample of some authentic pot stickers?" finally gets me a taker, a tall brown-haired woman wearing Lululemon yoga pants, who pops the sample into her mouth without much of a thought, and then does a double take.

"These are amazing. How much are they?" She gets two orders.

"Thank you so much for your business!" Jocelyn says as she cashes her out. "Here's a coupon for a free appetizer at A-Plus Chinese Garden restaurant. We're just a few blocks away."

When the woman leaves, Jocelyn gives me a high five. "Two down, two hundred and ninety-eight to go." With just over 1,500 pot stickers, we have enough for about three hundred orders depending on how many free samples we have to give.

Priya flashes out her iPhone yet again. "Here, let me take a picture of you two with your first dollar. Or ten dollars, as it were."

We hold the edges of the bill up like we're getting an oversized check from some philanthropist. Priya waves us in with one hand.

"Get a little closer, and bring the money to your face. I want to really zoom in on you."

I have to crouch down so Jocelyn and I can lean our heads in together, and I smell a faint coconut from her shampoo. It's getting to be a warm day, and I'm suddenly worried that I'm too sweaty, that I didn't put on enough deodorant this morning. We're close enough together that, if I were with my buddies, I'd just sling my arm over their shoulders. But neither Jocelyn nor I makes a move to do so—instead we just hover at the borders of personal-space invasion.

JOCELYN

I am going to kill Priya. Not because she and Will get on like a house on fire (of course they do). I am going to murder my best friend because she is trying to produce my life as if it's some reality show.

"Angle yourselves in so you're facing each other," Priya says, all smooth and businesslike. People who don't know her would think that she's just being professional, but I know the smirk she wears when she's trolling someone, so I stay put.

Will, on the other hand, shifts his stance obediently, so our faces are just about the width of a dollar bill apart. I can feel the air move as he breathes, and I have to use every ounce of mental strength not to stare at his lips, which are smooth and perfect, not all chapped up like mine always are. Instead, I focus on Priya, trying to communicate to her without words that she needs. To. Stop. After my attempt at telepathy fails, I try not to sound too annoyed when I ask, "You done?"

She has the gall to look innocent when she scrolls through

89

the images on her phone and says, "Just a couple more shots. J's eyes were closed."

"They're not closed, I'm just Asian," I say. Will chokes down a laugh and my resolve breaks—I look at him, he looks back, and I'm trapped. Frozen by how intensely he's *seeing* me.

It maybe freaks me out a little. I wonder if he's noticing that one of my eyebrows is less straight than the other, or if he clocks the scar on my left cheek that I got in sixth grade from a zit that I couldn't stop picking at and eventually got infected. I should have worn lip gloss or tried to pluck the fine baby hairs on my lip that make me look like I have a mustache that was inexpertly photoshopped out.

Finally, after what seems like a hundred shots, Priya is satisfied.

"I'm going to totally keep that picture for your wedding slide-show," she whispers to me while Will helps another customer.

I snort, tearing my eyes away from Will to concentrate on the boiling pot of water. As if he could be remotely interested.

"Let's focus on cooking and selling, okay?" I plead. "We've got three hours and more than a thousand dumplings to unload."

WILL

My friends like to rag on me a lot. I'm Will the perpetually picky eater (dairy makes me feel bloated), the teacher's pet (so sue me if I like to turn my assignments in on time and occasionally give them thoughtful end-of-the-year thank-you gifts), and the envirofreak (seriously, why don't they understand, I keep used plastic utensils in my backpack because of the children—do they even know how much energy goes into creating our disposable culture?).

The point is, they'll really have a field day when they find out how much it turns me on to watch Jocelyn cook.

She's a whirling dervish of efficiency: talking while frying, tossing the perfect amount of oil into pans straight from the bottle, wielding the spatula as if she's a fencer, shouting out orders like she was born to do it, which I suppose she was. There is not a single millisecond of hesitation in any of her movements. Watching her, I feel this buzz under my skin, a constant awareness of where she is, a little hiccup in my heartbeat when she's close.

They don't tell you in life skills class how hard it is to work with someone who you're attracted to. I'm simultaneously drawn to her and afraid to get near out of fear of the train wreck that is Will When He Tries to Get His Game On. But we're colleagues, right? I need to be her right-hand man. I need to take things that she hands to me hurriedly, so that our fingers brush in a completely unsexy way that nevertheless makes my blood rush (just a little bit) into very unhelpful body parts.

It's hot and it's sweaty and there are so many people lining up to place orders that my chub never completely materializes, but I do take a bathroom break to readjust when Jocelyn gets overheated and takes off the T-shirt she's been wearing, revealing a black camisole with just enough lace to make my mind short-circuit a bit.

The pace picks up, and Priya and I both give up on prep work for a bit to take orders and run the register. The line in front of our little stand gets longer, which attracts more customers.

Jocelyn gets a pinched look around her eyes as she looks out at the rows of people. "We're going to have to cheat," she says flatly. "Can you take over for a sec?" We talked about it beforehand, that deep-frying the dumplings would be an option. She walks over to the Wu's van and brings out the deep-frying unit, then fills it with oil with a grim face. In the twenty minutes it takes for the fryer to get hot enough she tells us to offer boiled dumplings until we catch up to demand.

"If you'd like them panfried it will be an extra ten minutes, but it's actually healthier without all that oil," I reassure any customers who look askance at the pale boiled dumplings. Admittedly, they do look like they could use some sun.

Whether they're panfried, boiled, or deep-fried, folks keep coming. It's a steady stream of people unlike anything I've ever experienced in the restaurant.

JOCELYN

By noon things are so busy that we don't have time to give out samples, let alone chitchat. The world narrows down to the seven-by-nine-foot area of our booth, to the sound of boiling water and the sizzling of oil. We have a line for ordering, a line for cashing out, and a line of people waiting for fresh pot stickers that gets longer and longer, until we have to make them in batches of twenty to keep up with the pace. We run out of the thousands of quarter-sheet flyers that we copied on the Xerox machine at Will's father's law firm.

When I slide our last bag of pot stickers out of the wok into a serving container, I feel a boneless, aching relief.

We're done.

I collapse onto an overturned crate. It's the first time I've sat down since our first sale, my hair reeks of the smell of panfried oil, and I'm probably as dehydrated as the runners are going to be during the actual race.

When Will finishes checking out our last jiaozi customer, he glances at the heating lamp and then peeks in the empty dumpling cooler.

"Holy shit!" he exclaims. "We sold out! Jos, we did it. We knocked it out of the park." He puts his fist out and I barely have the energy to raise my hand to bump it, but his euphoria is infectious. I allow myself a brief moment of victory.

We did it.

I only have a minute to savor it, though, before a middle-aged woman comes up with two teenage boys. "I'd like four orders of those dumplings everyone is eating, please."

Within seconds, all my euphoria bleeds away, and a knot of dread forms in my belly.

"I'm sorry, ma'am—we're out of dumplings." Will says. "Would you like some fried rice?"

"No, that's okay." The woman sighs heavily and turns around to her kids. "They're all out, kids. Guess we have to go to the pizza cart instead."

Crap.

Just like that, disappointment sucks all the air from my lungs. We've underestimated demand and are leaving money on the table. Every person who stops by asking for dumplings only to pass when we can only offer fried rice is another blow. When I can't stand the thought of any more lost revenue being shoved in my face, I send Priya out to scrounge up some masking tape so we can hang up a SOLD OUT sign over her amazing dumpling photo. A few people come looking for pot stickers anyway, like we have a secret stash squirreled away for VIPs.

"We shouldn't have given out so many samples," I say the tenth time someone frowns and walks away. That's probably hundreds of dollars we left on the table. "We should've made more dumplings. They don't go bad when they're frozen. We could've used them up later if we made too many."

Will is silent for a minute, like he's thinking of the old adage: If you can't say anything nice, don't say anything at all. Then he says, "We've been making dumplings practically nonstop since we found out we had a booth."

"Maybe it doesn't matter if they're homemade," I fret. "For an event like this, we should've just bought premade dumplings and marked them up. We could have made thousands more."

"Jos, we did the best we could with what we knew, and it's still a huge success."

But we could have done better. I don't say it out loud, but I hear the voice—a combination of my dad's and my uncle's—in my head anyway.

WILL

The thing about fake news is that it preys on the truth. There's always a kernel of reality that gets watered with misinformation and deliberate misinterpretation until it mutates into something hateful, hyperbolic, and divisive.

Last fall, Mr. Evans had a whole unit on the journalist's role in a "post-truth" society. He had to explain the term—named the 2016 International Word of the Year by the Oxford Dictionaries!—to us: "relating to or denoting circumstances in which objective facts are less influential in shaping public opinion than appeals to emotion and personal belief."

In other words, the whole world's starting to process news the way my brain does life.

Watching Jocelyn crumble into self-loathing, I realize that she has a post-truth brain, too.

My excitement at selling out trickles into unease when I realize that Jocelyn isn't smiling. Instead, she's staring out at the few people who are still milling around. I can practically see the moment when her brain morphs an objective fact (we ran out of dumplings) from something positive (we were so popular that we sold out) into something negative (we failed at capturing all the customers that we could have).

I glance at my watch—it's almost one o'clock and we've been working nonstop through lunch. I grab a carton of the fried rice. "Hey, I don't think any of us has eaten since this morning. We'll all feel way better if we have something in our stomachs."

"Thanks, I'm not hungry," Jos mumbles, still looking out at the people lining up at the other food carts.

I start cleaning up the serving area in silence. Jos joins me eventually, packaging up the fried rice into take-out containers that we sell for two dollars each. It's still a moneymaker, given that it's concocted from yesterday's fried rice and leftover veggies, but Jocelyn's distress hangs over us like a darkening sky before a thunderstorm.

Maybe she just needs perspective, some cognitive reframing.

"You were amazing today," I tell her as we pour the dumpling water into a bush by the parking lot. "I can't believe how many customers we had. This is such a win for the restaurant."

She glances away and gives a half-hearted shoulder lift. "Sure." I know someone deflecting praise that they don't believe when I see it. "I can't take credit for it. It was your idea."

"But it was your execution," I insist. I recognize the disconnect between what I see and what she thinks of herself, because I do it, too.

"Then the execution was shortsighted. I can't believe I set our expectations so low," she says, her voice cracking. She sniffs and rubs at her nose angrily. "You were right that we shouldn't have worried about not having enough customers. We should've made twice as many dumplings, and boiled them all beforehand to save a step. Our price point should have been higher, or maybe we could have given out only four dumplings per order, not five. And I should've gotten one other person to cook so two people could run the register when we fell behind on orders."

"Don't be so hard on yourself," I tell her. The irony of my using that phrase on someone else does not escape my notice. "This was the first time A-Plus has ever done something like this, right? Even if it wasn't perfect, we definitely turned a profit, and the exposure is priceless."

"You can't pay rent with exposure," Jocelyn says. "I don't know if it'll be good enough."

"The fact that I'm getting a hernia picking up our cash box suggests that it will," Priya says, making a show of struggling to lift our register. "Hey, Catastrophe Girl, let's wait to do the math before you beat yourself up."

It's then, when I watch Jocelyn shake her head and go back

to cleaning up, as if she can't bear to watch the blow-by-blow of the accounting, that I realize our crucial mistake: We made such a conscious effort to keep our expectations low that we didn't set ourselves up for maximal success.

I'm used to setting myself up for small potatoes, informed by years of therapy and lectures from my father about how "unrealistic expectations breed disappointment, perfectionism, and anxiety."

But Jocelyn? She can't bear to count how much money we made, because no amount would be good enough to make up for opportunity lost.

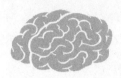

This Is My Brain
on Fatigue

JOCELYN

After I do the math, we make back the entrance fee plus an $800 profit, which seems good until we count the time it took to fold all those goddamn dumplings—forty-plus hours of work? We barely break even, even if we only pay ourselves minimum wage.

What a bust.

As we load our equipment into the van, Priya and Will chatter quietly behind me, but I can't bring myself to join in. I know I'm the wet blanket—God, I always know it, but there's nothing I can do to get rid of the sensation that my head weighs too much for my body.

Failure doesn't need to be spectacular, like with that face-planting ski jumper they show every time the Olympics roll around to illustrate the agony of defeat. Actually, I'm beginning to realize, it's usually pretty boring, sometimes even masked by a thin veil of achievement. We sold out of dumplings. Woo-hoo. I don't know why we thought it was so crucial to have handmade dumplings in the first place. People at the Boilermaker couldn't care less if the thing they cram into their mouth is a handcrafted piece of exotic culinary art. All they want is fuel.

As I pull out of the Mohawk Valley Community College parking lot, Priya snaps a picture of me. "Hashtag Mopey McMopeface."

"Hashtag Too Exhausted for My Homicide Filter to Work." I snap back.

"I get it," she relents. "But we had a great day on social media. One hundred new followers, a couple of retweets by the official Boilermaker account. And hey, two sign-ups for our e-mail list!"

"Wow, what does that brings us to? A grand total of five?" My voice isn't dry. It's just dehydration. "The spambots are going to be hacking into us any day now, I mean, we're major influencers."

Priya's used to ignoring me when I'm like this, probably because she's got two older brothers. Snark just rolls off her like water off a duck's back.

"Will's a good guy," Priya says then. "He was totally trying to drag you out of your funk, but you wouldn't have any of it."

I think of the way Priya and Will clicked right away, of how effortlessly they worked together taking orders while I did all the food work. "Well, if you like him so much, maybe *you* should marry him." I pitch my voice to sound like a whiny eight-year-old, aiming for irony but missing it by a mile.

Priya stiffens in the seat next to me, and I apologize before she can reply. "I'm sorry, that was out of line. I'm a shit human being today." I know that she would never take Will from me. Not intentionally.

She doesn't say anything for a few seconds, and the pause while she composes her response is the only thing that hints at how much I've hurt her feelings. Priya and I never have to worry about what we say to each other. "It's been a long day," she says finally.

"Thank you for helping," I say in a small voice. "I know there are more fun things to do on a summer Friday."

"Psht. Fun is for the lazy," she says. She pauses and looks out the window for a second. "It was important. And you did good."

The closest I can get to accepting her praise is silence. But that's the thing about best friends: Priya understands me anyway.

♡

The next morning I wake up feeling like I've been run over by a cement mixer and then baked in a pizza oven. The tip of my nose burns like it's had an encounter with that character on *Game of Thrones* who skins his enemies, and my neck aches so badly I can barely turn my head to see what time it is.

I lie in bed for a few minutes after I wake up. Maybe closer to an hour, who's counting?

My brother, apparently. At nine o'clock exactly he starts banging on my door at just about the same tempo that my head is pounding.

"Jiejie," he yells. "I need you to help me with my homework."

I burrow my head farther into my pillow. "Jesus Christ, it's Saturday morning."

100

"Dad says I need to get it done before I can do any screen time. The guys are doing an epic multiplayer today, but Mom says I have to help out downstairs for lunch because it's going to be so busy. Baituo, Jiejie, bangwo?" It's a low blow for my brother to switch to Mandarin, and he knows it. Nothing triggers my guilt and filial piety more than my formal title of "Big Sister."

"Only because you said please," I grumble as I roll out of bed, muscles screeching. After I brush my teeth I pop some ibuprofen and splash some cold water over my face before staring at myself in the mirror. I don't have bags under my eyes—I've got suitcases, and my hair has the opposite of body. It lies like a corpse on my oily scalp.

At the breakfast table, while I'm helping my brother with his homework, I have coffee and youtiao, baseball bat–length sticks of fried dough that Priya once described as a chubby churro without the cinnamon sugar. It's basically Taiwanese comfort food, and I can't help but think that if Will tasted one he'd probably try to get me to sell them in the restaurant, too.

It's sweet how excited he is about "authentic" Chinese food, but right here and now I resolve to keep youtiao under his radar for as long as possible, because it's just not worth the weird looks, the disbelieving chuckles, and the times we'd have to explain what it is and how to eat it. We're a crappy Chinese restaurant, not a Ten Thousand Villages. Our food will never come with a pamphlet celebrating its exotic origins.

I polish off one youtiao and reach for the remaining one only to have my mother slap my hand away gently. "Aiyo, Xiao Jia. Chi taiduo, duzi pang." She pinches my belly fat and I give an indignant yelp. "That for your brother to eat."

"What, so it's okay for Alan to be overweight?" I protest. My mom, empress of Fat Shameland, just shrugs and moves her size-two waist over to the sink to do dishes. It's like she doesn't care that people die from eating disorders every year.

Since the day I hit puberty, my mother's been on my case. On a daily basis, I'm told that my belly's too big (duzi tai pang), that I'm a hunchback who needs to stand up straight (ting xiong yidian), and that my hair is a mess (toufa luanqibazao). I'm surprised she hasn't hit the trifecta already in the half hour I've been downstairs.

My teachers at school would never call me a rebel, but I find little ways to act out: sneaking bites of food when my mom isn't watching, savaging my hair with rubber bands when I forget hair ties, and generally perfecting my lady sprawl in mixed company. It's not even like my mom has time to really police me—she's too busy, which takes a little away from my satisfaction with my rebelliousness, but not too much.

"I don't get it," my brother whines when I make him show his work for a problem. "I got the right answer. Why do I have to go through all these steps?"

"It's for your own good," I say, cringing a little at how much I sound like my dad. When he rolls his eyes, I throw my hands up in the air. "Look, I'm the cheapest tutor you've got, so deal with it. You can either take my advice or ignore it and flunk the class again."

He seems to choose the latter option, gluing his eyes to the back of our generic Cheerios box.

"Earth to Alan. Hello?" When I grab the box away from him, he gives me the same innocent smile he's had since he was a four-year-old getting into trouble with our parents. "Do you want to play your freaking *Fortnite* or not?"

"Fine," he groans. In the next hour, Alan has to go to the bathroom twice, prepare himself a mid-morning snack, and go upstairs to bring down his window fan, but we finally get his worksheet done. Then he's in his room logged onto his computer within ten seconds.

For the first time in what seems like forever, I can just do nothing. My parents and Amah are already downstairs doing prep work. I know they'll call up when they need me, or pound on the ceiling with a broomstick if the landline downstairs is being used to take orders. For these few minutes before the lunch rush, I can sit.

♡

"So there's good news," I tell my dad while we clean up after lunch. "We sold all the pot stickers, and literally thousands of people stopped by and now know about us." My dad grunts with approval, and his eyes practically light up with dollar signs. "Once we include all our expenses, we net about eight hundred dollars, which I think is great considering it's our first year—"

"Dengxia, dengxia. Ni shuo shenme?" my dad interrupts. "How you sold out, but only get eight hundred bucks?"

"Well, there's the cost of food and equipment rental, and there was the Expo booth fee…." I don't mention the labor costs.

"How much this booth?" my father asks suspiciously, his Wasting Money Warning System blaring.

I'm glad that he's been too busy to ask the question until now. I try not to have my voice wobble. "Well, it was four hundred dollars, but as you can see we really made it up."

His eyes bug out and he opens his mouth to say something, then stops. His brow furrows and his gaze grows distant before he squints at me. "You still make eight hundred dollars. You sell more than twelve hundred dollars' worth of food?" he asks.

"Yeah."

My dad does his "not bad" frowny face, the one that makes him look like a surprised catfish, and my heart does a little flip. That's practically his version of a high five.

"Overhead too high," he grumbles as he takes a stack of flat take-out menus and turns them into trifolds. "Next time work on cutting expense. How much you charge per order?" he demands.

"Five for five dollars, but next time I think we can do four for five dollars at an event like this."

"Also next time sell egg roll. Cheap and easy, make good profit."

I sit down next to him to help fold. It isn't until we're almost done that I realize the phrase he used twice to critique my business plan:

"Next time."

This Is My Brain on Stew

WILL

As bone weary as I am when I get home from the Expo, I still can't sleep. So I open the file that I've titled "The Restaurant at the End of the Strip Mall" and do something I haven't done since the creative writing module in my seventh-grade English class: I freewrite. I try to capture all the granular details of the day: the smell of sesame oil just before it starts smoking, the sound of a metal spatula scraping against a wok, the feel of a worn twenty-dollar bill as you slide it into a register.

On Saturday, the day of the race, my family drives by the restaurant on our way to Red Lobster, and I notice a few more customers than usual sitting in the red-cushioned chairs by the counter, waiting for takeout. One of the storefronts in the strip mall is vacant, and I take a picture of the sign so I can look up the developer who manages the complex.

The next day, when my family is knotting up ties and slipping on sandals as we get ready for church, I wonder whether the Wus ever have a day of rest. Unlike a lot of other small restaurants in the area, A-Plus isn't closed on Sunday or Monday. From what I understand, their backup cook is Grandma Wu, and their substitute waiter/busboy/delivery person is Jocelyn's brother.

Sunday night is family night in our house. It's the one day a week my mother cooks dinner, when she's not on call, and she uses it as an opportunity to make some of her favorite childhood dishes. It's so my sister and I develop a taste for Nigerian food, since there aren't really any African restaurants in our area. I'm her sous chef this week. Grace is nowhere in sight. My mother taught her to cook (after all, my nne nne would have been scandalized if she hadn't) but recently Grace has started opting out. Part of me resents Grace for having the guts to leave and then not get in trouble for it, but in the end it isn't half bad having some mom time for myself.

I take out one of the bags of tomato puree that my mother keeps in the freezer for jollof rice. When I measure out the actual rice grains, I'm struck by how the long-grained rice we use is so different from the stubby short-grained rice they use at A-Plus.

My mother prepares the fish and meat for the egusi stew and grinds up the melon seeds and crayfish. This is my mother at her best—relaxed, centered, and focused on a singular task. It's when she's cooking that I feel most comfortable talking to her; maybe it's because her attention is turned elsewhere, so I don't feel as much like I'm under a microscope.

Of my two parents, my mother has always been the one who expects the most of us. Unlike my father, who used to take

106

my sister and me out for Dairy Queen whenever we got a good report card, my mother would just nod and give a faint smile at our assumed excellence being confirmed. Doubt just isn't in her vocabulary. There isn't a problem that she can't solve.

My father always mentions my mother's confidence when he's telling people how they met—a common occurrence, because everyone wants to know how an Italian American patent attorney with male-pattern balding and a Grade A dad bod ended up with a gynecologist who's a dead ringer for Danai Gurira.

He also says, jokingly, that it was the noodle connection.

That's how my father describes it. He was a law student. My mother was in med school. They met at a party thrown by one of my mother's church friends. Within a few minutes of their first conversation, they found out they lived on the same street, which was how they ended up in my mother's apartment with her roommates as chaperones, eating glorified ramen.

This is the point of my parents' love story where my nne nne raises her hands to her temples and moans "chineke meh." It's like my grandmother thinks she can use mind control to wish away my mother's rude breach of etiquette, that she would dare to fete a potential suitor with instant noodles, even if they were spruced up with yam, carrot, and egg. "How does she expect to catch a husband by cooking indomie? Only by the grace of God."

To which my father simply gives a rumpled shrug and a nostalgic smile. He grew up eating some variation of spaghetti with red sauce four days of the week with fish on Fridays. The indomie was a hit: "A pasta by any other name tastes as sweet."

The only thing sweeter is the kiss that my father lays on my mother's forehead whenever he tells the story. Their tenderness always sets off a lightning-quick pang in my chest, as if my body is processing the briefest panic that my father could've judged my mother by the dinner she served him. There are so many things that need to fall in place for two people to get together, and even more things that need to happen for them to stay together.

I know that you can't go through life like that, imagining your life stretching ahead of you as a series of missed connections. I know that with so many billions of people in the world, chances are there's someone out there who wouldn't mind hanging out with me and maybe making out a bit. And I know that even if I don't find "the one"—if there's even such a thing—it's still possible to live a fulfilling and happy life.

That's always been my problem. Knowing something is going to be fine doesn't ever stop my body from acting like things might turn out badly anyway. So it's not my fault. I can't help it: Each time I witness the force that still draws my parents to each other, I worry that the random sequence of events that leads to love will never happen to me.

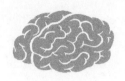

This Is My Brain on Food Joy

JOCELYN

I send Priya my first draft of our screenplay the second I'm done with it. It's the deal we've made: "You have so little faith in yourself that you'll throw out anything that's not one hundred percent perfect. Let me tell you the ninety percent that works so you can fix the ten percent that doesn't."

Within minutes she pings me back.

> Got it. BTW, made some vids that I think you'll like. I have a little more editing to do and then we can post them.

The link she sends to me is literally a sizzle reel, with close-up shots of onions bubbling in oil and of Jin-Jin doing a stir fry, the kind that leaves a film of grease over you when you're done. She's got a beautiful single shot of my amah making a dumpling, her quick fingers making it look like magic. There's a sped-up action video of me panfrying the pot stickers where I look completely badass.

The best part, though, is a montage that she made of people's reactions when they had the pot stickers. Priya's videos are proof positive that eating my amah's dumplings is a cross between a religious experience and a sex act.

There's the burly middle-aged man who looks skeptical when his wife hands him a dumpling on a fork (heathens). His eyes are narrowed when he moves in for his bite, but the second his teeth sink in his eyes open in surprise before they close shut while he chews, as if he doesn't want his other senses to interfere with his ability to savor the pot sticker.

There's the twenty-something woman wearing NYU shorts who makes a beeline to our booth with her friends. "Pot stickers, yessssss! I get them all the time in the Village."

"Really?" you can hear one of her friends saying in the background. "I don't think you should trust a Utica dumpling any more than you trust a Utica bagel."

NYU girl tears into the jiaozi despite the fact that they're fresh from the pan and jumps up and down beckoning for a water bottle when it's too hot. "Holy shit, these are awesome. Totally as good as Dumpling Kingdom."

My favorite clip, though, is one of a toddler clutching a blue *Observer-Dispatch* balloon while her mom is hand-feeding her bits of chopped-up dumpling. The girl is putting them down like a champ—every few seconds she squeezes her fingertips together and moves her hands in and out until they bounce off each other in the baby sign for "more." She looks like a little bird flapping its wings.

She looks like pure joy.

I think back to the dozens of hours we spent rolling out dough, coming home with flour caked in my cuticles, dusted over every article of clothing including my shoes; I think of the days of anxiety leading up to the Expo and the exhausting, bone-wearying crush of cooking and serving, the lines of people that seemed to blur into a sea of waiting, disapproving, disappointed faces. How had I missed all the food joy that Priya saw?

On my laptop, Priya's interviewing the toddler.

"Is this your first dumpling? Did you like it?"

The little girl gives a big nod and her blond curls flutter as she gives a big two-thumbs-up.

And that's how Priya ends the video—with a freeze-frame of this little girl who can barely talk, who's fallen in love with jiaozi.

And goddammit, those are not tears in my eyes.

When Will comes in on Monday, he's carrying two green Tupperwares and looks faintly tentative, almost nauseated.

"Everything okay?" I ask.

"Yeah. I brought you some Nigerian food my mom made. Have you ever tried jollof rice?"

"There's no such thing as a bad carb in my book," I say, peeking under the lid of one of the containers. It's a riot of different colors and smells like curry.

"That's egusi stew. It's made out of crushed melon seeds and beef, fish, and all sorts of veggies." Will's acting super nervous. I can relate. "My mom likes it because it reminds her of home. I like it because it's more interesting than pasta, which is what my father usually cooks."

I steal a place setting from one of the booths and take a bite. Will's right: It's a wonderfully satisfying and complex mix of curried spices and textures. And the experience of eating it doesn't end in my mouth—it sends a thrill of satisfaction through my entire head before traveling down to settle into a warm glow in my stomach.

"This is amazing," I tell Will, as sincerely as I've told anyone anything in years. "My taste buds are just exploding. Do you think this is the first time anyone's ever eaten Nigerian food with chopsticks?" I ask.

"Probably not. There's actually a Chinatown in Lagos. My cousins talk about it all the time. It's where they go to get bootleg American movies before they come out on DVD."

I eyeball the Tupperwares Will brought—they probably have three or four servings. I know Amah would love it. "Do you mind if I share this with my family?"

"I'd be honored," he says, his eyes crinkling.

I have to turn away to hide my blush at his smile.

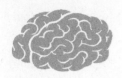

This Is My Brain on Success

WILL

Jocelyn's grandmother loves the egusi stew.

"Hen tebie," she says, nodding approvingly.

"She says it's very special," Jocelyn translates, and I finally relax. Grandma Wu polishes off the whole bowl, asking me if there is onion in it, and what kind, and tell me again what fish we used? I felt my cred rising with each answer I give.

"Are there any Nigerian restaurants around here?" Jocelyn asks after we put away the leftovers and go back to prep for lunch.

"Not really. There are a couple of African restaurants in Syracuse, but for specifically Nigerian food you need to go down to the city." Once a year my family takes a New York trip to see a Broadway show, always making sure the next day to make a pilgrimage out to Jamaica or Harlem to eat at a restaurant that reminds my mom of home.

"Funny, when you can go to any little town in the middle of nowhere Nebraska and find a Chinese take-out place. Did you know there are more Chinese restaurants in the US than there are McDonald'ses?"

"No. That's ridiculous." That's the kind of fact that I'll need to research for my feature—one that will make the story universal and not just specific.

"Never underestimate the ability of my people to sacrifice everything to bring the gospel of moo shu pork to the unbelievers of middle America. And to make a buck. I read a book about it, how this one Chinese restaurant in Manhattan was the first one to deliver, around the time when more women had started to join the workforce. It was a total revolution. Now Chinese food is literally more American than cherry pie. I can think of at least three movies off the top of my head where someone is eating Chinese food out of the take-out box. It all goes back to Woody Allen and that scene from *Manhattan* with him and Mariel Hemingway." When I look confused by her reference, she explains, "It's kind of old, his first movie after *Annie Hall*. Priya's life goal is to watch every movie on the AFI 100 lists, and it's on the comedy one."

I shake my head. "My family mostly watches Marvel and Pixar, or more hyped-up blockbuster movies. I have watched a lot of films about journalism, though: *The Post*, *All the President's Men*, and *Spotlight*."

"Have you seen *Broadcast News*? It's a 1980s film with Holly Hunter and William Hurt. Also on the AFI 100 Laughs list." Jocelyn pauses for a second and fiddles with the napkin she's wrapping around a pair of chopsticks and a fork. "We could watch it.

Here in the restaurant on a slow day," she adds quickly, without looking at me.

"That'd be fun," I say. Every once in a while my parents have the family watch what my father fondly calls "the classics of my youth"—*The Princess Bride*, *The Breakfast Club*, and *E.T.* "I get a kick out of eighties movies. I think it has something to do with the fact that movies weren't digital yet, so all the special effects are so... earnest."

That makes Jocelyn quirk a smile in my direction. Eye contact at last. "Exactly! They're trying so hard. How can you not appreciate the craft that movies used to take?" She grimaces. "Nowadays, an elementary school kid with an iPhone can shoot a decent short film."

"It's like that with journalism," I say. "Any blogger can build a platform and get as many hits as a legit newspaper with paid reporters. It's scary, even though some people would say it allows for more viewpoints." I stop myself before I start ranting about how the biggest papers have become worshippers of the search engine optimization gods, and how Google has lowered the bar for research to the point where the wrong journalist can find "data" to support anything.

"Yeah, it's the same with movies. It's just too easy," Jocelyn says. Suddenly, she sits back into the booth, her body language relaxed but controlled. The uncertainty she had when she asked if I wanted to watch *Broadcast News* is gone, replaced with a wide-eyed, raw expression. She's not shy about looking at me right now. I feel a bit like I'm a firefly that she's captured in a mason jar, and that she's waiting for me to light up.

In sixteen years, I've never been the focus of a girl's attention like that, and my body responds to Jocelyn's stare as if this is the most important, life-changing cold call I'm going to make in my life.

"Does it ever scare you…" She pauses, and I can feel my pulse fluttering in my neck as she gathers her thoughts. "Do you ever find it terrifying to think that with so many billions of people who have walked this earth, there is no way that your thoughts are unique? I mean, everyone pretty much agrees that at this point Hollywood is just a recycling bin of ideas. Do you ever wonder, what's the point?"

Jocelyn's brown eyes are impossibly dark and liquid. I can feel myself begin to flush. Somewhere above us, the central air turns on, but I can hardly hear it over the roaring in my ears as I struggle to formulate a coherent response, to say something that's meaningful, because it's so clear how much my answer matters to her.

What I want to tell Jocelyn is: I wonder all the time. About everything, which is why I'm so awkward at parties. I'm a writer, not an improv guy. If you need someone to come up with a cutting remark approximately seven minutes after one would've been useful, though, I'm all over it. The seconds tick by as I start to say something, then bite it back. Then I bark out a laugh.

"Okay, how ironic is it that I'm struggling so hard to say something original about how impossible it is to have unique ideas?"

It takes Jocelyn a moment to parse out my meaning, but when she does she giggles.

I grin back. "If you haven't figured it out yet, the answer is yes. I wonder, 'What's the point?' all the time, and not just with writing." I balance a pair of chopsticks on my fingers, testing their weight before deciding to make my next statement. "I mean, a lot of the times it just seems like everything I want to do, my sister or my mom or my dad have done better already."

Jocelyn lets out a huff of sympathy, and we sit in silence. Then she laughs and shakes her head. "I don't usually do this, but you look like you need a hug. Can I give you a hug?"

My response is to step out of the booth and open my arms.

In my family, my dad's always been the hugger. Grace and my mom are queens of the arm's-length embrace. My dad, on the other hand, learned from the gold standard: my grandma Domenici, whose hugs are like falling into a down pillow of love and safety.

Jocelyn's hug is fierce. The squeeze of her wiry arms knocks the air I have remaining right out of me. She's such an outsize personality that as our bodies meet, I'm startled by how the top of her head barely comes to my chin. I can feel every angle and curve of her body, and the heat of her breath against my polo shirt. She smells faintly of mint, and it shouldn't be a surprise that my jeans start feeling a little tight as my mind registers how curvy her figure is.

I don't want the hug to end, but I shift a bit and rest my cheek on the top of her head so I can move my waist away from her a little— just enough to prevent any embarrassing escalation. Jocelyn seems to take the movement as me pulling away, though, and she lets go.

As she steps back, I'm acutely aware of a sense of loss. Suddenly the space between us feels like a solid object, heavy and impenetrable. I want to reach out to bring her in close again, but I hear my mother's voice in my head, scolding me on the impropriety. I hear my friends' voices, jeering at me for my permanent membership in the Got-No-Game Club. And almost ominously, I hear Mr. Wu's first admonition to me: "No hanky-panky."

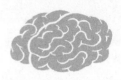

This Is My Brain on Touch

JOCELYN

It won't surprise you to find out that my family is not really the hugging type.

My mom likes to show affection with small pecks on the forehead, sending us off to school with a hand on the shoulder and a "Work hard today! Respect your teachers!" My dad basically just grunts and scowls at us. Amah prefers to shower love by pushing food.

If I had never met Priya Venkatram, there is no way I would have asked Will for a hug. But after several years of friendship with Priya, who dispenses hugs like Tic Tacs, I know how amazing it feels to have someone put their arms around you when you've just shown them a piece of yourself. I hug Will to thank him for being vulnerable, the way you can't help but scratch the belly of a dog who rolls over for you.

Hugging Will is nothing like hugging Priya, and I savor it the way I would a new kind of sweet, closing my eyes and pressing my face to his chest with a sigh. It's a slice of paradise—he's so warm and tall and muscly(!). I'm really leaning into it, and Will isn't shying away, circling me with those forearms that feel just as good touching me as they looked.

But then he pulls away from me just a little. Just enough that there's a sliver of air in between our bodies, enough that I open my eyes and realize that I'm showing PDA in the dining room of my family's restaurant, with a boy who doesn't even realize that I like him, and oh my God, what was I thinking?

My dad could walk out of the kitchen any minute.

I let go of him as if I've been stung by a spray of hot oil, and my arms flap awkwardly at my side. "Um, I hope that wasn't too uncomfortable."

Will doesn't look unhappy, though. "Not at all." He lifts his hand up in an abortive gesture, as if he's not sure what to do with his appendages, either, and ends up sticking it in his pocket. He shrugs and gives a little grin. "I fully consented to the hug. I won't file any complaints with HR."

It's a relief to turn back to work and dial things down a little. For the next hour, I try to keep my eyes on my computer screen, even as a tiny voice in my head keeps whispering, "Look at him, look at how cute he is! He's right there!"

Will and I tag team our social media sites—I respond to our Twitter mentions, and he curates our Instagram account for the college students and our Facebook page for people over forty. I can barely concentrate, and my peripheral vision seems to register every single time Will moves his hands up to scratch behind his ear, heck, every time he freaking swallows.

I finally give my brain a good shake. Will and I work together. I cannot ignore him, even if talking to him (worse, looking him in the eyes) makes me feel faintly sick to my stomach. So I close my laptop, grab my legal pad, and look at him head-on.

"Want to brainstorm outreach to the colleges? Not just MVCC, but University of Utica. I'm thinking it might be good to have a 'Study Group Special'—something like a fifteen-dollar meal for four. It can be high-yield dishes like pork fried rice, egg rolls, and chicken vegetable delight."

"One of my dad's friends is a professor at Utica," Will says. "He can give me some advice on the best way to reach students. I think they have an activities fair every year. Maybe we could leave some coupons there."

I open up a new file and design a flyer for our new Study Group Special. As I draft some copy, Will pauses from the e-mail he's composing to send to the college.

"By the way, it's called 'the anxiety of influence,'" Will says.

"Huh?"

"What we were talking about before, the fear that whatever you create is going to be crap, or just derivative of everything that's come before it. When I was writing my first feature for the *Spartan*, I kept on worrying that my angle wasn't unique. So our adviser told me about this Yale professor, Harold Bloom, who essentially said outright that there's no such thing as an original poem. That you can't escape the influence from all the art that's come before you."

"That's...depressing."

"Yeah, well, I don't think Mr. Evans meant that you have to give up. He was just saying that it's okay to be anxious, it's okay to be worried, but that there are a million ways you can be influenced by a past work, yet still make it your own. What do they say, there are only five basic stories in the world? Just because what you write is influenced by something that came before doesn't mean it's not still notable."

I make a face. "Are you saying that I'm a special snowflake?"

Will's laugh makes a little thrill of happiness run down my neck. "You are totally a special snowflake."

Somehow, this is not reassuring. "Just because something's unique doesn't mean that it's good." Art is not like toddler soccer, where everyone gets a trophy just for showing up.

"Of course not. I think what Mr. Evans was trying to say was that something's uniqueness has nothing to do with its quality. So we don't need to stress. We just need to worry about it being good."

"But what makes something good?"

Will thinks for a second. "Well, I'm not sure about other things, but for journalism, it's not just facts that make an article stand out. It's the truth of a story."

Slowly, I nod, thinking of the movies that have made my own personal top one hundred: *Amadeus. The Big Sick. Black Panther. When Harry Met Sally…. Toy Story.* Comedy or drama, fantasy or thriller, Will's hypothesis hits the nail on the head.

I think out loud, "So many truths to tell."

"We've got time," Will says hopefully. And something about the way he says it, like a question, in a voice that somehow gets across all his doubt and anxiety and need to tell these stories, makes the air thicken between us. I want to hug Will again, and somehow communicate with touch what I can't with words— that I believe in him. That right now, he is one of the truest things in my life. But then our kitchen door swings open and Jin-Jin comes in bearing the first load of takeout for the afternoon.

I put the finishing touches on my handout and go to print out a copy upstairs. As I'm getting up, though, Will asks in a small voice (is there a little bit of a shake in it?):

"You know, if you want to watch *Broadcast News*, are you free Wednesday night?"

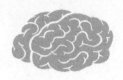

This Is My Brain on "Friendship"

WILL

Waiting for Jocelyn to answer is the most excruciating thing I've endured in years, and that includes the hour of mental gyrations it took me to get up the nerve to ask her in the first place. It's been obvious how important movies are to Jocelyn ever since my interview, when she jokingly offered her friend's Netflix log-in to me. And isn't that the classic first date? Dinner and a movie?

Not that this is officially a date or anything. It's just two friendly colleagues getting together after work....Right?

God, I hope Jocelyn thinks this is a date. But am I supposed to clarify, or ask if she expects it to be one? What if she doesn't?

Suddenly I feel feverish. I can feel the sweat rising on my forehead as the seconds tick by without Jocelyn answering. She's stood up to go print a flyer, so we're almost at eye level, and she doesn't have any of the expressions on her face that I initially feared (shock, pity, disgust). She just looks…thoughtful, and perhaps, a really optimistic part of me thinks, a little pleased.

"Wednesday nights are pretty slow, so it's as good a day as any, I guess. I can ask my dad if I can have it off," Jocelyn finally says. She cradles her laptop in her arms and runs her fingers along the seam a couple of times. "Did you…I mean, where should we meet?"

I suddenly realize how little I thought this through, and my throat starts closing up. It seems too forward to invite her over to our house, but it's not appropriate to ask if I could come to hers, either. Am I supposed to suggest a neutral location? "Uh, would you want to come over to my house? Or I could just come here, or we could meet at the library or a café or something."

Jocelyn's eyes widen, and that's *definitely* pleasure. "You'd invite me over to your house?"

"Of course," I blurt out. "You're my friend." The minute the words leave my mouth and I realize that I've implied that it's just going to be a friendly get-together, I close my eyes and let out a silent, internal scream. I almost don't want to see the expression on Jocelyn's face (Disappointment? Confusion? Relief?).

But when I open them again, she's smiling at me. "That'd be really cool. I'll tell my dad that I'm at Priya's—she'll cover for me. She loves that movie. You will, too."

Then she turns and runs upstairs, leaving me with a whole new experience to stress over.

JOCELYN

When I finally get up the nerve to ask my dad for the night off, he's in a super-good mood because on Sunday and Monday alone, ten new customers came to the restaurant bearing coupons from the Boilermaker Expo. They all ordered pot stickers, and he was fairly giddy with glee.

"Aiyo, Xiao Jia, you see? Ten customer ordering twenty, forty bucks each, that almost make up that fee you pay," he says, as though it was all his idea.

"That's great, Dad! Since things are going so well, can I have Wednesday night off? Priya and I are going to work on our movie."

"Sure, sure," my dad says, still smiling, waving me off. I wonder if he's actually delirious. "I get Alan to help. He can study in restaurant."

Tuesday night, Priya comes over to help me choose what to wear to Will's house.

"I can't believe you didn't ask him if this was a date," Priya moans after complaining for the third time that giving me advice would be so much easier if she knew the terms of my "engagement." It's kind of embarrassing—I've totally fallen into the "Not a Date" trope.

"And I told you, he looked like someone who was about to walk the plank, Pri. He was so nervous he would've passed out if I had given him the third degree." He wouldn't be that stressed out over something friendly, would he?

"Okay, so you don't want to wear this, then?" Rummaging through my closet, she pulls out a yellow knit cardigan set that Amah gave me for Christmas last year. "It'll be perfect for bingo night in another seventy years, though."

"I should choose something nice. I think his family's kind of well-off," I say. "He lives in that development off Oxford Road with all those big McMansions."

"Do you want to do a dress?"

"Nah, trying too hard." I only have three dresses, anyway: two from Goodwill and a hand-me-down from my mother, which she gave me after my father told her she looked "too young" in it. "I feel like the Constance Wu character in *Crazy Rich Asians*, when she's trying on formal wear for the Khoo wedding? Except that my entire wardrobe is probably worth less than the strap of one of those gowns."

"That's us," Priya chirps. "Crazy Poor Asians!"

"It's funny because it's true." I sigh.

Ultimately we decide on jean shorts and a peasant-style blouse that I bought at T.J.Maxx with the hong bao money I got from my relatives this Chinese New Year.

"It's perfect," Priya declares. "You look nice but not too formal, and the shorts plus the neckline of that shirt give him enough skin to be intrigued, if that's where his mind is going."

I look at myself in the slightly distorted full-length mirror on my closet door. "You really think his mind will be going there?" I stare at my boobs (too small), my knees (too knobby), and my waist (too close to a muffin top for my liking). Maybe Will didn't want to watch the movie on the clock because he felt uncomfortable about me paying him. Maybe he ended up offering his own house because he didn't want to spend an extra minute in our crappy restaurant.

"What if he's not straight?" I ask.

Priya nods. "That's always a consideration. But if he's straight, or bi? Trust me, I have two brothers. I'm pretty sure his mind is going to be going there."

WILL

Wednesday night, I pick Jocelyn up at the library. It's the cover story she gave her dad, and she wants her bike to be there in case he passes by during a delivery.

The entire ride to the library, my body felt itchy with nerves. But as Jos gets into my car, I realize that the most amazing thing about her—better than how competent she is, how bitingly funny, how cute—is how it quiets my brain just to be around her. I don't know what kind of alchemy it is, whether the smell of her pheromones somehow triggers a receptor in my nervous system, but having her sit in the passenger seat hits the reset button on my mind.

I feel like a blinking cursor on a screen. Full of potential. Anything could happen.

JOCELYN

When I get into Will's car, I have to bite back a laugh, because Will looks as nervous as I feel: eyes just a little too wide, shoulders practically at the level of his ears.

"Hey," I say. And as he looks at me—as he really *sees* me—I watch the little crease on his forehead disappear. His shoulders relax, and he smiles back at me.

"Hey," he says.

It's a quick ride to the Domenicis' development. I've been here before for deliveries, but this is the first time I've been here as a guest. I let myself ogle the ginormous houses and the occasional glimpses of fenced-in pools and huge, tree house–like play structures.

Walking into Will's house is a bit like walking onto an HGTV set. Everything is immaculate, from the cream-colored sofas with artfully casual pillows to the sparkling kitchen with stainless steel appliances. There's a curio cabinet in the dining room with some sculptures that look like they're from Africa, and framed family photos on the wall of the massive stairway leading up to the second floor. I wonder where all the stuff of living that seems to proliferate in our house is. Maybe his family carries a gene that makes them immune to clutter.

Despite how perfect everything is, Will looks just a little anxious as I peek around, like he's worried that it won't be up to snuff. He has a glass of water ready for me, and some popcorn that I stuff into my mouth so I won't say anything inappropriate like, "OMG, you guys have a concert grand piano?" or, "Holy shit, is that an eighty-eight-inch QLED TV?"

None of it really surprises me. The fact that Will hardly batted an eye at the four-hundred-dollar Expo fee kind of tipped his hand. Will pulls up his family's iTunes and rents the movie. "I hope you like it," I say. I'm pretty sure he will. Recommending movies is my superpower.

I've watched enough teen movies to anticipate what comes up next: couch sitting awkwardness. Will seems to be waiting for me to sit down, so I take the recliner on the left side. The only problem with this arrangement is that the Domenicis' sectional is huge—pretty much the opposite of intimate, and there's an entire stationary seat in between the two sections that recline.

Will doesn't even blink and chooses the seat without a recliner. I do a mental fist pump.

Will's laughing from the first scene, when Holly Hunter's asshole boss snarks, "It must be nice to always believe you know better, to always think you're the smartest person in the room," and she replies, "No, it's awful."

He looks over at me, still smiling. "I'm glad this is about network news, because it's so much easier to make fun of. That other reporter guy"—he means Albert Brooks's character—"has the soul of a print journalist."

It's my second time watching the movie, so I watch it for technique and structure instead of just plot. I take note of the framing devices in the beginning and how they establish the main characters' personalities so quickly.

I'd forgotten how the movie ends—with none of the people in the love triangle ending up with each other. The lack of a typical happy Hollywood ending makes it feel kind of old-fashioned, and for a minute I worry that I've made a bad call for a first non-date.

Here's my dirty secret: When it comes to movies, I'm not an auteur like Priya is. I like good stories, but I don't go into raptures over a film's cinematography. I watch movies to be manipulated. I watch them to cry, to laugh at inappropriate jokes, to get indignant over injustices, to experience romance that bubbles through my skin and makes me hopeful that one day I'll find someone to make me feel that way for real.

I love that movies can take a burned-out, cynical person like me and make them believe for just a short while that romance can happen to them. I love that movies keep my dreams alive.

This is, of course, the exact reason my parents hate movies. My dad thinks they're a waste of time, pure escapism. "So unrealistic, they fill your head with such fluffy nonsense," he says. My mom is more neutral about them, which is almost more upsetting to me. How can she just not care? Are my parents really that dead inside?

Inviting Will to watch a movie with me was, I admit, kind of a test. I wanted to see whether he could fall under a cinematic spell the way I do. Because there's a reason movies are such classic dates—they're an instant shared experience. They give you something to talk about.

But *Broadcast News* isn't your typical romantic comedy. It wasn't designed to make two people believe in the power of true love, or to be the entry point for a good make-out session. It was meant to make you laugh and be pissed off about people manipulating the truth. It was meant to show you how sometimes you can be attracted to the wrong people for the wrong reasons. So...maybe not an auspicious movie for a non-date?

WILL

Broadcast News is a good flick. Scratch that, it's kind of an amazing flick. Funny but bittersweet, and totally spot-on in the way it captures the drama of being on deadline and the drive to tell a story the right way. It was kind of amazing, too, that in the end Holly Hunter's character didn't end up with either William Hurt or Albert Brooks. I can't think of a single movie that I've watched where a romance ended up this way. It's brave, and probably it's true.

"Did you like it?" Jocelyn asks carefully as the credits roll.

"Yeah, it was terrific." I talk about all the little things it got right, and a smile lights up her face. "They really don't make movies like that anymore, do they? With endings that don't tie up in a nice bow?"

"Not the major studios, really." She shrugs. "I don't blame them. People like to leave a movie theater believing in happy endings. Why not, when the world seems like it's such a shit-show?" She pulls one of my grandma Domenici's afghans over her knees. "Sometimes you just want to laugh."

Idly, Jocelyn leafs through the coffee-table photobooks my mother made after our family trip to Nigeria a few years ago. She stops at a picture of us on safari at Yankari Game Reserve. "Does your family go to Nigeria often?"

"Not really," I say. "It's too hard for my mother to schedule enough time off, and most of my extended family is here in the States now. That trip was my first visit there since I was a baby." After I came back, it was the first time that I started thinking of myself not only as "black" or "mixed race," but also as Nigerian American.

"Why did your mom come to the US?"

"For graduate school, like a lot of other Nigerians. When my mother was a teenager there were years of military rule and attacks on the press, and most people who had the means to— even a lot of people who really didn't—sent their kids abroad to study. It's easier for Nigerians to do that than people from other African countries, because the official language is English."

"I didn't know that."

"Not many Americans do. It's one of my mother's pet peeves, when people tell her that she 'speaks English very well.' English is her first language, and she went to boarding school in the UK. Her 'English' is better than ninety percent of Americans'."

"Oh, I get that at least once a month at the restaurant," Jos says. "I enjoy that almost as much as when customers say that I'm a credit to my people."

"Do you have that thing happen where people confuse you with another POC in your school? Because that happens to me about once a week." I've gotten so used to people mistaking me for Andre Jones that I automatically respond to his name.

"Oh my God!" Jocelyn simpers. "I love it so much when that happens! Microaggressions are *the best*."

I laugh, feeling giddy at how natural it feels to have Jos in my home, sitting next to me, shooting the breeze. I fiddle with the TV remote, flicking it with my finger as I rack my brain for something else to do so we can hang out longer. The idea, when it comes to me, is a no-brainer. "Do you want to watch any of the extra features?"

Jos's face lights up. "Now you're speaking my language."

The first featurette we watch is an interview with Susan Zirinsky, the TV producer who partly inspired Holly Hunter's character, Jane. It turns out that Jane's daily crying jags—the ones I'd just chalked up to Hollywood overdramatization—were real.

"I often have these moments when I don't think that I'm the right person for this job, and that somebody who's smarter should be doing it," Zirinsky says in the interview. "I'd like to say that I grew out of these thoughts when I turned fifty...but I didn't."

I'm not sure if this is reassuring or crushing, coming from a woman who's now president of CBS News. All I know is, for a second, it's pretty nice to not feel alone.

JOCELYN

Watching bonus features is definitely my jam—in fact, I'm kind of surprised I didn't think of it myself—but eventually I have to take a bathroom break. Afterward, I maybe linger a few seconds too long in the hallways to look at pictures of baby Will, cradled in the lap of his sister, who looks about two years old. The photo album confirmed that his dad is definitely white. I can tell by the pictures on the stairway—a steady march of festively clothed portraits—that the Domenicis are the type of family to send out tastefully designed holiday cards each year. I bet they're on thick cardstock, not like the flimsier photo paper ones my Big Uncle sends out to his more prominent business associates, complaining about the cost every time.

When I get back from the bathroom, Will is flipping through the remaining extras.

I blink as I sit down. "What? There's a bonus ending?" Priya would freak out if she knew. "We have to watch that."

The alternate ending is introduced by James L. Brooks, the film's director. He explains that when they first gave test screenings of the movie, it did really well, except that everyone wanted a more satisfying resolution to the romance, so they reshot a reconciliation scene at the airport between the producer, Jane, and the pretty-boy anchor, Tom.

"Hoo, boy," I say as I settle back into the couch. "This is going to be good."

While I was in the bathroom, Will made another batch

of popcorn, which he brings in a ginormous bowl that he puts between us. It's a bit of a balancing act, and I move my right leg a little bit farther to the right to steady the bowl, just as Will does the same with his left, and our knees touch.

Who knew your knee had so many nerves? My toes curl at the contact, and I remember what it felt like to hug him, how warm he was.

Next to me, Will has gone completely still. He doesn't move away, but he keeps his eyes focused on the TV, where Tom has just thrown himself in Jane's cab.

Holy mother of God, William Hurt and Holly Hunter can act. There's a grainy unfinished quality to the cut, a rawness that triggers a tightness in my chest as the characters argue and fight and ultimately kiss in a way that's angry and vulnerable and frightening and hot enough that I can feel something unfurling in my belly.

I take a deep breath and try to calm my hormones.

The room is so quiet that I can hear Will's breath hitch a little, but I don't dare look at him because I can feel my face flushing. The place where our knees touch feels like it's generating enough energy to power the city of Utica for the next decade.

Finally, after approximately four decades, the characters on the screen break their lip lock, and Jane grabs Tom's head, shakes it a bit, and tells him, "I could kill you."

"Yes, you could," Tom mumbles.

The line is so good, I have to make a joke about it so I don't cry. "Nothing says I love you more than whispering sweet homicidal nothings," I say.

134

Will turns to grin at me. I smile shyly and intend to go right back to watching the scene and listening to James L. Brooks's genius commentary, but I can't. I'm transfixed by Will's lips, the *nearness* of them. The air between us feels like a live thing, vibrating with tension.

And that's when I break down and make the cheesiest, tropiest move ever: I do a kickass classic arm stretch, ending up draped over Will's shoulder with my head nestling into his very, very nice bicep.

"I'm so glad you're not an asshole," I sigh, the words traveling straight from my hindbrain to my mouth.

I have the best pickup lines.

WILL

One minute I'm watching deleted scenes, stressing out over everything: Should I have gotten Jos her own bowl of popcorn? Is this just a friendly movie night, or is it a date? If I make a move, will it ruin things forever? The next minute, Jocelyn is leaning into my shoulder, and I don't think I have ever been more present, or more alive, in a single moment. Ever.

For a split second, I wonder if she's feeling light-headed and just needed to lie down. But her eyes are open and fixed on the screen. She's smiling faintly, and when she looks up to see what I can only imagine is a completely flummoxed expression on my face, her grin gets wider, and she says, "I'm so glad you're not an asshole."

Me too, Jocelyn. Me too.

It takes me a few minutes, but right around the time that my left arm falls asleep I realize that I can make a move, too. I wiggle my arm out from under her and slide it around her shoulders, pulling her in to what can only be described as a Grade A, 100 percent bona fide cuddle.

It feels like when you've been playing outside all day in the winter, and you've got snow inside your socks, and your snot's frozen in your nose, and you come inside your house and your mom has hot chocolate already made for you with pastel-colored mini marshmallows, and fresh warm clothes that she's just run through the dryer.

It feels like when you've been working on a story for weeks, and there's this one source who you really need who isn't returning your e-mails, and there's a huge gap in the narrative where you have nothing to show for your research, but suddenly, the day before your deadline, the person responds and gives you exactly the information you need to deliver a kickass piece.

It feels warm. It feels true. It feels right.

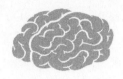

This Is My Brain on Tension

JOCELYN

James L. Brooks is a legendary director, but I've got to admit I barely register the featurette on his career due to my brain being on a continuous loop of: "He likes me! He put his arm around me and we're snuggling! Holy shit, I think this is now officially a real date, not a non-date! OMG, Priya is going to. Freak. Out."

At the end of the night, we still haven't really said that we like each other, but it seems pretty clear to me. This is uncharacteristically optimistic, I know, but it's not like I can't think positively. I just prefer not to, to avoid disappointment.

When we're out of extras, I rack my brain for how to further confirm my hypothesis that he is into me. Honestly, though, the longer we stay glued to each other like this, the more I feel like I've met the burden of proof.

"Did you like it?" I ask, though what I'm really asking is, "Do you like me?"

"I thought it was awesome," he says, which is a satisfactory answer on all counts. "And I was thinking…" Will swallows, twice, and the edge of his cheek sucks in like he's biting the inside of his mouth.

I hold my breath, not wanting to say anything that will mess up my data collection.

"…well, I was thinking how I've never watched *When Harry Met Sally…*, but my dad's always talking about what a classic it is. Have you seen it?"

Have I seen it? How am I supposed to answer that question, without lying, in a way that doesn't make him think that I'm a psychopath? Also, the fact that he chose a rom-com definitely supports my hypothesis that this is a date.

"Yeah, I've seen it," I say. "It's one of my favorite movies. But I'd love to see it again with you."

Will's smile transforms him into another person. It's not that he's normally a sourpuss, but before I've only ever seen him smile politely, or grin enthusiastically. The way he looks now, beaming like he can't help it? It makes me feel like a freaking revelation.

"All right." Will stands up, tidies up the couch cushions a bit, and holds his hand out to pull me up. "*When Harry Met Sally…* next Wednesday. It's a date."

"Yes." I reach my hand out to seal the deal (and confirm the results of my scientific method). "A date it is."

The air is as thick as butternut squash soup on the drive back to the library. After we pull into the now-empty lot, Will turns off the car, but neither of us moves to get out. With the engine turned off it's so quiet I can hear the squeak of leather as he turns in the seat to face me.

It's in that silence that in a flash of panic, like a switch flipping, my confidence evaporates. All of a sudden I'm certain that I've read Will all wrong. Maybe he's going to turn to me and say, "Jocelyn, I think you're getting the wrong idea."

I've been waiting all night for this moment, when all of our plans run their course, and we're alone and done with any activities or distractions, and there's nothing else between us but air and words and potential.

Honestly, I'm terrified. Because now's the moment that Will's going to make his move, but if he doesn't, if this opportunity passes us by, I know that I will never have the nerve to create another one.

WILL

The entire drive back to the library I have a buzzing under my skin that's almost unbearable, like that moment after you get stung by a mosquito where you feel a vague tingling but can't see the welt or feel the itch yet. I feel as if someone's bottled me up and shaken me, but I make myself concentrate extra hard on the drive, as getting into an accident would be a less-than-optimal barrier to my endgame.

We've both moved our chess pieces onto the board, and I am convinced that I have a chance, as long as I don't trip over myself getting to checkmate.

By the time I turn off my car and face Jocelyn, I've rehearsed a hundred lines in my head and discarded them all, starting with "I'm so glad that I got to work with you" (too formal; also, I should not remind her that I literally work for her), swinging all the way to "I think I'm in love with you" (which maybe comes off a bit too strong) to "So, was this a date?" (vaguely whiny and desperate sounding) to "I think we should take this relationship to the next level" (a little too on point to sound spontaneous).

I'm still trying to process what I really want to say other than "Jocelyn, I really like you," when I realize that almost a minute has gone by since we parked. With the air-conditioning turned off, the air stills and thickens. As seconds pass I watch Jocelyn's face morph from excitement to nervous anticipation to an emotion I never, ever want to see on her face again.

Fear.

It takes me a second to realize that the thing she's afraid of is this unspoken thing between us, and another to understand how easily I can address it.

"Jocelyn," I blurt out, because I can't stand to think of her being afraid. "I really like you."

Her eyes widen, her breath catches, and the frown that was just beginning to form flips into a watery smile.

"Oh, thank God," she whispers.

Then she starts to cry.

For as long as I can remember, my mother has impressed upon me the importance of my words. "Remember, Will, your words have weight, and the capacity to harm." Like I said in my interview at A-Plus, though, being thoughtful can be a double-edged sword.

Simple questions like, "What do you want to do?" stump me.

I think about what I actually want to do, of course, but then I worry about whether the person who asked the question really cares about what my desires are, or whether they are just being polite. If that sounds exhausting, it's because it is.

All this is to say that I am not known for speaking before I think. Which is why it's so amazing for me to realize that with Jocelyn, it's the best thing I've done all night.

"You took so long to say anything, I was sure you were going to tell me I was barking up the wrong tree," she says, laughing through her tears. Tears of relief, I realize.

"Nope, the rightest tree in the forest," I say, which doesn't make any sense, but I'm feeling kind of giddy, like my heart is beating so fast and so inefficiently that it can't get blood to my brain. My lungs can't seem to pull enough air, and I don't know where to look, or what to do with my hands. If I didn't know better, I'd think that I was starting to have a panic attack. I finally decide to stare at Jocelyn, even though it kind of hurts my brain to, as if I'm a circuit that's overloading. There's something I need to tell her: "I'm sorry it took me so long to get my act together and tell you how I feel."

"No, it's okay," she says, grabbing a tissue and swiping at her eyes.

"I mean, there shouldn't be a double standard," Jocelyn continues. "It shouldn't always be the boy making the first move. I could've told you." She squeezes the tissue in her fist, and her voice is kind of nasal when she says, "I really like you, too."

My chest tightens, then it swells. All the emotions from the past hour, from the past week, month—from my lifetime, really—seem to surge through my body at once. And I understand why Jocelyn was crying.

JOCELYN

So, my vision of my reaction when a boy finally (FINALLY) said that he liked me did not include actual tears. But Will doesn't seem to mind that I've turned into a snot factory. In fact, his eyes are kind of glistening in the streetlights, too, which quite possibly means that we are made for each other.

I feel like I've been lugging around this crush for so long, trekking through deserts and scaling mountains of feeling, so much feeling. And now I feel almost weightless.

Here's another metaphor: I've been holding back my affection for Will for weeks now, but it's been building up day by day like water beating up against a dam. And now there's nothing keeping my feelings back anymore.

Will holds his palm out to me again, and I shiver at the tingle that goes down my back when our fingers touch. This time he puts his other hand over mine, and I've never felt so safe, so protected, and then he curves his wrists open, leans down, and I swear to God he kisses my palm tenderly (that's the only word to describe it) like we're characters in an Austen movie.

As my cold, angry heart melts, I realize: I am so gone for this nerd.

If my life were a CW show, this is the point where a croony song by Ariana Grande would start playing. If it were an arthouse flick, it would maybe break into an animated riff where line drawings of Will and me would take flight to blandly inspirational piano music.

But my life is barely Instagram-worthy, let alone Hollywood-ready, so instead Will and I just sit holding hands like the chickens we apparently are for what seems like eons. In my peripheral vision I see a jogger run by the parking lot with a running stroller, and a car pulls in to dump some books into the after-hours return box. When the stillness becomes unbearable I move my thumb so it brushes over one of his fingers in the briefest caress, and I hear Will's breath catch, see his lips widen. His hand spasms as if he's been shocked, but he doesn't move. I don't move. It's as if we're both afraid the moment will shatter if we try anything else.

But you know what? Screw fear.

"Can we just kiss now?" I ask.

Despite the fact that my voice sounds like I've lost a war with about a billion tons of pollen, Will doesn't laugh.

"Yes, please," he says fervently, and he leans in. I tilt my head slightly to the right the way I've seen on screens big and small, digital and projected. And because Will is suddenly overwhelmingly close, impossibly real, I close my eyes to protect my brain from exploding from sensory overload as my mouth finds its target.

Will's lips remind me of the flour-covered mochi rice cakes my mom sometimes brings home as treats from her Chinatown runs. They're soft but firm, and warm in a way that makes my whole body sigh, that makes me want more, and suddenly it makes sense to me why books always use food metaphors when they describe kissing, and desire, and love. All of a sudden I'm ravenous for Will, and this is just with a chaste touch of the lips that would almost certainly still qualify a movie for a PG rating by the Motion Picture Association of America.

When it all gets to be too much—I haven't really gotten the

knack of kissing and breathing at the same time yet—I break away and finally open my eyes. Will's looking at me wide-eyed, and I'm surprised to realize that I know him well enough by now to guess what he's thinking. So I know what I can say to help him relax.

"I had to catch my breath," I explain. "That was almost too amazing." Then I lick my lips, and his eyes get heavy lidded as he stares at my mouth, and I can hear his breath hitch as I move in for round two.

I'm not sure where to put my hands, so at first I just keep my left in his, and my right on my leg. But as my hunger deepens, as we try our damnedest to actually meld the atoms in our faces together into a single molecule, my hand creeps up to touch Will's thigh. His very well-toned thigh. He groans, and as his mouth opens, I do the thing. The French kiss thing that I always told Priya sounded gross as hell, because spit.

In reality, French kissing is actually not too bad, which may explain its popularity.

Will is certainly a fan. And if I thought that lips were incredible, tongue is mind-blowing. It's like, you've had this body part your entire life, and it's a nice enough organ, one that allows you to experience both wasabi peas and chocolate peanut butter ice cream. You use it every day, and maybe you start taking it for granted a bit. I mean, it's not as if the tongue is something you need to pay attention to, or maintain, like your fingernails or hair or God forbid your bladder or bowels.

But for the first time I'm realizing the tongue is a muscle. It can move. And no one ever talks about how much it can feel.

Using tongue is some next-level shit, and all I can think

144

about is the YouTube video I once saw on how Hollywood special effects people use accelerants to turn ordinary fires (which are perfectly great for roasting marshmallows and boiling water) into spectacular conflagrations that make Tom Cruise/Vin Diesel/any actor named Chris look like total badasses.

Tongue is totally an accelerant, and not only for my heart rate. All of a sudden, Will's hand is feverishly clutching at my waist, and when his thumb brushes a sliver of bare skin I feel a heavy, twisty sensation in what my mother calls my womanly areas, and seriously, why am I thinking of my mom right now?

WILL

Kissing Jocelyn is a little bit like jumping off a cliff and a little bit like sliding a puzzle piece into place. I don't know if it's possible to feel completely unmoored and completely grounded at the same time, but that's the only way I can describe it.

Thank God she had the nerve to make the first move. I was sitting there like a complete doofus wondering if it was too soon to lean in for a kiss, trying to figure out whether it was still cool to ask a girl for permission to kiss her, or whether it'd make me look like I was trying too hard.

I'd just decided that consent is always sexy, when Jocelyn bulldozed through all my doubts. She planted her flag. And I, obviously, had no problems with being claimed.

Well, maybe one problem. In my pants.

It turns out that wearing jeans was a strategic error, as was waiting until I was crammed in the front seat of a Nissan Leaf to get my game going. But I make do, and when Jocelyn snakes her hand up around my neck to press me deeper into our kiss, it's impossible for me to concentrate on anything other than the softness of her lips, the heat of her tongue, and the feel of the curve of her hips under my hands.

The trouble with being labeled the quiet kid in school has always been the massive contradiction between my rep with the outside world and how freaking loud my thoughts are in my head. It's like when people look at me they think I'm just a pot sitting on a turned-off stove, but really my mind is constantly at that point just before a simmer—where you can hear the rumbling of water vapor evaporating against metal.

I feel like I've finally, finally broken into a boil. There's a crack in the facade of reserve that's kept me back, held me on the sidelines all my life. It's possible to see myself doing so many things, if I'm here kissing a gorgeous, smart, funny girl. If she's kissing me back. If she likes me.

I feel expansive. Invincible. I feel like I can control time, and that I'll live in this moment forever, in this bubble of warmth and skin like silk and stuttered breaths.

And then:

Crack

I'm sure it's a gunshot at first, and I break away from Jocelyn. It takes just a fraction of a second for a vise to close around my chest, and I'm breathless for an entirely different reason. The world closes around me.

CrackCrackCrack

The sound is too close, and I realize it's someone pounding on Jocelyn's window with something metal the same time a blinding light shatters my night vision. I close my eyes against the physical pain.

My hands are already up, the gesture automatic. Because if my mother has told me once, she's told me a thousand times: Always remember to show my hands.

JOCELYN

My first thought is that it's a cop, and I almost want to laugh, because how cliché is it to be caught necking in a parking lot? Not that we went that far. Next to me, Will freezes and puts his hands up. In the light that suddenly shines from behind me, I can see the whites of his eyes, and the terror I see there pierces my chest like a sliver of ice. Of course he would have a different reaction to seeing a police officer than I would.

"It's okay," I whisper, "we haven't done anything wrong." Will has turned his head to shy away from the sudden flash of light, so he doesn't look at me. His eyes are tightly shut, the muscles in his jaw rigid.

I wince at another sharp rap on the window that's so loud I can feel it in my bones.

"Hello, hello." It's a man's voice, impatient, and heavily accented. An icy ball of fear forms in my stomach.

If my life were a feature film, this is the moment when things would drop into super-slow motion and the heroine's eyes would open in recognition as a distorted voice suddenly sharpened into clear words:

"Xiao Jia, Xiao Jia, ni zai gan shenme?"

Then the camera would cut to the shot of an irate, slightly balding Chinese man trying to break down the car window with a handful of keys while waving around his cell phone flashlight in a furious attempt to get the attention of the dead-in-the-water teens inside.

"Hey, Dad," I say weakly.

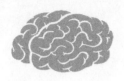

This Is My Brain on Consequences

WILL

When I first realize it's Jocelyn's father and not the Utica Police Department banging on my car window, I almost pass out with relief. My hands tremble as I lower them; I can feel my heart still racing as I force myself to take deep breaths.

Then embarrassment floods in, warming my cheeks, as I think of Mr. Wu's "no hanky-panky" warning. Thank God my hands were well above Jocelyn's waist and over all articles of clothing.

Mr. Wu raps on the door again, gesticulating wildly, and Jocelyn sends me a pained look before pulling at the door handle. "Later," she mouths as the night air fills with rapid-fire Mandarin. The door's not even open an inch before her dad is reaching in to haul her out. When she's gone it's like someone's vacuumed out the life in the car.

Then the door swings wide open and Mr. Wu leans in to get a look at who's in the driver's seat. His eyes widen with shock, then the surprise turns into a complicated expression halfway between disappointment and disgust.

Then he's gone, probably on his way to dig me a hole so deep I may never see sunlight again.

JOCELYN

My dad sits in stony silence the entire ride home, which is how I know that I'm in deep, deep trouble. Everyone knows that my dad is a blusterer, so my family's learned to just let his ramblings roll off our backs, and his fits of loud outrage tend to burn out quickly. When he's quiet, though, it means that his anger has so entrenched itself that it's become part of the very marrow of his bones.

The last time I saw my dad this upset was when he found out that Alan was falsifying my mom's signature on the math tests he'd flunked. Failing a test was bad enough. I had to admit to being kind of in awe that my kid brother had leveled up to forgery. For a while I couldn't decide whether to feel good that I was suddenly the golden child or pathetic that I seemed like such a Goody Two-shoes in comparison.

Months later, my dad still has a short fuse when it comes to Alan, and they do a lot of ignoring each other when they are in the same room, which suits Alan just fine. His big punishment was summer school—he's happy to fly under the radar for the rest of the time. I can only hope that I will be that lucky.

As we drive home, I pray that my dad will yell. I just want

him to tell me what he's most mad about, so I can feel bad about that one thing, instead of all of it. He could be mad at me for not doing my summer project with Priya, or that I lied about where I was. He could be upset that I was kissing a boy, or pissed that I was alone in a dark parking lot with said boy. When you put it all together, it's just a freaking Niagara Falls of bad decisions, and I want to hit the undo button of my life so, so much right now.

But my dad stews, and my guilt simmers.

"I'm sorry," I say in a small voice after a few minutes of silence. My dad doesn't even look at me, just stares straight ahead. There's a jerky acceleration as he puts on more gas, but he doesn't respond.

I am in so much trouble.

When we pull into the lot behind A-Plus, my dad brakes harder than he usually does, and I wince at the crunch of gravel. He doesn't spare me a glance as he yanks the keys out of the ignition and opens the driver door. After my dad disappears into the rear entrance of the restaurant I sit for a couple more seconds, bracing myself for the reckoning.

They don't still make chastity belts, do they?

By the time I've finally dragged myself upstairs, my dad has broken his vow of silence. My poor mom, who probably just sat down on the couch to watch one of her beloved *Law & Order* episodes, eyes me with a pinched expression when I walk in before turning back to my father, who is standing in the middle of the room gesticulating wildly as he enumerates my transgressions in Mandarin. Alan is slouched on the floor by the coffee table, making himself as physically small as possible while pretending to do work. I was hoping that the minutes I spent sitting in the car would have given my dad time to get the whole story out, but he's just getting started.

"Nide nuer pianle women." Your daughter lied to us, my dad tells my mom. She wasn't at the library at all. She left her bicycle at the library unchained, after all the people were gone! It could have been stolen! I had to get out that stupid bike rack that is such a hassle to put on. And then a car comes in and just sits there, and when I go up to see if our daughter is in it, she is kissing. A boy!

"Aiyo," my mother exclaims, glancing over at me. For a split second she seems almost excited. Then her eyes narrow, and she asks my dad who it was.

"Will," my dad says, making a disgusted face.

"Shi shenme nan ren?" asks my mom with a confused expression on her face. She apparently doesn't even know what Will's name is, even though he's worked for us for weeks.

My dad explains, impatiently, that Will is the boy I hired to help out with the restaurant.

I see the exact nanosecond that the penny drops, that my mother connects the name to the face. Her eyes widen, and her hands cup her mouth and nose as if she could block out the news if she doesn't breathe in any of the air it was spoken into.

"Nage hei ren?" she asks, the words like a sucker punch. My chest clenches up, and I can barely breathe with bewildered outrage.

"The black boy?" is the most generous way for me to interpret my mom's words, but my second-generation brain translates her Mandarin more literally at first, so what hits me initially is the word-by-word translation, which is "that black person."

It's a quirk of the language that in Mandarin a person isn't "American" or "British"; they're "that American person" or "that

British person." It's a lot like the subtle difference between saying that someone's "Jewish" versus calling them "a Jew."

I want to say, "Hey, Mom. Your bias is showing." At the same time, my instinct is to make excuses for her. The first-generation Chinese community I grew up with in NYC didn't have the time or energy to give a damn about cultural sensitivity. Like everyone else in the world, she's just internalized a shit ton of racist ideas, right?

None of this is an excuse, though. None of it makes it any easier to hear the mixture of contempt and panicked scandal in my mom's voice. And let's face it: Even as I try to justify my mom's comments, I know in my heart that it's more than innocent fresh-off-the-boat confusion. I think of the summer days when my mother insists on slathering me with Dollar Tree suntan lotion, not to prevent melanoma but because she's worried that my skin will "be too dark." When I tried to explain to her that some people in my school spent hundreds of dollars trying to get artificial tans, she scoffed. "You know who have dark skin in China? Peasants!"

All of a sudden I've reached my limit. I've played the role of the silently guilty child for as long as I can.

"I'm sorry for sneaking around, okay? But I'm not sorry for kissing Will. He's a really good guy who's already done a ton to help the restaurant. And let's just cut to the chase. You're maddest at me because he's black. That's bullshit, and you know it." I'm loud. I have to be, to cut through my dad's tirade. I hate that I don't sound sorry at all. Somewhere underneath all the rage, there's a part of me that's terrified by how little I actually care. "Can we just move on to how I'm grounded?"

My punishment is pretty much what I expected: no cell, no internet for two weeks. I'll basically be a prisoner to the restaurant. Not like that's so different from my summer so far. The worst thing, though, is that Will's fired. My dad eyes me suspiciously when I don't argue, or cry, or stomp off in a fit. I like to think it's a sign of maturity, but really it's a sign of not giving a flying fig about their arbitrary restrictions.

I'm already calculating how I'll contact Will behind my parents' back.

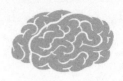

This Is My Brain
on Radio Silence

WILL

Fake news expands to fill the space allotted to it.

The days after kissing Jocelyn are torture. After getting an e-mail from her father saying that I won't be needed at the restaurant anymore, I have to explain to my mother that I was let go because I was caught fraternizing with my boss. Jocelyn hasn't responded to my e-mail or texts, and by Sunday night my brain is so saturated with worst-case scenarios that I'm desperate enough to actually call her. As usual I have a couple of false starts, but on the third attempt my thumb hovers over the green call button for only a minute before I close my eyes and tap it.

It's probably the first time in my life that I've ever been disappointed to get a voice mail. If that isn't proof positive that I've got it bad, I don't know what is.

I don't leave a message the first go-around. Instead, I call again after writing down a few notes, a loose script that I largely abandon as soon as I hear her cheery message: "This is Jocelyn. You know what to do."

It throws me, hearing her voice again. When I look down at my notes, they don't make any sense anymore. After the beep I just start rambling.

"Hey, Jocelyn. This is Will. I'm calling because I haven't heard from you, and I wanted to make sure you're okay, and that you're not in too much trouble. I…"

I curse myself. What can I do if she is in trouble if I *am* the trouble?

"If you're satisfied with your message, please press two. If you'd like to rerecord your message, press three."

My palms are so sweaty I nearly drop my phone in my rush to press three.

"Hi, Jocelyn. It's Will. I wanted to check in and see how things are going. I hope things aren't too busy at the restaurant, and that your family's okay. I had a great time last week, and…"

Ugh. I sound like a creep fishing for some action. I jab the button to delete the message before the completion recording even plays. Then I throw my phone onto my bed, as far away as I can to avert voice-mail disaster, and put my face in my hands the way my dad does when the Jets make a particularly boneheaded play near the line of scrimmage.

In the darkness, with my fingers pressed tight against my closed eyes, I remind myself why I'm calling. I'm not calling to stalk her, or push an agenda, or to rush in like a knight in shining armor to solve all her problems.

I'm calling to show I care.

Before my third attempt at leaving a message, I take half a dozen centering breaths before dialing. As the phone rings, I remind myself how it felt to hold her hand, and remember the feeling of her forehead pressed against mine, how it grounded me and gave me a place to land.

"Hey, Jocelyn. It's Will. Just wanted to call and say that I'm thinking about you. I miss you. Hope we can talk soon."

In the first hour after leaving my voice mail, I check my phone twice to make sure the ringer is on. My clock tells me that it's time to sleep, but my body is restless, buzzing with a physical need to hear Jocelyn's voice.

I scroll through my curated news feed until my eyes sting. There's another think piece about the Two Americas, and an investigation into yet another episode of police brutality. I read some analysis of recent events in the Middle East, and a feature on a couple whose baby was born intersex—with biological characteristics that don't fit neatly into the definition of male or female—and their efforts to prevent unnecessary surgery on intersex kids. I read about campaign finance reform. Fracking. Islamophobia. The responsibility of the media in a post-truth society. Noise. Noise. Noise. What to say? What can I do?

Eventually, I sink into the darkness of sleep.

After another twenty-four hours incommunicado, I finally crack and tell Manny the whole sob story over a can of Pringles in the Amazing Stories break room. If any of my friends are going to sympathize, it's the guy whose case of unrequited love is essentially a chronic condition.

"That's shitty, man. I can't believe you got canned, and then she ghosted you. Just when you were about to get some action, too. You have the worst luck."

I don't want to argue over the definition of "ghost," but I'm reasonably sure that's not what happened. "I think her parents may have just put her in total lockdown. The A-Plus Twitter and Facebook accounts have gone completely dark."

"What shows up in your e-mail tracking?"

"My what?"

Manny practically sprains his eyeballs rolling them. "Have you learned nothing about how to obsessively follow someone over the internet, young Padawan?"

In less than five minutes he's set me up and I've sent Jocelyn another e-mail:

> Subject: Still thinking about you.
> Hope you're okay.
> -Will

After I hit send, I stare at the little circle showing that tracking has been enabled until my eyes burn, half hoping it will turn into a green check mark, half dreading that I'll finally get confirmation that Jocelyn has been actively ignoring my e-mails. It doesn't take long for my brain to come up with scenarios where the program fails. For instance, if the tracker does show that the e-mail has been opened, it's not guaranteed Jocelyn was the one who opened it, right? What if her dad made her give him her password and is vetting all her e-mails? Or worse, what if he's logging into her e-mail and deleting my messages without even opening them?

"Dude, you've been staring at that screen and rocking back and forth in a modified fetal position for fifteen minutes."

I look up, and Manny's got the empty can of Pringles in his hand. He tosses it into the trash can with a hollow clank. He's got pity in his eyes, and I want to say something, but instead my gaze shoots right back to the computer screen. I hit the refresh button before I even realize what I'm doing.

"Man, you are so far gone."

I don't even bother arguing. Instead, I check to make sure the Wi-Fi connection is still on. Manny sighs and reaches over to slam my computer shut.

"Hey!" I sputter. "At least let me shut it down properly." Keeping computers on standby is a waste of electricity; Manny knows that.

"Listen, Will, I know you're new to this game, but you've gotta learn how to make like Elsa and let it go. If she's into you, she'll find a way to let you know what's going on. If she's not, she's not worth it anyway." Apparently I don't look convinced, because suddenly, he brightens and puts on his faux innocent face, the one that means my goat's about to get gotten. "You know what Javier would say in a situation like this. If you love something…"

My eyes widen. "No! Manny, don't say the bird thing! Anything but the bird thing."

"…set it free. If it's yours, it will come back. If it doesn't, it wasn't meant to be."

It's a running joke in our group that Javier Diaz is the king of inspirational refrigerator magnet wisdom. His kitchen is littered with them, the majority purchased by his spinster aunt Maritza, who dispenses them to everyone in his extended family as stocking stuffers each year, along with saint-themed Christmas ornaments. Javier first trotted out the "If you love something" chestnut in seventh grade, after Tim became the first one in our group to get to first base when he made out with Natalie Silverman in the coatroom of his cousin's bat mitzvah. Since then it's been endearingly, annoyingly applied to dozens of "relationships" ranging from e-mail flirtations to friendly text messages with lab partners to that time when Manny had a lunch date with Madison Nguyen when they both represented Turkey at a Model UN conference.

"Screw you, Manny," I say. "I'm not going to get Jocelyn back by listening to advice that came off a refrigerator magnet."

"Aw, Will—don't knock the wisdom. And I don't think it was from any of the Diazes' appliances—I think it was from a poster. Or at least a button."

At the beginning of high school, Javi upgraded from magnets to buttons, which eventually covered every bit of canvas on his backpack, even the straps. This past year he convinced the school librarian that a button maker would be a good purchase for the media department, and he started making his own. This was also the year his school counselor gave him exercises to study irony and humor: He ended up making buttons of a smiling Captain America saying things like, "I'm so happy that the POTUS appreciates the 'very fine' Nazis in America today!"

"I don't think the bird quote was from a button," I tell Manny. "You know what a button would be great for, though?" I ask in a burst of inspiration. "I bet we could make some kickass swag for A-Plus to use the next time we have a booth. Something like, 'Use Your Noodle, Order Chinese Tonight,' or 'Keep Calm and Eat Dumplings.'"

160

Manny gives me a weird look. "Yeah, I'm sure they could do that. You gonna be okay, buddy? I know it can be tough to move on sometimes...."

"It's not like that," I say. "I'm not in denial or anything." If anything, I'm experiencing the opposite of denial: I'm hyperaware of every possible negative outcome from being caught parking by Jocelyn's dad. I know things are messed up right now and they might never go back to the way they were—but I can't just turn off my brain when it comes to ways to help their business. If the business fails, and the Wus move to New York City, Jocelyn and I will never have the chance to see what we could become.

The button idea is the thing that gets me through the days of uncertainty that follow. I spend hours making three different designs, and when I'm done I e-mail Javi to see if he can hook me up with some prototypes. I can't talk to Jocelyn, or text her, and the green check mark that's supposed to come up next to her e-mail whenever she reads it never appears.

Once the buttons are done, I open up my "Restaurant at the End of the Strip Mall" file. I looked up the developer online and have had the name and number of the property management contact for days. I even have a list of questions I've been planning on asking her: What's the average duration of tenancy? Is it lower for restaurants than for retail outlets? How much does your rent typically rise each year?

I pick up my phone and input the number, ignoring the single buzz of my watch. I know that my pulse is up.

I take a deep breath and hit the call button. With each ring, the pressure builds in my forehead. My watch makes a double buzz.

There's a click as the call connects, and my throat seizes up.

161

It's an answering machine.

I hang up without leaving a message, telling myself that I'll call back the next day.

That evening, after an Xbox marathon, I let Javier get a ride home with Tim. I call in a take-out order and walk down to A-Plus. They may have fired me, but that doesn't mean I can't go there as a customer. As usual, there's only one booth occupied by a solo diner but a line of take-out bags ready to go behind the counter, where Jocelyn's brother is checking the orders. I see at least four stapled printouts indicating someone who ordered online.

I jiggle the paper gift bag I'm holding to settle my nerves.

"Hi, Alan."

When Alan clocks who I am, his baseline deer-in-the-headlights look is replaced by a brief moment of happiness at seeing me, before morphing into an uncomfortable shiftiness.

"Uh, hey, Will. Long time no see."

"How's it going?"

"Not bad. We're past rush hour." His eyes flit nervously to the door to the kitchen.

"So, is Jocelyn around?"

"Yeah," he says at first, before shaking his head and stuttering, "I mean, she's busy. Actually, I think she went out on a supply run. We, uh, we're running out of sugar. And, uh, I don't think she's going to be back for a while."

I get the message, which sits like a chunk of sour pineapple in my gullet. It's not like I'm surprised. I just thought that Alan would be able to come up with something better than an emergency sugar run when the night's half over.

"Well, I'm glad you guys are *busy*." I try to be gracious, try to moderate my tone, but I can still hear the resentment in my voice. "Can you just give this to your sister? I made some buttons for, you know, a little promotion. I think she could have a lot of fun with it."

Alan looks panicky when I try to hand over the bag, but eventually he takes it and stuffs it into the book bag that's in the booth strewn with his homework. Suddenly I feel rotten for putting him in a situation where he could get in trouble with his dad. Not rotten enough to take the bag back, but bad enough that I want to show him that I'm grateful.

I nod toward his homework. "Things going okay with summer school?"

Alan's shoulders slump and he moans. "It's so painful. And my teacher's a sadist. We have to do fifty problems every night."

"How many have you done so far?"

"Twelve. And I can't just make up answers. She wants me to, like, show my work."

I take a look at the clock, and at the familiar counter. It's only half an hour until closing. Usually at this time the Wus are busy getting a head start on cleanup in the kitchen.

"That's rough," I say. "So here's the deal. Why don't you do your homework. It's getting late. I can cover the counter for a little while. And if you can't get a question, just ask."

"Really?" Alan's eyes are like saucers, and I can't help but grin as I nod. "Yussssss."

It's not a hardship to give out bags when people come in to get their takeout—most of them have already paid online, which is part of why it's such a no-brainer. I even fold a few menus for old times' sake and worry a little bit about the fact that I only have to pick up the phone twice in half an hour.

"Have you had any other people come in with Boilermaker coupons?" I ask Alan.

He shrugs. "Maybe one or two a week."

"We need to keep on tracking that. How about the e-mail list? Is anyone updating that?" The little spiral notebook I left at the front of the restaurant where we leave the magazines for people waiting for pickup has at least two or three new names.

"Uh, I don't think so," Alan mumbles. He's squinting down at his homework like it's written in hieroglyphics. "I don't get this problem," he whines. "What do you know about proportional relationships?"

The seat of the booth squeaks as I sit down and try to remember the finer details of seventh-grade math. Alan's mind reminds me of those gel-filled slippery snakes—as soon as he catches on to an idea, he's slid on to another topic. About halfway through solving a multistep word problem he'll start blinking more often and spinning his pencil around. His eyes will flit to the wall-mounted TV and the silent CNN tickertape. Invariably he'll make a multiplication error, or forget to carry when he's adding. As he muddles his way through the problem set, I hear my mother's voice in my head, judging him (judging me). *Stop being so careless*, she would say. *You need to focus. Pay attention to the work, or the work will not pay.* And then finally, when I've just given up on the problem and moved on to the next assignment: *Not to know is bad. Not to wish to know is worse.*

My dad would be gentler. He'd suggest moving to a quieter room without distractions, and he'd bring me some mint tea to help me concentrate. I was lucky—I only struggled with math once in all my schooling, when I had a particularly ineffective

164

fourth-grade teacher. After that, things started coming easier, but I'll never, ever forget my first mixed fractions quiz and how the edges of my vision seemed to white out in panic when I realized that I just didn't understand. I'll always remember how helpless—and worthless—I felt, how utterly betrayed by my brain.

The homework that Alan's been assigned is the worst kind of math—problem after problem with no progression of difficulty, no creativity in how concepts are presented. It's busywork, pure and simple, and it's painful to watch Alan struggle through it.

"Okay, hold on. Can you explain to me what you're doing with this problem?"

He stumbles through about two-thirds of a half-hearted explanation before trailing off and shrugging.

"That's a good start." In Big Brothers Big Sisters they always emphasized the need for positive reinforcement. "You've got the big picture—we just need to work out the little steps and the order you need to take them in...."

It's past nine by the time Alan's done with his homework, but he actually does the last ten on his own. I've handled a few more pickups, and a group of five college students came in and ordered two dinner specials to share among them. At least they left a 20 percent tip. On my way out, I slip the money into the COLLEGE FUND jar when Alan isn't looking.

I don't see Jocelyn. But I manage to avoid Mr. Wu, too, and when I leave, Alan makes sure to tap his book bag as he mouths, "I've got your back."

The next day Priya shows up at my door.

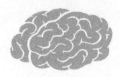

This Is My Brain on Communications Lockdown

JOCELYN

It takes me a while to get a message to Will. I've got to give my parents credit. Neither of them has a college education, but they clearly have graduate degrees in soft incarceration, surveillance, and obstruction.

Then again, it's not rocket science—they just don't let me out of their sight. Literally. They managed to get my amah on their side, which is frankly unfair. Because she isn't as distracted by the business as my parents, she's the perfect (read: worst ever) babysitter when they're at the restaurant. When we're in the living room she parks herself by the router so I can't sneak by and turn it on. She even makes me put Priya on speakerphone when I call her on our landline to schedule time to work on our project. I don't know what exactly Mom and Dad said about my infraction when they made her their enforcer, but Amah doesn't say anything when I give her my best "et tu Brute" look, just clucks her tongue and shakes her head.

So I resort to the old-fashioned way to communicate. Snail mail. It makes me feel like I'm in a Victorian novel, engaging in an epistolary relationship with Will. It's scarily vulnerable, writing my thoughts out by hand. I wonder what he'll read into the shape of my letters, the way they don't quite travel in a perfect line. I think of the thank-you cards that Peggy Cheng always sends after her birthday parties, and her immaculate handwriting that is literally straightedge (you can see the faint marks from where she couldn't quite erase the pencil lines she drew on the card).

My dad isn't quite awful enough to make my amah sleep in my room with me, but he does make me leave my door open the entire night, as if Will could climb through my second-story window. The rule is: lights out once I enter my room. So I write my letter by moonlight. How romantic is that?

> Dear Will,
>
> So I guess you've figured out by now that I'm on lockdown. No cell, no internet. They've even turned my grandma against me (she's my babysitter when I'm not at the restaurant). Sorry for going AWOL.
>
> You've seen a lot of my parents in the past month, so you know that they're kind of—

I have to think hard about the word I want to use. "Conservative" makes it sound like they've got a religious opposition to me dating. "Protective" might be more accurate, but it might be too generous. What are my parents? They're fearful, and out of touch with American culture. They're super suspicious of anyone not related to us by blood, regardless of their race or religion. And they're desperate that Alan and I not make any mistakes that will affect our future—the future that they've worked so hard to create.

> You've seen a lot of my family in the past month, so you know things are kind of complicated. My parents' priorities are different from a lot of other people's. It's an immigrant family trope, right? The "Overprotective Parent"? But it's a trope because there's a kernel of truth to it.
>
> I'm working on getting back to how things were. Or to even better than they were. It might take a while. But I hope you know that—

What do I hope Will knows? I hope that he knows that I miss him. That I really, really like him. That I want to kiss him, and to run my fingers along his forearm and make him shudder. That I want to figure out what comes next.

I'm too chickenshit to write this, of course. It's been over a week since we kissed, and there have been no grand gestures or attempts to break my family's barricade. He hasn't shown up under my window with a boom box, a la John Cusack in *Say*

Anything.... For all I know he could have taken one look at my dad's Rage Face™ and decided that no girl was worth it. Let alone me.

I hope we see each other soon.

I put it in a security envelope, the kind you use to send bills that don't come with a self-addressed one. I'll give it to Priya, because I don't want to get Alan in trouble for aiding and abetting if my parents catch him with it. He's on almost as short a leash as I am, and I don't want to make him my mule.

Color me surprised, then, when he shows up in my room before bedtime.

He shuffles into my room. "Good night, Jiejie," he says loudly, turning his head so his voice projects into our hallway. "I'll see you in the morning. Do you think you could check my homework?"

With his face still turned, making sure no one else is coming in from the family room, he hands me a crumpled gift bag, whispering, "Actually, I don't need you to look over my math. Will stopped by tonight looking for you, and he helped me with it." He grins, then scuttles off.

I grab my bathrobe and wrap it around me to hide the bag pressed up against my chest as I go to brush my teeth and get ready for bed. I can practically feel my heart beating against the heavy paper of the bag. A shivery thrill of excitement starts in the back of my neck and electrifies my body. Will came. He brought me something. And he tutored Alan before he left.

My hands shake as I open the gift bag and dig through the

purple tissue paper. The card is one of those over-the-top laser-cut three-dimensional cards that's basically a work of art. I never really understood why someone would want to pay the price of a matinee movie ticket for what is, for most people, really just a label for a gift, but now I get it. When you package something like that, it's basically fanfare for your words. It's a neon sign flashing: HEY, LOOK, HERE'S AN IMPORTANT MESSAGE. Before you even open the thing, your antennae are up, you're eager to see what's inside.

It makes me embarrassed by my own letter, written on college rule. Does it mean that my words are worth less?

I open the front flap, with its intricate cutout of a garden superimposed on a lattice background. There are butterflies with purple plastic gemstones on their bodies, and if I framed it and put it on my wall it would be the prettiest thing in my room.

My heart's pounding when I open it, but thank God, it's a blank card. There's no sentimental platitude, no trying-too-hard-to-be-funny joke. It's just Will's words.

> DEAR JOCELYN,
>
> I MISS YOU AND HOPE THAT YOU'RE OKAY. I DON'T WANT TO PRESUME THAT YOU EVER WANT TO SEE ME AGAIN, AND I DON'T KNOW WHAT YOUR PARENTS HAVE TO SAY ABOUT YOU AND ME BEING MORE THAN JUST FRIENDS. BUT I ALSO DON'T WANT ANOTHER DAY TO GO BY WITHOUT YOU KNOWING THAT I'M THINKING OF YOU, AND THAT ALL I WANT TO DO IS MAKE THINGS RIGHT.
>
> SO, WHAT'S IN THE GIFT BAG? IT'S NOT THE MOST ROMANTIC GIFT IN THE WORLD, BUT THE OTHER DAY I WAS TALKING WITH ONE OF THE GUYS AND I CAME UP WITH THE

IDEA TO MAKE SOME BUTTONS FOR THE RESTAURANT. YOU AND
YOUR BROTHER COULD WEAR THEM, OR YOU COULD GIVE THEM
TO YOUR FAVORITE CUSTOMERS, OR HAND THEM OUT IF YOU EVER
DO ANOTHER BOOTH SOMEWHERE. I DON'T KNOW IF THEY'LL BE
USEFUL, BUT IT MADE ME FEEL BETTER TO MAKE THEM.

    YOURS,

    WILL

I pour the contents of the bag into my hand and stare at them. It's been days since I've smiled, and I can feel the strain of my face muscles as they pull into a grin so wide I could be in a toothpaste commercial.

Will misses me. And screw John Cusack and his boom box, these pins are even more of a grand gesture. Best of all? They get my wheels turning on a Big Idea.

Head buzzing with ideas, I package up the gift bag, brush my teeth, and go back to my room. I have a sales pitch to create. But before I start that, I add a postscript to my letter to Will.

    PS: Got your buttons. They're amazing.
    I have a plan. Come to A-Plus tomorrow
    afternoon at 4:30, with your game face on.

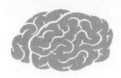

This Is My Brain on Business

JOCELYN

With how disorganized my dad's accounting is, it takes me almost a whole day to pull all the numbers together. I spend another couple of hours following up on our old leads at MVCC and then make a call to a dear old frenemy.

When my plan—my business plan—is ready, I rummage through my closet and find some of my ninth-grade English honors projects. That year, one of my group learning partners was Brenda Litwin, who insisted that presentation meant everything. "If your work looks professional, teachers take it more seriously and they're more likely to give you extra points for all the intangibles, especially for something as subjective as English."

I don't know if the five-dollar frosted polypropylene report covers really helped us get As on all our projects, but they were pretty and are really easy to repurpose.

By the time four thirty rolls around I've put on the outfit I used to interview Will and have three copies of my plan bound in Brenda Litwin's supremely professional manner.

When Will comes in, he looks as if he's ready to run the gauntlet. Nervous but determined. But the second he sees me, his vibe changes from anxious to excited. His eyes light up, and for the first time I actually understand the idiom. I always thought it was the stupidest phrase—like, it's not like people's eyes actually illuminate? But when I see Will, and see his reaction to seeing me, I can understand where the saying comes from. It's like a switch flips—his spine is straighter, the muscles in his jaws tensed and ready to speak.

There's a part of me that's kind of smug to see what I do to him—I'm a switch flipper. And if the acceleration in my own chest is any indication, so is Will.

I wonder if people can see it in me, too: the crackling of electricity under my skin, the slight flush in my cheeks that I can already feel, like I've got the beginnings of a fever. I can hear it in my voice, grainier, breathier, when I lick my suddenly dry lips to say, "Hey."

Will's eyes go to the button I'm wearing ("Show them your love. Buy them Chinese tonight."), and he smiles, getting impossibly brighter. He glows. "You like them?" he asks.

"They're perfect, and you know it." I can't be serious with him right now. I'm giddy, buzzed with emotion. "They're part of the plan."

"Yeah, tell me about this plan."

Wordlessly, I hand him the report.

My dad is the first to walk in, and I brace myself for the thunderous scowl he normally wears when he finds that Alan or

173

I have been bu guai (literally, not good). He never explicitly said that he didn't want me to see Will anymore, but it was certainly implicit. So I'm shocked, and maybe a little unsettled, when his eyes flicker to Will, and my dad's expression barely changes. "Hello, William. Xiao Jia, ni ganshenme?"

Just barely, I stop myself from blurting out, "I have a plan." Instead, I take a deep breath and say, "I've got some ideas for how A-Plus can increase profitability even more. I wanted to run them by you and Mom."

"Ta weishenme lai zheli?" he asks, head nodding to Will.

"You know that Will has some skills that can really take A-Plus to the next level. He made these pins, you know—I think they'll be a great advertising tool." I hand him a cheery red button that says, "Choosy Moms Choose A-Plus."

My dad grunts noncommittally and nods as my mother finally joins us. He looks suspiciously at Will and switches to English. "You know no money to pay you, right?"

"Well, Mr. Wu, I have to say that I'm not really doing this for the . . ." Will says at the same time I raise my hand to cut him off. My dad is playing right into my hands.

"Remember, Baba"—I always call him by his Chinese honorific when I want something from him—"we've got a new source of passive income through the website. The convenience fee should more than cover a modest salary, plus it's a built-in incentive— the more online orders he drums up, the more he makes."

To my own ears, I sound like a child trying to be a grown-up. The business school jargon that I whispered to myself yesterday evening in front of the mirror in the bathroom sounds stilted, so obviously trying too hard. I kind of hate myself.

174

My mom is nodding, but my dad looks unimpressed, and Will clears his throat and jumps in. "Mr. Wu, I've got a lot of experience writing copy and crafting headlines. The buttons are only the tip of the iceberg—I can work on some ads to place at the college, and I think I've got a good shot at placing a personal essay in the *O-D*. One of the things I've been kind of reading up on is how restaurants can drum up publicity, basically marketing that you can't really buy, that you have to earn. One of the things that a lot of the local restaurants around here do is take advantage of special events—like how Senorita's has a Cinco de Mayo party, and the Celtic Harp has a Saint Patrick's Day fest. If we worked with the local Chinese Association to plan some programming around Lunar New Year and the Moon Festival in the fall, we could increase awareness significantly."

I nod, taking a deep breath. These are all ideas Will and I have tossed around before, so it shouldn't surprise me that he's bought into my business plan 110 percent. "Basically, Baba, we need to increase our profile. These tent pole events will raise awareness, and there are two main areas that I think are growth targets: the college population and the catering population.

"You'll see on page two that we have a lot of actionables." This is one of the catchphrases that I know will get my dad's attention. Whenever we had family gatherings in New York, he would always find some way to mock my cousin Yi-Ping for being a stuck-up NYU MBA, but there was always a twinge of envious resentment in his voice. "We've already gotten a little bit of a foothold in MVCC just from the Boilermaker, and this fall we can really push our study group special." I tell him about how Will's contact at University of Utica said we could pass out flyers at their activities fair, and how we would make a push to try to have a food booth there.

"An even bigger untapped revenue source, though, is the catering aspect. One catering job a day would be the equivalent of five to ten walk-ins. I've reached out to someone in the medical field who gave me contacts for the pharmaceutical people who bring lunches to doctors' offices almost every day." In what seemed like karmic retribution for six years of putting up with her Little Miss Perfect routine, Peggy Cheng came through for me in a big way with a copy of her mom's office manager's drug rep list.

WILL

Jocelyn is on fire. She's blazing with ideas and so passionately ambitious I can actually see her father's skepticism thaw, despite his best efforts.

As she lays out her ideas, her energy fills the entire room. After working at the restaurant for several weeks, I'd gotten used to the vibe of the place being—well, "homey" is the nicest way to put it. There always seemed to be a frenetic kind of desperation in the air: Were they going to hit budget? Did they have enough broccoli/green beans/carrots? Every day seemed to hum with a baseline level of anxiety.

With Jocelyn on stage, though, I've never felt more hope in the room. Her mother's looking at her with a quiet pride, and her dad's moved on to nonverbal communication that almost sounds approving.

I feel like I'm in the middle of a hurricane of hope and

desperation, of ambitious calculation and passion, all of it with Jocelyn at the center. I feel unhinged. I feel alive. I am absolutely, terrifyingly in love.

JOCELYN

When I finish my presentation, my fingers clutch at the edges of my report like it's a lifeline. I'm afraid to look up at my parents. My mom, always so stoic, didn't make any noise at all while I was laying out my plan, just listened and waited with that half smile that she plasters on whenever she is at the restaurant, no matter how harried or tired she is. I don't know if it is something she learned from TV or that was drilled into her in her first job, that Americans don't like to buy things from people who look unhappy, as if dissatisfaction can taint a product.

I can't read my dad's expression, though there was a moment or two during my presentation that his frown could've been read as grudging approval. He makes a show of flipping through my report before running his hand through his thinning hair and sighing. Finally, he swivels his head toward me and waves his hand at Will.

"So what, all that is so you can see this boy?"

I stiffen, indignant on Will's behalf; I'm ready to snap at my dad that Will's not just some *boy*, but something stops me when I see the expression on my dad's face. It's not the thinly veiled contempt that I'm used to seeing there. It's a mix of curiosity and maybe even something bordering on respect.

"No," I reply, lying only a little. "I still believe in this restaurant, and that we can do better."

My dad's shaking his head already.

"Dad, just listen. My plan..."

For the first time all afternoon, my dad raises his voice. "Your plan?" he says, scowling. "Your plan. You keep talking about your plan. Remember, it still *my* restaurant. Still *my* family."

I feel like I've been slapped. Of course his stupid pride is in the way. But then my dad sighs and brushes his hair back one more time.

"Xiao Jia, your plan, it not bad plan, but risky. Risky because you be distract. Big men in Chinatown say, business takes much *dan.*" It takes me a second to place the word, pin it down as the Mandarin word for guts.

"So. I will let you do this plan, but you must stay focus. It too much risk if you get distract. You and Will, you cannot do hanky-panky. No kiss. No hug. No nothing. All business, you understand?"

Wordlessly, I look over at Will, who gives me the slightest shrug, the barest smile. It galls me to have my dad telling me what I can and cannot do, but it's honestly better than I expected. So yeah, I'm okay with no PDA at A-Plus. But my dad's got something coming to him if he thinks he can stop me from doing what I want.

"Got it," I say. "No hanky-panky." *In the restaurant*, I add in my head.

My dad eyes me a little more shrewdly than I'd like, and then his eyes flit over to Will. "How about you, Mr. Domenici? I know you are man of honor. You also say no hanky-panky?"

Shit, I think.

Will looks at him with big brown eyes. "Yes, Mr. Wu. Of course, sir."

"Good." My dad turns back toward me, knowing triumph in

his eyes. He knows that I might sneak around behind his back, but that Will won't, now that he's promised not to.

For a moment, all I can do is stare at my father in shock. He can't hide his faint look of satisfaction, and a bubbling fury builds up in my chest. I want to scream with frustration, that my dad of all people could outmaneuver me like that. I had a *plan*.

Then my dad leans forward and gestures at Will.

"The day after I catch you in your car, my friend Mr. Cheng come see me." That's Peggy's father. "I so mad he can tell straightaway. When I tell him what upset me, he tell me I need to be more modern, accept that boy and girl in America go on date. Everyone has boyfriend or girlfriend, he say. If you don't, other people think you strange. Is that true?"

"Um," Will says, his eyes flitting back and forth in panic between my dad and me. "Well, kind of, but not really. Sure, a lot of the social scene in high school is about people pairing off, but there are some people who are single, too."

Dad is laser focused on Will, like he's an anthropologist interviewing an obscure indigenous tribe. "But if you no have girlfriend or boyfriend, people think you…" He scrunches up his face. "…what is called, 'loser'?"

At that point my anger fizzes out into a level of confusion and embarrassment that I have never in my life experienced, and hope to never experience again. I have no idea what my dad is getting at, why he's torturing Will like this. Poor Will looks completely baffled but is too polite to cut off the conversation.

My dad plows on anyway. "Mr. Cheng say that if I don't let Xiao Jia go on date, she will become rebel. She will learn to hate me, will get angry and do thing behind my back."

The truth is a hot, stinging pain that I feel not in my chest, but in the place just behind my ears where the worst headaches start. My dad's eyes sharpen when he sees the guilt on my face, and he looks over to my mom, who nods.

"Your mother and I am decide. Xiao Jia can date when she prove that dating will not be distract. So this is *my* plan. Three thing must happen."

Wait, what?

My father waves at my report. "Number one. If A-Plus revenue increase by thirty percent." Next, he points a judgy index finger at me. "Number two. You need to show you serious about your future. If you get University of Utica Junior Business Program Scholarship, that is second requirement." Finally, he turns back to Will. "Number three. Alan must get B plus or higher in summer school."

"Wait, what does Alan have to do with this?" I don't get it; how do I have control over what my brother does? I look over to Will, who doesn't seem fazed at all. He's nodding in acceptance, in fact.

"This business plan is only start," says my dad, staring at Will. "You must earn right to date Jocelyn. I see you working with Alan other day. He need lot of help, and tutoring too expensive. If you keep helping him, and he passes his math, I will approve you to date my daughter."

For a second I just gape at my father, who is looking at Will with a wary respect. Will is still nodding.

"Wait a second, so you are literally proposing that Will do three tasks for the 'Standard Hero Reward' trope?" I'm still processing things—how could Will have come to terms with my dad's "plan" so quickly? "Are you sure about this, Will? Isn't this kind of extortion?"

"It's not coercion if I volunteer to do it," he says slowly. He rubs the inside of his wrist absentmindedly for a moment, pausing before he continues. "I did a little bit of work with your brother last night when I dropped off the buttons, and he's a good kid. I'm happy to tutor him." He looks at me, and—God help me for this metaphor, which is so cheesy, why is my brain making me barf—it's like staring into a well of love. "I'm happy to do anything I can."

There's not much I can protest about after that. The phone rings in the background, and my mother excuses herself to take the first order of the evening. My father picks up his copy of my report and puts it in the file folder we have next to the cubby where we put bills and kitchen catalogs.

So the only things left to do are to negotiate with Will when he'll come in tomorrow and to pack up my stuff. As I go back to help put together our first order, I tell myself that I've won. That they're going to go with my plan. But can you blame me if I can't help marveling at how perfectly I was played?

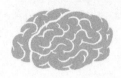

This Is My Brain
on Second Chances

WILL

The morning before the first day of my second life at A-Plus, I'm thrumming with nerves, ping-ponging back and forth between euphoria and anxiety. I'm going to do this. I'm going to prove myself worthy. Or, I'm going to screw up massively, and play the fool.

When I tell my sister that I'll be working all summer and tutoring Alan, too, she gives me her patented boy-are-you-shitting-me stare. "Didn't you say that they didn't have enough money to pay you for more than a month?"

I hedge a little and tell her about the commissions from the online ordering.

"Little brother, that's work you already did. They should have been paying you for that all along. Haven't you heard Mom complain a gazillion times about how white people always expect brown people to do things for free?"

"Mr. Wu's not white," I say, trying to keep a level tone. I do not want to get into this argument with my sister.

Grace waves her arms. "White-adjacent. Same thing."

"You did an unpaid internship with dad's firm."

"That was the summer after freshman year," she scoffs. "Plus, that job paid for itself with the letters of recommendation and networking. Who're you going to schmooze with at a Chinese restaurant? The guy who delivers the fortune cookie shipment?"

"It's all research, remember?" I insist weakly. If I told Grace the real reason I was going back to A-Plus—for Jocelyn, plain and simple—she'd just tease me for being a desperate pushover schmuck who has no concept of self-worth when it comes to relationships with the opposite sex. And there's part of me that would wonder if she was right.

When I call to ask Manny if I'm doing the right thing, he's more direct in his assessment.

"I'm happy for you, man. That's what you wanted, right? To be able to see her again?"

"Yeah," I say. That is all I really wanted. And to be honest, I'd be willing to do a lot more to prove to her father that I'm datable.

The minute I walk into A-Plus, my nerves settle. I don't know if it's the underlying redolence of garlic, soy sauce, and sesame oil that's so comforting, or if the slightly off-tune *beepbeep* of the electronic door sensor triggers my relaxation. It's all familiar and associated with laughter and good food and a girl who is as sweet as she is sharp.

Jocelyn is waiting for me. So is her father.

"Hey," Jocelyn breathes, standing up. She takes a step forward, then rocks back. Her hands spasm like she wants to reach out and hug me, then she glances over at her dad and lets her arms hang to her sides.

No hanky-panky.

"Hey," I say, with a great big grin on my face like a big dork. "It's great to be back."

"Great to have you," she says. Her answering smile is smaller, more cautious, but she's still radiant. "We've got some good stuff planned."

"I expect daily progress report," Mr. Wu interjects sternly from where he's filling the register. "And Xiao Jia still have no cell phone when she is not at work, so don't be expecting any more secret meeting."

"Yes, sir. I understand. When did you want me to work with Alan today?" I ask.

"He get back around three thirty. Will come straight here to be chaperone when I go for supply."

"Got it."

Mr. Wu goes back to his work, and I walk over to Jocelyn to drop my book bag at the booth that serves as her workstation. I sit down across from her, almost aching with the desire to instead be sitting next to her, feeling the side of her body pressing into mine.

No distractions.

This summer may very well kill me.

JOCELYN

In theory, my dad's plan is pretty reasonable, almost enlightened when it comes to Asian parenting culture (thank you, Mr.

Cheng). I tell myself to think of it as delayed gratification, as hoops we have to jump through so my dad can save face.

Approximately thirty seconds after Will comes in for work, though, I realize that it's just torture, plain and simple.

I can't hug Will. I can't sit next to him and feel his heat as we pore over advertising ideas. (My dad has demanded a one-foot rule, as if he wants us to leave room for the Holy Spirit.)

And you know, that would all be fine if I didn't also have to sit across from him and look into his eyes as we discuss financials, and listen to his laugh while we brainstorm more slogans.

This is why I'm an atheist. Any God who thinks hormones are a good idea should be shot.

I try to sublimate my feelings into spreadsheets. After we've been working an hour, Amah comes down to be my parents' eyes and ears as they run a few errands. By then the tension between Will and me has come down to a simmer, which is good because I'm looking through my plan and panicking a bit about where to even start.

"Do you want to divide and conquer with these groups?" I ask him. "You should do the college communications, and I can work on the consumer outreach." We'd decided to make bookmarks to give out at the bookstore, as well as flyers emphasizing our "Healthy Choices" steamed menu (with brown rice and sauce on the side) that we could post at the LA Fitness down the street. "We can work together to cold-call the drug reps."

I'm surprised when Will's expression flattens and he seems to physically fold into himself. When he replies his voice is off. Higher pitched. Nervous? "Actually, I can hand out the flyers at the bookstore and the LA Fitness, since I have a car and can go around. Do you mind handling the calls?"

"Fine." I shrug. His mother is a doctor—he got us a few more names from her, after all—maybe he had a weird interaction with a drug rep.

Will swallows, and I watch his Adam's apple bob. "I'm sorry," he says in a more natural voice. "I just...I don't like calling people I don't know. Face to face is fine, I'll drop off the samples at the offices, I'd just prefer not to make calls to the reps."

"Sure." I mean, he's doing all of this for free, basically, so I shouldn't ask him to do anything that makes him uncomfortable. "It makes more sense for me to call from the restaurant, I guess. More official."

Will has turtled into a little huddle in front of his computer. "Thanks for understanding," he says, staring at his keyboard.

"No prob. I'm making the fitness flyer now—we should drop some off at the Y, too. What were the numbers again for what the protein-to-fat ratio is supposed to be after a workout?"

Will is back to normal within a few minutes, and I forget about the little blip in an otherwise clockwork afternoon. It isn't until weeks later that I look back on that moment and wonder: What if I'd noticed earlier?

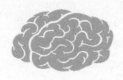

This Is My Brain
on Solicitation

WILL

The next day, I print off a set of flyers at my mom's office and head over to LA Fitness. They won't let me put the flyers up in their locker rooms, but there's a community bulletin board at the front entrance, and I have enough menus in my trunk to put one under the windshield wipers of each car in the parking lot. My family are regulars at the bookstore, so the people there let me leave some A-Plus bookmarks at their counter when I promise to put out their monthly newsletter with the magazines our customers read when they're waiting for take-out orders.

When I get back to the restaurant, I'm starving. "Did you have lunch already?" I ask Jos, who is portioning food out for the bento boxes I'm going to distribute in the afternoon.

She shakes her head, concentrating on her work. "Nah, I'm not hungry." Surprised, I glance at the clock—it's past two, and

I didn't see her eat anything in the morning. I go back to grab some of the chicken and broccoli that's always premade for lunch specials. "I don't know how you can be around these amazing smells all day and not constantly have the munchies."

Jos shrugs and starts on another sampler. Each office is going to get a dozen jiaozi, an extra-large order of pork fried rice, and two cucumber avocado rolls. We're dropping off three a day based on geography and which drug reps Jocelyn was able to get in contact with.

I'm still embarrassed that I had to pawn that part of the job on Jocelyn, but I console myself with knowing that she's 1,000 percent better at it than I would be. I'm happy to be the food mule, and though it does ratchet my anxiety up to knock on people's doors and talk to them, it's a type of nerves that I've gotten used to.

Having spent a significant part of my childhood doing homework with my sister in a storage room in my mom's office, I know my way through medical buildings. I know enough to dress up in a suit so they know right away I'm not a patient, and to wait until there isn't a line at the front desk to politely give them the business card I made up on Vistaprint and leave them one of the ribboned tiers of take-out containers that Jocelyn made.

One of the reception ladies at the surgeon's office actually moans when she smells the tower of goodness. "Oh my god, I love dumplings."

"We're definitely one of the more affordable catering options out there," I say. "Make sure to order extra dumplings so you can take some home. Gotta have fringe benefits, right?"

"You said it," she says, glaring at an elderly patient who's been giving her the stink eye since I walked in. She calls in our first catering job that afternoon.

When we get the order, Jocelyn and I exchange high fives without thinking, only to hear Mr. Wu's shout of outrage from the counter.

"No hanky-panky!"

Later on in the afternoon, two identical Post-it notes show up on our laptops:

A-PLUS RULES

* No touching allowed (any body part)
* Will use nanny cam if hanky-panky continue
* Also no secret whispering or messages

PS, We expect revenue report on Friday.

I can practically hear Jocelyn's teeth grating when she sees the note.

"It's okay," I say, glancing over at Grandma Wu where she's pretending to snooze at a booth at the far end of the restaurant. "It's kind of funny—I'll have to tell my friends that I have a rep for being handsy now. They'll think it's hysterical. Do you think your dad would lay off if I gave him their names as character references?"

"I think my dad's going to lay off when I've reached meno-pause," Jocelyn says sourly. She tears the note off her computer screen with extreme prejudice and crumples it up into a tiny dense ball before tossing it into the trash.

I shrug and stick my note in the little blank spot to the right of my touchpad.

For the next few minutes Jocelyn just takes her anger out on her keyboard, hammering out quick violent finger strokes with a scowl on her face. I see her look up at me a couple of times in my peripheral vision, but I keep my eyes on my own work. I've never been good at defusing other people's moods.

Finally, Jocelyn slams her laptop shut. "I just don't get how you just sit there and take it," she says, and it's like the blast of heat you get when you open the door of a car that's been sitting outside all day in August.

"Why aren't you more angry about this?" she hisses at me. I don't know what it means that my first concern is that she's breaking rule number three. "Shouldn't you be resisting? Or fighting back? Is it because you assume that you have something to prove, that my dad's right and you're not worthy to date me unless you fulfill some sort of bullshit arbitrary contract?"

"Ummm…" It makes me slightly breathless, not only to see the depth of her rage, but to have it directed at me all of a sudden. I blink heavily, like I'm trying to ward off smoke, or tears. "I mean, it's his prerogative as your father…"

"What about your prerogative as my…kind-of boyfriend?" She stutters over what to call us, and it makes my heart hiccup at the idea of even having a kind-of girlfriend. "Shouldn't you stand up for yourself?"

I have to admit that I never really questioned the deal I made. I accepted it at face value, because it never crossed my mind that Jocelyn wasn't worth it. Maybe another guy would've bargained for a better "dating contract," but I just didn't see the point. It wasn't worth losing Mr. Wu completely by pushing back.

I try to explain. "It's not that I don't want to stand up for myself, it's just that I'm choosing my battles. I didn't want to put up a fuss only to have your dad shut me out completely. I'm happy with the deal I made. You're worth it. I might not be fighting, but I'm persisting. He's not going to get rid of me." I offer a tentative smile as Jocelyn seems to deflate, like a cat smoothing down its hackles. "You're not going to get rid of me."

Jos sighs. "I don't want to get rid of you." And like that the storm's over. "The scary thing is, I think he really does have a nanny cam somewhere," she says, resigned instead of furious. "We had this one checkout clerk that he was convinced was siphoning money on the side. Also, I don't know why he's asking for revenue reports so early. It's barely been a day since we started our outreach."

"We did already get those two catering orders," I offer. "Also, my mother saw my flyers lying around and gave me a tip. You know who orders out a lot? Shift workers. We can make up a bento box for the ER and each nursing station, and I can drop them off tonight with some menus."

"Maybe we need a hospital-specific flyer," Jocelyn says. "How about something like, 'You worry about your patients. We'll worry about your food.'"

"Yes! We can highlight the low-sodium and low-carb choices, too. And put a 'No MSG' callout."

"Ummmm..." Jocelyn looks a little shifty.

I raise my eyebrows. "You guys use MSG?" I mean, it isn't

like there are huge kegs labeled "monosodium glutamate" lying around.

"You know that MSG is in, like, everything?" Jocelyn says. "Most soup bases have it, and any soy sauces that aren't Kikkoman, which is super expensive. And it's not just a Chinese food thing, either. KFC and Chick-fil-A use MSG in their seasonings. There's natural MSG in Parmesan cheese, for God's sake. Heck, it's in freaking Doritos. I don't know why Chinese food gets such a bad rap for it—sinophobia, anyone? Besides, recent studies show that it's not actually that bad for you."

I blink. My mind whirs, wondering if I can leverage this into a blog, an op-ed in the *O-D*, or even a longer think piece revealing common misconceptions about ethnic food. Mr. Evans might even be proud of me. He wanted me to dig deep for material? You can't get more behind-the-scenes than this gig here.

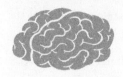

This Is My Brain
on Personal Statements

JOCELYN

Perry High School has a Rising Stars of Business club that's basically composed of tools. To the best of my knowledge, it's an all-white group of six boys and two girls who sit around playing at being grown-ups. They wear ill-fitting business suits to their meetings and tote around giant flip boards so they can brainstorm shit and talk about "economies of scale," play with imaginary money, and brag about how much they won in the Stock Market Game. I am never going to fit in with that group and don't want to try.

What my dad wants me to do is the University of Utica Junior Business Program, which allows high school students to take a college course each semester during their junior and senior years. A lot of people get into the program—basically, it seems like if you can pay tuition and string together sentences for an application essay you are in. What interests my dad, of course, is a scholarship program where the person who plans the best business project gets free tuition, not to mention access to a faculty adviser and $5,000 seed money for their proposal.

I know at least one of the people applying, this guy Geoff from my school, who is student council treasurer. He's apparently trying to start up a solar power assessment company.

As it turns out, Geoff is dating Priya's friend Sophia, so Priya was able to give me intel. "Basically Sophia tells me that his parents told him to play up the clean energy angle because it's hot now, not because he's really interested in it. It's all just résumé fodder for him; he doesn't actually want it."

I'm not sure if that makes it better or worse, to feel like some scrappy underdog battling a faceless group of overachievers. Actually, there's no question. It makes it worse. I know the people applying for these honors—I pirated the frosted polypropylene report covers that one of them bought for our group project, for God's sake—and they are not to be underestimated. They probably have recommendation letters from VPs of Fortune 500 companies or something. Who am I supposed to get my recommendation from, my amah?

Just scrolling through the application for the scholarship gives me hives. The program's general application just requires a transcript, a statement of purpose, and two recommendation letters, one from a teacher and one from another supervisor or counselor. But the scholarship application asks questions like, "Tell us about a leadership position you have volunteered for." and "What was the most challenging ethical dilemma you've ever had and how did you resolve it?" It also calls for a third recommendation, from a colleague or someone else who has witnessed me in a leadership role.

I reluctantly admit that this third letter is going to have to come from Will. He's the obvious choice, not only because he can string more than five words together in a sentence. I'm already stressing out that my "supervisor" is also my dad, until I realize that I can probably ask my middle school librarian, Mrs. Morgan, whose media section I reorganized and curated.

My biggest problem is that it's going to take me at least a week to produce enough bullshit to populate a seven-hundred-word statement of purpose. "My dad's making me do it" probably isn't going to cut it.

"I don't get it," I whine to Priya as I pump her for more information about Geoff and his project. "What do these admissions people really expect from these essays? I mean, isn't it obvious that people's purpose when they go into business is to make money?"

"Maybe this is the part of the application where you have to do some ego stroking. I mean, you have to appeal to their idea of B-school having a higher purpose. You can spout off about how prosperity brings growth or something like that. I don't know, talk about how thriving companies mean thriving communities. I think I've heard that on a commercial somewhere."

"I guess I need to watch *Wall Street* again." I sigh. "Greed is good."

"No, just google 'best business school essays,'" Priya says. "Find the one that least makes you want to vomit into your own mouth and model it after that."

"Ugh, why do these sites all give you advice that essentially amounts to 'be yourself' and 'just remember not to be a jerk'?"

"It's good practice for college admission essays. It took my brother seventeen drafts before he came up with one that my dad approved of. He basically became the king of the humble brag."

"A lot of people say you should mention your failures," I note, browsing through a few summaries. "That'll be kind of easy."

"Yeah, schools like you to show that you have 'grit,'" Priya says vaguely. "It's like in interviews where you have to talk about your biggest weakness and somehow make it into a strength."

"Hey, I think I asked Will that one," I exclaim. "Maybe I am meant to go into business after all."

"Of course you are," Priya says, like it's completely obvious. "You're the OG get-shit-done-woman. I'd want you to be CEO of my company any day."

It's such a Priya thing to say. I love that about her. "You're just saying that because Excel gives you hives."

"No, I'm not," she insists. "Stop deflecting, or I'm going to make you do your daily affirmations again. University of Utica is going to accept you because you're ridiculously organized, have experience with creative ways to run a business, and because you've been raised to have an unreasonable work ethic that will probably give you a heart attack before you're thirty."

When I don't say anything, Priya grumbles, "Jocelyn Wu, don't make me ask you to repeat after me."

I laugh so I won't cry. "I don't know. Will I even make the cut for an interview? My GPA isn't exactly stellar." It's not the worst. I don't take enough honors classes to get above a 4.0, so it's a 3.8, which sounds good but is basically an Asian C.

"Hey, it's better than mine," Priya says cheerfully. She loves that her parents have already given up on her and labeled her The Child Who Will Not Get into MIT. "Seriously, don't stress out about the app."

It's the only time Priya's advice ever chafes me, really. Because it's like she doesn't even know who I am, to think that there's ever a moment in my life when I'm not bummed out over one thing or another, or stressed in some way.

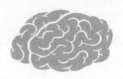

This Is My Brain on Delayed Gratification

WILL

"Dude, you're hanging out with the wrong Wu," Tim said the first time I begged off Xbox night because I was helping Alan study for a quiz.

Tutoring Jocelyn's brother is exhausting sometimes. The first time it was easy. There weren't any stakes—I was just helping a friend out—but now that I know what is riding on it, well, that is a whole new level of urgency. For Alan to get a B, he has to average at least 85 percent on all his tests, which means he can only afford to get about three questions wrong on every twenty-question exam.

The first time we did a practice quiz, Alan got three problems wrong just because he didn't actually read the questions all the way through. Another two were calculation errors—his writing was such chicken scratch he got the columns messed up when he did his division. Only twice did he actually not understand the math, which was both awesome and nerve-racking. I can teach concepts, and even the general test-taking strategies that I learned from the SAT tutor my mom set me up with, like circling the verbs in word problems and taking the time to read every question twice. But half the time Alan's biggest obstacle to doing well just seems to be his own brain, which has the focus of a plastic bag blowing in the wind.

"Does Alan have an IEP?" I ask Jocelyn after Alan gets a 70 percent on our second practice test. She gives me a blank look. "You know, an Individualized Education Program, for kids who have learning differences."

"Well, no," she says. "He's not, like, dyslexic or anything."

"Do you know if he's ever been tested?"

Jocelyn screws up her face and shakes her head. "I remember this time when he was in third grade, my parents got mad after a teacher conference because his teacher recommended that he see a psychologist. Dad was so pissed that he wrote the principal."

"So they never diagnosed anything?" I ask.

"No, my parents just yelled at Alan and took away some privileges and eventually he got his grades up. That's kind of their MO." She chews her lip. "My dad went off about how Chinese people didn't have dyslexia and how ADHD was something made up by pharmaceutical companies to sell drugs."

I grimace. It doesn't sound too different from stuff my mom has said about anxiety. I know about IEPs because Javier has one that lets him take tests in a separate, quiet room without bright signs or any noisy vents. All in all, it's the closest thing to a sensory deprivation chamber you can get in a high school. It was a simple fix, but he went from Cs and Ds to As and Bs when they started making accommodations for him.

When I tell Jocelyn as much, she shrugs. "I mean, that sounds good. I think my dad just thought it meant he'd get an asterisk on his diploma or something. He went off on this big rant about how administrators just want an excuse so they can do better in the rankings. Typical Dad conspiracy theories." There's a resignation to her tone, a sense that she sees a problem but doesn't know what to do about it, that makes me suddenly very sad. For her and for her dad, but mostly for Alan.

"Do you think he'd reconsider if I told him that it'd help Alan's grades?"

"If you want to fall on that sword, be my guest."

I start off by writing an e-mail to Alan's summer school teacher, introducing myself as Alan's tutor and sending her the results of an online ADHD screening tool that I had Alan take. I tell her that I know that it is the summer session, and there is no time to institute a formal IEP, but ask if there is any way to consider even the smallest accommodations, like allowing him a fidget device, moving him to a corner seat, or giving him noise-canceling headphones for tests. I give her Mr. Wu's e-mail address for if she has any questions, because I'm just a tutor, and she probably can't institute any changes without Alan's dad's permission. What I'm hoping, though, is that when Mr. Wu sees the accommodations the school can make, he'll realize that it can only help.

As I read my e-mail after typing it up, I hear a voice in my head that is some imaginary combination of my mother and Mr.

Wu: *Don't coddle the boy. If you keep propping him up he'll never be able to make it on his own.*

I press send anyway.

JOCELYN

Aside from that time in fourth grade when Alan needed four stitches on his temple because I shoved him into our coffee table accidentally on purpose after he broke the cultured pearl necklace Amah had given me for my birthday, I've always thought that I was a pretty good big sister.

After seeing Will with my little brother, though, I'm not so sure. I have to wonder if I could ever have the patience that he has in walking him through his homework. Just watching them struggle their way through problem sets, I can feel myself getting annoyed at Alan's space cadet act, but Will always stays calm, and his voice doesn't get condescending the way I know mine sometimes does when Alan's not listening to me.

Today, they're working on basic probability, and it's like Will's learned to speak in Alan's native language.

"So you know how in a game of Magic, if you don't like your library, sometimes you can decide to mulligan?"

Alan nods, about 500 percent more engaged than he's ever been when I've tried to slog through math with him.

"Right." Will continues, "When you do that, you're changing the probability that you'll get an artifact...."

It stings just a little bit, the connection they have. Isn't he *my* brother? Isn't he *my* not-boyfriend? Part of me also feels guilty that I didn't figure out how to teach these concepts so they stick to Alan's Teflon brain. I guess I just didn't try hard enough. It leaves a sour feeling in my stomach.

But that's the thing about Will. Watching him work with Alan, I start to realize that it's not that I necessarily suck as a big sister—it's that Will is a kickass big brother. He's smart enough to be able to break down a complicated subject so it makes sense, but humble enough to tell Alan that he had trouble learning it, too. He notices when Alan's energy is getting low and makes sure to bring out a snack or crack a joke, his wide genuine smile so infectious that it makes me grin across the room, where I'm staring at him like a creeper.

So sue me, I can't take my eyes off him, especially now that he's preoccupied with my brother. When he's talking with me, no matter how good our conversation's going, there's always this barely visible layer of reserve over everything, like he's so afraid of saying or doing something to turn me off that he's holding back a bit. With Alan, he doesn't hold anything back, so he can be as goofy or earnest or dorky as he wants.

He's cute when he's nerdy. When he comes across a problem he can't solve right away he has this nervous tic where he makes a tiny, rapid head shake, like a dog throwing off water after a dunk in a pond. Then when he figures it out he does a little shimmy with his left shoulder. He likes to drum with the eraser end of his pencil to make a point, and he can do that pen-spinning trick that I can't seem to get down no matter how many YouTube tutorials I watch.

The point is, Will is sure as heck more interesting than my Junior Business Program essay, which is why so far I only have the following haphazardly typed up:

1. Grew up with family business
2. Not afraid of hard work
3. Learned to be organized to balance school and the restaurant

I decided early on in the process that "have sacrificed any semblance of a life" would not make a good bullet point. I'm also not convinced that I should do what Priya suggested and talk about my recent "innovations" to help the restaurant. Making social media accounts and ramping up outreach to the college sound pretty basic. What if bringing those things up just makes it more obvious that A-Plus is the loser business that it realistically is?

After five minutes where I mostly stare at a blinking cursor, Alan starts pacing nervously around the kitchen table like a Doberman puppy waiting for its owner to take it out for a walk. Will's hunched over a question sheet, grading a practice quiz.

"I can't watch," Alan says, trotting over to me and bouncing up and down. "I hate this. This sucks so bad. Why can't I just quit school and join the circus?"

"I…actually don't think Ringling Bros. is in business anymore," I say. I'm pretty sure I looked that up after watching *The Greatest Showman*. "Even when they were, they didn't exactly have the best 401(k) plan."

Just then Will lets out a whoop. "That's what I'm talking about! Only three wrong! Eighty-five percent, baby!" Alan lets out a long "Yusssssss" and raises his hands up in the air, and the two of them do some sort of male bonding ritual dance that involves some disturbing bodily gyrations that will be burned in my eyeballs forever.

"I gotta go show Dad," Alan says, and rushes off downstairs.

With Alan out of the room, it's jarringly quiet, except for the sound of Amah's Taiwanese soap operas in the background. Will takes in a shaky breath in the silence and smiles at me, coming closer but not too close, mindful of Amah, who's sitting on the love seat just a few feet away.

Suddenly, I'm aware of how warm it is in our apartment. The baseboard heating and wall-unit air-conditioning have always made the temperature impossible to control, especially with all the hot air rising from the kitchen downstairs. I push up the sleeves of my shirt nervously as Will hovers a couple of feet away, glancing at my computer.

I push Alt-Tab automatically to toggle to my desktop. It's an instinctive maneuver for me whenever any of my family members get near my laptop. I hate the creepy-crawly feeling of someone looking at my unfinished work. It's like they're seeing me in my underwear.

Will blinks and looks away when he sees my screen flicker out, as if he's embarrassed, but he covers it up with a rushed, "So, your brother's doing really well."

"Guess it helps to have an actual academic star teaching you." I hate myself for the hint of bitterness that comes through in my voice.

"I'm hardly a star. The opposite, kind of. I have to work harder for my grades than people like my sister, so I know all the tricks."

That might be true, but there are plenty of people who work hard and don't have an above-perfect GPA. It bothers me, a little, that he can be so blasé about being exceptional, like it's just another thing that you can guarantee if you put in the hours and do the right things. It just doesn't work that way if you don't have the God-given brains to begin with, or don't have the resources to do things like starting up solar power companies.

"Know any tricks for applying to business school?" I ask, only half-jokingly.

"You, uh, working on your application for the U?" he asks awkwardly, looking down while rubbing at his wrist. "I mean, I don't want to pry."

Aaaand I feel like shit for making him think that I don't trust him. "No, pry away! You're welcome to…" I shake my head. "What I mean is, it's okay to talk to me about it. I was actually thinking about asking you to read my essay."

He perks up at that. "Really?" he asks with a smile that is so delightedly sweet that it should come with a warning for diabetics. It should definitely come with a sign for me—CAUTION: ELEVATED HEART RATES AHEAD.

God, he is so cute.

"Of course," I say, a little unsteadily. I have to stare down at my laptop to get my voice under control. I run my middle finger over the blank space where the "E" has worn off my keyboard. "Who else am I going to have go over it? You're the editor after all."

"Well, whenever you're ready," he says firmly. And there's something in his tone, a certainty, a steadiness, a patience, that makes it impossible for me to keep my eyes away from him anymore. I look at him, at his head held high, a respectable foot and a half away from me even though he's leaning in subtly toward me like I'm pulling him by an invisible thread. And I know with the utmost certainty that he's going to give me—he's going to give us—all the time in the world to get it right.

This Is My Brain on Numbers

WILL

Friday is our first day of reckoning.

I try to set expectations low as I bring out the spreadsheet. "Remember," I tell Jocelyn, "it's only been a few days since we started catering, and we're not even fully implemented. But we've already had a ten percent increase in online orders compared to two weeks ago." I pause. "The tricky thing is to figure out how much we're cannibalizing from in-person ordering, which can be hard to get a handle on. Speaking of that, I've been asking around, and Manny says that when Amazing Stories switched to an iPad-based system for checkout they got lower credit card fees, and cash-flow and inventory tracking got a heck of a lot easier."

"Fine, let's get it in writing," Jocelyn concedes, biting her lip. "Sure as heck would be amazing to get rid of all this paper. Half the time Alan forgets to stick the receipt when it's paid and then the register's all off."

"I'll start a proposal right now." I've already opened a Word document to type up a pro/con list for Mr. Wu.

"I love it when you talk dirty to me," Jocelyn whispers, glancing over to the propped-open door leading to the kitchen, where her mother is chaperoning while prepping vegetables.

For a few minutes the only sound is the lightning-fast click of fingers on the number pad Jocelyn's hooked up to her laptop and the scratch of a ballpoint pen when she marks each one registered. When the noise stops, she's beaming.

"No drop in in-person orders," she says. "In fact, we're up five percent."

"Total customers, or cost of average order?"

"Both." She scrolls through her calculations. "But average orders are up a bit."

I bite my lip. "Do you itemize every sale, to see if some things are more popular? Like the pot stickers?"

Jocelyn shudders. "Are you kidding me? We can't go into that level of detail. Two years ago my dad still did his accounts in a spiral notebook."

I nod. "Another benefit of cloud-based point of sale. Your dad won't know what hit him."

JOCELYN

Who knew that a random set of numbers on a screen could make you feel so good?

I feel giddy, like I can't get enough air in with each breath, electric at the idea that, according to the math at least, we're doing it. A-Plus is doing better. Because of what we've done.

I want so badly to lean over and put my hand on Will's cheek and see if he's feeling it, too. Is there the tiniest ache in his muscles, as if they're coiled with anticipation and ready to spring into action with the next step in our plan? Does he feel like his skin's too sensitive, so that he feels the rub of his shirt too acutely when he moves his shoulders too much?

I want to do something spontaneous. I want to run a 5K. I want to go crash a kiddie party and jump in a bounce house. Trouble is, I can't leave the restaurant to do anything because I can't go out alone with Will. I look at him, studiously typing away at his freaking pro forma with an adorable crease between his eyes, and realize I'd rather stay here with him, both of us hamsters in an endless spreadsheet wheel, than be out and alone.

If that's not a sign of true love, I don't know what is.

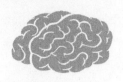

This Is My Brain
Off Script

JOCELYN

I'm still buzzing with low-level anticipation when Priya comes over bright and early Saturday morning to start shooting our submission to the All American High School Film Festival. I don't know if I've ever had so much going on in my life: a new movie project, trying to save the restaurant, a not-boyfriend. Why does it feel like I'm at the top of a mountain, staring off a cliff?

We have a tradition now on our first official day of production: a selfie with our script. Every project has a working title that's basically a code word; this one's is *Pot Sticker*.

Amah, my chaperone for the day once Will gets in and finishes his tutoring session with Alan, is all set for her star turn, having traded in her around-the-house cardigan set for a somewhat newer one that doesn't have frayed sleeves and a stain of unknown origin on the hem.

"I am ready for my close-up, Priya darling." She puts her hand up to her mouth and whispers, "I put on rouge and steal some old lipstick from my daughter, do not tell her."

"You look fabulous. The camera's going to love you." Priya fiddles with her camera, making sure that Amah is standing at the precise area I did when we did all our checks. "Mrs. Wu, can we start off with you just walking in? Okay, *Pot Sticker*, act 1, scene 1."

I whack Priya's homemade clapboard once, and we're off.

Amah walks in the side door, shimmying down in a geriatric approximation of a model on the catwalk, and oh my God, the struggle to keep myself from bursting into laughter is real.

Priya carefully schools her face. "That was wonderful, Mrs. Wu, but can we take that again, where you just pretend that I'm not here? You don't have to smile or anything; a neutral expression is actually best. And feel free to slouch a bit, like you're already a little bit tired."

"Buyong ting xiong," I offer in Mandarin. It feels like payback to be able to tell her *not* to stand up straight.

"Okay, okay, I act natural."

It requires about four takes for Amah to stop looking up at the camera when she walks by, but eventually Priya gets her B-roll, and we switch to taking close-ups in the kitchen. Around lunchtime we call it a wrap and head upstairs to our home kitchen to make some peanut butter sandwiches and go over our footage. Which is awesome. Somehow, the way Priya framed things, pulling in tight to the food, to the actions, makes our dumpy, badly-in-need-of-renovation restaurant look artistic, even cinematic.

"You're a genius," I proclaim. "This is amazing. I can't wait until tomorrow. You said your brother and Lauren can come, right? So we can shoot some of the black-and-white scenes?"

"Yeah, I just need to go out today and get the last few things for a waitress uniform."

I review the script to think of any additional props I need to get. I should bring my laptop down so we can shoot some scenes where Mr. Regular is working while he's eating. And then there's the scene where the waitress is really tired and he offers her an aspirin, so I should probably bring a medication bottle or something...

I blink. Turn one or two more pages. Flip back.

I turn to Priya. "What happened to the scene where the waitress has a headache?" It was the most dialogue-heavy scene of the script and honestly the one I felt most proud of.

Priya takes a sudden interest in the microphone attachment to her camera. "We-eell, remember when we talked about not needing so much dialogue? It just seemed a little forced, a little too on the nose. Plus, we only have seven minutes. It's a super-compressed timeline. I mean, our deadline is in three weeks."

Basically, she says a lot but doesn't actually answer my real question, and I can feel a sourness in the back of my throat. "Why didn't you tell me you cut it? I thought we were coproducers."

"I'm sorry! I honestly thought we had talked about it when I edited the final script." She finally at least looks at me, pursing her lips the way she did when she was trying to placate the kids she used to babysit. "You know what, just because we don't film it this weekend doesn't mean we can't add it in. Let's just see what our run time is."

I stuff the last of my PB&J in my mouth before I say something I regret, as if I could chew up my hurt and swallow it like the obedient daughter/student/friend I am. God, I know that Priya just wants what's best for the film, but...it was my favorite part, their first real bonding moment before the food connection. It was kind of Mr. Regular's "Save the Cat" moment, the little character-building act that made the audience think, gee that Mr. Regular's a swell guy.

Priya's still fiddling with her microphone, swearing under her breath when it won't stay right where she wants it to be and casting me occasional little worried glances.

She cares about what I think, I realize. If I really wanted to, I could fight for the scene to stay in.

But if Priya couldn't see it when she read it, it probably wasn't good enough. The thought settles in my chest like a heavy stone, solid and shameful and immoveable. I'm not a good enough writer. We'll hopefully get into the festival mostly on the strength of Priya's genius with the camera, but with no help from my shitty script.

Priya finally puts the microphone down and fiddles a bit with her video program, tagging the shots that she thinks will make the final cut. Every once in a while, she asks me if I like one shot better than another, but I'm still hurt that she edited my script, and I don't think I could stand it if she overruled me again. After the third time I answer, "Whatever you think," she stops asking.

"Well, I've gotta get going. The Patel wedding is tonight, and my mom wants us to go do Mehndi and hair with the cousins." Priya rolls her eyes. Normally, I would groan and commiserate with her about how annoyed she's going to be by her cousins, but today I can't do more than just smile tightly. There's something raw festering inside me, and I'm afraid that if I open my mouth, all that ugliness will ooze out.

I had planned on doing a script breakdown after Priya left, maybe double-checking her shot list, but just seeing the *Pot Sticker* file on my desktop is like picking at a scab. Instead I bring up Word and look at the draft that I wrote of my statement of purpose for JBP. I stayed up well past midnight to finish it, using a strategy one of my English teachers gave us for dealing with writer's block: She told us to turn off our monitors so that we didn't let what we had already written interfere with what we were going to write next.

Mrs. Wilson had a lot of other pithy little things to say, little literary pep talks. "Remember that the enemy of good is better. Don't let your quest to be perfect stop you from being great. Never be afraid of writing a cruddy first draft."

Me, perfect? As if.

Still smarting from Priya's comments on my script, I can feel the sense of inadequacy welling up inside me as I look at my personal statement. Except maybe that's the wrong metaphor. It's not a hole that I need filled with positive reinforcement; it's a gap in the weave of my life—something that affects my whole fabric.

I'm staring at my mess of a first draft, wondering how the heck I'm supposed to turn it into a marginally readable second draft, when there's a knock on our door.

It's Will, and seeing him makes my heart do a little jig despite my mood. It makes me feel off-kilter to have my soul in the dumps when my heart is singing. I glance at the clock when

I open the door. "Alan should be back in a few minutes. His friend's birthday party should be winding down. I know my mom was on her way to pick him up."

"No, that's okay," says Will, grinning crookedly. "It's nice to see you. Does that mean…" He glances around our living room.

"Yeah, no chaperone for the next few minutes. I finished a draft of my essay, I think."

"Really?" Will says, eyes wide. "Want me to take a look at it?"

On the one hand, I feel so vulnerable that I can't stand to expose any other parts of myself right now. On the other hand, Will's a writer. And inexplicably, he sees the best of me. Maybe he's the only one who can help.

The instant I blurt out "Sure!" I second-guess myself. But there's no going back—Will's already leaning toward my laptop, eyes glued on the screen. I feel a faint sense of nausea. I'm suddenly terrified that he'll think that it's horrible, that it will completely and irrevocably ruin his opinion of me. I mean, what could be more of a turnoff to an editor than a piece-of-shit writer?

"You know, maybe this isn't the best time," I say as he sits down. I reach out to shut my laptop, but it's too late. Will's hand gently holds my arm away, and he exclaims, "That's a terrific lede. What a great first line."

I watch helplessly as he hunkers over my laptop, brow furrowed, eyes darting. He's concentrating so hard his mouth opens a little. After a grand total of five seconds, I have to look away. I walk over to pick up the catalog on our coffee table and page through it.

I can tell when Will sits back in his chair that he's done. He doesn't say anything at first, and I want to die on the spot. He must have hated it. My eyes are fixed on the stupid little hangnail on my left thumb, and I'm a millisecond away from saying that I have to go to the bathroom and curling up in the fetal position on my bed, when Will calls my name.

"Jocelyn." His voice is so soft, so filled with wonder that it stops my cycle of self-loathing in its tracks. But when I turn to him, he's staring at me solemnly, and so seriously that my heart races, waiting for the hammer to drop.

WILL

Reading Jocelyn's personal statement is frightening. That's a weird word choice, I know, and it's not something I'd ever tell her, because it has nothing to do with her essay and everything to do with how I feel when someone lets me read a piece they've written.

I've always thought that writing down one's truth is one of the most vulnerable things a human being can do, second only to the act of sharing that writing with another person. That's why the literary device of reading someone's diary is so effective— it's a complete violation of one's privacy and trust. When a friend—or non-girlfriend—gives you a piece of writing that they care about, it's one of the most intimate things they can do. Lucky us that it doesn't fall under Mr. Wu's definition of "hanky-panky."

I'm frightened that Jocelyn trusts me this much. It's like I've been given an egg and asked to juggle it with a pile of rocks, and I am so, so terrified that I will drop this egg, shatter it into a mess of shell fragments and yolk that's impossible to salvage.

When I'm editing something, I usually read it two times in a row before even forming an opinion of it. Once to get an overall take on how it makes me feel, then a second time to track back and parse out the components that pop and the ones that could be brought out more.

After my first pass of Jocelyn's essay, I breathe out a sigh of relief because, thank God, it's good. I won't have to lie by omission or make up positive comments to soften any criticism I give. The writing is clean, her points salient, her word choice solid. As a personal statement it's the perfect reflection of who she is: smart, honest, and witty.

The second pass is where I notice how it can get better: Jocelyn's too modest. The essay focuses mostly on her experiences growing up and brushes over everything she's done with A-Plus in a single sentence. She talks about her grades almost apologetically and doesn't mention how she can add up five orders in her head within seconds, or tell just by looking at a shelf how much inventory she needs to order for the next month.

It's not ideal to have the person you're critiquing hovering over you as you formulate your thoughts, so that's one thing I would do differently. When I finally look up from the essay, Jocelyn's retreated to her living room couch, sitting with her shoulders hunched up and her leg bouncing, a wholesale supplier's catalog on her lap. She's not really reading it, though, and is focusing on her hands. She's as frightened as I am.

"Jocelyn," I say, in the same voice I use when my mom's resting in her room with a migraine. "It's really great."

In an instant her brow unfurrows, her legs still. "You think so?" She looks up at me with a hopeful smile.

"Yeah. My guidance counselor once said that if a personal statement makes you want to grab a cup of coffee with the person, it's done its job. You nailed it."

Her smile is real now, radiant. I want so badly to go over to her, not even to kiss her, just to be able to put my forehead to hers so I can feel her warmth.

"Thank God," she says. "I had no freaking clue what I was doing. I don't know what they're looking for. I'm not like some of the other people who are applying. I can't talk about how I'm starting my own sustainable energy business or anything."

"Well," I say brightly. This is where I have to be careful about how I start juggling. I've weighed the egg in my hand, and I think I know how hard to toss it. "You've got your own strengths. I can't imagine that anyone else out there has done as much as you have to sustain a business."

"Okay." Jocelyn shrugs, turning a little pink with my praise.

"Can I make a suggestion?" I turn her laptop over to her and point out a sentence I highlighted. "See here, where you say, 'This past summer I've learned an incredible amount about how to grow a business, having taken the reins to improve my family restaurant's bottom line.' This is where you can really dig deep, knock them out with the details of what you've done with your advertising, outreach, and innovative campaigns."

She nods slowly as her eyes move across the screen, but the furrow between her brows is back. "So you're saying I need to dig deeper," she says neutrally, the radiance gone.

I suddenly feel off-balance, like everything is one or two degrees off its axis. I blink and think back to what I said. "I guess what I'm saying is, you've done all this stuff. Now you just have to show it." I'm grasping at straws to say what I mean, and I latch on to the stuff I'm working on with Alan. "It's like I tell your brother, sometimes you know how to do a problem, but it's not quite enough to just put down the answer—you have to show your work to get full credit."

It's the wrong thing to say. I know it the instant the words leave my lips. Jocelyn's mouth tightens and she looks away. Her hand makes a fist, as if cracking an invisible egg.

JOCELYN

Will pretends to like my essay. I mean, he says he likes it, and that it makes him want to get coffee with me, but of course he's biased. Then he says what he really means, which is that it needs work. Specifically, I need to "show my work," like I'm some kind of failed middle schooler who has to take summer school.

I feel sick with embarrassment. I sit on my hands to stop them from shaking. "Okay," I say to Will, who is looking at me concernedly as I melt down. "I get it. I have to rewrite it. That's fine, it was just a crappy first draft anyway."

"No, that's not what I'm saying," Will insists. "Most of it, like eighty percent of it, is perfect…."

"There's no such thing as perfect," I simper, parroting every elementary school teacher, ever. Because it's true, at least for me.

He puts his hand to his head and sighs, and it reminds me so much of my father that I want to puke. "What I mean," he tries again, "is that there's so much that's pure gold. You don't have to redo the whole thing. Just don't be afraid to put in specifics about what you've done. The committee will eat it up."

I take a deep breath, as if it'll buoy me from the sinking sensation that threatens to overwhelm me. My legs feel like they're fused with our thinning gray carpet and the sagging cushions

218

on our secondhand couch. I couldn't stand up if I tried. "But…" I struggle to put it in words, how it's not going to be that easy, he makes it sound so easy. "I tried to. I wrote it out, what we did this summer, and it looks…it looks like I'm pretending to be a grown-up. I might as well be using plastic coins."

"No one expects you to be fully formed," Will argues. "These programs can't expect anyone to be ready to lead Fortune 500 companies. They're just looking for potential."

"Potential that I don't have!" I can't help it, I'm yelling, because he just doesn't get it. He has this weird faith in me as if I'm worth the effort, as if I'm not just some bargain-basement wannabe who's going to disappoint everyone who ever put faith in me.

"Oh my…" Will covers his face with both hands to muffle a scream of frustration. "Jos, everyone has potential. You most of all. No one works harder than you, and you're so smart…."

"Well, my PSAT scores don't really support that," I mutter.

"Because you haven't taken a hundred hours of SAT prep courses. Plus, there are studies showing that they're not the best predictor of success in college—grades are."

"Those aren't exactly anything to write home about."

"They're not horrible, either. They're okay." When I glare at him—does he really believe that?—Will throws up his hands. "I don't know what you expect me to say. Do you want me to tell you to quit, not to bother? Is that what you want?" I feel a heavy thud as Will slumps to the couch next to me, just inches away from where I'm still picking at that hangnail.

I don't say anything, because I don't know the answer to his question.

Will's voice is low when he finally breaks the heavy silence.

"I'm sorry. I just remembered that it wasn't your idea to apply to this program. It was your dad's. You're doing it because it's part of that contract." He pauses. "Jocelyn?"

The ache in his voice pulls me out of my spiral. I hate that I made him sound like that. I hate that when I look him in the eyes I can see the hurt in them.

"Jocelyn, you know that if you want to pull out of the contract, I won't hold it against you, right?"

WILL

In the beginning of her freshman year, my sister started to act even moodier than usual. The only thing that would make her smile at any family gatherings was when one of our younger aunties cooed over her, "Look, Grace, when did you become so fit! Sha, are you a model now with that waist?" Invariably this would spark controversy with my nne nne's generation, who grumbled that she was too skinny and should gain weight, and Grace's resting frown would come back. She was always a picky eater, but that year she started to prepare her own food, mostly raw vegetables and soups. It wasn't until she fainted one day after tennis practice that her coach took my mother aside and told her that she'd caught Grace purging in the locker room the week before.

"I do not understand it," my nne nne vented to my dad on the way home from the hospital. She had flown in from Chicago as soon as she'd heard that my sister was sick. "Why does the girl think she needs to lose more weight? She is stick thin as it is." She was truly flummoxed, completely unable to comprehend how her perfect grandchild had suddenly become the problematic one. "Such a waste. There are people going hungry in parts of the world, and yet children in America are vomiting recreationally."

"They don't do it for fun, Mmá," my mother said sharply. "It's a disease."

Dr. Rifkin had introduced me a long time ago to the concept of cognitive distortions—those moments when your brain is an asshole and misinterprets your world. It was kind of the same thing with Grace—she had something called body image distortion, so that whenever she saw her body reflected it was like she was looking into a funhouse mirror.

I've been able to recite the cognitive distortions I'm prone to since fourth grade. That doesn't mean that I have total control yet over how I personalize (in short, my tendency to feel responsible for bad things that happen to other people), how quickly I jump to conclusions, and my apocalyptic-level ability to catastrophize.

It's always easier to see fault lines—both your own and others'—than to fix them.

So when I realize that I've been listening to Jocelyn and silently ticking off the ways that her brain is tricking her (polarized thinking, overgeneralization, disqualifying the positive), I know that just pointing them out isn't going to be helpful. Even after pretty much half my life in therapy, I still bristle when my dad gently points out a distortion or suggests that I write in the workbook Dr. Rifkin gave me for the days in between sessions.

What I can do, though, is relieve one of her stressors. She's only doing that stupid business program for her father, and maybe because she doesn't want to let me down.

I think I'm doing the right thing by giving her an out, I really do. But I really, really should have given more thought to how her asshole brain was going to interpret what I said.

JOCELYN

If I felt like lead before, now I feel like ash. All it would take is a puff of wind, and I'd blow away.

"You want me to break the contract?" I whisper. I hate the way my voice breaks. I hate how pathetic I am, that we're less than a week into this stupid plan and Will already wants to bail.

"No!" Will practically explodes in horror, and for the briefest moment it's as if he's reached out a hand to physically steady me, even though we haven't touched. I know in my gut, in the release of tension in my chest, that he means it, and I wish I could bottle the intensity of his emotion and squirrel it away somewhere.

It's funny how your brain works, isn't it? How it can warp reality like Silly Putty, pulling your emotions this way and that, so that you can think that something is absolutely true one minute, only to have doubts about it the next.

I just want to know what to think. How to be. I don't want my life to be a shapeless, endlessly changing plaything at my brain's mercy. Is that too much to ask? For things to hold their shape for a little while?

"I'm so tired." Saying it feels both like I'm finally releasing a breath and like I'm admitting defeat. It's the worst kind of confession: Weak. Pathetic. Selfish. I think about all the work my parents have put into giving Alan and me a fighting chance. I think of my amah, seventy years old and still waking up at six in the morning to prepare my lunches and start with veggie prep. And I'm the tired one?

"I get it," Will says softly. "I am definitely one hundred percent absolutely on board with the contract...." He takes a deep breath, shakes his head.

I brace myself for the "but." When it comes, though, it's not what I expect.

"But I know that it's a lot of pressure. It's okay to be stressed. It's okay to have doubts about the right things to say in the application."

It's a good thing I'm sitting down, because the realization that this is the first time anyone has given me permission to be stressed? It's a knee-wobbling revelation. My parents always look at my freak-outs with impatient exasperation and basically tell me to get over it. Priya always just tries to talk me down, tell me how everything's going to be okay, which just winds me up because I think of more evidence to argue that it's not. No one's ever just agreed with me that things suck. It's refreshing.

"I wish I could just take a nap and have everything be all better when I wake up," I say finally.

"You and me both," Will says. As we've talked he's inched in closer to me, and I swear I can feel his body heat and smell the scent of his shampoo, something sweetly sharp that makes my brain whisper, *Closer, closer.*

My mom and brother will walk in at any second so I resist the urge to lean into him, bury my face in his shirt so I can be surrounded by his smell and shut out the jumbled mess of my thoughts.

Instead I just whisper, "Thanks," and wrap my hands in my lap.

"Always," Will says. He's quiet for a minute, unsmiling, and

I feel a growing anxiety as I watch him start to say something, then stop.

"Have you ever…" Will purses his lips and shakes his head. "Okay, there's no way to have this conversation without sounding like a jerk, except to come clean to you." He visibly steels himself.

"What are you talking about?"

"So you know those doctor's appointments that I told you I had to go to?"

"Yeah." A couple of times over the summer Will had told me that he was going to have to be late for work.

He grimaces and picks at the cuticles on his left hand. "Well, they weren't dermatology treatments like I said. I'm sorry I lied to you."

"O-kay?" It's weird. Instead of being apprehensive, I'm just confused and a little curious. It's just another sign of how much I trust him, despite my brain's best efforts.

Will takes in a deep breath before blurting out, "I'm…They were therapy appointments. I've been seeing a psychologist since I was eight. Anxiety."

I can't help it, but my knee-jerk reaction to the word "therapy" is to recoil and to wonder what Will's been hiding from me. I blink and realize that I need to choose my words carefully.

Because I am hopelessly pathetic, those words do not materialize.

WILL

Among my closest friends, it's well known that I'm kind of neurotic. It's a running joke, even, but I've never actually told any of them that I see a doctor, or that I have a diagnosis. Or two of them, really: generalized anxiety disorder, with a side of social anxiety disorder.

It's not that I'm hiding my mental illness, exactly—it's out there in the open. I couldn't conceal the lengths I'll go to avoid certain situations, even if I tried.

Besides, like Dr. Rifkin says, anxiety is a spectrum. Every single person who has ever existed has felt nervous over something at some point in their life. Which means, when I'm doing my exercises and using my coping skills, I can pass for normal well enough, even though my sister would lecture me and say, "There's no such thing as normal." She would tell me, "Everyone has their own shit to deal with." I guess she should know.

Still, I've never labeled my shit to my friends, because giving it a name pathologizes it, turns me from someone who can be a little anxious to someone who has anxiety.

I've seen firsthand, with Javier, what that kind of label does to people. Not that his diagnosis of autism spectrum disorder really changes who he is, but it changes how people interact with him. That's why I don't volunteer the fact that he's on the spectrum to people who have never met him. The couple of times I've seen him meet someone who knew beforehand that he was autistic, they saw everything he did through the lens of autism, using his diagnosis as an excuse, or an explanation. Even now, it's rare that someone sees him as just a kid, instead of that kid on the spectrum.

I've never wanted my teachers and friends to see me like that, to treat me with kid gloves because of the flashing neon ANXIETY sign over my head. So I've never said outright that I'm being treated for it, even though I think Manny, at least, probably assumes.

It's terrifying, then, how quickly I decide to tell Jocelyn, how after knowing her for mere weeks I'm willing to reveal something that I haven't told people I've known for a decade. It's a calculated risk, but one I'm willing to take because I truly don't know how to help her—or really, whether she'll accept my help—without my first admitting that I've got problems, too.

I'm looking straight at her when I tell her what my appointments really were, so I see the confusion in her face replaced by something that's a cross between disappointment and pity before she straightens her face into concern.

In the silence that follows I can hear my heart pounding in my ears. Each of Jocelyn's microexpressions seems to confirm all the fears I've had about coming out with my anxiety. I flash ahead to the next few weeks, imagining that Jocelyn will stop asking me to do things for the restaurant. Maybe she'll take more things on herself, not wanting to stress me out. Or perhaps she'll be like my grandma Domenici when I was growing up, constantly coddling me after anything that could remotely hurt my feelings. "Oh, Will, is everything okay? Can I do anything to help?"

When Jocelyn finally speaks, it's tentative, stilted. "Wow. Um, thank you for telling me."

I don't know what to say. Am I supposed to say, "You're welcome"? Then I remember why I told her in the first place.

"I just thought... I thought it'd help you to know. Because I wanted to say that it helps, sometimes, to talk through things. Is there anyone you trust? Would you want to talk to a... a professional? It wouldn't have to be mine. I'm sure he could refer you to some other people."

JOCELYN

Of course that was where he was going to go, I think, as I feel the anger building inside me. Anger coming from a little bit of hurt with a hint of shame. I should have known. Why else would he have made a confession like that out of the blue? It was smart of him. I'll give him that. I can't be mad at him for suggesting that I should see a shrink if he is seeing one, too. Except…

"Why do you need a therapist?" I ask sharply. I have to grit my teeth to keep resentment from bleeding entirely into my voice. "You're, like, the most stable person I know."

"Only because of eight years of therapy," he says with a smile that borders on bitter. "You should have seen me before. I had these stomach pains that the doctors said were psychosomatic— literally in my head. I would cry before I went to school some days. Then I would cry when I got home because I was worried that I'd done some little thing wrong."

I feel a pang in my chest, thinking about grade-school Will curled up in physical pain because of his anxiety. "I'm sorry about that," I say. The heat in my cheeks subsides as I wonder whether Will's a quiet crier, or an ugly one, like me. "I'm glad life got better."

"That's the thing, it's not that life got better, I just got better at coping with it. There are mental exercises you can do to change your thinking patterns. It's called cognitive behavioral therapy. The techniques are really helpful when you're going in circles in your head." Will looks at me hopefully, and I know he wants me to jump on his idea. If he could pick up a phone and make me an appointment with some mental health clinic this minute, I think he'd do it.

But that is not going to happen.

"That sounds nice. No, really it does," I say when he gives me a dubious look. "But...what you're describing doesn't really sound like me. I'm not having, like, stomach pains or anything. I'm just having a rough day. I'll get over it. I don't think I need to, like, talk to anyone."

WILL

There's so much to say after Jocelyn brushes off my suggestion. I want to tell her that no, she doesn't have the same symptoms that I have, but that's probably because it's not anxiety that's her issue, but some kind of mood disorder. I want to tell her that I've noticed that she only picks at her lunch these days, and that her cheeks are less full than they were even a month ago. I want to remind her that twice in the last week she's been late in the morning because she said she had trouble getting out of bed.

Most of all, I wish I could show her how worried I am to see her being eaten up by guilt and low self-esteem. I wish she knew how much I wanted to see her happy.

This is where my father would insert, "But it's okay to be sad sometimes." And my mother, who would argue that grief and hardship is a normal part of the human condition, would agree, quoting that Nigerian proverb about how, no matter how long the night may be, the day is sure to come. It's like my anxiety. Depression is a spectrum, too. Every single person who has ever existed has felt sad about something at some point in their life. So who am I to push Jocelyn when she says she doesn't need a therapist?

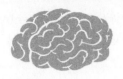

This Is My Brain on Mute

JOCELYN

The next morning, Lauren White is the first one to show up for our casting call. When she comes in her nose gives a little wrinkle at the smell of lingering cleaning solution, and I feel an instant surge of dislike.

"Hiiiii, you must be Jocelyn! I'm Lauren. Is Priya here yet?" She searches around the empty restaurant, as if Priya's going to be underneath a booth or hiding behind the counter. She's only a little bit taller than I am, with a pixie haircut and dirty-blond hair with highlights. Priya told her to feel free to do her makeup at home to save time, so her face is all red lips and rosy cheeks, with heavy mascara and eyeliner that make her look like a real-life Bratz doll.

When Priya comes in with her brother Pranav, who is dressed up in a sharp navy business suit, I help Priya set up some shots while Pranav mercifully picks up conversation with Lauren. I've got to hand it to him—he's pretty smooth, and even I can see the chemistry he has with Lauren.

Priya notices me frowning at Lauren and comes over to me. "You okay?" Priya whispers as she raises her external lights.

"Yeah, just tired," I say. It's as honest as I can be right now. I don't want to bring up the scene she deleted. My heart feels sore still, but it's not bleeding anymore, so I'm going to just let it be.

"I think today's going to be really fun."

And it almost is. Lauren, it turns out, is a freaking amazing actress, the type who can control her body language on the turn of a dime. One second she is her normal peppy, self-absorbed self, and the next second she is a world-weary waitress just passing the days until her next paycheck. I wish I had her talent—it would've made sneaking around so much easier.

Priya and I gradually slip into our working rhythm—her the close-up person, me the eye in the sky and facilitator, pointing out wide-angle issues and running for everything we need to make the shoot go smoothly. Things are almost right—or at least, they're never exactly wrong. The day is just…muted.

After Pranav and Lauren leave, we run through the dailies, and they're great, possibly even better than the day before. Priya's practically glowing with satisfaction.

"Jocelyn, almost every take we made is usable. Can you believe it? I think we might be able to do this on two days of shooting. One day for reshoots, tops."

"Good for you, that's awesome." Usually I'm charged when we go over our footage. Every single time it's amazing to see my storyboards come to life with the actors' interpretation and

Priya's framing. But today I feel like my brain is in one of those mesh foam wrappers they use to keep Asian pears from bruising in transit.

Priya stares at me as if I've just slapped a baby in the face. "Good for us," she says.

"That's what I meant," I say, trying to muster up a scrap or two of enthusiasm. "Good for us."

Sundays are usually pretty slow in the restaurant, so Will only works for a few hours that afternoon to hash out a plan for the week. At first, things are kind of awkward, like we're tiptoeing around the conversation where he basically called me a head case. There's enough shit to do, though, that we get over it quick.

We're going to hit another slew of doctors' offices tomorrow, and we start working on an idea that I had as I was cycling past one of the sports fields a few days ago: a post-practice special.

Will gives a thumbs-up to my idea, which involves free on-field delivery with a full set of utensils and three dollars off a twelve-pack of Powerade instead of our usual two-liter soda. "Great idea to tap into the sports industrial complex. If you get a hungry high school lacrosse team hooked on A-Plus..."

"...Thirty percent, here we come." My eyes flick over to where my dad's "dating contract" is taped behind the counter. "How did Alan do today?"

"Not quite as well as yesterday. Eighty percent."

"Hey, at least he'll pass."

"How was your day?" Will asks. "Did you guys have a good shoot?"

I pause for a second. "Yeah, it was good."

"Only good?" Will asks, his mouth bending toward a frown.

"No, it was fine," I amend my statement. I hate that he can read me so well. "Priya did a great job. I just don't really want to talk about it."

Will's brow furrows. "Hey, you know what we should do," he says after a minute or two of silence. "We need to start having a regular movie night. What's next up in your tier-one movies?"

"I'm not sure." Tier-one movies are films that I really want to see that are either on Netflix or available through interlibrary loan. And I'm lying, I know the dozen or so movies that are in that group, I just haven't had any interest in opening my spreadsheet to figure out what's on top. "I haven't really been all that into any of the movies I've seen on my own lately." I glance over to where my mom's counting the cash register. "Maybe it's because I've been seeing them on my own," I whisper, giving him a half-hearted smile.

He doesn't smile back, like he recognizes it for the excuse that it is. "Maybe..." His eyes go unfocused for a second. "Or maybe...never mind."

There he is, holding back again.

"What?" I ask, suddenly irritated. "Spit it out."

Will grimaces sheepishly. "You're going to think I'm a broken record."

"Spit. It. Out."

He sighs, and his head drops into a hangdog position. "Okay, so my aunt Mary is a nurse at the U," he says, his voice pitched so my mom can't hear. "She's really into mental health, always has been. She knows issues run in my family, so she's always, like, screening us during holiday gatherings and talking about warning signs. And she says that one of the first signs of depression is losing interest in activities that you once enjoyed."

I bristle and turn on Slacker Radio, angling my laptop to face the counter and block our conversation a bit. "My not being impressed by Ben Affleck's first attempt to revive his sputtering career is not a sign that I'm depressed," I hiss.

This time, Will doesn't roll over the way he usually does when I give him pushback. "It's not *not* a sign that you're depressed, either," he argues, though he has the grace to look uncomfortable doing it. "I know you've been under a lot of stress lately; there have been a lot of ups and downs. It's natural for—"

I cut him off. "You're right." His mouth snaps shut, and God help me but he looks like a puppy waiting for its chew toy. I almost feel bad. "You are absolutely correct, going through stress and having ups and downs is perfectly normal," I say coldly. "Would you freaking stop with trying to mother me? I am not depressed."

WILL

Jocelyn's words are like a slap.

There's a civil war going on in my head. Team Chill is telling me, again, that nothing good will come of me trying to push someone into therapy who isn't ready. Team Mayday is freaking the heck out. How can she not see it? Feelings of guilt and inadequacy. Check. Decreased appetite. Check. Altered sleep patterns. Check. Now loss of interest in movies and filmmaking. Short of printing out a copy of the DSM-5 guidelines from my mom's old psychiatry textbooks, I can't think of anything that would be more convincing. Or more futile.

Jocelyn and her family clearly have some sort of mental block against talking about psych issues, and I get it, I really do. My own family, open as it is, doesn't bring my anxiety and Grace's anorexia up in casual conversation.

We don't pretend it doesn't exist, either.

Team Mayday is running circles around my head, screaming at me that I have to say something, that stigma and denial are dangerous, that they can kill.

Team Chill retorts that arguing with someone who doesn't recognize that they've got an issue is only going to cause resentment and further entrench them in their denial.

As my thoughts war, my body is the battleground. If someone were looking at me they might notice that I'm starting to look spacey. Maybe they'd see that my eyes are darker, because my pupils are dilated from the stress. People who know me would recognize my more common tics—the tugging at my sleeves, the way I rub my wrist as if I could slow my pulse manually, as if there's anything I can do to calm my stupid, skittish, runaway horse of a heart.

Jocelyn looks pissed, as if my using the "d" word is a personal affront. Part of me is reflexively, defensively, mad in return. I mean, I opened up to her about my own anxiety. Does she really believe I'm the type of person to think less of her just because she might have depression?

For a few seconds, I let myself feel angry. Angry that it seems that Jos is upset with me for caring. What, does she think I'm confronting her because it's fun? Does she think that I'm taking joy in this intervention, like I'm some sort of psychiatric superhero swooping in to help the poor, screwed-up damsel in distress by ferrying her to a therapist?

Then, because my brain is a freaking pinball machine, a memory burns away my anger in an instant: I remember how mad I was at my dad the first time he took me to a psychologist, how betrayed. I was only eight at the time, but even then I had a sense of the stigma, what with the white lie that my dad told my teacher to excuse my absence. The worst part was when my dad left me alone in the consultation room for the first time. Dr. Rifkin asked me, gently, "Did your parents tell you why you're here?" And the only response I could think of was "Because there's something wrong with me."

JOCELYN

For a moment, Will's eyes narrow in anger, and it's such an unfamiliar expression that I can feel a thrill go down my spine, a flash of dangerous recognition. I've seen Will indignant, passionate, and even outraged, but I've never really seen him match the dark resentment that always seems to simmer inside me. I feel a weird mix of triumph and shame to have goaded him to that point. *See*, I think, *he's not perfect. And now he'll realize that I don't deserve him.*

Part of me wants to cry, already anticipating the loss of our relationship. He won't quit A-Plus; he's too goddamn professional for that. He'll keep doing his best to fulfill the contract. I'm sure he'll whip Alan into shape if only to prove that he can. But at the end of the summer, he'll look at our spreadsheet, feel satisfaction at a job well done, and say good-bye.

And for what? Because I'm too proud to admit that I might have depression? My mind does that familiar acrobatic loop-de-loop where all of a sudden my anger implodes onto myself. It's all my fault for jumping to the attack so quickly. Will was just trying to care, and now I've driven him away, cut him

235

with my sharp edges the way I've alienated everyone from Peggy Cheng to that girl Megan who shared her Babybel cheeses with me in sixth grade, only to have me complain about how they tasted gross and gave me gas.

Suddenly, I feel empty, as if all my emotions have canceled one another out. I'm a zero sum.

The stone in my chest is back. The rest of the summer stretches out in front of me as an endless dark corridor: being a spectator as Priya takes over our film, watching helplessly as Will goes from being something more than a friend to something much, much less.

I can't look at him, so I stare at the lame-ass flyer that I've been making for our floundering restaurant. It's a pointless effort—what, I think a bunch of hungry lacrosse bros will save our restaurant?—but I don't even have enough energy to scroll my mouse over to delete the file.

My mom walks back to the kitchen to shout out an order, the familiar *thump-squeak* of the swinging door resonating in the lengthening silence between us. I want to tell Will that I'm sorry, that I know that I'm screwed up and shouldn't have taken it out on him. I'm trying to pull together the courage to apologize, really, I am, but there's no reserve of grace for me to draw upon, when Will—my heart jump-starts, despite everything—speaks first.

WILL

Jocelyn is so upset she can't look at me, and I don't blame her. I remember the hot shame I felt during that first therapy session, remember not being sure whether to turn all that pain inward or outward.

I breathe in through my mouth, count to five. Breathe out through my nose, count to five. And then I speak before I can think too much.

"I'm sorry. I didn't…I don't mean to be pushy." My words break the surface of the quiet but don't quite dispel the tension that still fills the room. At least Jocelyn looks at me again. She's got this hollowed-out expression that I can't read.

"It's okay. I know you were trying to…" She waves her hand to fill in the blanks. "I didn't mean to snap." She swipes her palm over her face and sighs. "You don't have to stay, I mean, I understand if you want to leave."

"What? No. I don't want to leave," I say, shaking my head. Then, my voice cracking a little, "Unless you want me to leave?"

"I don't know. Yes? Maybe? No?" Jos lets out a groan. "Everything's a mess in my head, I'm so sorry."

"Don't be.… You don't have to apologize. We're good."

She looks up at me, frankly disbelieving. "Why?"

That's all she says, just the one syllable. She could be asking me why I'm staying, or why I'm forgiving her so quickly for her outburst—that makes the most sense. But I'm crap at mind reading, if you couldn't tell already.

"Why what?" I ask.

"Why do you care about me?"

It's the essential question, and my anxiety level goes up the way it has for every test I've ever taken, from my third-grade spelling tests to the SATs. "Do you trust me?" I ask.

"Yeah?" she says. It sounds like a question.

"I need you to know, you mean something to me." At my words, Jocelyn's lips curve halfway to a smile, before she gives a little shake of her head and her mouth crumbles back into a frown.

That's just it, though, right? I can say whatever I want, but what will make Jocelyn's post-truth brain believe me?

My father has always liked to express his love for my mother with things, because he knows that she doesn't always have the time to shop for herself. At least once a month he'll come home with expensive chocolates (the kind that are hand decorated and displayed in boxes with gold elastic string), or hand-selected flowers (dahlias are her favorite, big and vibrant and long lasting).

In the end those kinds of things are easy to pass off as fake news, insincere thoughts that are bought and paid for. I need to give Jos tangible proof that I care, something so undeniable that it'll break through the noise of her own doubt.

And then my watch buzzes, and I know what I can do.

JOCELYN

When I ask Will why he puts up with me, it doesn't shock me that he struggles to answer the question, that at first he just says something generic about how much I mean to him.

But then he gives a little start, and his lips part in surprise. He looks at me, laser focused, his eyes wide. "I know how I can show you."

He reaches for his wrist—I've noticed that he does that a lot. He unbuttons his sleeve and pushes it up. He's got an Apple Watch, of course, and he's swiping through screens until he finds the one he needs. He angles his hand over to me to show me an EKG tracing. Instantly, I can tell from a lifetime of watching medical shows that it's too fast, the waveforms filling up the screen frenetically instead of being a calm, steady rate.

And I realize: Will is literally showing me his heart.

"My mom got me this program a few years ago," Will says. There's a breathlessness to his voice, like he's struggling against a strong wind. "She's a scientist. She likes data. She uses it to show me how I can use mindfulness techniques to control things like my breathing and heart rate. So I know from months of observation that my resting pulse is sixty-eight."

Right now, his heart rate is 102.

Mine is probably the same, and I'm already trying to explain it away. "We kind of just argued," I pointed out. "Doesn't that explain it?"

"Pfft." He waves his hand. "This kind of talk? It's not the easiest thing in the world; I understand that it sometimes doesn't go perfectly. If I had the same conversation with one of my buddies and he blew up at me, I wouldn't be tachycardic."

"Tachy-what?"

"Sorry, using my mom's medicalese. Tachycardic. Fast heart rate." He's already poking at his watch, scrolling through some numbers. "You see this here? This is from the day of my interview. Heart rate a little higher in the ten minutes before we're scheduled to meet. Then when I saw you? It jumps to one hundred five."

"Couldn't that just be that you were stressed out about the job?" I ask.

"Sure, that's a theory, but let's see what it is on my first day at A-Plus, when I should've been more relaxed. I already had the job, right?"

101.

"But I know what you're going to say," he says. "That's just first-day-on-the-job jitters. So, let's look at the next day."

103.

"And how about this, the day I was working on trying to get the ordering system up and running. You were out making deliveries, I barely saw you."

88.

"Then, the night we saw *Broadcast News*."

That night, he maxed out at 110.

As the numbers scroll by, I get a surreal sense of displacement, as if I were viewing my life through the wrong end of a set of binoculars. It seems ludicrous to have, all of a sudden, so much evidence for how Will feels about me. I have to resist the urge to giggle.

I've only ever been to anything resembling an amusement park once in my life, last summer, and it wasn't even a real one. Priya invited me to join her family at the Booneville-Oneida County Fair. Her parents bought me an all-you-can-ride wristband, and I milked that piece of plastic for all it was worth. Priya and I rode the Tilt-A-Whirl (affectionately called the Tilt-A-Hurl by her brother) four times, and I still remember how jarring it was to step back onto solid earth after three minutes of dizzying, nonstop multidirectional twirling on uneven ground.

That's how I feel right now. Unsteady. Not able to trust that the spinning of my emotions has stopped. Kind of euphoric. And kind of like I want to hurl.

WILL

I've played my last card, and I am so afraid that Jocelyn is going to pull out another ace.

Then she says, "Okay. I believe you."

She doesn't ask for my list of therapists. She doesn't say she's going to look anything up or call to make an appointment. But I think—I hope—she's finally come to terms with the fact that I have a stake in what's going on in her head.

After eight years of therapy I'm used to the idea of taking two steps forward and one step back. It might seem like I haven't gotten anywhere, but I'm resolved to play the long game. I can only pray that it's enough.

This Is My Brain
on Notice

JOCELYN

The morning after Will shows me his literal heart, I bite the bullet and submit my application and references, as well as the request to waive the thirty-five-dollar application fee. When my e-mail notification dings, I feel my heart skip a beat even though I know it has to be an auto response.

> Thank you for your submission to the University of Utica Junior Business Program. We look forward to reviewing your application and contributing to the growth and success of many future leaders in management and entrepreneurship.

> Should you be selected for an interview, you will be contacted via e-mail in approximately one to two weeks.

"I probably won't get an interview," I tell myself out loud, even as a voice in my head that sounds suspiciously like Priya says, "Of course you're going to get an interview!" the same time a voice that sounds exactly like Will says, "Don't be so down on yourself. You have so much to offer."

To distract myself from the peanut gallery in my brain, I volunteer to go pick up my amah's med refills after lunch while Will does his afternoon tutoring session with Alan. It's one of the first times I've been out of the house by myself since I was grounded, and let me tell you, there's nothing more pathetic than having a five-minute bike ride to CVS be the highlight of your week.

I enter pharmacy-line purgatory. I'm scrolling through my Instagram feed trying to come up with ideas for the A-Plus account, when along comes everyone's favorite nemesis.

"Jocelyn! It's been so long since I've seen you! We missed you guys at the last MVCA potluck."

"Hey, Pegs." I muster my most convincing smile.

"Did my mom's drug reps come through for you?"

"Actually, they did. I owe you one." My smile gets 200 percent more genuine when I'm reminded that she did me a favor recently. Two, really, if you count her dad showing mine that Asian kids can date. I glance over at her shopping basket—it's full of travel-sized toiletries. And is that an honest-to-God disposable electric toothbrush? "So, you, uh, leaving for a trip?" I ask. I feel beholden to at least have our conversation last more than thirty seconds.

"Oh, yeah! I'm leaving on Friday for a trip to California. I applied to this Women in STEM program at Stanford. My mom is super worried about me being so far away, but it was just too good to pass up. Room and board is free, and there's even a travel stipend."

"That sounds great!" I say, even though what I really mean is, "Does it come with a 'Feel free to tell me to STFU' T-shirt, too?" Because of course Peggy Cheng, who has never been denied a thing in her life, gets a free ride to study at one of the most prestigious universities in the country. Mercifully, the pharmacist calls my name next, before I start to actually emit fumes of toxic bitterness.

When I get back to A-Plus I have a black cloud over my head, and only about half an hour to snap out of it before Will's finished with Alan. That's the thing. Now that I'm 100 percent conscious of how aware Will is of my every mood, it's impossible not to be super careful about my vibe.

It's a little stressful, honestly. I mean, sixteen years into life in the Wu family, I've gotten used to the weight of my parents' expectations. It's like a backpack that I wear every day; I barely notice it. The only other person whose opinions I care about is Priya, but she's easy. She's used to my peaks and valleys. She's also enough of a go-with-the-flow person that she just deals with the drama. Not that Will wouldn't want to, but he's pretty sensitive, to use a word that I hate when it's used to describe me. It's a little bit easier for guys, of course; when people say a dude is sensitive, they use it as a compliment, to show what a great catch he is and how in tune he is with his feelings. When people say a woman is sensitive, they say it with an eye roll, like she's one malfunctioning pair of period panties away from rabid hysteria.

People say it as if it's a burden to have to think about other people's feelings, and for the first time, I kind of get it. Because as I'm waiting for Alan and Will to get done, I wonder: What if I accidentally trigger an anxiety attack with my worrying? Do I now have to be happy, in order for him to be happy? Should I start hiding the things that get me down, burying those feelings to protect us both? And are all these questions a huge, blinking warning sign?

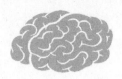

This Is My Brain on Placebos

WILL

This is what kept me up last night: wondering if I pushed Jocelyn too far. Wondering if I didn't push her enough. Freaking out that Alan has kind of plateaued in his progress, and that Jocelyn implied from the beginning that there is no way in hell her family would ever get him tested—let alone treated—for ADHD.

I've trotted out every test-taking strategy I have. Alan has gotten better, but he still makes too many unforced errors. So, I got up and did a two AM search on natural remedies for ADHD.

The first time I ever googled medical advice for a tennis injury, my mom (1) shot me the hairy eyeball and (2) delivered a lecture on fake medical news and how to detect it. She gave me her log-in to an online resource that doctors use when they need to look up reliable information on treatments. She took me to her medical school's library site so I could see how many freaking different publications there are and understand why a few of them are like rock stars (the *New England Journal of Medicine* and *Nature*) whereas others are more like garage bands.

She then gave me a miniseries of talks with episodes on concepts like peer review (essentially, your frenemies get to gleefully tear apart your research before you can publish it), double-blind randomized controlled trials (the best and most scientific way to compare two treatments), and of course, conflicts of interest (because, news flash, scientists who are paid by pharmaceutical companies tend to unconsciously favor those companies' drugs).

My mother gave me these fact-checking tools to show me how complicated the search for medical truth can be. I was taught in school that science is objective, but she wanted to illustrate that scientific research isn't always perfect, which means that the conclusions that people draw from it can be flawed, too.

It was a frightening realization, and one that explained why my mother has always hated taking any medications. When she comes home with her neck and shoulders aching from standing over an operating table, she just warms up a heating pad and waves off my dad's offer of ibuprofen, muttering about wanting to protect her kidney and how she doesn't want to get an ulcer. She chastises my nne nne, too, for the metric ton of dietary supplements she consumes every year. "You are just wasting your money," she says. "Most of those pills are essentially expensive placebos!"

Of all the things that my mother has tried to teach me about the ins and outs of medical research, I've found the idea of the placebo effect to be the most fascinating. I'd known for years that the mind has far more control over the body than most people realize. So, it came as no surprise that, to a certain extent, people can sometimes think themselves better, and that taking a sugar pill can improve everything from chronic pain to an overactive bladder to someone's perception of how bad their asthma is.

The next morning before work, I go to our drugstore and get some fish oil tablets. The evidence, my mother would tell you, is not convincing that omega-3 fatty acids can help prevent ADHD symptoms any more than, say, eating a fiber gummy.

That does make it a pretty perfect placebo, though.

And oh, hey, placebos have been shown to improve ADHD symptoms at about 50 percent of the level that actual drugs have. With none of the risks.

A couple of years ago, the sisters at St. Agnes started talking about Ritalin abuse in their health lectures, and there were the occasional rumors of kids stockpiling them to give away at the kind of exclusive parties that I wasn't invited to and would probably have hated in the first place. We've all seen those ads for ADHD drugs that end with a dulcet-toned voice-over artist rattling off twenty side effects in as reassuring a tone as possible. But I've also seen how they turned around my cousin Lonnie when he started meds in eighth grade. One year at the family Thanksgiving dinner he broke three wineglasses on two separate occasions and left in screaming tears at the end of the night; the next he was like a mini-adult. Was it maturity or was it the drugs?

The problem is, on a case-by-case level, there's no way to really know. So, the people who don't have access to their parents' medical journals can only go by their cousin's story, or their friend's mother's nephew's, or by a glossy magazine's human-interest story about celebrity X's recovery from stimulant addiction.

Still, I'm desperate. So for our next study session I bring snacks that are free of food dye and print out a five-minute mindfulness/yoga plan to do before the study session. I filch a Days-of-the-Week pillbox from our medicine cabinet to repackage the fish oil tablets as a "traditional Italian concentration enhancer" that boosts focus.

Alan turns up his nose when I offer him some snacks. "What is that, rabbit food?" He breaks his yoga poses to scratch his elbow, or behind his knee, or (once) at his butthole. But he fidgets with the rainbow-colored pillbox, opens the Monday compartment, and pops two tablets like they're M&M's.

I'll take it.

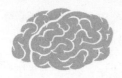

This Is My Brain on Interviews

JOCELYN

Exactly forty-eight hours after I submit my application, I have a heart attack.

I log in to my e-mail at lunchtime to see if our contact at MVCC has come through with our query about providing food for the student activities fair, and I actually feel chest pain when an e-mail from UUJBP@uticauniversity.edu pops up. The subject line is: "Request for Interview."

I look so stricken that Will is immediately concerned. "Are you okay?" he asks.

Mute, I flip my laptop around to show him the e-mail. It only takes a few seconds for him to break out into one of those smiles of his that I love so much, the kind that are so radiant, so focused on me that I have to look away.

"I knew the admissions committee would love your essay!"

I bite my lip, and it stings a little, so I know I'm not dreaming. Okay, so I've jumped through the first hoop. I'm still a long way from a scholarship. "It's only an interview," I remind Will, and myself. "They didn't say how many they offered. They could be bringing in everyone."

"But it shows that they're interested at least. You're not even a little proud?"

It's a tougher question than it should be. It's a relief to not be rejected, but I'm already stressing out about what I'm going to wear and imagining how badly I'll flub their questions. It's hard for me to envision any scenario other than one where they realize the minute I open my mouth that I'm not B-school material.

I haven't said a word, but all of a sudden Will nods, as if he understands. "Did I ever tell you how I felt when I got your e-mail to come in for a job interview?"

"No."

"Kind of elated. And kind of like I wanted to vomit."

"That pretty much sums it up," I say.

"You know who's sickeningly good at these kinds of things? My sister. Can I ask her if she wants to help you prep?"

Aaaand now my anxiety is replaced by a different kind of panic. Will has met every single one of my immediate family members and my best friend. But I've yet to meet anyone in his life. On the one hand, it's thrilling to know that he wants me to meet his sister. On the other hand, it's basically another interview, except this time it's not some college administrator who I'll never see again if they reject me; it's the person who has known Will as long as he's been alive, who he's probably closer to than anyone else.

I am so screwed.

"It's about time you and Grace met. You kind of remind me of her, you know. Both of you have that older-sister-who's-always-cleaning-up-after-their-screwup-younger-brother vibe."

I scoff. "You? A screwup? Please."

"Everyone's a little screwed up. Some people are just better at hiding it. Grace, for example. She's always given me good tips, even if I can't always implement them."

It's a measure of my terror that I'll crash and burn in my interview without some serious coaching that I finally say yes.

♡

The day I first talk with Grace, I wear the outfit I threw together for Will's interview. It was her idea to have our meet-up be a run-through of the real deal.

Since I've already been to the Domenici house I don't feel the same level of intimidation that I did before, but it's still a nerve-racking decade before Grace opens the door.

"Hello, Jocelyn. I'm Grace. Nice to meet you." She reaches out her hand and I do my best to avoid the "limp noodle" grip described by Forbes.com as implying a "weak inner-being." When I was reading up on good first impressions for interviews, they talked about the perfect handshake, and they could've been describing Grace. Within two seconds (confident posture, direct eye contact, smile, firm-but-not-too-firm pressure) she gives off the impression of being competent, trustworthy, and likable.

It's kind of annoying.

Grace is a little taller than me, though not as tall as Will of course, and slimmer. She's wearing a blouse with three-quarter-length sleeves that shows off bangled wrists. Her skin tone is a shade lighter than Will's, and she's rocking a gorgeous Afro.

I think about my own lank hair and wish that I had at least thought to blow-dry it this morning. Grace ushers me to an office in the back of their ground floor, overlooking their pool. It's got chestnut-stained built-in bookshelves filled with legal textbooks—basically it looks like a stock photo office or an old-timey home "library" like the one that Don Corleone presided from in *The Godfather*.

Grace takes a seat behind the massive glass-covered oak desk. I have to hand it to her—this definitely feels like an interview. Or an interrogation.

"So, Jocelyn, Will says that you're applying to some sort of scholarship program and are trying to get ready for the interview?"

"Yeah, it's the University of Utica Junior Business Program." When she smiles and raises her eyebrows for me to elaborate, I struggle to come up with a good description. "It's, like, you can take some courses at the college. And you come up with a project. They have mentors and stuff."

"I think I've heard of that," Grace says. "One of my friends did it last year—it develops future business leaders and encourages creative entrepreneurship."

It's like she memorized their website, and it's hella intimidating. "That's the one," I say weakly.

"So, tell me about your proposal. Will says that you've been doing some amazing things and really turning your family business around. A-Plus, right? Your dumplings are to die for." When she smiles she reminds me so much of Will that I instinctively relax.

"Yup. My grandmother's pot stickers are our claim to fame." That's as good a segue as anything. "I'm looking to expand the business, using the pot stickers as the kind of concession-friendly food that will allow us to do more catering and events. I think what we need to do is eventually buy a mobile unit, a food truck really, so we can participate in things like farmers markets and big sports events. We have a decently loyal customer base, but not much foot traffic. And you know how it is. Rent goes up every year.

"My real dream, though?" I pause. I've never said this out loud to anyone, have barely allowed myself to think it. "My real dream is for us to move beyond the daily grind of food service. There's a huge market out there for affordable, ready-to-eat meals and frozen dinners, particularly with the growing Asian population in the area. That would give everyone in my family a break from having to run a storefront twelve hours a day, seven days a week, three hundred sixty-five days out of the year just to scrape by."

I'm thinking of my amah and the way the skin on her fingers cracks every winter from the constant hand washing and forced-air heat. My mom has started to fill old pillowcases with rice to make hot packs that she slings over her shoulders every morning after she wakes up and every evening before she goes to bed. My dad has always complained about everything from his worsening nearsightedness to indigestion to his "whole body ache" without ever bothering to see any sort of medical professional, but even he broke down recently and visited a primary care doctor, who prescribed him some blood pressure medications that he reluctantly takes every night.

Grace looks at me thoughtfully for a while after I finish. "Well, you've convinced me that you want it," she says at last. "You've got a great story, clear motivation. What you and I have to do today is figure out how to maximize their confidence that you'll follow through with your ambition. Here's what you've got to do. First of all, you should make sure to review the program so you can make clear to them how they're going to help you."

She explains what she means: I need to know specifically what courses I want to take, and why. I need to have a mentor picked out already and be able to show them that I've done the research to find the faculty member who's the best fit. I need to be able to parrot back the program's mission statement, making sure that I know exactly which points of my story align with their "core values."

Then she takes me downstairs to a closet off the basement where she sorts through a pile of shoes that she's grown out of, and she finds me a pair of Mary Janes that are the right size if I wear thick socks. Afterward, we go upstairs to her room and she comes up with a camisole and a black blazer that matches my pants almost perfectly.

"I don't know how to thank you," I say when it's time for me to leave. I'm clutching my bag of spoils like it's a lifeline. "I don't even know what to say to tell you how amazing you are."

Grace smiles, looking even more like her brother than she did earlier. "You can thank me by kicking their asses and showing them that women of color are the hardest-working Bs in B-school." Then she shakes her head. "But I should be thanking you. Will hasn't been this good for years. All the luck, okay?"

"I kind of feel like someone just gave me a massive cheat code," I confess to Priya that night. "Also, like I'm some kid playing dress up."

"That is literally what we do when we go to college, J," Priya says. "We try to figure out how to adult. Why are you feeling bad about it?"

"Because I put on that outfit that Grace gave me, and at first I think I look really good, and five seconds later I feel like a giant fraud. I mean, I look in the mirror and I don't even recognize myself. It's just not me."

"Not yet," she says. "But it could be. Isn't that what you want?"

"What, the JBP?" I snort. "It's what my dad wants."

"But what about you?"

The thing is, I have no idea. Priya and I have always had that dream of moving to LA, but I've also recognized that as the tropiest small-town desire ever, and if I'm being honest, it's one that Priya is more likely to realize than I am.

The things I want more than anything are simple. I want to get out of this town, and I don't want to be tied to the restaurant forever. Anything else is just gravy. Considering that, JBP isn't the worst idea ever.

"I don't not want it. I mean, it's part of that damn contract," I say after a moment. I think of the rush I got when we sold out at the Boilermaker and the humming satisfaction in my chest when I saw those spreadsheet numbers spike. "I guess I could live with it."

Priya's quiet for a minute then gives a huff of breath. "I guess we could all do worse than having lives that we can live with."

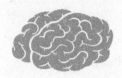

This Is My Brain
on Unsolicited Advice

WILL

I'm at A-Plus when Jocelyn has her "interview" with Grace, because we still aren't allowed unchaperoned time together. The lunch rush is slower than usual, which makes me feel a faint anxiety about whether we'll hit our target for the week. It's as good a reason as any for me to finally pull up the contact info for the plaza's property manager.

Just looking at the number on my phone makes me feel nauseated. I take a lap around the restaurant, doing my breathing exercises, pepping myself up by saying phrases like, "You've got this" and "She's not going to know what hit her."

Like Dr. Rifkin once suggested, I come up with a script to use. It's supposed to give me control over the situation, something to fall back on if my brain short-circuits the moment the conversation gets awkward and turns me into a stammering mess.

"Hello, Ms. Ross," I practice. "My name is William Domenici and I'm a staff writer for the *Spartan*. I'm working on a feature article on the microeconomics of Waterford Plaza." I know I have to reveal my conflict of interest, so I rehearse what I'm going to say about working for A-Plus.

I end up with a five-hundred-word speech, and still, when my thumb hovers over the green call button, I'm flooded with self-doubt. No way Rebecca Ross is going to give an interview to a high school student, even if I mention that previous *Spartan* articles have been picked up by the *O-D*. She probably couldn't tell me any meaningful intel anyway. What, do I think I'm going to do some investigative reporting and come up with something to save the Wus' business?

I close out the Word file with my script.

News flash: I don't make the call.

When Jos comes back to the restaurant, she has no apparent signs of trauma and is carrying a shopping bag full of clothes.

"She didn't eat you alive?" I ask, only half joking.

"No, she was great. I feel a lot better about the interview."

Later on, at home, Grace says pretty much the same thing. "She seemed a little nervous at first, but then she settled down when we actually started talking about what she wanted out of the program."

"Thanks for meeting her," I say.

"Naw, she's a good egg. I can see why you two get along."

There's something in the tone of her voice that feels like a tiny barb—something flippant, almost indulgent. Lately, Dr.

Rifkin has been working with me to try to "verbalize my sensitivity in order to defuse its consequences," which is a fancy way of saying that I should speak up when something bugs me, so I ask, "What do you mean?"

Grace looks up from the *New Yorker* she's reading on our couch and sets it on the coffee table. She shrugs. "Your neuroses complement each other."

As my eyes begin to narrow, Grace puts her hands up. "Don't get upset, it's an observation, not a criticism." She takes in a deep breath, a sign that I've always teased her to mean that she's gearing up to expel a lot of hot air. "The way I see it is that she's probably got some self-esteem issues—as do we all—and that you're a really good fit with her because you're super sensitive and aware of other people, so you're less likely to play into said self-esteem issues."

She's not exactly wrong, though it still irks me that she's so right.

"Also, Jocelyn seems like a straight shooter, which is good because she doesn't feed into your tendency to overanalyze everything. Plus, she seems super loyal. So, perfect for you."

I turn her words around in my head like I'm examining a puzzle box, looking for the right combination of touches for it to fall apart. "And how much are you charging for today's psychoanalysis?" I ask.

"Consider it pro bono," she says, ignoring my sarcasm. "And, little bro, no overthinking, okay?"

She goes back to her magazine. And I wonder how my sister can be as smart as everyone says she is if she doesn't realize that she said the exact combination of words to guarantee that I'll start overthinking.

♡

This is the question that keeps me up tonight, with all its codas, postscripts, and permutations:

Does Jocelyn only like me because she has low self-esteem?

It's not as if Grace's observation wasn't something I hadn't already cottoned on to, but it's the first time I've ever put it in the context of Jocelyn wanting to date me. Could it be true that Jocelyn settled on me because I was safe and unthreatening and clearly so into her that she didn't need to feel insecure?

And even worse, could it be that I only liked Jocelyn because some calculating, manipulative part of me noticed that she was vulnerable and didn't have many other choices? Did some primitive part of my brain look at her and think, *Oh, easy prey. We should go after her*?

My instant, visceral reaction is, *No, it's not like that.* I can feel my muscles tensing up in reaction to the thoughts that dart in and out of my brain, this rising horror that the attraction that Jocelyn and I have is something built from newspaper and matchsticks, ready to go up in flames at any instant.

At some point I realize that my breath is stuttering, barely enough to move any oxygen. It's too hot under my sheets, and I fling them aside and stumble into my bathroom, where I gulp in huge lungfuls of cool, stale air. It's three AM.

"It's not like that," I tell my reflection sternly. "Pull yourself together."

I drag myself back to my room and grab the notebook on my

nightstand. I start to write, only stopping when I can't keep my eyes open.

♡

The next day at A-Plus, Jocelyn is in such a good mood I almost feel guilty for my middle-of-the-night decompensation.

"Okay, ask me something, anything that might come up in an interview."

"Uh, okay. What's your biggest weakness?" I ask, thinking back to the day we first met.

She pulls a face, knowing exactly what I'm doing. "You can't think of a better question than that?"

I shrug. "It's probably the most commonly asked question. Can you answer it yet?"

"Ugh, you're the worst. Okay." She stands up straight and looks me right in the eye. "My biggest weakness is probably that I could do better at delegating. Sometimes when things get busy at the restaurant, and things come up, I find myself thinking, 'Oh, it's just easier to do that myself,' even when it's something simple that anyone could do, like cutting vegetables. The thing I have to realize is that just because I can do something, that doesn't mean that it is my job. Teams work the most effectively when everyone works as a unit, with specialized tasks."

"Not bad." I think about other likely questions. "Okay. How will a UUJBP scholarship fit in your future plans?"

Jocelyn rolls her eyes at first, then gets a mischievous look. "Well, sir," she says, honest to God batting her eyes. "It'll allow me to fulfill my potential by dating this really cute, sweet guy, so I'd appreciate it if you'd just sign me up."

I'm so flustered that I fumble the plasticware I'm wrapping into a napkin. When I bend down to pick it up I can feel my face heat up as my mouth pulls into a smile I can't suppress.

"Xiao Jia! How many times I say, no flirt!" Mr. Wu complains from the propped-open storeroom.

"I'm not flirting, I'm practicing for my interview!" Jocelyn yells.

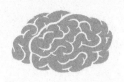

This Is My Brain on Blank

JOCELYN

The first time I step onto the University of Utica grounds, I'm pleasantly underwhelmed. It's an urban campus, so it doesn't have a lush, manicured college green. It's basically a bunch of loosely affiliated parking lots and high rises. It looks almost unassuming, I think.

My dad drops me off and I find my way into one of the taller buildings. My borrowed shoes are the right size, but slightly too wide, so I have to scrunch my toes a little to keep them from slipping when I walk. A receptionist gives me a name tag with a UU lanyard and points me to some couches in the atrium, where two pasty-white guys and one slightly darker-skinned girl sit.

The other three are ignoring one another, which is fine by me. I open the leather folio that Will lent me and skim through the key talking points Grace had me write down.

"Once they start asking questions, remember to make like a politician on Fox News, and be ready to pivot, pivot, pivot!" Grace told me.

"Won't they be mad if I don't actually stay on topic, though?"

"Nah, they don't really have an agenda other than wanting to know more about you. So it's okay for you to be proactive and dictate what they discover."

She gave me a bunch of pivot phrases, like: "That reminds me of _____" or "My personal experience of _____ led me to _____" or "It's important for me to always remember _____."

I whisper the words under my breath and try not to feel like a tool.

Eventually the other girl tries to start a conversation with me. "Excuse me," she asks, "are you here to interview for the JBP, too?"

She's wearing an adorable navy skirt suit that makes me feel like a classless ogre, even in Grace's jacket, and her dark brown hair is up in a high ponytail that's so perky I can't help but be irked by it.

"Yeah," I say cautiously, not able to figure out if she's being genuinely friendly or just sizing up the competition.

"Oh, cool, me too. I'm Laura. This is such an amazing program. My older sister did it a few years ago. She's at Syracuse now, and this summer she got an internship at Bain. Can you believe it?"

I smile as appreciatively as I can, as if I could tell Bain from Adam. "That's great. She must be a rock star."

"What school are you from? Are you going to be a junior or a senior?" she asks, her eyes flicking over my ensemble. Sizing me up, then.

"I'm from Perry High, just about to start junior year. How about you?" I ask.

"St. Agnes. And I'm going to be a junior, too!"

Will's school, I realize with a jolt. They must know each other—I remember Will saying once that St. Agnes is small, only about one hundred kids in each grade, so it's like a family. "A really incestuous family," he said once. "I think the coeditor of our paper has dated literally every girl in the school at some point. Some of them twice." When I asked Will how many he had dated, he'd gotten squirrely and said that he'd mostly had crushes. Now, of course, I can't help but wonder if Laura was one of them.

She's got that look of someone crushable, wearing just enough eyeliner to make her hazel eyes pop while still looking professional and expertly applied lip gloss that make me just want to stare at her mouth when she talks. And she's likable, too?

Thankfully, before I can obsess for too long, a middle-aged woman with a clipboard walks over and leads us to a conference room. The two guys, Brad and Jonathan, jump up first. Laura follows, and I trail behind as the caboose. It suits me just fine to hang back. That way I can see the subtle wave Jonathan throws to one of the two white guys sitting at the head of the table when we enter, and catch the way Brad chooses a seat directly across from Laura and stares a little too long at where her name tag hangs at chest level.

Each of our seats has a glossy JBP brochure, a UU water bottle, and a UU pen laid out like a table setting. The older of the two men introduces himself as Dr. Harris and goes through a PowerPoint about the program.

It is, I realize, a recruitment pitch for the three of us who don't get the scholarship, to entice us to enroll in the program anyway. Dr. Harris uses the phrase "tremendous opportunity" at least four times in his presentation, clearly going for the hard sell. At the end of his PowerPoint is a scrolling list of previous JBP students along with their colleges and current jobs; when I glance over at the others, they're transfixed. Jonathan is slack jawed and actively mouth breathing, and Brad is leaning forward, lips moving as he silently mouths out the names of Ivy League schools like he's reading a holy text. Even Laura is smiling and nodding.

Me? I've turned to the last page of the brochure, to the "tuition and fees" section, where it shows that I, too, can have the privilege of this "tremendous opportunity" for the low, low fee of $7,500. There are testaments from former graduates talking about "recognizing growth potential" and from parents gushing about how it was a "priceless experience."

"Priceless" is one of those words that I've just never understood. It took me years to figure out that some people use it as a passive-aggressive faux-pliment ("Oh, yes, he's just priceless"). But even when people use it as the *Oxford English Dictionary* intended, it doesn't make any sense—at least it doesn't to me, because in my world, growing up, everything had a price. Usually one that my family couldn't pay.

So that's the shitty position I'm in: I have to gear up enough enthusiasm for JBP to rock my interview and convince them that I am the person who deserves the scholarship the most, but also be ready to walk away if I don't get funding.

They wrap up the presentation and pass out our itineraries— we're each going to interview with both Dr. Harris and his colleague Professor Wisneski. As we gather our things I feel a little hollow tickle in the back of my throat and swallow. Silently I curse Will for bringing me an omelet for breakfast. He said that his sister told him I should eat a full breakfast, so I don't get a sugar low during the interview, but I'm not used to having such a heavy meal first thing in the morning. My stomach feels like it's trying to digest a baby hippopotamus.

I've already broken into a light sweat by the time I walk into Professor Wisneski's office, which throws me into a panic, because one of the components of the perfect handshake is that your hand isn't too clammy. I don't have a purse, so nope, no tissues. I have to frantically rub my right hand along my pant leg and hope that the professor doesn't notice.

"I'm so honored to be here, Professor Wisneski," I say as I sit down. That's one of the openings that Grace suggested, because even though it's kind of obsequious (I mean, seriously, an honor?) it reminds the interviewer that they've selected you for a reason and, well, suggests that you deserved it.

I can tell from his slight smile that the professor eats it up. "No, thank you for coming, Ms. Wu. I must say, your personal statement really stood out among the others'—not many of our applicants have lived and breathed the business world like you."

"Um, thank you for saying that," I say, heart pounding, because this isn't how it was supposed to go. I was supposed to come in, fists raised, full of passion, ready to explain to them how my life experience makes me the most qualified person ever for the JBP. To have him spit out my party line is both validating and completely deflating. It's like I walked into a confrontation wearing full body armor only to realize that it was actually a water balloon fight, and what I really needed was a poncho.

There's an awkward pause where I probably look like a

complete Looney Tune as I rack my brains for a new game plan. The exact moment Professor Wisneski opens his mouth to say something, I blurt out, "I always try to remember that business is really all about relations."

It takes about two seconds of dead silence for me to realize that that didn't come out right.

The twitch of Professor Wisneski's lips clues me in, too.

My face is on fire as I stutter out a correction. "Relationships, I mean. I meant relationships, not nepotism, or that type of relations—like Bill Clinton." I manage, barely, to stop myself from saying "the sexual kind" during the most important interview of my life, but the damage is done. I'm such a disaster I couldn't draw a tic-tac-toe board, let alone a game plan.

Fuck my life.

Professor Wisneski puts his hands over his mouth to cover a cough that I'm 99 percent sure is just a disguised chuckle. I'm so flustered that I can't even look at him, so I open my folio with numb hands to furiously study my page of notes in a desperate attempt to avoid death by mortification.

Must. Get. Shit. Together.

Except, before I can think of some line of conversation to save the interview, Professor Wisneski pretends to leaf through my file and goes on as if nothing happened.

"Ms. Wu, you say in your personal statement that your family restaurant recently made moves to expand. Would you care to talk about that?"

It's the interviewing equivalent of an underhand slow-pitch, and his kindness feels like a failure. "Sure," I say, in a voice that sounds defeated even to myself. I shift around in my seat in an attempt to redistribute blood that's decided to spend an extended vacation in my hands, feet, and rear end (basically every organ in my body besides my brain).

It's a good thing I practiced. The gears in my head creak a bit, but eventually they get turning. "Well, to give you a bit of background, the restaurant my family owns was originally built in the eighties, and we inherited an infrastructure that was a bit dated...."

I limp through the rest of the interview. The professor must take pity on me—he asks me two more questions, one about my "management style" and one about what I hope to get from the program. I dutifully rattle off my talking points.

There's a point where it seems like the professor is looking at the grandfather clock on his wall every fifteen seconds. Finally, he closes his right hand into a fist and knocks twice on his desk. "Well, it looks like our time is up. It was truly a pleasure speaking with you today, Ms. Wu."

"Thanks, Professor." I reach out to shake his outstretched hand and try to approximate a smile. It's only polite, since it's probably the last time I'll see him.

When I walk out of the interview room, clipboard lady shepherds me back to the boardroom, where she trades me for Laura, telling me that Dr. Harris should be ready for me in half an hour. I excuse myself to the bathroom, lock myself in a stall, and proceed to sit on a toilet seat, head in my hands. I breathe and let myself be hollow.

There's something strangely comforting about losing hope. Or maybe comfort isn't the right word—it's more like relief. Because the hope that I've been holding on to for the past two weeks was just plain stressful. Hope comes with aspirations and the need to expend energy. Hope comes with expectations that weigh down your every thought and action. Hope comes with the never-ending fear of disappointment.

Well.

I don't know how long I've been here when the door opens and someone comes in. I peer under the stall and see sensible shoes and ankles like dumpling dough. Not Laura, then. I check my cell phone and am surprised to find that it's only been twenty minutes.

For a brief moment I run through possible excuses to bail on the second interview: Cramps? A migraine? Could I pull off a convincing faint? There's nothing sharp enough in the bathroom for me to produce enough blood to require an ambulance.

I realize after a minute that I don't have the energy or presence of mind to come up with an escape plan. So, I do what I've been doing my entire life. I pull on my big girl panties and soldier on. If nothing else, I know how to follow a script.

Dr. Harris's interview passes in a blur. I think I'm polite. I think I avoid any more major gaffes. I think I manage to trot out one or two ungraceful pivots so I can parrot out some of the stock answers Grace and I came up with.

After I pick up my stuff and check out with clipboard woman, I go out to meet my dad, who's waiting at the curb. I shrug when he asks me how it went. Then, once we get home, I claim a headache, go to my room, and lie down in my bed, where I don't have to think at all.

This Is My Brain
on Hold

WILL

After five minutes of navigating a phone tree and ten minutes on hold, I finally reach our MVCC contact. My heart rate's 108, and I probably need to change out of my drenched T-shirt as soon as the call is over.

"Hello, Blanca Sanchez here." She's harried. Distracted.

I take a deep breath and rub the wrist holding the phone. "Hi, Ms. Sanchez! I just wanted to follow up on our previous e-mail and see if we could still help you out with the catering for your student activities fair."

"Yeah, we're working out the details for that. I still don't know if I even have the budget for food."

I close my eyes and look down at the script I prepared for this very reply.

"Oh, that's totally understandable. There are quite a few

other institutions that have the same problem, which is why A-Plus has a program to augment your event with a hybrid of free and low-cost items. Essentially, we'd be able to provide the event with free fried rice and beverages, with the option for your students to buy egg rolls and crab rangoon for a nominal fee."

"You can do that?" Ms. Sanchez asks suspiciously.

"Oh, yes," I say, trying to sound as welcoming as possible. Jocelyn and I both agreed that when it came to telling her dad about the plan, we'd ask forgiveness instead of permission. The goal is to have the profit of egg rolls balance out the sunk cost of the fried rice. But even if we end up in the red for the afternoon, if we pass out a couple hundred flyers and coupons to a captive audience? It'll definitely be worth it. "I can send you a sample contract. All we would require is a fifty-dollar deposit against cancellation, which will be refunded after the event."

"Huh." I can tell that Ms. Sanchez is trying to figure out if the deal is too good to be true.

Time to seal the deal with the part that I practiced with Jocelyn a dozen times. "A-Plus is very excited about the ability to offer this service to MVCC, because your students have been terrific customers. This year's booth at the Boilermaker Expo at MVCC was our most successful ever."

"Oh, yeah, I think I remember some of the people in my office coming back with dumplings." She pauses, and I cross my fingers. "Okay, why not. Sounds like a win-win. You can e-mail me the information."

"Thank you, ma'am," I say after I do a silent scream and fist pump. "You won't be disappointed, and I look forward to your event."

272

I'm practically buzzing as I put the activities fair up on the whiteboard we got to keep track of upcoming catering gigs. We already have six contracts for the next two weeks, and the four meals we did last week are almost singlehandedly driving the 25 percent increase in profits we've seen lately.

I can't wait to tell Jocelyn, but she only left for her interview an hour ago. I look down the rest of my to-do list for the day. I already did a deep dive into the past week's numbers, isolating the catering and online orders as the sources of increased revenue. Next up is some website stuff I wanted to do so people could select the Healthy Choices option for individual items.

A little more than halfway through my coding, I hear Mr. Wu and Jocelyn get back. Charged up with the good news, I head into the kitchen only to see the door swing shut as Jocelyn goes upstairs. My heart drops.

I turn to Mr. Wu, who's muttering in Mandarin. "Did it not go well?"

"She very moody." He frowns. "So, probably no go well."

I turn to stare at the door leading up to the apartment upstairs. It's just a piece of wood with a few bits of metal, but with no one upstairs to chaperone and Mr. Wu glaring at me with his best "don't you have work to do" scowl, it's impenetrable.

I walk back to the front and grab my phone to text Jocelyn. I can already feel my heartbeat pounding with worry in my ears.

You okay?

I stare at my phone for two agonizing minutes before it's obvious she's not going to respond right away. Briefly, I consider pulling a fire alarm to clear the building or going out to buy a grappling hook so I can scale the outside wall up to her room, something smart or heroic that'll pull her out of whatever funk she's in. Then reality sets in as my thoughts shrink down to a realization that's small and sharp: Obviously, she doesn't want to talk to me.

I'm dizzy with disappointment for a moment, unmoored, and I try to find steady ground by piecing together what must have happened.

The interview didn't go well. Was it my fault? Did I set her up for a fall by forcing her to meet with Grace, whose level of perfection was probably unattainable? Did the omelet I made for her give her indigestion? Should I have walked her through my breathing exercises this morning? I must have failed Jocelyn in some way for her to close the door on me like that.

I go back to my laptop and consider sending her an e-mail, even though it's unlikely she'll check her e-mail if she's not responding to texts. I'll give her the good news about the catering business to try to cheer her up. And I'll apologize for whatever I did, or whatever I didn't do.

As I type through the message my hands start shaking, and the typos build up. The edges of my vision start to blur, and I close my eyes.

Five seconds in, five seconds out.

When I open my eyes my vision's gone back to normal, but there's still the slightest tremor in my hands, and my back feels like I'm a strung-up marionette. I continue my e-mail, only to be interrupted by a text chime.

Don't want to talk about it, is all Jocelyn writes.

It's like being sucker punched. I look down at my watch. I've been sitting on my ass for the past ten minutes, but my heart rate is 120. Another cramp hits then, as if someone's stuck a fork in my liver and twisted. For a moment I struggle to breathe through cement-filled lungs. It's been a long time, but I know what to do. I put my hands around my mouth and nose like a baffle and force my shoulders up and down, squeezing and releasing the muscles, willing them to relax.

Then, when I have a modicum of control over my body, I open up a new message and type slowly, reluctantly:

"Hi, Dr. Rifkin. Do you have any emergency slots this week?"

It turns out that Dr. Rifkin had a cancellation, so I slide into an open appointment at three thirty. Mr. Wu gives me permission to leave for a while after I promise to come back for the dinner rush. Jocelyn still hasn't woken up from her "nap."

When he opens his door to let me into his office, Dr. Rifkin has a gentle look of concern on his face. "I'm so glad I could get you in, Will."

Left unspoken is the fact that it's been years since I've called for an acute appointment. I'd been doing so well, in fact, that I'd cut down from weekly visits to twice a month, and now monthly. It just made more sense with how many commitments my parents had to juggle.

He leads me to the familiar couch, with its array of textured pillows. As always, I pull over the one covered in flip sequins, smoothing them down so they're all green then drawing patterns in them to change them over to their blue side. I stare at the pictures on the wall of Dr. Rifkin with his husband and their two kids. They had just adopted their oldest daughter when I started therapy. It is wild to think that she is in grade school now.

"So, how can I help you?" Dr. Rifkin asks.

Well, might as well go with the headline. "I almost had a panic attack today."

"Almost?" he asks.

"Well, not almost. I had one—the abdominal pain, the elevated heart rate. But I was able to control it with some relaxation techniques and mindful breathing. So it didn't...I didn't feel like I was going to die, or anything."

Listening to myself, I think: That's a pretty low bar.

Dr. Rifkin seems to agree, his forehead creased in concern. "Did you feel like you needed any medical attention?"

"No, not really. It was exactly the same symptoms I had before, and it went away within five minutes." My doctors always reinforced to me that panic attacks are almost never dangerous, no matter how frightening they feel.

"That's fabulous, Will. You've done an incredible job working on a lot of exercises and techniques to help you in this situation. I know that you know that, if this becomes recurrent, or if you have any new symptoms that you can't explain, you should call me or go to the ER..."

I'm nodding before he even finishes his sentence, because I've been to this rodeo before. The next thing he's going to do is offer pills.

"...and you know that if you ever get to the point where you don't feel like you can control your physical reactions," Dr. Rifkin says, right on schedule, "there are medications that might help to decrease the frequency of these attacks."

I nod, because God, I've wanted those meds before. There was a point in middle school when I could barely go a week without getting another panic attack, when I wanted nothing more than a pill I could take to make me able to step on a school bus without fear of hyperventilation.

My mother had been frank about her opinion. "Those drugs, William, they can be good, but they can also be very, very bad." She ticked off their evils on her fingers. "They can give you headaches, they can disturb sleep patterns, they can make you wish to harm yourself. Some of them can make you an addict." She didn't expressly forbid me to take them, though she warned me, completely unnecessarily: "You know that if you are thinking about taking drugs, you should not mention it to your nne nne or to your cousins, right? It's better to keep these things private."

In the end, I'd held off on the meds, and to this day I'm not sure if it was out of pride or because of my mother's warning.

"Thanks, Dr. Rifkin. I'm good for now."

He gives his usual nonjudgmental nod. "All right. Were there any triggers that you can think of for this most recent incident?"

The AC in Dr. Rifkin's office is on full blast, and it's nice when you first walk in from the August heat, but it creeps into a chill the longer I'm here. I look down at where I've tucked my hands in between my legs to keep them warm, and stretch my shoulders, preparing for the heavy lifting about to begin.

"I told you about my summer job at my last appointment, right?" He nods again. "Well, there's this girl...."

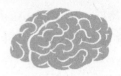

This Is My Brain, Powerless

JOCELYN

When I wake up to the pounding at my door, I look over at my alarm clock, see that it's four thirty, and almost go back to sleep. Then I see the little red dot lit up by the PM, and I realize it's my dad hollering something about how I need to come down now because Will had to leave for a doctor's appointment.

"All right, all right, I'm coming," I yell, not budging from my bed. Five minutes later the knocking starts again, and I can tell by the knock (softer, but regular like a metronome) that it's my mom, whose knocking is not to be denied. When I open the door, my mom looks me up and down, expressionless, before she motions to our bathroom. "Kuai yidian, shu tou, xi lian."

I look in the mirror, and I'm a living, breathing "Hangover" trope. My hair is a rat's nest, and the makeup I had put on is a ruddy, streaky mess from my post-interview cry. I'd made it up to my room feeling a calm numbness. I'd told myself that I was okay, that I wasn't going to freak out until the decision e-mails were sent out, and then my phone had buzzed, and it was Will, and he asked me if I was okay, and I realized with an ugly flash that, no, I was not okay.

And I'm still not.

After Will's text message I cried myself to sleep, wallowing in a freaking tsunami of disappointment and self-loathing. Now that I'm awake, as I survey the wreckage, I have no idea how to rebuild. I have no idea what to hope for anymore. I'm not going to be able to fulfill my dad's contract. And what then? Do I wait for college? Do I sneak behind my family's back (again)? Do I strike another bargain?

Or maybe I do nothing and accept the things that I cannot change, like that stupid motivational quote that every teacher posts on their wall that's supposed to be inspiration, but in the end just reminds you that you are, in the end, powerless over a lot of the things that matter most.

I grab a bar of soap and scrub all traces of my interview off my face, but there's nothing I can do about the slight puffiness around my eyes. I comb my hair, scrape it into a ponytail, and slink downstairs.

♡

It's a strange relief to get back to A-Plus, to the knowable repetition of taking phone calls, checking orders, and packing take-out bags so the containers don't spill in transit. At around six o'clock Will comes back.

"Hey. Something wrong?" I ask. There's a stiffness to his

walk, a flatness in his face. "My dad said you had a doctor's appointment."

"Nah, just a checkup." He rubs his wrist and doesn't meet my gaze. "Hey, can I help you with some of those orders?"

We work in silence. Even though part of me is grateful that he doesn't ask me about the interview, a bigger part wants to spill everything like a confession, as if he could pardon me for my ineptitude. Then, when Will leaves to make some deliveries and we still haven't said more than three sentences to each other in a row, a niggling voice in my head asks, *What if he doesn't even care if the interview went well?*

My mom goes into the kitchen once she's relieved of her chaperone duties, and once I'm alone my thoughts continue to degenerate. It's my fault Will's acting weird. He did ask me if I was okay, and I said I didn't want to talk about it. I know how sensitive he is, and I still blew him off. How did I think he would feel? Maybe he's finally seeing what a bitch I am.

The truth of it all cuts through me with a howling sort of pain, and my hand spasms over the plate I'm clearing. It's so obvious what he must be feeling: his coolness, the way he held back and couldn't look me in the eye, how quickly he volunteered to go on a delivery and leave me behind.

My throat closes up and my still-swollen eyes prickle again. I want to take the plate and do something dramatic with it, like smashing it into the ground only to collapse keening into the shards like the actresses in the Taiwanese soap operas my amah watches.

The door opens. A customer comes in. And I don't do anything, just swallow and say, "How may I help you?" like always.

That's not true: There's one thing I do for myself. After a few minutes, I call up and make Alan come to finish up my shift and close out the register. He whines, of course, but he comes down because he will owe me until the day he dies, and by the time Will comes back I'm safely in my bed upstairs, trying not to cry, and not succeeding.

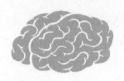

This Is My Brain, Helpless

WILL

The next day before I get to A-Plus Jocelyn sends me an e-mail telling me she'll be out most of the morning on a supply run, then going out right away to drop off one of our catering orders.

> Could you go through Priya's most recent footage from the restaurant and see if you can come up with an Instagram video or a YouTube channel idea?

When I reply, I say that I'm happy to do it, because of course I am. After that, though, I'm stumped. I think about adding, "I miss you." Or, "Are you avoiding me?" But I chicken out, because I'm almost certain that she is, and that my pushing her will only drive her away.

In my session with Dr. Rifkin yesterday, my story started with, "There's this girl," and ended with, "I think she has depression and I don't know what to do."

Dr. Rifkin responded with a question, the way he always does. "So how does that make you feel?"

Because we've been through this before, I started answering almost before he finished asking.

"I feel responsible," I blurted out, "like it's somehow my fault, that I pushed her to this point. I've been trying to, you know, get her to acknowledge her own feelings and maybe talk to someone, but it's like the blind leading the blind. How can I help her if I can barely get my own issues under control? I feel so helpless."

Dr. Rifkin hummed and nodded in the gentle low-key affirming way he always does, then asked, "Why do you feel responsible for Jocelyn's happiness?"

"Isn't that what the Little Prince said we should do?" I said, half joking, half not. Maybe "responsible" is the wrong word, but of course I want Jocelyn to be happy.

Dr. Rifkin took his own calming breath and shook his head. "You're talking about the line where he says you're responsible for the things you've tamed? That darn quote is the basis of more unhealthy relationships than I can count. It probably single-handedly paid off my graduate school debt."

"So, what you're saying is I'm being codependent?"

"I'm not the biggest believer of codependency as a negative trait, actually. As you know, I prefer to frame relationships in terms of attachment theory."

I've been working with Dr. Rifkin long enough to know what he's referring to. Essentially, attachment theory started with the study of the interactions between babies and their caretakers and then morphed into a way that psychologists can categorize relationships into four main styles of attachment: secure, anxious-preoccupied, dismissive-avoidant, and fearful-avoidant.

You can guess which one I tend toward the most.

I've always felt like it's unfair that there are three insecure types of attachments and only one secure one. It's as if the deck is stacked against us from the beginning.

Security is the anxious person's Holy Grail, and I'm no exception. What Dr. Rifkin's worked on with me for years is how to trick my brain so that I don't automatically respond to insecurity by overthinking things. He's taught me—well, if I'm honest, he's still teaching me—ways to establish closeness in the face of panic.

The journalist in me understands the idea that most brains are really, really prone to confirmation bias. My head is a veritable fake news factory: Hyperbolic statements of distress. Unconfirmed catastrophes. Thinly based assumptions that things are all about me.

So, every once in a while, I need someone to help me with some fact-checking. Someone to give my brain a Pinocchio rating of five so I can laugh for a bit and see things more clearly. There's only so much you can do in an hour, but yesterday Dr. Rifkin did help me sift out one central truth from the tangle of my emotions, which was that I can't fix Jocelyn, but I can support her. For today, that means giving her space and helping her family's restaurant.

It doesn't mean I can't miss her, though. As I go through Priya's footage I keep forgetting myself and looking over to where

Jocelyn usually sits to share each clip that grabs my attention. Without her, A-Plus is depressingly quiet except for her father's incessant throat clearing and the occasional phone call.

The sensation that I'm missing a part of myself takes me by surprise. I've always been an introvert, confirmed by every stupid internet permutation of a personality test I've ever taken. I'm a Ravenclaw. C-3PO. Ned Stark. Vision. I like my friends, they keep me grounded, but I've never been lonely when I'm not with them.

What I feel now, though, is more than just loneliness—it's a restlessness, an itchy desire to move from where I am, to find her, to be with her. I spend an hour looking through videos, and after each one, my default thought is to try to guess what Jocelyn would think about them.

It's become impossible for me not to see the world, at least partially, through her filter, so my favorite clips are the ones I know would also resonate the most with her. One is a single shot of her grandmother deveining shrimp with knife work that would make an assassin proud. Another is time-lapse video of the checkout counter over the course of a day that animates the literal dinner rush, making me appreciate the number of people we feed on a daily basis in a whole new way. But maybe my favorite one is a single moving shot Priya did where she circled around the staff sitting down for their evening meal long after the doors were locked. The camera pans fast enough that you get an almost dynamic sense of how much food is made and shared family style, but slow enough that you can see the fatigue in the slope of Mr. Wu's shoulders as he props his head up with his hand, in Miss Zhou's distant stare as she sucks the last threads of chicken off a bone. Not much is said during the meal, and it would be easy to watch the shot and find it depressing, but there's something about the way Priya frames it that captures how it's almost a sacred ritual, this last breaking of bread of the day.

I tag the best clips and, instead of just uploading them to our Facebook site, I share them with Jocelyn in an e-mail, just to make contact. Just to create an electronic link between the two of us, a digital lifeline to remind her of me. Maybe it's pathetic. Maybe it's exactly what she needs. I guess the fact that I only spend ten minutes freaking out about it is a sign that the thousands of dollars that my parents have spent on Dr. Rifkin haven't gone to waste.

This Is My Brain
on Edge

JOCELYN

After I leave my shift, I sleep for thirteen hours and am still exhausted when I wake up.

My room faces east, though, and I was too tired to draw my curtains when I fell into my sleep-wallow last night, so I drag myself out of bed just to get the sun out of my eyes, which are so filled with sleep grit that it hurts to squeeze them closed.

At first, I think the hole in my belly is left over from the yesterday's disappointment, but then my body growls like a disgruntled cat and I say, fine, I'll feed you. I didn't eat dinner last night, what with all the weeping. I grab a cover-up, lumber over, and crack my door open, listening. It's quiet enough that Alan's probably already on his way to summer school with one of my parents. Which just leaves the other one, and Amah.

Please let it be Dad's day to drive Alan, I think. I can't face him yet. Not that my mom will be much better, but our lives are too small to avoid them forever.

In the kitchen, I brush past my mother, who is already at the sink washing dishes, and make a beeline to the cabinet where we keep our cereal.

"Zao shang, Xiao Jia. Ni yao xifan ma?" My amah calls out from the kitchen table, gesturing at me with a bowl of rice porridge. Our kitchen table is crammed full of small plates with dried fish, salty egg, seaweed paste, fresh-cut scallions, rou song, and fried onions. I look at the cereal box in my hand and realize that I can't answer the most basic question about what I want to eat. I'm gripped by an inexplicable panic, like I'm going fifty miles an hour on a highway that's forking and I'm headed straight for the median because I can't figure out where my GPS wants me to go. It should not be terrifying to have to choose whether you want a hot meal or a cold one. And yet here I am.

Amah takes one look at me and wordlessly starts making me a bowl. I collapse into a chair, watching her swirl the porcelain spoon in the porridge to get just the right consistency, and for this one moment I am so grateful to be taken care of. So I watch Amah use a fork to scrape the salty egg into tiny flakes that don't overwhelm the other flavors; she skips the dried fish that I've hated since I was little and gives a generous dollop of the seaweed paste, a handful of scallion, and onion for texture.

Amah fumbles a bit putting the lid back on the jar of the seaweed paste. The lid's a little too wide, her fingers not quite nimble enough to manage the twist. Tears form in my eyes—again with the waterworks, dammit. I rub my face as if I'm trying to wake up, trying to hide how much the simple act of someone serving me food breaks me. As empty as I felt when I woke up suddenly I'm so full of conflicting emotion it's overwhelming. Love. Gratitude that there's someone, anyone, who knows me so well they can make me a congee without asking. A sudden stab of awareness that I don't know how many more breakfasts Amah will have with us.

Warm food was a good choice. I close my eyes and focus on the flavors mingling in my mouth, salty and neutral and a little bit sweet, and I pack away my feelings, one by one.

By the time my bowl is empty except for a little bit of rice water at the bottom, I'm almost steady. Controlled enough to actually go up and pull on the jeans I wore yesterday and a V-neck T-shirt lying at the foot of my bed. When I brush my hands through my hair and throw it in a ponytail it looks almost presentable.

Here I am, ready to face the world. Or something like that.

Before everything went to shit, my plan for the week had been to work with Will to post some of Priya's videos on Instagram or YouTube, maybe even try to brainstorm ways to spruce up our anemic Yelp page.

Now? That's not going to happen. The thought of spending all day sitting next to Will at a computer, even with a chaperone lurking in the background? It makes me light-headed, makes a muscle just under my breastbone clench. I would literally rather do anything than go downstairs and have him avoid my gaze, or worst of all, look through me again the way he did last night.

So I take the coward's way out and type up an e-mail, telling him that I am going to make some runs to new doctors' offices, and can he look through Priya's videos?

that if he sends me a message back right away, we're
takes a while, there's something wrong, and I'll have to
what he says to figure out where we stand. I can't envi-
world where he wouldn't respond—he's too fastidious,
an SAT word that I would never in a million years have
ght was remotely attractive in a boy. But somehow, on Will,
attention to detail doesn't seem picky or calculated. It seems
reful. It seems kind.

After I hit send, I go downstairs to put together some of our
samplers. When I'm done putting together the food and tossing
in our new catering brochure, I open my laptop and bite my lip
in disappointment when there aren't any new messages, even
though I know it's only been about ten minutes.

I grab my bike and hit the road at ten thirty. We're just hit-
ting the dog days of August, so the air is thick, and I break a
sweat within seconds. Maybe it wasn't a good idea to do this. I
should have just left the job to Will, who could drive around in
his air-conditioned zero-emissions car and show up all calm and
collected with his J.Crew attire and trustworthy attitude.

I push through anyway. Just as I turn onto Genesee Street,
my phone buzzes. At the next stoplight I pull it out. It's Will, and
a flood of relief pours through me even as part of me worries that
it took him twenty-five minutes to write back, which might not
sound like a big delay, but it is practically blowing someone off
in Will time. He almost always responds to e-mails right away,
unless they're something that he needs to think about, that he's
not sure of.

What if it's me he's not sure of?

His e-mail doesn't give me anything at all.

Happy to help. I'll start looking at the videos
right now. See you soon.

This is from someone who regularly sends me five-hundred-word texts that make my phone blow up because my texting app still insists on breaking messages into 140 characters.

An old pickup truck belches past me and I swing my leg back up to pedal grimly on. Every breath I take feels like I'm inhaling a furnace through a straw. What does he mean that he's happy to help? Is that some sort of passive-aggressive statement that's supposed to imply that I'm being demanding? And how is it that he still hasn't asked me how the interview went?

Maybe it's because he assumes that it didn't go well, a voice in my head suggests, and boy, does that thought have the sting of truth.

When I walk into the first office building, I chain up my bike and sigh with relief when I step into the blessed AC. There's a bathroom where I freshen up a bit so I look less like I've just ridden the Tour de France. As I turn on the faucet to rinse the street grime off my face, a woman with a Samsonite rolling bag and two-inch high heels clomps in. She has a name tag that IDs her as Brittany from East Coast Pharmaceuticals, and she is wearing a suit dress that shows off her perfectly toned calves. She doesn't have a drop of sweat on her but still dabs delicately at her face with a thin blotting paper before touching up her powder and relining her pouty lips.

Ugh, why do I even try.

So maybe I'm not in the most confident mood when I stop into the first office, an obstetric practice.

"Can I help you?" The woman behind the counter is a middle-aged white woman wearing a floral blouse with a matching cardigan, and she eyes me warily, maybe like I'm a bit young to be looking for a baby doctor.

"Hi, I'm Jocelyn Wu from A-Plus Chinese Garden," I say, rattling off the script that Will and I developed with as much conviction as I can muster. "We've just expanded our restaurant to include a catering menu, and I wanted to bring some sample dishes over to give you a sense of what we offer. We deliver every day of the week and have low-sodium, gluten-free, and low-carb options."

I put the bag on her counter, and she eyes it like it might be laced with anthrax.

"What's the catch?" she asks bluntly.

"Um, there's no catch."

"So you just go around giving free food? How do I know I'm not going to get food poisoning?"

I blink. If you think about it, I guess it's surprising that no one's ever asked this before?

"Well." It's a real head scratcher. Does this woman turn down the little bites of bourbon chicken on toothpicks they hand out in the Sangertown Food Court, too? More importantly, if someone believes in conspiracy theories, is there really anything you can say that will convince them otherwise? "Our restaurant is approved by the New York State Department of Health."

"What's in there again?"

"Some dumplings, egg rolls, fried rice, chicken with broccoli. And some cold cucumber salad, perfect for the hot weather."

The woman's nose wrinkles and her mouth twists into an honest-to-goodness scowl. "Chinese, then," she complains.

I'm ready to bolt but a younger woman wearing scrubs comes in. "Hi, Linda. I'm ready for the next chart." Her eyes go immediately to the bag on the counter. "What's this? Smells good."

"It's some sorta oriental food," Linda says, her tone still heavy with suspicion. "Apparently they cater now. She brought some samples."

"Well, that's lovely," says the younger woman. "Thank you very much."

I make a hasty exit.

The Latinx woman at the front desk of the next office I go to is a little more excited to get our package, and the office manager at the gastroenterologist's is so thrilled that he books a lunch next week. And yet, on the way back to the restaurant, I can't get rid of the sour feeling in my stomach. I can't stop seeing the disgust in Linda's face.

I know it's stupid, and I know I shouldn't take it personally. It's quite literally a matter of taste. But Linda's stank eye seemed bigger than that.

Back at the restaurant, it's the lunch rush, and my mom is scrambling in the kitchen, so even though I want to peek out front to see what Will meant by his "see you soon," I stay behind and work the deep fryer until the lunch specials finally taper off. By then my clothes are spattered with oil and my hair is matted with sweat, and my mom shoos me upstairs to take a shower.

When I come back down, Will has started to work with Alan already. They're huddled up in a booth but barely glance at me when I push through the kitchen doors. They're too busy staring at a trio of men who are huddled by the main entrance.

The three men are all blond. Two of them look to be in their forties and the third a little younger. They all have stocky builds and noses that are so similar I assume they're related.

One of the older men with a little more gray in his hair has his phone out and is taking pictures. Wide angle shots, held at waist level. The other one, I realize as my heart races, has a tape measure half-hidden by a beefy hand.

"Can I help you?" I ask. My voice sounds too loud for my ears. Too hard. Out of the corner of my eye I see Will start and turn toward me, but I can't turn away from these men. I don't want to give them any kind of opening.

The youngest blond saunters over to me first, left hand in his pocket, right hand reaching out to me. My lip curls as he gives me a lazy handshake. Forbes.com would not be impressed.

"Hey, you must work here," says Limp Noodle, flashing me a charming smile that raises my hackles even higher. "What can you tell me about the heating and cooling in here? Think you would mind showing us around the back so we can bang on the pipes a bit?"

"Excuse me? Would you like to place an order? We're a restaurant." I deliberately play dumb, because if I acknowledge what I know, that they're here to scope out the property because my landlord anticipates that my dad won't be able to make the lease, I'll either scream or cry, or both.

"Not for long," Tape Measure whispers under his breath.

"Shut up, Nate," Gray Hair snaps when he sees my stricken look. "I'm sorry, miss, that was uncalled for." He runs a broad palm over his face. "I'm Gary Brennan. My brothers and I were under the impression that this building was looking for new tenants. I apologize for the disruption if we were mistaken. We'll be leaving now."

They shuffle out, exchanging whispers that are too low for me to hear. In fact, I can hardly hear anything through the sound of blood rushing though my ears. For a minute everything whites out in panic.

Then I become aware that my brother is shaking me by the shoulder. "Jiejie, what's going on?" From the impatience in his voice I gather that it's not the first time he's asked.

"I have no idea," I mumble, turning my head so I don't have to face him, except now I'm looking at Will.

Will, whose mouth is pressed into a tight frown, whose dark eyes are filled with understanding.

It hurts, but I turn away from his pity. I don't look at either of them. They're not the ones who will have the answers.

"I'm gonna go find Dad," I croak out finally, though I'm pretty sure he won't have the answers I want, either.

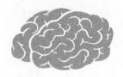

This Is My Brain, Trying

WILL

"Is that about...Is our landlord gonna kick us out?" Alan asks in the silence after Jocelyn leaves. There's a resignation to his tone that unsettles me. He's too young to be so weary.

"I'm not sure," I say. I'm too much in shock—a tape measure, for heaven's sake—to come up with anything more reassuring.

"I don't wanna move," he says, but he's not whining; it's more like he's stating a fact. "I've got friends, and now I'm getting better grades. I don't wanna have to start all over again. What if other schools don't do all the stuff you made them do for me?"

"If you get an IEP they would have to," I say. "It's the law."

Alan still looks skeptical, and I don't blame him. I've lived in the same house for all sixteen years of my life, and even the thought of leaving for college makes my throat tighten.

"Plus, it's not written in stone yet. We've been trying...." I shake my head, and it's like I knock loose my thoughts, because all of a sudden, the mental hand-wringing starts. How could I have been so complacent as to think that we were succeeding? I didn't try hard enough. I should have made more calls, more visits, really pounded the pavement as if my life depended on it. Because it did, my life with Jocelyn depended on it. And now it might all be ruined.

Stupid, stupid. I'm always so stupid.

Maybe their landlord could be convinced to make more favorable terms on the lease, or we could make a GoFundMe to cover the shortfall in rent. We could make the restaurant a co-op, like the Utica Bookstore did when it almost went under a year ago.

I need to call Rebecca Ross. Or, maybe, her boss.

"Do you know your landlord's name?" I ask Alan.

He screws up his face. "I think it starts with a 'B' and ends in an 'er'?"

"I'll ask your sister." If I ever get to talk to Jocelyn again, that is. I feel bereft. Panicky on her behalf. "Do you talk to her much?"

Alan gives me his "my tutor's really smart but also kind of a dumbass" look. "I talk to her every day."

"No, I mean...does she confide in you?"

Alan screws his face up. "You mean, *talk* talk?"

I nod.

"Not really. I'm her younger brother, not her BFF."

"Priya," I say. Of course. "That's who she confides in?"

"I guess." Alan shrugs. "My mom's always yelling at Jocelyn for spending too much time on the phone at night."

It's not that hard to do some investigative work. The restaurant and the apartment upstairs share the same line, and there were those two weeks when Jocelyn was grounded when she lost cell phone privileges, so I'm able to easily find a number that I assume is Priya's.

I actually type out what I'm going to say and practice it a couple of times into the voice-recording app on my computer. I can't risk underselling my argument—or overselling it, either.

After I finally key the number in, I flip my phone over four times vertically and three times horizontally before making the call.

Five seconds in, five seconds out.

With each ring, my lungs feel tighter, even as I berate myself. This is ridiculous. Priya's cool. But she's also Jocelyn's best friend. What did Jocelyn tell Priya about me? I check my watch. Pulse: 125.

"Hello?" Her voice has that expansive sound, as if she's outside. I can hear the staticky blow of her breaths. I figure she's walking somewhere.

"Priya, this is Will. You remember, from the Boilermaker? I'm calling because I'm worried about Jocelyn."

"Um, hold on for a second." The sound is muffled for a moment, and there's the sound of walking as if she's pulling herself away from a group. "How so?"

"Has she seemed different to you in the past few weeks?"

"A little stressed, maybe. There's a lot going on with the restaurant, with her application...." Her sentence trails off a little, and I wonder if she's holding off from adding on, "with you."

I take a shuddery breath. "I don't know. I feel like she's not eating as well, and I know she's always tired. And she doesn't seem as interested in things she used to enjoy."

Priya hums. All of a sudden, I want to take everything back. It feels presumptive to suggest that I've known her long enough to know what she's always enjoyed. "Do you think she's been down lately?" I ask, doing that thing that my sister hates, using euphemisms for sadness. "Just say depressed," Grace would say. "Ask if she's depressed."

There's a moment of silence as Priya thinks. "It's hard to tell. I mean, yeah, that's just the type of person she is. Melancholic, you know? Sarcastic, gallows humor. I wouldn't trust her so much if she didn't always see the worst in people."

"That's funny," I say, trying to fit this in with the small interactions I had with Priya. "You seemed really positive at the Expo?"

"Meh, that's different. I can be positive for other people. So can Jocelyn, at least for the people she really cares about."

I nod to myself, then forget that Priya can't see me. "Yeah, she's hardest on herself. Sometimes I just wish she'd cut herself a break."

Grace's voice in my head whispers, *Pot, kettle.*

"I guess I haven't seen her quite as much with how busy the restaurant's been," Priya admits reluctantly. Her voices tinges with concern. "You definitely see her more than I do. So you really think she's depressed?"

"I don't know, I can't be one hundred percent sure...." Despite everything, when confronted by the word, my instinct is to pull back. Hedge, and protect Jocelyn from the baggage that label brings. "I just want it to be on your radar, that's all. Because the way that she's been acting since the interview, it doesn't seem like it went that well."

Priya swears under her breath. Suddenly, I feel like a jerk, dragging her into all this. Now I've got her worried, too. I need to shift gears.

"So the reason I called was, I was trying to think of things we could do together to maybe cheer Jocelyn up a bit. She showed me some of your video clips, I think there's a lot of potential for a longer piece, something to put on the A-Plus website and Yelp page, maybe even Facebook. But I don't have the greatest video-editing software."

"Anything you think will help. I'll try to give her a call, too. I haven't heard from her since yesterday. My family's going away this weekend, but I'm free to tool around with the video tonight if you want."

"Sure, I can come after I close up the restaurant. Do you want to meet at a café or something?"

"Well, my best editing software is desktop based," she explains. "Do you mind coming to my house?"

Priya gives me her address, and I tell her I'll forward the e-mail I sent Jocelyn with the clips I thought were most promising. For the first time all day, I don't feel like I'm sliding slowly down a steep cliff. I've found purchase. I'm barely holding on, but I have a plan.

Jocelyn never comes back after going off to find her father. The last contact I had with her was a terse response to my e-mail, sent right after she left.

Thanks. I'll look over them tomorrow.

It's not what I want, but it's a lifeline. I swear to myself that I won't let it go.

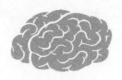

This Is My Brain on Rage

JOCELYN

My dad is on the toilet when I find him, and I don't care if it's his safe space, or his only time to sit down and be alone all day. I bang on the door until my palm is a raw pink and my dad opens up with a shout. "Xiao Jia, ni ganshenme?"

On the sink behind him is the most recent *World Journal*, his usual bathroom reading. It's been folded so the classified section is on top (who even reads paper newspapers anymore?) with the most prominent listings circled with a blue ballpoint pen. For some reason the sight of it (was he looking through it to try to find new jobs in New York or other restaurants in different towns to buy?) puts me over the edge. The whole last-ditch effort to save A-Plus was a lie. We had no chance.

"Did you know?" I demand, already almost breathless with anger. "Why didn't you tell me Berger was kicking us out? He already has someone ready to sign a new lease. There were people in here just now taking pictures, ready to freaking tear out the pipes." I make a ripping motion with my hands and my dad flinches away.

Just like that, all my dad's puffed-up indignation deflates. He sighs and rubs his hand over his face. For a moment as he pulls the skin on his cheeks down, the bags under his eyes disappear, then when his hands fall away, they're back, gray hollows making his eyes look sunken, creases and folds in his skin that are too deep and permanent to be laugh lines.

"Lease expire at end of month," my dad admits finally. "Berger say we can go month to month until he find another tenant, but he just tell me today that he find someone who want to sign."

I stagger with the weight of the news, can feel it pressing into my chest, hard and immovable. I grab at the doorframe to keep myself upright.

"What, then. Is that it?" I croak.

Dad shrugs, and I want to punch the passiveness out of him. "Berger give us until Friday to decide. But he want us to sign two-year lease."

A two-year lease. That'll take me through high school, up to my leaving for college. If I can even afford it.

"Is that even legal?"

"It his property, he do anything he want."

"How much does it cost to break the lease again?"

"Ten thousand," my dad says grimly.

"Jesus," I groan. That's practically two months' profit. I slide down the wall and sit with my legs out, hands in between my knees. "But I thought we were doing better."

"We are, Xiao Jia. Ni shuo duile," my dad says. Then he sighs again and waves me out of the hallway. "Wo xi shou, zai jianghua." I haul myself out as my dad washes his hands, and I walk back to the kitchen table. My dad's laptop is there, along with a mess of papers.

"You do good, Xiao Jia." My eyes prickle even as I think, *Not good enough.* "Things much better. This July we make maybe ten percent profit. But June, July, August, they best month of year. Winter months, not so good. And January, *ppft*. Fangpi." He makes a farting sound, and I let out a mirthless laugh.

"We can still do better," I insist. "The catering business is just getting off the ground, and there are still plenty of ideas for outreach, plus I haven't really had time to look into how we can streamline operations better...."

My dad starts shaking his head halfway through my speech and cuts in. "Xiao Jia, ni tai stressed. Tai overworked. In one month you need focus on school work again. This most important year, that what your counselor say. We need focus on your future. That why we need to move."

I can only gape at my father, because he isn't making any sense. "Are you kidding me? My future's here. It's not in the city anymore. You can't yell at me for not caring about the restaurant, then turn around and tell me that we need to move because I'm working too hard to save it."

My dad's face hardens, and he shifts like he's planting his feet in the ground. "We do what best for you."

And it's like he's pushed the lever to put me into hyperdrive, because, just like that, all the complicated emotions that I've stuffed away mix together and combust.

"Excuse me?" My voice rises, and I drink in the sense of danger that I feel whenever I yell at my parents. I know I'm playing with fire. "Can I have a say in what's best for me? You can't say that you're moving for me, then get mad at me when I don't want to do it."

I can see the blood rush to my dad's face, turning it a splotchy pink. "Wo shi ni de baba. I know what best for you." He's yelling now, too, his voice deep and dark, that tone he gets when he tries to play alpha male. It makes me want to laugh. He's an omega if I ever met one.

"You know nothing about me or what I want," I spit out. "Have you ever once asked me what I want to be when I grow up? All you know is your own shitty life, and your own shitty ambitions. Do you think it's Alan's and my dream to run ourselves into the ground managing a crappy Chinese restaurant in Podunk, New York?"

My dad reels back and raises his hand, and for a split second I'm sure that he's going to hit me. I brace for the blow, then actually lean toward my dad, daring him to do it. I can already taste the blood on my lip, am ravenous for it, it's going to be so satisfying....

"Shenme gaode?" Suddenly my amah is standing in the doorway leading up from the kitchen. She's wearing gray pajama pants, a short-sleeved silk top, and an expression of such bewilderment that I feel my anger shrivel up in shame.

Amah clutches at her chest, wrinkling her blouse with a liver-spotted hand, and a panicked hysteria bubbles through me. This is the moment. This is that tropey TV climax where the beloved grandparent walks into an "End of the World" argument and has a heart attack that leads to a swift reconciliation.

Slowly, my father drops his hand. Amah lets go of her blouse, sighing heavily but still breathing.

For a moment there's absolute silence, except for the sound of pots clanging downstairs.

"Xiao Jia," my dad says quietly. "Qu nide fangjian."

I go to my room.

I sit on my bed for a long time before I feel anything. The hollowness is back, and I pick at a scab on my leg, then use my fingernails to worry at some ingrown hairs on my knee.

At first, I wish I could cry. I wish I could feel sadness, a sense of loss, but I'm still numb. I wish I could rage at my dad, or Mr. Berger, or whatever schmuck started A-Plus in the first place, but it doesn't make sense to scream into the void. No one cares, anyway.

My phone pings—I left it up here in my book bag after I got home from my errands. It's a message from the college.

The subject line reads: "Congratulations."

For one moment, I feel hope. It's like a Disney movie where the clouds part and rays of sun shine down on Bambi in a forest, and treble voices trill, giving you reassurance that everything will be okay. The Mouse House will provide a happy ending.

With my heart pounding, I open the e-mail.

Dear Ms. Wu,
Congratulations! The trustees of University of Utica are thrilled to accept you to our Junior Business Program. We had many superb applicants, and we believe that you are uniquely qualified to benefit from everything our program has to offer.

> Unfortunately, we are not able to offer you
> a scholarship at this time, but our office
> of financial aid has several loan assistance
> programs. . . .

I can't read any further. The pit in my belly has opened up again, a vortex too powerful to escape. A voice in my head whispers a reminder that I never wanted to do the program in the first place.

I delete the "acceptance."

After I send the college's congratulations to the trash bin, I immediately notice another one below that Will must have sent earlier in the day. Because I can't catch a break.

I almost delete his e-mail, too. Because what's the point? But there's still a sliver of longing that's resisting the undertow, a part that can't bear to let Will go even when it seems to make sense to cut bait.

So I open it.

Ever the honors student, he's turned his homework in early and even sent Dropbox links to a few of his favorite videos. It's a short message, but every word seems to sharpen my loneliness.

> There's some amazing stuff here. Priya's
> really talented! Some of my favorites are
> linked below. We should definitely try to make
> a video. Call me when you want to discuss?

When I hit reply to thank him for sending, I don't have the heart to tell him that it's probably not going to matter, that my contract is null and void because I fouled up my interview. And even if I'd aced it, it wouldn't matter anyway. Because…three days. I have three days to change my father's mind about renewing the lease before Limp Noodle and his brothers come in and turn the place into a juice bar, or whatever kind of trendy thing they think will make them money.

Or maybe I should just give up.

I close my eyes and try to imagine what it would be like to fail. Would it be a relief to close A-Plus's doors for the last time? Wouldn't it be amazing to move to an apartment that doesn't perpetually reek of sesame oil and garlic? What if Will decides to go to college wherever we end up. Maybe that will be our happy ending? I'd have to say good-bye to Priya, but she'd go on with her life. She has other friends. Jin-Jin and Miss Zhou would need to find new jobs. It would suck for Alan for a bit, but he's always been adaptable. He is good at letting things slide off his back. Better than I am.

And me, I only have two years left before I graduate, anyway. I can do anything for two years.

Right?

My wall AC unit kicks on and a blast of cold air sends me burrowing under my covers. I curl into a ball and let myself drift off. My family will wake me up if they need me.

True to form, Alan comes knocking on my door just before five.

"What'd you say to Dad?" he asks me, kind of awestricken. "He is pissed."

"I didn't tell him anything he didn't already know," I say, brushing past Alan to go downstairs. Like last night, I stay in the kitchen to avoid Will up front. The times he does come back to ask about an order, I duck into the storage rooms or under the prep station to get one of the pots we store underneath.

Tuesdays aren't particularly busy nights at A-Plus usually, but tonight we're hopping. Seeing our team cook, churning through order after order, it's like watching someone bailing out a ship that's sprung a leak. There's just no end.

I help out with cleanup just enough to not look like a slacker and then plead stomach cramps and retreat to my room. I can't face my family even as I'm antsy enough to finally talk to someone. But when I call Priya her voice mail picks up after just a few rings. Did she really swipe me off? A couple of seconds later a text comes through:

cant talk rn, call you in 30?

I surf around a bit on the net, typing in searches like, "how can I break my lease," and "legal to require two-year lease," but nothing's all that helpful. I bring up Will's contact on my phone, and my finger hovers over his name for a moment, but I don't hit the green button.

After about fifteen minutes I remember the bits of equipment that Priya left behind after our last shoot. Maybe I could drop her stuff off and talk to her IRL. Kill two birds with one stone. I need to get out of the house.

Alan is in his room playing a video game, and my parents are finishing up downstairs. It's not that long before Amah takes a bathroom break that allows me to slip out the back door.

It's a quick ten-minute bike ride to Priya's house. It's past rush hour, so the roads are clear, and it's just about dusk so things are cooling down to bearable levels. I'm hardly sweating when I pull up to their development.

I skid to a halt when I reach their driveway, because Will's Nissan Leaf is in it.

"What the…" I can only think of two reasons for him to be here: (1) He's following up on his task for today (if so, then why didn't he mention this in his e-mail?), or (2) They're talking about me (if so, then why didn't she mention this in her text?).

I don't bother locking up my bike. No one would steal that piece of crap in this neighborhood. I let it drop onto the Venkatrams' lawn and go to their front porch to peer in the decorated glass bordering their giant oak door. I don't see anyone sitting in their living room, so I hop down to a side window. No one in their den, either, or in their kitchen.

Priya's bedroom is on the second floor on the other side of the building, and when I look up I can see the curtains are pulled tightly shut, but there's a sliver of light shining through.

I realize I'm shaking. There's a throbbing starting to develop in my right temple. I don't know what to do. Do I call them so they can ignore me? Do I make like a psycho and throw rocks at Priya's window? Do I just run away? Do I just give up on everything?

I lean over to pick up a pebble from the ground, weigh it in my hand. But who am I kidding? I have terrible aim. I'm about to turn tail and just leave when my eyes catch on movement in the window just below Priya's room. It's her father's office, but sometimes she does work there, too. My heart leaps. Maybe my first theory was true.

I creep in closer and see that the two of them are both at the main desk, but they're not looking at the screen. They're looking at each other, bodies angled close enough together that they look like conspirators. Will's back is facing me, so I can only see the hint of his profile, but I can tell from the curve of his cheek that he's smiling. And Priya? She's glowing and blushing in a way I've never seen her look when a boy's involved.

I think back to Will's e-mail. That little exclamation point after "Priya's really talented!" And the big question mark after "Call me when you want to discuss?" And then I imagine walking back to my bike, forgetting to put my bicycle lights on, and taking the main roads back to A-Plus. Maybe when I crossed one of the more minor intersections, one without stoplights, someone would run a stop sign and there'd be an accident. A shiver runs through me at how delicious this sounds, what a relief.

I wonder if Priya would still put together my tribute video when I died. Maybe Will would write my obituary, maybe my death would tear them apart? Or maybe it'd drive them closer. With my luck, I'd die and everyone would just end up happier.

Well, misery loves company.

Before I know it, I'm hammering on the window to the Venkatrams' office with the pebble I picked up from the ground. At the sound, Priya and Will jump back from each other, heads swiveling to the window. Will is wide-eyed, terrified, like the day when my dad caught us parked in his car. Priya looks startled at first, then relieved, but then oddly guilty. And that look of guilt? It sets off a jealous righteousness like it's the freaking Olympic flame.

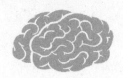

This Is My Brain on Panic

WILL

Priya's house, it turns out, is in the same development as Tim's, so I get a weird sense of déjà vu when I walk in. The place has the exact same layout, except it's inverted, so the office she takes me to is facing south instead of north.

"I think it's really special, what you did," I tell her as she pulls an extra chair up to the office desk. "It's clear how much love you have for the Wus, and the food they cook."

Priya smiles and busies herself with pulling out some sheets of printer paper to sketch a storyboard on. "What can I say? Jos is my bestie." She fidgets with a pen for a while, leans forward until she's close enough that I can see the flecks in the iridescent blue eyeshadow she's wearing, blinks, then leans back again like she was repelled by a magnetic field. "So, what is it that you wanted to do with this video?"

"I've been thinking a lot about what the A-Plus brand is. It's a different place to eat than, say, a Panda Express at a food court. Of course, it's not going to be fancy Chinatown dim sum, either. That's a different thing entirely, not that most of the people here in Utica are that familiar with that. A-Plus isn't quite 'Authentic' with a capital 'A,' but it's real food made by real people, like Jocelyn's grandmother, who loves to cook. What I'm hoping viewers will see in this video is the sense of family that you get in the restaurant. That love. I mean, that single shot you took of everyone sitting around after the day, eating? Wow."

As I talk, Priya stares at me with an intensity that has me worrying if I have something on my face, but she smiles when I mention the tracking shot, and blushes. "Jocelyn didn't tell me you were a film nerd, too."

"Oh, God, I'm totally not. I just remember her pointing out that technique in something we watched together. She says I watch too many superhero movies and is trying to reeducate me," I explain. "Anyway, what I'm trying to do is make the viewer love A-Plus as much as we do."

"So, I'm not sure if this is what you had in mind, but I put something together really quickly using the vids you sent me." She clicks on a new file, which opens up into a longer video that she's cobbled together with some music in the background. Except the music isn't at 100 percent volume, so you can still hear the sounds of the restaurant. It's amazing.

"That's fantastic!" I say, and I'm so excited I lean over to cover Priya's hand with my own. Priya beams. "What you did with the overlay and the cuts is exactly what I—"

And then another déjà vu moment:

Crack

I'm sure it's a gunshot at first and break away from Priya. It takes just a fraction of a second for a vise to close around my chest, and the world closes around me.

CrackCrackCrack

The sound is too close, and I realize it's someone pounding on the Venkatrams' window with something hard, like a rock. My hands are already up, the gesture automatic. Because if my mother has told me once, she's told me a thousand times: Always remember to show my hands.

Then my eyes focus on the figure outside—it's dusk, so it takes a second to parse out the person's features from the reflection of what's inside.

"Jocelyn?" Priya calls out, squinting.

After a second, I can see it, but I can understand why it took me so long to figure it out. Because it's Jocelyn like I've never seen her before: mouth twisted downward, eyes pinched as if in pain, forehead knotted up as if she's going to cry.

Vaguely, I'm aware of my watch buzzing, warning me that my heart rate is elevated.

Five seconds in, five seconds out.

That's about how long it takes for Priya to drag Jocelyn in through their side door, and it's not enough time. I'm still a hyperventilating yard sale, a fully activated fight-or-flight system at your service.

"Hey, are you okay?" Priya is saying to Jocelyn. Priya's got her hand out, as if to steady her, but Jocelyn shies away and ignores her question. Instead, she turns to me, and I greet her with joy the way I always do, but then feel my smile crumbling when she doesn't smile back.

"What are you doing here?" she asks, her voice like a slap.

"We're just going over some of the footage. I...I had some ideas for a video to put on the website. Kind of like a trailer."

Jocelyn's face curls in on itself even more. "You guys didn't even bother looping me in?" Her voice breaks at the end of the sentence, and the disappointment there triggers my Mayday response.

"Well, you...you seemed busy," I stutter. "Preoccupied."

"How would you know? You haven't even seen me for more than ten seconds in the past two days." It comes out like an accusation, and the way my mind works, of course I grind myself down with what I must have done wrong. I should have reached out. I was wrong to give her space. If I had been real boyfriend material, I wouldn't have let her push me away.

"But that's okay," she continues. "I understand. After all, Priya is so talented and I'm such a loser." The words are meant as a sneer but the pain behind them is so obvious, they don't have an edge.

"Hey. Hey, Jos, don't do this," Priya interjects gently.

"Do what?"

"That thing you do..." Jocelyn stiffens and Priya stops herself, tries again. I can almost see the years of friendship weighing the conversation down, making every word, every inflection mean more than I can comprehend. "Don't put yourself down like that."

If anything, it makes Jocelyn angrier. "Oh, so now you're my

314

life coach again? Is the Great Priya Venkatram going to tell me how to dig out of my shithole of a life?" She turns on me. "Is that why you're here, Will? To get some free therapy?"

She's needling me, but she should know better than that. No one's going to hurt me anymore by suggesting I need counseling. "Nah, Priya invited me here because that's where all her editing software is...."

Jocelyn turns back to Priya, a look of disbelief on her face.

"You have got to be fucking kidding me. You used your line?"

Priya blushes. "I told you, it's not a line," she protests. "It's totally legit....My laptop is, like, so slow when it runs those programs."

Jocelyn rolls her eyes. "So you put on some makeup, bring your prey into a room with mood lighting...." She gestures to the dark wood paneling and low-watt lamps, and then her expression contorts. "Well, if that's the best game you've got, I guess I shouldn't get too worried. It's not like it's ever worked before."

The shot's not directed at me, but I feel the hit anyway. Jocelyn's always been sarcastic, but this is the first time I've ever seen her be truly cruel. I don't expect it to be so devastating being on the opposite side of the court from Jocelyn, staring down her serve.

I so do not want to play this tournament, and I signal this by making a feeble attempt at the universal stop sign. "Hey, guys, I think everyone should just take a step back and calm down." I turn to Jocelyn. "I get that you're upset that we didn't tell you we were meeting, but..." I can think of all the different ways to phrase what comes next: You're overreacting. You shouldn't make a mountain out of a molehill. We meant well.

Everything that first comes to mind makes her seem like the

unreasonable one (*But she is*, an unhelpful voice in my head supplies), and even I'm not such a kamikaze conversationalist that I keep flying in that direction.

Jocelyn, on the other hand.

"What, Will?" she challenges. "But what?"

Since I started working at A-Plus, and, obviously, since we kissed, Jocelyn and I have shared a lot of glances. Every one of them has been almost as good as a touch—okay, maybe not quite as good—in the way they set my nerves tingling with amusement, or warmth, or just plain joy. The way she's looking at me now, though...If she were a bird, she'd be the kind that ate her own eggs.

I move to rub my wrist and realize that my palms are clammy with sweat. My watch buzzes again, and I swipe it silent without looking.

"You look nervous, Will," Jocelyn says, piercing me with those cannibalistic bird eyes. "Do you have something to be anxious about?"

I'm trapped. If I tell Jocelyn what I really think, she'll go off the handle. But if I hedge she'll think I'm hiding something. I swallow once, twice, three times and lick my lips, hoping that if I do, the words will come.

Finally, Priya takes pity on me and jumps in. "Jos, why are you being so mean?"

Something feral blazes in Jocelyn's eyes, and she turns on Priya. "Just use the word you want to use. Just say it. Ask me why I'm being such a bitch."

"Okay, you asked for it." Priya's voice gets shriller. "Stop being such a bitch. Will was just trying to make a good video for your restaurant."

"And of course you had to be all altruistic and help, right? The perfect excuse to move in on my boyfriend…"

What? No. That couldn't be. I swivel my head to Priya, and she looks pissed.

My watch buzzes again, twice, and I barely register it. I'm too busy thinking back to how I was surprised that she was wearing makeup on a Tuesday night, when I'd never noticed it on her before. Then there was how she pulled my chair so closely next to hers that I had to adjust them so we were farther apart.

How could I be so stupid? Is this all my fault?

My breath is coming in short gasps. I try to count, but my lungs won't pull air. One, two, three, and I'm suddenly wheezing, choking on acid.

The world tunnels, grays out at the edges. I can feel my chest fluttering, trying so hard to deliver that oxygen, but failing, falling short the way everything…

"Will? Wait, what's wrong?" Priya's facing me so she's the first one to see me flailing for the desk when my knees buckle. As the room spins around me, Jocelyn turns, too, and I feel the vertigo thick and dark in my throat as her scowl morphs into something more uncertain, then melts into fear.

There's a roaring hiss in my ears, and I hear her words as if from a distance. "Oh my God. Will, are you okay?"

I can't feel my fingertips anymore. Everything is sepia toned and creeping darker, but there's no helping it: I gasp out a laugh. And my last thought before I pass out is, isn't it obvious that I'm the furthest I could possibly be from being okay?

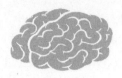

This Is My Brain on Guilt

JOCELYN

Will doesn't so much faint as crumble onto the Venkatrams' rug. The fall is slow enough that I catch his head before he hits the ground, and my first thought is, *This is the first time I've touched him in weeks*. I'd forgotten the texture of his hair, the smoothness of his skin.

"Dad! Help!" Priya's shout, though, brings me back to reality pretty quick.

I just broke Will.

For a moment I just sit there with my hands cradling his head and think about how I've never understood how heavy a person's head is. It just seems so easy for the neck to hold it up, but it's only when a person's passed out on your supposed best friend's dad's office floor that you realize that it's basically a bowling ball held up by a lollipop stick.

Meanwhile, Priya's freaking out for the both of us. "Oh my God. Oh my God. I got a first aid badge in Girl Scouts, but I don't remember what we're supposed to do? Do we do chest compressions first? Or mouth breaths?"

"He's still breathing," I say, still numb. "I think the first thing we're supposed to do is call 911." Maybe the thing that strikes the most fear in me is how lax Will's face is, erased of any expression. While Priya calls for help from the landline in her dad's office, I can't stop myself. I take his hand in mine and fumble at his wrist until I find his pulse, closing my eyes when I finally feel it, steady and firm.

"I'm so sorry," I whisper. Then I turn to Priya, who's still giving out directions to the ambulance. "I'm so sorry, Pri," I tell her.

She doesn't respond, just puts the phone receiver to her chest. "They say to lay him on his back and raise his legs. Loosen any constrictive clothing." She listens to the dispatcher again. "No, he's not bleeding," she says. "Oh, hey, he's waking up."

I turn back to Will, and his eyes are blinking open and closed, deliberate, like he's checking to make sure the muscles still work. They're unfocused, blank. Then, in a heartbeat, he gives a start, his gaze sharpens into terror, and he turns his head, eyes darting, scanning the room and trying to place his surroundings.

"Hey, Will. It's okay. It's Jocelyn. I'm here. We're in Priya's house. There's an ambulance coming."

"What?" He gasps and struggles to sit up. "No, I'm fine. You don't need to do that."

"Will, you just passed out," Priya says severely. "I swear to God there were, like, ten seconds where you weren't even

319

breathing. They're on the way. Give me your parents' number so I can tell them to meet us at the hospital."

"No!" Will scrunches his face, as if to reset it. "I'm fine, guys, I'm breathing just fine. Look, my lungs are great." He takes in a huge breath, puffing his mouth out like a fish, and lets it out. "Panic attacks aren't actually life-threatening," he says, sounding like he's reciting something from a book.

When the EMTs come in, they find that his heart rate is okay but say that he still needs to be checked out by a doctor. They cart him out in a wheelchair even though he insists that he can walk out by himself, and they tell us that we can meet him at St. Luke's if we want.

"I can drive you both," Mr. Venkatram offers. Priya ran for him just after she got off the phone with 911, and he was the one who ultimately contacted Will's dad. He asked me if he should call my family, too, and I said no. They're used to me sulking in my room and probably won't even notice I'm gone.

We pile into the Venkatrams' Ford Explorer, Priya taking shotgun, leaving me alone in the back seat like a kid who's been told to sit in the corner and think about what they've done.

Let me tell you, my head isn't the most inviting place in the world right now.

All the life-and-death, having-to-call-911 shit hit the reset button on my anger, which is great in that, yay, no more feeling like I'm Hulking out on my supposed boo and BFF, but also bad because once the fury's gone, all that's left is guilt and pain and me wanting to hit myself on the head, repeatedly. Seriously, spying on my best friend and boyfriend and assuming that they're cheating on me? It's not like they were kissing or anything.

Up in the front seat, Mr. Venkatram's grilling Priya for details.

"What did you say was going on when he fainted?"

"We were just looking over some video footage."

"Maybe he had a seizure or something."

Priya just hums, and my stomach prickles with guilt over what she's not saying, over what she's hiding for me. I don't deserve her. I don't deserve Will.

When we get to the emergency room there are four people waiting in line just to check in. Mr. Venkatram waves us over to where there are two empty seats in the almost-full waiting room. "You guys sit. I'll go find out where Will is and when we can go see him. Then maybe I'll go get some coffee. It might be a long night."

Priya and I trudge over and squeeze ourselves in between an elderly man who's been there for so long that he's fallen asleep and a woman with a lethargic toddler draped over her shoulder.

We sit in silence for a while. The automatic door to the ER opens twice, and I catch a glimpse of stretchers and people milling around in scrubs and white coats. The TV in the waiting room is on CNN and I lose myself in the scrolling captions. More forest fires in California. Gridlock in Washington. The follow-up to a college admissions scandal. I try to numb myself with other people's problems, but it doesn't quite work.

The AC is jacked up to high, and I twist my hands together, trying to rub in some warmth. When I glance over at Priya, she's scanning the room, and I would bet a million bucks that she's making up backstories in her head, casting the people in the waiting room as characters in her Great American Movie.

"What do you think?" I whisper, jutting my chin out in the direction of a man with a bloody rag tied around his hand. He's wearing work boots that are chalky with dust. "Handyman who was sleeping with his client. Attacked with a chef's knife when her husband walked in on them doing the nasty on the kitchen counter?"

Priya huffs, and her mouth twists into a not-smile. "Have you got cheating on the brain, or what?"

I look at my hands and wish I could just disappear, but there's no running from this. I bite my lip and sigh. "I'm sorry things got out of hand. I wasn't...like, clearly I wasn't thinking. My brain was like that old Keanu Reeves movie, what was it, the one you made me watch where he's on a runaway bus that will explode if it goes under fifty miles an hour?"

"*Speed*. AFI Thrills list."

"Yeah, that one.

"That's what it felt like. Completely out of control. Like, if I stopped to, I don't know, work things out, I'd explode with jealousy."

Priya bites at her fingernails, searching my face. She sucks her cheeks in like she's just tasted a lemon. "Well, as you so kindly noted, it's not like there's much for you to be jealous about," she says bitterly.

And oh, I feel sick to my stomach when I remember the things I said to her. They were like targeted missiles directed straight at her worst insecurities.

I am such a shit friend.

"Pri, you know that was all BS....That was just the crazy speaking. You know I'm crazy, right?" I say it like it's a joke, a parody of the way people say that they're "reclaiming" the words "crazy," "insane," and "bonkers." I say it like it's the most central truth of my life. It's the first time I've even hinted that I might suffer from mental illness.

"That's not an excuse," she says sharply enough that I feel it in my gut. "You can't say stuff like that to people, then apologize and expect them to forgive you right away."

"I know." My voice comes out wheezy now, because my throat is closing up. I feel that all-too-familiar pressure in my sinuses that means I'm going to cry.

Yet another thing I can't control.

"Pri, I don't know what's wrong with me," I say with a gasp. The waiting room blurs, and I sniff loudly in a valiant attempt to stop the snot dripping down my right nostril. I fail and have to stand up to grab a tissue from the hand-sanitizing stand by the reception counter. My nose blowing startles the little girl in her mother's arms and she starts to whimper.

"I'm so sorry, ma'am," I hiccup as the woman stands up.

"Don't apologize! Take care of yourself," she says, and turns to make a rotation around the room, bouncing the girl up and down to soothe her.

Somehow, that little kernel of forgiveness calms me down. It only ends up being a three-tissue cry.

Once I'm all cleaned up I draw in a shaky breath. "I don't know why I'm so fucking insecure all the time."

Priya doesn't laugh, or say, "Me neither." Her silence is worse than that.

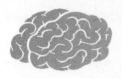

This Is My Brain on Recovery

WILL

I've only been at the hospital for five minutes when my mom makes her entrance. I, and probably everyone in the ER, can hear the moment she walks through the door. Her voice cuts through all the background noise like a hot knife through butter. Sometimes I think she missed her calling as the female James Earl Jones.

"Hello, I am Dr. Ogonna, ob-gyn. I would like to know what room my son, William Domenici, is in. Sixteen-year-old male here for syncope. Oh, hello, Eric."

If I strain, I can hear a male voice mumbling something about lab tests. I barely wince when the nurse putting in my IV knots a tourniquet around my arm, but I have to steel my expression when my thin privacy curtain parts and my mom strides in.

"Oh, thanks be to God, William." She comes immediately

to my side and whispers a silent prayer before touching her forehead against mine.

As it always does, my mom's presence fills the enclosed space. It's not that she's that big of a woman, although she's not tiny, either; it's that she carries so much kinetic energy within her that everyone else seems slower and less significant.

She glances up at the monitor and nods. "I was so afraid when that man called. What was his name? Venkatram? He said something about you losing consciousness." The questions keep coming before I even have time to answer. "Tell me what happened. Were you inside or outside? Was it the heat? Have you been drinking two liters a day like I told you? Did you have a seizure?"

The entire ambulance ride, I tried to get my story straight. I wasn't planning on lying, exactly—I'm a journalist. I'll give my mom the facts and make her fill things in. So I tell her that I'd had a long day at work, and then I'd gone straight over to Priya's to do some video-editing work. The girls had gotten into an argument, and I'd started to feel light-headed. I was probably hyperventilating as I tried to resolve the conflict. And then I fainted.

"These girls." My mother emphasizes "girls" the same way she stresses words like "problematic" and "supposed." "One of them is the daughter of the A-Plus owner?"

"Yes. Jocelyn." I make sure to keep my voice as neutral as possible. I know how to keep my cards close to my chest when I need to.

"Eiiyaah!" my mother murmurs, shaking her head. "That is unfortunate. It will take some time for you to recover in their eyes, no?"

I know without asking that my mother doesn't mean physical recovery. The last time I had a panic attack this bad was years ago, at an Ogonna family picnic. We'd set up in the biggest gazebo in our municipal park, and you could probably hear us from the town over. Nigerians are not known for throwing quiet parties.

Just after the grilling had started, while most of my cousins and I were playing soccer, a police car pulled up in the parking lot closest to our gazebo. A blond-haired officer sauntered over, and he eventually had a "friendly" conversation with my uncle Akunna about local noise ordinances that led to some not-so-friendly shouting, and my aforementioned panic attack.

Except my mother never called it a panic attack. Instead, she made a big fuss about my being dehydrated and scolded my cousins for not having Gatorade before playing. She whisked me away to our car so I could sit in air-conditioning and "rehydrate," at which point she made sure I knew that under no circumstances was I to mention to any of my cousins, aunties, or uncles that I was seeing Dr. Rifkin, or that I had been diagnosed with anxiety.

"People from Nigeria, they are not as understanding about these issues as people here," she explained. I remember thinking it strange that she never used the phrase "mental illness" when she talked to me. "They consider anxiety and depression American diseases."

I'm pretty sure that Mr. Wu would agree with my uncle Akunna, so maybe my mom's right. Maybe I'll look like damaged goods in his eyes, the way his son does. The way his daughter would if he could see what is right in front of him.

The curtains slide open with a metal screech, and Dr.

Warren, the doctor who did my initial exam, walks in. "Ah, hello, Eric. Thank you for taking care of my son," my mother says graciously.

"Of course. I'm happy to say that there wasn't much for me to do. His labs and EKG look great. Everything seems to have stabilized."

"Does that mean I can go home?"

Dr. Warren turns to speak directly to me for the first time since he walked in. "Pretty soon. I just wanted to ask you a few more questions to figure out what kind of follow-up I recommend, then I'm going to print out all your discharge instructions."

I nod, and Dr. Warren's eyes flicker over to my mother briefly before coming back to me. "So, Will, when I took your history you mentioned that you'd had something like this happen before, and that it usually presents after some external stress, with some hyperventilation, visual changes, accelerated heart rate. That sounds a lot like a panic attack to me."

I lick my lips and reflexively look at my mom, who gives me a single nod.

"Yeah, that's about right," I say.

"Have you ever seen any school counselors about anxiety? Or your pediatrician?"

"I see a psychologist over at the college."

"Oh, good, I'll make sure that gets documented in your chart." Out of the corner of my eye, I see my mom stiffen the tiniest bit. Not enough that Dr. Warren would notice. Just me. "As I'm sure you know, panic attacks are uncomfortable but rarely dangerous. Have you ever been on any medications for anxiety?"

"No. For the past few years I've been okay with breathing techniques, mindfulness, that kind of stuff." I shift around in the hospital gurney. My whole body aches. No specific muscle group. Just overall, like someone's wrung me out from head to toe. "I have a heart-rate tracker on my watch. That helps. I haven't had a . . . an episode in a while."

"He's been through CBT, if that's what you're asking," my mother tells Dr. Warren. "William gets a full evaluation every year and it's never been determined that medications are necessary."

My mom's crafting her story the same way I did. It isn't quite true that no one's ever told me I should take meds. Dr. Rifkin's always been clear in telling me that I could take meds, if I wanted to: "The choice to start medications is a very individual one. If you're struggling I can make a recommendation, but every drug ever made has potential side effects. In the end it's your choice."

Here's the rub: If you leave the choice up to an anxious and avoidant person, there's a high probability that they're going to come up with reasons not to decide. So I did nothing, by default.

I don't tell this to Dr. Warren, who's nodding at my mother, all smiles, as if relieved that he can go ahead and write my discharge. "Well, nice to see you again, Rose, and wonderful to meet you, William. There's still some paperwork for you to do, so it will be a minute. The nurses tell me you have some friends out in the waiting room. Would you like me to let them in?"

I glance over at my mom, who must have called in my buddies. She just shrugs. "Sure, you can send them in." Maybe Manny and Tim brought me some new comics to distract me. Or actually, it's probably Javier. He's not fazed as much by medical stuff, so he wouldn't mind coming to a hospital to see me.

But when my curtain opens, it's not the guys. It's Jocelyn and Priya.

All of a sudden, I'm acutely aware of how thin the hospital gown I'm wearing is, how it doesn't quite close up completely in the back. My monitor goes off, shrill and insistent, and when I glance over I can see the spikes in my tracing getting tighter and tighter. My mom notices, too, her eyes narrowing as she flickers back to look at Jocelyn and Priya.

"Hey, you feeling better?" Priya's the first to say something. Jocelyn's hanging back, her gaze tracking everywhere except to me.

"Yeah, they're going to spring me soon. Thanks for coming," I say weakly. "Sorry to ruin everyone's evening."

That gets Jocelyn to look at me. "Don't you dare apologize," she says, almost angrily. "It's not your fault." She looks miserable, and I know whose fault she thinks it is.

"Okay, it's no one's fault except my brain's, then," I counter.

Priya barks a laugh. "You could say that about every disaster in the history of the world. It wasn't my fault, it was my brain's!"

"If the shoe fits." I shrug.

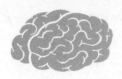

This Is My Brain
on Tropes

JOCELYN

We don't get to see Will for that long before he's discharged and sent home with his mother with strict instructions not to work until he makes a follow-up appointment with his pediatrician and psychologist. It's not enough time to apologize to him, to try to begin to make amends. It's barely enough time to see that he's well enough, and that he already blames himself for what happened.

So when Priya and I go back to the waiting room and wait for Mr. Venkatram to bring the car around, I feel like a shaken-up soda bottle, with so much pent-up emotion that I just want to scream.

"Will looks like he's going to be okay," I say, to break the unbearable silence.

"Okay enough," she answers. She doesn't even try to hide the blame in her voice.

"I said I was sorry," I blurt out, both wanting to scream that it's not my fault and wanting to cry because it is.

"Just saying you're sorry isn't going to cut it, Jos. You have issues. You need help."

"I know," I whisper. "I swear…I'll talk to someone."

And I mean it. I just don't know who.

I'm staring at a muted video of a protest in Eastern Europe when Priya nudges me with her elbow.

"That woman in the pink cashmere shirt," she whispers. "Society wife whose son had a football injury. What she doesn't know is that he's just faking it so he can quit the team and try out for the school musical."

I close my eyes, feeling them prickle with tears of relief. "He's read up on all the signs of a concussion, and he's going to pretend that he can't remember what happened and stumble when they make him walk in a straight line."

"We could pitch it as *Friday Night Lights* meets *Glee*," Priya says. "Oh, there's my dad. He's at the front."

On the way home, I take my seat in the back and am surprised when Priya waves me over and slides in next to me.

"Dad, can you put on some Bollywood music please? We need something upbeat."

As Mr. Venkatram fiddles with the stereo I turn to Priya and whisper, "So, is this the 'Third Act Misunderstanding'? The 'Mistaken for Cheating / Not What It Looks Like' trope?"

"Of course," Priya whispers. "I'm not a jerk. Yeah, I put some makeup on. Sue me if I don't want him to think that I'm a schlub.

He's not interested in me, though, so no, there's nothing for you to be jealous of."

She makes it sound simple, but deep down I know it's not. There are layers there that I'm going to have to pick apart some day when I can see more clearly.

For now? "I can't believe that I'm re-creating bad romantic comedy tropes in my life." I sigh.

"It's normal," Priya reflects. "Tropes resonate because they play on our hopes and fears, and if we see them over and over again it becomes part of what we expect in life."

"That is so messed up," I moan. "I guess if you recognize the pattern, though...."

"Yeah, knowing is half the battle and all that."

I guess half is better than none.

By the time I get back to Priya's house, grab my bike, and get home, A-Plus is completely dark. I slink up the stairs, and my father is asleep on the love seat, newspaper in his hand, while my mother watches house porn, aka HGTV, aka swooning over life-styles she'll never be able to afford. It's her one pleasure at the end of a work day, and I hate to ruin it.

"Xiao Jia?" She's shocked to turn around and see me setting down my helmet. "Ni hui zai nali?"

"Duibuqi, Mama," I say. "Will was in the emergency room. I was too distracted to send you a text." It's kind of the truth?

"Ai yo!" My mom's mini-scream wakes my dad up, and he snorts and startles, his newspaper falling to the floor. "Baba, ni tingdao mayo? Nege Will, ta qu jizhenshi. Xiao Jia, shenme yang?"

"He passed out. He was totally unconscious."

My mom's eyes open wide, almost a parody of horror. My dad makes a loud "tsk tsk," and I use this sympathetic opening, because it's the only thing I've got to work with. "Mom, Dad, I'm going to try to go over there during lunchtime and maybe bring some dumplings for Will. I know you'll be busy with the restaurant"—in fact, I planned on it—"but I think I should go support him. Obviously, he's taking the day off tomorrow."

"Of course, of course!" My mom starts babbling about how she'll also make Will her special medicinal soup and goes to our kitchen to rummage for goji berries and red dates.

Which leaves me with my dad, who glares at me once, then leans down to pick up his newspaper and starts to read.

I go up to my room and send Will an e-mail saying that I am sorry, so sorry for acting so weird tonight and giving him a heads-up that I'll drop by for lunch tomorrow. After I send it, I catch sight of the e-mail I ignored from earlier, the one with the video clips that started this whole mess. It's the least I can do to actually watch them. But before I can open them up, my laptop pings with a message from Priya.

> Just FYI, here's what I've done so far with the videos. I think it'll really draw some customers in. It's honestly one of my favorite pieces ever.

That's when I remember that I didn't actually tell Priya that my dad is ready to give up the restaurant.

My mouse arrow hovers over the link that Priya sent for

almost a full minute before I finally click on it. It takes me to Priya's Vimeo channel, where the thumbnail image for her video comes up—it's a close-up of Amah's liver-spotted hands holding one of her picture-perfect pot stickers. It's the background that catches my eye—I'm in it; I recognize the hot pink of one of my favorite T-shirts. The focus of the shot isn't me, it's the dumpling, so you can only see my head from the nose down, but you can see most of my smile, and that I'm angled toward my left, where there's another, darker set of flour-covered hands, and another fragment of a smile.

This is going to hurt, I think as I click on the play button.

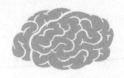

This Is My Brain on History

WILL

The day after my panic attack, my father gets permission to work from home so he can babysit me.

"I'll be fine by myself," I insist. "You don't need to take time off."

"I should drive you to Dr. Rifkin's this morning," he says. "Just in case."

I huff in frustration. "I don't get panic attacks when I'm alone in the car," I say.

"I get it. I still want to come. Aren't I allowed to get some quality time with my son?"

The funny thing is, I actually believe him. Unlike my mother, he usually doesn't have an ulterior motive other than just spending time with me.

Except that this time he does.

We've just left our neighborhood when my father starts up. "I feel like we haven't really had much time to just talk lately, Will."

The thing is, my father did a lot of stuff with us growing up—he took me to movies and baseball games and kiddie water parks where he was the long-suffering father who sunscreened up and did double-person tube rides with me when I was too afraid to go on them alone. He was a participatory dad in every sense of the word, and he was the one who really diagnosed my anxiety and got me into therapy. But it's been years since I've confided in him. I have Dr. Rifkin for that, and it's a good thing, too, because there are a lot of things I just wouldn't want my father to be worried about.

"It's been a busy summer," I say, because it's the best excuse I can come up with. "You know I love you, right?"

"Hey, isn't that my line?" He chuckles ruefully. "In all seriousness, I know that part of the definition of being a teenager is that you start to develop an identity that is separate from your parents. Your mom and I love that you're getting more independent. But we also want you to know that we're still here for you. Whatever you need, anytime you have questions about anything, we're here."

"I know." And I'm not lying. Deep down, there's a core of security there, even among all my fears. Doesn't mean it isn't nice to hear it said out loud.

"Did your mom and I ever tell you what happened when we first started dating?"

"I know about the instant noodles."

He gives me a crooked smile. "Your nne nne always likes to play that up, doesn't she? It's her moment of drama, her time to shine. It also allows her to throw shade on your mom without talking about the real reason she disapproved of our relationship."

"Why? Because you were a poor grad student?"

"No, Will." My father gives me a sad, indulgent grin. "Because I'm white, of course. Or perhaps more accurately, because I'm not Nigerian."

I can feel the veracity of his statement in my gut, but it takes a little longer for my brain to make sense of the more complicated strands of truth. It's important that my dad pointed out that my mother's family would probably have had the same suspicion of anyone who wasn't Nigerian, even if they were black. It's a prejudice born, I guess, out of a combination of memories of colonization and the fear of further loss of tradition.

Yet, it's a bias that can be overcome. "They accepted you eventually. Everything's fine now." I feel like a little kid begging his parents to reassure him that everything's going to be okay.

"We've learned to code switch, play traditional Nigerian gender roles when we're with her side of the family. But for a while your nne nne wasn't even speaking with your mom. It wasn't until Grace was born that they really allowed your mother back into the fold. There's no way those aunties could resist her, you know. By the time you were born everything was pretty much back to normal."

I shake my head. "I had no idea."

"It's all water under the bridge, but it's just something that I thought you might want to know: Your mother and I will always trust your judgment when it comes to who you love. We will support you no matter what."

337

"Thanks, Dad," I say, my voice thick.

We drive a few blocks, and my dad looks over at me twice, as if he's waiting for me to say more. Finally, he clears his throat.

"So, Will. I'll come clean. Your mom, she seems to think that you may be dating one of the girls who was there when you had your panic attack."

"What?" I replay the whole interaction in the ER to figure out what gave me away. And I want to kick myself as I realize. "Ugh, the heart-rate monitor."

"She was right, huh? I'm amazed by her intuition sometimes. So when can we meet her?"

I groan and throw my head back against my seat. "You know that phrase 'It's complicated'?"

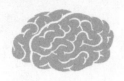

This Is My Brain on Surprise

JOCELYN

Another day, another morning when I can't get out of bed.

This time it's my dad hammering on my door that wakes me up. "Xiao Jia, qu gongzuo!" When I don't come out after five minutes, the banging starts up again, until it stops abruptly. There's whispered Mandarin that I can't quite make out, and then my door opens.

"I'm up, Dad, just give me some time to..." I whine, coming out from where I pulled my blankets over my head, only to stop short when I realize it's not my dad. It's my mother.

"I can come in?" she asks me in English, which is strange enough that I say yes. My mom doesn't usually speak English except when she's talking to a customer at the restaurant, on the phone with a vendor, or at a parent-teacher conference. That's usually okay, because Alan and I are fluent in Mandarin to about the third-grade level. It's when she tries to engage us in deep conversations that it's a problem.

She walks in, her slippered feet shuffling against our worn carpet. She's clutching a small silk pouch shaped like an envelope, the kind that Chinese people put jewelry in.

"Xiao Jia," she says as she sits down on the edge of my bed. I shove myself up so I'm at least upright. "Xiao Jia," she repeats, reaching out to hold my hands in hers.

In my entire life, I don't think my mom has ever reached out to hold my hand.

"Is…everything okay, Mom?" It's a stupid question. Things are definitely not okay in my family. But somehow, I figured that my mom was the one who was the most okay, if that makes sense.

"Shenme?" My mom gives me a deer-in-the-headlights look. "No, no, I just fine." This just makes me more suspicious, especially when my mom works her jaw a bit, as if gearing up to say something.

When my mom finally speaks, it's in this robotic tone she gets when she's saying something that she's practiced in her head a bunch of times but never said out loud, like when she went on a MVCA trip to Lake George and she had to struggle through "May I have a meatball sandwich, please?" when she ordered lunch from a food truck. It's the kind of thing Alan and I like to make fun of. For instance, when she pronounces fettuccini alfredo "feh-TOOK-knee AL-fredo." It's less amusing when my mom recites:

"I feel like you has been very sad lately."

My mouth literally drops open.

"I want you to know," she goes on bravely, "that I always

here to listen." Then she looks at me expectantly, like a freaking dachshund jonesing for a treat.

"Mom," I say helplessly. "Okay, thanks."

When that's all I say, my mom kind of crumples into herself a little. But then she clutches the little silk purse tighter, takes a couple of deep breaths, and jumps once more into the breach.

"If you are feeling depression, it is okay. If you ever feel like hurting yourself, that is something you should tell me and I will not get upset."

I'm so embarrassed for both of us that I want to crawl back under the covers. Or open my window and shout, "Help! I've fallen into a bad PSA, and I can't get up!"

The only thing I can think of that will end this horror is to give her what she wants, so I gear up to say, "I have been feeling a little down lately, but I don't have a plan to die by suicide," which is pretty much true. My fantasy about riding home without lights and getting hit by a car doesn't count. Does it?

Before I can get the words out, though, my mom unbuttons the silk purse and pulls out an orange plastic prescription bottle. The words freeze in my mouth.

"Just after you born," my mother says, "I very sad. Cry all day. That why your amah live with us now, because she have to help. I get better eventually, but when I have Alan, I very afraid same thing happen, so my doctor send me talk to someone, and they give me these pills. At first, I scared to take them. But then your amah tell me, I cannot have postpartum again, I have two kids take care of. And wha!" She throws her hands up in surprise. "I better. So much more happy."

With a shaking hand, I take the bottle and stare at the label.

FLUOXETINE (PROZAC) 20 MG
TAKE ONE CAPSULE DAILY.

I check: It's my mom's name, and the date of the prescription is two weeks ago.

"You've been on antidepressants for years," I say, stunned.

My mother nods. She looks relaxed now that she's said her piece. She always looks relaxed, though—it's something that's always made me feel kind of broken, that I'm "so emotional" and constantly "making a big deal about things" when my mom's always so calm.

"I can't believe..." My voice breaks, and my mom straightens, as if she's bracing for a hit. "I've always wondered what was the matter with me. And now to know that you..." I pull my knees up to my chin and shudder. "Does Dad know?" I whisper.

My mom shakes her head.

I wish I were surprised.

♡

The minute Will opens the door I blurt out my news. Best to tear the Band-Aid off.

"I got into the JBP program, but I didn't get the scholarship. My dad has until Friday to renew his lease, but Mr. Berger already has a taker for the space and they're offering ten percent more than our current rent. So, I don't know how much longer I'll be here."

Then I drop the bag of food in his foyer, throw myself into his arms, and start weeping.

Will staggers back, caught off guard, but steadies himself. "Hey, hey. It's going to be okay." And for that moment, warm and safe in the circle of his arms, I allow myself to believe that, somehow, it's going to be okay.

Because I have a plan. One that I'll implement just as soon as the fountain show is over.

Somehow Will hauls me back to his room, where he sets me up in his bed, curled up around a box of Puffs. When most of the snot has been delivered, and I can draw in a breath without it sounding choppy as a helicopter, I lie there like a limp kitten staring at the ceiling. Then I swivel my head over to Will, who's gathering up my tissues to throw in the trash.

"I'm sorry. I was jealous."

Will sits on his bed with a sigh. "Well, I've never had someone be jealous over me before. I guess I'm moving up in life."

He's deflecting. I've noticed that he does that a lot, gives people free passes because he doesn't like to dwell on the past, just brushes things over to avoid more conflict.

I'm not going to let him sweep things under the rug this time.

"It's not funny, it's embarrassing. It's kind of dangerous. I totally became a...a stereotype. I said some really awful things, and I triggered something, right? I made things bad for you."

Will rubs at his wrist. "Yeah. It's. It's something I'm working on."

That sounds...not specific. I look at him with raised eyebrows, and he has the grace to look chastened. "Did the doctors in the ER give you any...Is there anything they could do?"

He shakes his head. "No, they just told me to go to my therapist."

"So when are you going? To your therapist?"

"I went this morning." That's all he says. He looks away, and God, I would give anything in the world now to have him trust me, if trust were something that could be bought.

This Is My Brain on Answers

WILL

It's something I've fantasized about for years, having a girl alone in my room, but not like this.

I'm already emotionally drained from my appointment with Dr. Rifkin, but that seems like a gentle summer drizzle of feelings compared to the hurricane that Jocelyn brings in.

There's her guilt about wrongly accusing Priya and me, and her grief over her father possibly letting go of the restaurant, and her fear that she may have caused my panic attack. And then there's something else that I can't put my finger on, an unease that's almost anger, but not quite. It's a lot to deal with when all I want to do is batten down the hatches and curl up in a storm shed with my supply of bottled water and canned goods.

So when Jocelyn starts pushing me about what I'm going to

do—everyone's always so focused on what to *do* to prevent these panic attacks—I might drag my heels a bit.

"So when are you going? To your therapist?" She asks in a carefully neutral tone, like she's asking me whether I prefer half-and-half or soy milk in my coffee.

"I went this morning," I say, not volunteering more because once I start, I won't be able to stop.

I must have been too abrupt, though, because Jocelyn's face falls, and she bites her lip like she's trying not to start crying again. She sits up and yanks out a tissue with maybe a little more force than is necessary, and blows her nose with a deafening trumpet sound.

When she's done, she gets up and throws her own tissue away. She takes her time walking back to the bed, scanning my walls—the family pictures from our trips to Montreal and Jamaica, the Nigerian masks hanging over my desk—like she's looking for clues to a mystery.

I'm the mystery, I think.

Finally, she sits down heavily next to me, folding her arms tightly against her chest.

"Will, you know I want us to work out…"

I close my eyes, waiting for the "but."

"…but I think we're both going to need help."

"Both?"

"I mean, obviously we can't go on like this, right?" She swallows, purses her lips, and looks me in the eye. Her eyes are puffy, red-rimmed, but they still manage to look fierce. "You've got to be straight with me. Do you want us to work out or not?"

I don't even have to think about my answer. "Yes!"

Jocelyn closes her eyes and slumps. "Thank God." When she opens her eyes they're brimming with tears again. "Do you think we could talk, then? About what your therapist said? Please?"

I groan and rub my hands over my face. "Ugh. It's nothing personal, I swear. It's just…" My heart rate's going up. "You know that confidentiality's, like, the basis of the whole therapeutic relationship, right?"

Jocelyn nods, then shakes her head. "But I'm not your therapist."

"Exactly! But Dr. Rifkin is, and he's heard everything, all my screwups, my soft spots, every embarrassing thing that's riled me up or turned me inside out. But he's my therapist, so by definition he's a vault. Unless I say I'm suicidal or homicidal, anyway."

"So you don't trust me to keep a secret," Jocelyn says, her voice flat.

"No, it's not that…."

"Then what is it?"

"Dr. Rifkin's a nice enough guy, but when it comes down to it, I don't really care what he thinks of me. You, on the other hand?"

"Oh," Jocelyn says. She grabs another tissue and blows her nose. "All right, I get it, but let me tell you a story. I had a heart-to-heart with my mom today." She shakes her head and laughs. "You're not going to believe it. She's been on antidepressants since Alan was born. And guess what? My dad doesn't even know. She's been hiding it from him for over a decade. He thinks they're vitamins that she takes every day."

"That's weird," I say, but what I think is, that is so horribly sad.

"Anyway." Jocelyn taps my ankle with her foot. "You see?"

"Yeah," I say after a second. "I see."

I lay my palm up between us, and after a second, she takes it. But I don't just hold hands with her. Instead, I take her index and middle fingers and put them on the inside of my wrist. I take a deep breath and begin.

"So, Dr. Rifkin brought up meds again today. And on the one hand, yeah, I'm getting sick of this panic attack business. I'm also afraid of how medications might affect my personality. Plus there's all the controversy about meds increasing suicide risk."

"Can you just get a prescription so you can have it on hand, if things get worse?" she asks.

"That's what I did, but I haven't filled it yet. I mean, what's the point? I feel better now, and it can take six to eight weeks for it to work."

"What?" Jocelyn fakes a clutch at her chest. "Pills aren't a quick fix? What a rip-off." Then, after a pause, more seriously: "I talked to my mom and I'm going to try to get a therapist."

She looks almost frightened about it. I take her hand away from my wrist and wrap it up in mine. "That's great. That's really great. I think it'll help. And it definitely won't hurt."

Jocelyn shrugs. "I guess the only thing it can hurt is my pocketbook."

There's truth to that. It's completely screwed up that mental health care in the United States costs what it does. "There's a clinic attached to the college where you can get therapy on a sliding scale, and a lot of therapists accept insurance these days."

Jocelyn looks up to me again, wonderingly. "You really do have the answer to everything, don't you?"

"Hardly," I snort. "Isn't that obvious?"

She snakes her other hand around my waist and leans into me. "Okay, you don't always have the answer, but you almost always have *an* answer. Which isn't bad."

"That's usually a good first step," I agree.

This Is My Brain on Moving Pictures

JOCELYN

"Alan, Amah! Come on, it's all set up."

"Aiyo, dengyixia. Kuaiyao wanle." My grandmother doesn't budge from where she's watching the electrifying end of this week's episode of *Single Ladies Senior*.

"I'll just be a minute," Alan says. "Lemme just finish this practice test. I've got a good feeling about it."

"I'm giving you guys ten minutes," I say. "Jin-Jin has somewhere he needs to be. I think it's a date with one of the waitresses at the Vietnamese place."

I go back downstairs, where the whole A-Plus staff is finishing up their evening meal. Will and I have set up his dad's portable projector against the side wall of the dining area. I had to take down a couple of framed TRAVEL CHINA posters from the wall, and seeing the empty space gives me ideas. What if we replaced the decor with canvas enlargements of some of Priya's shots? I file the thought away and double-check that Will's Bluetooth speakers are still connected to my laptop and playing the most aggressively positive music I can find.

Halfway through the B section of Sara Bareilles's "Brave" we hear a loud shout from upstairs and my brother comes storming down. "Holy cow! I got one hundred percent! Will! I didn't get a single one wrong on my full-length practice test!"

"That's my man!" Will and Alan fist-bump as Alan does a victory lap around the room before plopping his worksheet next to my dad's plate.

"Bucuo," my dad says, nodding his head. Then he amends himself in English. Instead of saying "not bad" like he did in Mandarin, he says, "Very good." My brother beams.

A minute later, Amah finally comes down, and Will pulls over her special cushioned chair from behind the counter. I clear my throat.

"Thank you all for being here. You may not know it, but this is A-Plus's fifteenth anniversary week. Obviously, none of us were here when the original owners started the restaurant, but the fact that we're still thriving and doing strong business fifteen years later shows that Utica really loves its Chinese food!"

Amah, my plant, bursts out in spontaneous applause, and Will and Alan join her. My dad looks a little like he's opened a tin of cookies only to realize that it's been repurposed as a compost bin, but my mom looks genuinely happy. Miss Zhou actually cracks a smile.

It makes sense that the restaurant's lease gets renewed on the anniversary of its opening, but I didn't realize A-Plus had been open that long until I dug through our maintenance records.

"In honor of our fifteenth anniversary, my friends Priya and Will and I put together a little tribute to A-Plus and our customers. We hope you enjoy it."

Because I'm a drama queen, I turn off the lights. It's only dusk, so there's enough ambient light from the street so it's not completely dark, but it's enough.

It was Priya's idea to open with an old-timey movie countdown, and I have to admit that it gives me chills when the final beep sounds, the screen fades to black, and Sarah McLachlan starts singing.

"You don't think it's too on the nose?" I whisper to Will as "I Will Remember You" fills the room to a shot of my dad flipping the store's CLOSED sign to OPEN.

"What do you think?" Will says, smiling. I look over at my A-Plus family, and they're all riveted. Miss Zhou is leaning forward half out of her chair with her chin on her hands. My dad's the only one who seems even the least bit uncomfortable.

Good, I think.

"Hey!" Will nudges me as still pictures of the restaurant being built come up. "Where'd you get these pics?"

"I did some digging," I say. "Your dad's friend at the chamber of commerce was able to get the contact information for the previous owners. They live in Kansas City now. Can you imagine?"

"And you think I have all the answers?" Will says wonderingly, shaking his head.

When the scene changes to focus on Amah's jiaozi making, I

notice my mother dabbing away tears. After a minute we pan over to a shot of Will making jiaozi, at which point Sarah McLachlan finishes and is replaced by circus music augmented by whoopee cushion sound effects when his jiaozi lose their structural integrity. Alan and Jin-Jin really enjoy that part.

Then the Beatles's "With a Little Help from My Friends" comes on to footage of the Boilermaker Expo. Priya's cut together half a dozen reaction shots of happy customers, and when I look around the table I can see people lighting up as they see how much joy the food we make brings to people. Then there's the time-lapse shot of a full day at A-Plus to the refrain of "Do you need anybody? I need somebody to love."

The pièce de résistance, though, is the single-shot clip of the very same group of people who are watching the film, winding down at the end of a long week.

As Ringo Starr sings, "Oh, I get by, with a little help from my friends," I watch my mom, ever the bedrock, carrying in the rice, using a paddle to serve it steaming, right out of the pot. For once, Alan and I haven't scattered to our bedrooms at the end of the day, and we're putting out the tableware—gosh, do we look young, but also older than our years. Jin-Jin comes in with his dishes, then collapses into an exhausted sprawl, but then he says something that I can't quite follow and Miss Zhou laughs, the fatigue dropping from her face for just a moment. Will rounds out our motley crew, and Priya's camera catches the deference with which he spoons out a plate for my amah and tops off my dad's water when it gets low.

If Priya's video were a film, it'd be the kind that gets a Rotten Tomatometer rating from critics but scores off the charts in its audience rating. Even as I teared up the first time I watched her initial cut, the reviewer in me wanted to use words like "mawkish" or "sentimental." And the tropes! I stopped counting after a while: The "Family Restaurant" trope. The "Multigenerational Family" trope. And here I am, the walking "Your Tradition Is Not Mine" trope.

But the second time I watched it and burst into uncontrolled weeping, it occurred to me that the video works *because* the tropes hit so close to home, not in spite of them. That's when I called up Priya and told her that my plan was to make this the most manipulative video in the history of man. If my whole life was a trope, I was going to own it.

I've watched the video enough times that it doesn't make me cry anymore, but I can see Miss Zhou scrabbling in her purse for a tissue. Even my dad looks a little stricken. And yes, I'm a total atheist (or at least an agnostic), but at that particular moment I pray. I pray to an unnamed God or Goddess that my dad will see. That he'll realize that our family is so much bigger than him and Mom and Alan and Amah and me. I pray that he'll understand that now is not the time to give up, and that he'll see that he's not alone anymore, that I have just as much a stake in the business as he does. Most of all, I pray that he'll see that for the first time in my life I might have a chance at happiness—and that my dreams for the future might not look exactly like his.

I turn the lights back on, and my mother is the first one to burst into applause. Everyone joins in, even my dad. And as people blink back into reality, I turn to Will.

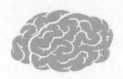

This Is My Brain on Pride

WILL

"I hope everyone enjoyed the video," I say. There's a chorus of approval and a grunt from Mr. Wu, who is giving off some very conflicted vibes from where he's sitting with his arms crossed. "It's the first time I've been involved in anything like this, and it was awesome because it was so easy to capture how much love people have for this place. I've only been working here for a couple of months, but thank you for opening up your hearts to me and making me part of the family."

"Thanks for making it so my math book doesn't seem like it's written in Dothraki," Alan yells. I fight to keep a straight face as I continue my speech.

"We've had an amazing summer, and Jocelyn and I wanted to show you exactly how amazing." Jocelyn pulls up the Power-Point that we made and turns on my laser pointer.

"The most incredible growth we've had has been in our social media," Jocelyn says. "We went from zero to one hundred in our presence online, and the number of check-ins and e-coupons we've seen has driven a twenty-five percent increase in revenue compared to last year. Thanks to Will's online cart, we've also been able to be more efficient with taking orders—there are hardly any days when people have to wait on hold, and of course payment processing is a snap."

Jocelyn pauses and clicks ahead to her next slide, which is a picture of the A-Plus storefront. "So, I know there's been some concern about rising rent costs."

Alan, who was there the day the men came by with the tape measure, grimaces. Mr. Wu just looks gloomily at a half-empty cup of tea.

"The good thing is," Jocelyn says, "we're hopeful that sales growth will be able to outpace overhead. And Will has an update on the status of our lease."

That's my cue. I clear my throat. Mr. Wu is staring at me with narrowed eyes. A month ago that look would have sent me scurrying. But today I eat that suspicion up like it's gelato on a hot day. It fuels what I say next.

"This morning I had the good fortune to meet with Mr. Berger, the landlord who owns a number of the businesses on the street. It turns out that he wasn't aware of A-Plus's anniversary, either, so I was able to share this video with him as well."

It took me five cold calls and twenty minutes of waiting on hold, but I finally got to sit down in the same room with the man. He wasn't really thrilled about sitting through the video—in fact, he sent at least two text messages while "watching" it on my laptop—but was super interested in a report that I put together on the three brothers who were hoping to take over the A-Plus lease from the Wus.

It turns out that exposure therapy is easier when you're motivated by the threat of someone you love having to move away forever. I lost count of how many cold calls I made to public records and former associates and clients of the Brennan brothers. Near the end of my investigation, I barely broke a sweat when I made a phone call. More importantly, I discovered that the Brennan brothers have been involved with some shady deals, to put it mildly.

"After watching the video and reflecting on how A-Plus has become a Utica institution, Mr. Berger told me that he is thrilled to extend our current lease for another six months," I tell the crowd at A-Plus, clicking through our PowerPoint and bringing up a PDF of the new contract. "It'll give us time to grow the catering business and further our ties with the local colleges, so maybe we'll be in a better place to negotiate next February."

"Yussss!" Alan gets up and repeats his earlier victory lap twice, high-fiving Jin-Jin and Miss Zhou along the way. Mrs. Wu gasps and puts her hand to her mouth in disbelief, while Jocelyn's grandmother beams and leans over to clasp my hand in hers, chattering away in Mandarin.

Mr. Wu is the only one who doesn't say anything, and the silence might be because he's almost stopped breathing. I watch as Jocelyn walks over to him. She hovers for a second when he doesn't seem to see her, as if she's unsure whether to talk, or make a move, or make a strategic retreat. And then slowly, tentatively, like she's reaching out to pet a shelter dog, she puts a hand on his forearm. He starts, as if seeing her for the first time. He closes his eyes. And slowly, tentatively, he hugs her.

That afternoon, I finally get my interview with Rebecca Ross. After I showed Mr. Berger how narrowly he dodged the bullet of the Brennan brothers, he was more than happy to put a word in for me.

Ms. Ross, it turns out, is an incredibly nice woman. I probably didn't need to rehearse my pitch quite as much as I did, but I know she responds to the part where I say I want to "shine a spotlight not only on stores that succeed, but on those that have failed. If I write about these losses to the community, it might prompt readers to get out there more to support local businesses instead of just buying stuff online." She's more than happy to put me in contact with businesses in the plaza that have closed down, as she's still in touch with a lot of the owners.

On my way home, I realize it's the first time I've had a list of phone numbers that I'm actually looking forward to calling.

I've just gotten back and am plugging in my car when my mom pulls in the driveway. It's starting to drizzle so I run out with an umbrella to cover her as she unloads her laptop bag, white coat, and a few bags of groceries. Because she's always the first one out in the morning, she never parks in the garage.

"Bless you, William," she says as we unload the bags in our mudroom. "The weather report this morning did not mention rain. I bought some yeast at the market. We have not made puff puff in some time, no? It used to be your favorite."

My mouth waters at the mention of the Nigerian fried dough balls. My mom used to make puff puff every year for my birthday, until I turned nine and begged for a "real" birthday cake to serve at my party. "I still love them, Mom. Can I make them with you? Learn the recipe myself?"

"That would be lovely, William. Why don't you get the flour and the big pot for frying? I will get the nutmeg and sugar. Oh, and I picked up your prescription for you."

I blink in alarm. "What prescription?"

"The Zoloft that Dr. Rifkin ordered for you," she says casually, as if she were commenting on how she got me a new tube of toothpaste because she noticed I was running low. "I saw it on the kitchen counter when I was cleaning up the other day."

"Um, thank you. I, uh, hadn't decided on whether to take it or not."

"Is that so? May I ask why you would not?"

I almost laugh. Why would I not? Because it still feels like a shortcut, like I'm being lazy. Because my nne nne would have a stroke if word got out that I was "mad" and was taking one of those American devil drugs. Because I thought my mother would think less of me if I did.

"Well, there are a lot of side effects." I say finally.

She flicks her hand dismissively. "William, if there is one thing I know as a doctor, it's that every medication has potential side effects. That does not mean that the risks outweigh the benefits."

"I didn't realize you were such a fan," I mumble. "You never even take Motrin when your neck hurts."

My mother sighs in response and smooths a finger over the bottle of vegetable oil that she's taken down from our cabinet. "Yes, well, I'm not the best role model. Doctors are always the worst patients, right?

"But this is about you. Of course I was reluctant to jump straight to medications when you first started having problems, William. You are right, there can be side effects, including a possible initial increase in suicidality that is well documented if poorly understood and controversial. I always like to start with conservative treatment, even in my practice. However, we've given nonmedical intervention the old college try, have we not?"

She turns to me and reaches out for my hand. Her palm is silky smooth; she's always been obsessive about the use of moisturizer because she has to clean her hands so often every day. "I am so immensely proud of you, of all the work you have done to keep yourself mentally healthy over the years. But a person—anyone—can only do so much with the biochemistry they were born with. I do not begrudge my diabetic patients medications when they fail to control their sugars by diet alone. If you feel like you are ready to turn to pharmaceutical management for your anxiety, it is your choice."

I duck down to get our big stainless steel pot from the cabinet, so my mother can't see the wetness in my eyes. Five seconds in, five seconds out. I'm proud that when I speak, my voice barely wobbles. "But how do I know if I'm ready?"

My mother smiles. "You'll know, William. You're the only person who will."

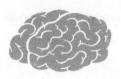

This Is My Brain
on Truth

JOCELYN

My dad drives me to my first appointment at the college's mental health center. Last night, my mom finally told him about her own depression, and he's been unusually subdued all day. Or maybe subdued is the wrong word—he's just talking less, and watching and listening more.

He looks at me intently when he drops me off at the clinic, and he swallows.

"Qinai de xiaohai," he says.

I turn around and gape at him, my fingers curled around the handle of the door. The phrase is often translated as "dearest child," but "qinai" has a much more tender feel to it—more like "beloved."

He's never called me that before.

"Shenme, Baba?" I ask, feeling wrong-footed. Raw.

"Ni yao…" He shakes his head and switches to English, as if

to make sure that I understand him. "You must always feel free to talk to me." He says it like a command, but I know it's not. It's an opening.

"Sure, Dad." I swallow. "I will."

My father drives away, and I square up my shoulders and shuffle into the clinic.

Will warned me that the initial intake visit can be, in his words, "unsatisfying." So I'm not expecting much. The shrink they match me with, Dr. Julie Cotton, is a thirtysomething white woman who is a personification of every psychiatrist stereotype I've ever seen on TV—soft-spoken, open-ended-question asking, nonjudgmental. I guess they teach that in school.

Our appointment starts out with me just talking, which I suppose is the point, but I don't think I ever realized how much deflection I do during normal conversations. Even with the easiest questions about my family, it's tempting to just skim the surface of the truth.

"Tell me more about ___," I discover, is one of Dr. Cotton's favorite prompts. Then, as our visit goes on, there comes a point where all she does is sit there and nod, and when the silence gets too uncomfortable I blurt out more detail just to fill the pause. It's like therapy magic.

After about half an hour of information gathering or, as Will put it, "creating rapport," Dr. Cotton asks me the million-dollar question: "So, what are you hoping to achieve with these visits?"

"Everyone's telling me I'm depressed, so I'm here to get help." If a little bit of resentment bleeds through my voice, it's because, okay, I know she can't wave a wand and make things better, but shouldn't she be the one who has answers here?

"Do you feel like you're depressed?" Dr. Cotton asks, face neutral.

I don't answer right away. First it's because I'm pissed, because, well, obviously, but after a second, it's because I realize with a shock that this is the first time anyone has actually asked me. Everyone has just assumed that it is cool for them to tell me how I feel. It's always, "It seems like you have depression," or "Here are some resources if you're feeling down." This is the first time someone's actually asked me, point-blank, if I'm depressed.

Maybe that's why, for the first time, I actually admit to Dr. Cotton: "Yes, I am."

After that, Dr. Cotton's questions change subtly, like she's a circling airplane that's just been cleared for landing. Have I been feeling hopeless, or like I'm a failure? About what? Her questions are so gentle that I barely feel a bump of surprise when she asks:

"Do you ever think about dying?"

Do I ever think about dying.

"Well, sure, doesn't everybody wonder?" I hedge, thinking of the night at the Venkatrams' and how close I was to riding home without my bike lights on. "But if you're asking me if I've ever thought about, like, taking a bottle of pills? No."

Dr. Cotton nods, somehow managing to just signal acknowledgment rather than approval or disapproval. "Do you ever think the world would be better if you were dead?"

"No." The lie sits there uncomfortably for a second until I nudge it straight. "Not exactly. Maybe. Sometimes I just think things would be easier if..."

I shrug, and Dr. Cotton goes on. "When people are sad and feel like nothing is helping, they sometimes think about what it would be like to just leave life to chance, by driving recklessly or not looking both ways while crossing the street. Have you ever felt like that?"

Have I ever felt like that.

The shiver of recognition that slides through my whole body makes my throat close up for a fraction of a second. When I can breathe again, the air comes out in a shudder of relief. I nod wordlessly.

"It's a common misperception that passive thoughts about losing one's life don't 'count,'" Dr. Cotton says, and that rings true, too. It's as if I'm so down on myself even my suicidal thoughts aren't good enough. "It's my job as your doctor to assure you that they're valid, and that they deserve treatment."

"What kind of treatment?" I ask through the lump in my throat.

"That's going to be your choice," she says. "Every person will have a different answer to that question. Want to go over some options and come up with a plan?"

Of course, I think as I nod, still dizzy with relief. *That's usually a good first step.*

♡

That evening when I go down to work dinner, I see it. The contract that's taped up behind the counter has been crossed out with a huge red "X" with the words *Contract Fulfilled* scrawled along the side. As if he thought it would make it more official, my dad has added his chop mark in red ink at the bottom.

"What the heck is this?" I say, holding the paper up so Will can read it. "We haven't hit thirty percent yet."

As Will takes the paper from me, our fingers brush, and I feel a Pavlovian sense of guilt that we've touched. It doesn't seem real that my father's honoring our contract. Will looks at the paper and smiles. "Well, last week's number was up to twenty-eight percent, and if you round up..."

"When has my father ever rounded up when it was in someone else's favor?" I demand. "Plus, what about item number two? I didn't get the scholarship."

Will looks shifty. There's no other word to describe it. "Well, have you checked your e-mail lately?"

I boot up my laptop, and my eyes widen as I find another message from the college in my mailbox.

The subject line is: "Congratulations on your scholarship offer."

I give Will the hairy eyeball. "Is there something shady going on, like your dad suddenly decided to donate to the college so they could create a new grant?"

"No," he says, rolling his eyes. "I may have stopped by the JBP administration office yesterday to plead your case, but when I did, one of the interns let it slip that they'd just accepted you after all. I'll bet one of the people they originally offered the scholarship to had something else lined up." Will pauses and grins. "What's really interesting, though, is that when I went to the office I ran into another one of your references who was there to update your application."

"Who, Mrs. Morgan?"

"No," Will says, looking up through his eyelashes. "Your dad."

"What?" I practically shriek in horror. "That's even worse!"

"Calm down." Will laughs. "He wasn't trying to bribe them or anything. He just wanted to drop off a letter of support with A-Plus's new numbers."

"What?" I say weakly. "It doesn't seem right."

"Okay. I see what you're getting at," Will says, sighing. "If you would rather be in breach of your contract—if you don't really want to date me—I guess you can reply to the college saying that you want to turn down the scholarship..."

"Fine, fine." I laugh. "Shut up!"

"...and you can go up and berate your dad for rounding up to thirty percent, and also tell your brother that he doesn't have to study for his final anymore...."

Seriously, this kid. There is, of course, only one thing I can do to shut him up: I kiss him.

His kiss feels like home, I think, even as I realize that it's the tropiest "Kiss" trope of all. But you know what? It's the truth.

I decide to own it.

This Is My Brain on Drugs

JOCELYN + WILL

We sit and we stare at the bottles in front of us. Both of them are full. Both are in our names. Both are unopened.

They're unopened because we worry that taking them will make us look weak (to ourselves, to our families, to our friends). But still, we have the bottles, and that alone seems like a Herculean effort. We went to doctors. We asked for help, and accepted it, partly for ourselves, but mostly for each other, because we're scared of what will happen if we keep going the way we are.

We've only known each other for months; still, somehow, together we're strong enough to know that needing help isn't weakness.

We don't know what the future brings, whether the medications in these bottles will ever be taken (and if they are, if they'll work).

We don't know if there will ever be a time when we don't feel insecure or anxious in some way, or whether we'll ever be able to trust our brains not to sabotage us.

All we know is that we're willing to listen. We're willing to talk.

We haven't made our happy ending yet, but we promise we'll try. We promise.

Author's Note

If I were to describe my relationship status with antidepressants, it would be: "It's complicated."

Like many people who are aware of the stigma surrounding medications for mental illness, I turned to antidepressants as a last resort, only after months of sadness, fatigue, and loss of interest in things I had previously been passionate about. I was in college and had started seeing a therapist, but it wasn't helping. I desperately wanted to feel better. Even so, when my doctor first mentioned drugs, I almost didn't take them. Aside from the possible side effects, it felt like taking medications was tantamount to admitting that I couldn't handle things academically and socially.

In the end, my desire to feel better overpowered my shame.

The first pill I took left me with awful withdrawal headaches when I forgot a dose, so my psychiatrist switched me to a medication with a longer half-life, which ended up working well.

However, at that point in my life, I wasn't ready for a relationship with a pharmaceutical. In a classic "it's not you, it's me" breakup, I stopped taking meds a few months after I started feeling less sad. I told myself that I didn't want to become dependent on the meds, but really, it was that I couldn't help worrying that being on drugs made me weak.

For almost a year, I did okay. I graduated and started a new job in a new city. I didn't seek out a new therapist, partly because I seemed to be handling the ups and downs of my new life just fine, but mostly because therapy costs a lot of money and I was just getting used to the idea of disposable income.

Then, I had a down period that didn't end.

I remember walking to work one day, crossing a busy intersection, and thinking that it wouldn't be a bad thing if a car ran a red light and put me out of my misery.

Going on pills a second time was a lot like getting back together with an ex. It was a known quantity. My boyfriend at the time was also on drugs for anxiety, which made it doubly easy for me to restart; he was the first person in my life who freely admitted to being on psychiatric meds.

The funny thing is, even with a partner to help normalize mental illness, I still couldn't get off my medications fast enough. This time, I told myself that the side effects weren't worth it.

Two years later, after a long, slow decline during which I stubbornly told myself that I was doing fine, I finally acknowledged the severity of my unhappiness and restarted meds again.

I tried one more time to quit antidepressants after my internship year. I figured the worst part of residency was over (wrong). The fourth time I came back to medications, my psychiatrist told me that I might need to be on them for the rest of my life. "Your brain just needs the serotonin," she said. And her matter-of-factness, combined with a burgeoning number of friends who had confided in me that they, too, were struggling and were taking medications, made me come to peace with the inevitable: Antidepressants and I were more than likely married for life.

What scares me most about how long it took for me to come to terms with needing medications is that I'm a doctor. I've read the literature. I know how prevalent depression and suicide are, and I'm aware of the medical guidelines that overwhelmingly support the responsible use of antidepressants. Sometimes I wonder: Why did it take me ten years to realize that taking medications does not make me a freak?

Part of the answer, of course, is that the medical community isn't immune to the stigmatization of mental illness. I've seen countless doctors and nurses throw out casual comments about how a patient is "crazy," or how a struggling physician is "going off his rocker." The biggest compliment you can give a surgery resident is to tell them that they've done "strong work"; implicit in this statement is that they're not just physically strong, but mentally so. When I cried during residency, I knew it was viewed by my colleagues not as a sign of compassion, but of weakness.

Another part of my struggle is cultural. I, like Jocelyn, was raised by immigrants from Asia. Mental illness was a subject of scandal. My grandmother spoke in hushed tones of a cousin, a girl, who died by suicide as a teenager. Making this tragedy even worse is that her father, my grand-uncle, was a psychiatrist.

In a culture where hard work and determination are considered panaceas for any ailment of the spirit, the silence regarding mental illness can be crushing. Studies show that Asian Americans are three times less likely to seek out mental health care than whites; when they do seek help, they're more likely to drop out of treatment. They're also more likely to consider and attempt suicide.

I've often felt that because I've never actively tried to harm myself that my depression wasn't severe. It wasn't until I was in my thirties that I first understood the concept of "passive" suicidal ideation, namely insidious thoughts like, *Things would be easier if I were dead* or, *It would be a relief if I just didn't wake up in the morning*. A lot of people have the misconception that people with passive suicidal thoughts aren't at the same risk for self-harm. In fact, recent studies have suggested that passive suicidal thoughts are just as important a clinical marker for suicide risk as having a plan to kill oneself.

If you have ever had suicidal thoughts, there are many hotlines staffed with people ready to help you through tough times:

- **Crisis Text Line** (Text HOME to 741741 from anywhere in the USA or to 686868 from anywhere in Canada, at any time)
- **National Suicide Prevention Lifeline** (Call 1-800-273-8255 from anywhere in the USA, at any time)
- **The Trevor Project** (Call 1-866-488-7386 from anywhere in the USA, at any time)
- For suicide hotlines by country: **International Association for Suicide Prevention** (https://www.iasp.info/resources/Crisis_Centres/)

Many people, however, hesitate to reach out to crisis resources, deeming their troubles to be "not that bad." Depression, like any other thing in life, is a spectrum. For those in the wide gray area between wellness and crisis, there are a number of "warmlines" and other services:

- **Mental Health America** has free online screening tools to assess your mental health as well as links to many resources (https://screening.mentalhealthamerica.net/screening-tools)
- **Substance Abuse and Mental Health Services Administration** has a national helpline to guide you through treatment options (1-800-662-4357) as well as numerous other online resources (https://www.findtreatment.samhsa.gov/)
- The **Anxiety and Depression Association of America** (https://adaa.org) has high-quality information on mental illness topics, an online community, and a section with hundreds of personal stories of hope from community members

Finally, when people from diverse backgrounds seek out mental health care, they often struggle to find therapists who can relate to their unique cultural backgrounds. Resources like the *Psychology Today* website (www.psychologytoday.com) can help—the site is one of the most comprehensive directories of therapists and psychiatrists in the United States and Canada, searchable by a number of filters, including cultural sensitivity training and languages spoken.

At the lowest points in my depression, the loneliness seemed impenetrable. The purpose of this book is to break my own decades-long silence and show you that, if you feel the same way, you're not alone.

You are not broken.

There is no shame in being who you are.

When you are ready to speak your truth, there will be people to listen.

Acknowledgments

Just over a year ago, the fake news running through my brain had headlines like, "You'll never write another book," "Stick to medicine, you talentless hack." There were months at a time when I couldn't bear to see the Scrivener icon on my desktop.

You wouldn't be holding this book in your hand if it weren't for the steady faith of my agent, Jessica Regel, and my two oldest critique partners, Abigail Hing Wen and Sonya Mukherjee. The instant I had anything remotely resembling an idea for a novel, they were there to cheer me on and shepherd me through the drafting process.

Just as important in the long gestation of this book are the gift of time and room service provided by the Writers for Young Readers Residency at the Betsy Hotel in Miami; my gratitude goes out to the Deborah Plutzik-Briggs, Jonathan and Lesley Plutzik, and Pablo Cartaya. The Madcap Retreats Writing Cross-Culturally Workshop spearheaded by Natalie C. Parker, Tessa Gratton, and Dhonielle Clayton provided me with the mental space and courage to tackle writing both Jocelyn's story (informed as it is by my own) and Will's, which required much more research to do it justice.

A huge thank-you to Winnie Adams, Edidiong Ikpe-Ekpo, and Adaobi Tricia Nwaubani, who opened up their networks to me. Immense gratitude to Rich Oyelewu, Uzoamaka Nwoye, Bassey Ikpi, Ngozi Onuohah, Toyin Erinle, Uduak Osom, and Ngozi, Sean, and Isaac Enelamah for answering my many questions and inviting me into their homes both real and virtual. I will forever be grateful to D.K. Uzoukwu and Regina Richardson for taking the time to read early drafts. All errors or misrepresentation that remain are mine alone.

Thank you to Corrie Wang and Jackie Lin for providing me insight into the day-to-day operations of restaurants and pop-up eateries. My mother, Justina Huang, provided indispensable advice about Mandarin phrases that the Wus may have used. Nothing but heart eyes for Lyn Miller-Lachmann, Rachel Simon, Marieke Nijkamp, Kelly Loy Gilbert, and Kacen Callender for their wisdom and expert reads. Kacen, of course, also gets special mention for writing the e-mail that made me finally think, "Yes, I can do this again." I consider them my first Fairy Godparent.

I can't imagine a more perfect editorial team for this book than Alvina Ling, Nikki Garcia, and Ruqayyah Daud, whose insightful editorial comments pushed this novel to new heights and whose palpable enthusiasm kept me going through the revision process.

Cookies and jiaozi to the whole brilliant and hardworking Little, Brown Books for Young Readers team, including Marisa Finkelstein, Bill Grace, Karina Granda (whose cover I simply adore), Valerie Wong (whose fantastic cover reveal was the stuff of dreams), Katharine McAnarney, Michelle Campbell, and

Victoria Stapleton. Particular thanks to the true superhero of this entire process: my copy editor, Kerianne Okie Steinberg, whose eagle eyes proved to be such an antidote to my sleep-deprived ones.

I remain grateful for the author friends who have made feel less alone during the solitary journey of publication. Mackenzie Lee, Natasha Sinel Cohen, Marcy Beller Paul, Amy Garvey, Anna-Marie McLemore, Mary McCoy, Becky Albertalli, Kathy Kottaras, Katherine Locke, Jerry and Eileen Spinelli, and Randy Ribay—thank you so much for your friendship. Group hug to the Fearless Fifteeners and Philly Kidlit Low Groggery crew led by Alex London.

Over a decade ago, when I started writing for young people, the industry was a different place. It's very possible that if it weren't for We Need Diverse Books I would have never even attempted to write this book, with its complicated intersectionality. When I think back to the earliest days of WNDB, I know that the intensity of emotion and activism is something that I might never again experience. To Ellen Oh, Stacey Lee, Sona Charaipotra, Miranda Paul, Lamar Giles, Mike Jung, Aisha Saeed, Meg Medina, Kristy Shen and Bryce Leung, Caroline Richmond, Jennifer Baker, Marieke, and Dhonielle—thank you for the difference you've made in my life, and in the lives of so many others.

Many thanks to my colleagues at UCCC for bearing with me when patients have had to be rescheduled or I'm running late because I'm being pulled in seventeen different directions. I couldn't have done this if I didn't feel supported in my day job, and I'm so grateful for all your cheerleading.

When I'm spiraling, when my mental news cycle gets the best of me, I call Libby Copeland, Nina Morgenlander, Pam Demnicki, Bridget McCabe, An-Lon Chen, and Eliza Auerbach. Someday they'll bill me for the therapy they've rendered, but until then...

People often ask me how I'm able to balance my medical career, writing, and raising two kids. The truth is, I don't do it alone. I would never be able to do what I do without my extended family: my brothers James and Eric; my parents and step-parents; and my in-laws, Marcia, Larry, Elena, and Julie; as well as the Pierces, Deppens, Harmons, Fiorentinos, and Kotarskis.

Then there's Joe. My best friend, my first reader, and the best co-parent anyone could ever ask for. Thank you for knowing exactly how much pharmaceutical-grade hot chocolate I put in my morning coffee, for not rolling your eyes too hard when I load the dishwasher improperly, and for dealing with all the feline indiscretions that have so recently permeated our life. Our kids are so lucky to have you for a father.

And O and G: Thank you for your understanding when I can't go on IKEA trips because I'm on deadline, for being my hot pack on cold nights, and for filling my life with shenanigans and laughter. Most of all, thank you for being the people who I write for. I know you haven't read *None of the Above* yet, but this book? This one is for you.

Finally, I must thank every reader, bookseller, teacher, and librarian who asked me, "So, what's your next book going to be?" I hated it every single time someone brought it up, but I'm glad they did.

Here it is.